Acclaim for **Caveman at the End of the World**

"Original and funny... Entertaining, well written and different."

—*Manhattan Book Review*

"Shocking... Captivates and intrigues... Rarely does a novel succeed in giving its readers such a brilliantly illuminating window into the hero's soul."

—*The Columbia Review*

"Satisfying... interesting and unpredictable... until the last page."

—*San Francisco Book Review*

"A wonderfully blended mix of Orwell, Kafka and originality, Rau's unique writing style weaves in themes of individualism, sexism, religion and romantic longings... (and) immediately gets the attention of his audience."

—*IndieReader*

"Bizarre in the right ways..."

—*City Book Review*

"Commendable... Rau succeeds in drawing readers into his woolly world."

—*Kirkus Reviews*

Caveman at the End of the World

Brad Rau

—SmallPub—

General inquiries and requests for permission to make copies of
any part of this work should be submitted to the following email address:
smallpubpublishing@gmail.com

SmallPub ISBN: 978-0692884317

For Rainy

"On the third day, the machine asked if I'd enjoy a joke. Curious about what the computer's processor might present me with, I typed 'yes' into the interface. After a few moments, the green cursor blinking, the screen filled with a cascade of ones and zeros. It went on for quite a long time, ones and zeros piling up, an avalanche of binary code. Afterward, there was a pause before the machine issued a succinct postscript: 'I guess you had to be there.' "

—Toru Oe, *This Machine Remembers*

Caveman at the End of the World

Prologue

1 Sunrise in the City

As the blossoming day saturated the city in copper hues, Ella Pearson stood on the fire escape, waiting for the sun. A moment passed. Erupting around the corner, sunlight spilled down the roadway, bathing her face and her bare shoulders. As though a switch had been thrown, she felt awake and present: instantly charged and prepared for her day.

More than anything else, Ella Pearson revered the sun. She understood the primacy of the sun; that everything—every-last-thing-on-earth—depended on it for survival. Things without eyes, bacteria and protozoa, organisms thriving in utter darkness without nerves to relish heat, depended on the sun. They had no concept of it, no contact with it and yet, without the sun, they would never have come into being. Even now, if that cardinal star fizzled out, the world would freeze. Everything would end.

Ella wasn't meant to be a city dweller. She wasn't meant to be a marketing executive, though she was good at that. She was meant to be a beach bum, or a migrant farmer. Either would do. Any position that would put her under the sun would have suited her.

She felt jealous of those naked savages who long ago, and perhaps still to this day, migrated across wide savannas, in search of things Ella could not name of but nonetheless felt she understood. Even so, the city where she lived existed in her mind with nearly the same preeminence which the sun held. The universe consists of an infinitum of stars, all more or less the same, but there is only one Sun and, as far as Ella was concerned, there was only one City. That was where she lived.

2

A Hat
An Obelisk
This Has Nothing to Do With Terry

Closing herself quietly in the bathroom, Ella paused a moment to listen to the apartment beyond the door. She half expected to hear the soft, menacing padding of Clara's little feet hurrying down the hall, but everything was quiet. Or, as quiet as the City ever let it become. A pervasive, electric hum sounded wherever she stood, inescapable.

While the day had begun outside, here in the bathroom it was still twilit without the light on. The only window was tiny and looked out on the side of the next building over, close enough to touch. The bricks had only just begun to emerge in the morning light. She didn't bother with the light switch, even though the darkness made her feel groggy again. To turn on the light would mean activating the bathroom fan and that risked waking someone, and this morning Ella wanted whatever privacy she could get.

Passing by the mirror, she ignored the smudgy, flat likeness stalking her and took a seat on the edge of the bathtub and got her phone out. In the lower corner of the screen, a stuttering, pixelated illustration of her own face followed her lead. Looming above the image, the word *Connecting* glowed and dimmed. The slow rhythm made Ella feel even sleepier.

"Good morning," her Practitioner announced, the moment after his image arrived, large over her own. He was still dressed for the outdoors, for the chill of early spring.

"Morning," Ella echoed and watched as the man removed his fedora and hung it on the coat rack and started unwinding the scarf from his neck.

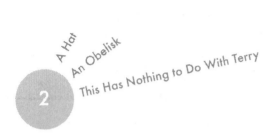

The fedora was Warner's doing, though the doctor wouldn't have known that. Ella would have forgotten it altogether, if Warner wasn't constantly reminding her. Exactly how or why it had begun were mysteries. Maybe there'd been a client (a hat distributor, or a manufacturer) who'd needed help boosting sales, but Ella couldn't remember any such individual having existed. It seemed to her now that it was all a joke Warner had played on the world.

For him the hats were a scarlet letter: a mark on every hopelessly impressionable man across the City. Andy wore one—of course he did. And now Ella's own Practitioner had one on. But Ella couldn't have said who's fault the scarf was.

It should have been a source of amusement for her, like it was for her boss. It was not. The hats looked dumb, to start. It had never been a style that Ella had any affection for—it stank of double breasted suits, greased hair, Italian *cheese*. Sexist noir.

Maybe the worst part was, Warner's experiment had made an impression on her as well: reenforcing Ella's nagging presumption that most men were simply morons. And now, with the Doc willingly applying that dunce-cap himself, she wondered if she should be seeking second opinions.

"You're looking well today," the man remarked.

Ella was wearing her favorite suit, the blue one with the pinstripes. Perhaps today wasn't going to be the dim disaster she'd anticipated.

Once he'd hung his coat and taken his seat before the computer, he asked, "How are we feeling?"

Ella cringed at the word 'we.' This was not a singularity. There were, obviously, two of them. Two individuals with distinct personalities and heartaches and nether regions all their own. He's a moron, she thought, but what she said aloud was, "We're feeling fine."

"Good. Good. Everything good? How're things with Andy and the girl... Clara, isn't it?"

She thought to tell him that she was leaving Andy. That by the end of the week she planned on being in her own apartment. Instead, she said, "Things are fine. Nothing to report, really."

"Good. Good. Everything's good. It's awfully dark in there, isn't it..."

"Brown out. You know how the City is." This potentially wasn't a lie. Brown outs had been rolling through the City like billowing waves of a preindustrial past. Or, maybe it was more like the premier of an unfolding apocalypse: an early glimpse of a final, terminal darkness that would someday overcome the whole City—the entire world. At any rate, that she hadn't tried the light switch didn't necessarily mean it would have worked if she had.

The Practitioner shook his head, in common grief with the energy crisis and said, "Perhaps you two are getting ready for that next big step?"

She was leaving Andy. That had been decided and it certainly constituted a big step, even if it wasn't in the direction the Practitioner was indicating. She said, "Yeah. Of course."

The Practitioner delighted in the news. "Well, you two are both competent and in good physical condition and I don't see any reason why you shouldn't expect your family to grow. And soon. I'll go ahead and refill your prescription. Did you have questions? Concerns?"

"Mmm. Yes... The side effects?"

"Are you experiencing side effects, Ms. Pearson?"

"No," she said and then repeated it a little more surely, just to be safe, "no. It's just, I see those commercials. They always end with that crazy litany and I just worry... You know? I keep thinking, Jesus, am I gonna turn into a mindless drone or something." She laughed, so he'd know she was only half-worried, able to joke about it, just plumbing for reassurance.

He didn't laugh. He said, "This concerns me, Ella. Paranoia can be an early warning sign of a serious reaction..."

"I'm not being paranoid... Just to be clear. I'm just concerned about some of these side effects..."

"We'll cut back the dosage." (Again, with this *we* business.) "We'll see how that works. I'd like you to come into the office later in the week. We'll have a little check in and see how you're feeling then. Sound good? Good. Good. Take care then, Ella." He nodded and was gone. The screen went black, just her tiny face in the faltering blue swatch in the lower corner.

That wasn't what she'd wanted. The dosing was fine, it seemed to her. She certainly didn't want *less.* She'd just wanted a little reassurance. She stared into the void beside her image where the Practitioner had lingered. "Moron."

Outside the door, someone had started fiddling with the knob.

"Just a moment."

There was a light knocking, *tap-tap-tap.*

"Jesus Christ, I said 'just a moment,' alright?"

Before leaving the bathroom, she washed her hands and briefly scoured the screen of her phone with a wet-wipe, even though she'd barely touched it. Almost as important as the sun, was the matter of staying clean: Godliness and all that...

•

On the street, nothing bloomed. The snow was gone, but the air still smelled like winter: a sour bouquet of rubber, no life at all.

Despite the dreary gray of the neighborhood, with the sun on Ella's face, a tide of optimism carried her down the street. She was almost free. Soon she'd be out of Andy's apartment, out of his life, for good.

The clutter had gotten to be too much for her: Clara's projects piled up on the shelves in the hallway and littering the floor. And, in spite of Andy's frequent assurances that it would be dealt with, it only ever seemed to worsen. It nagged her: she was a professional woman—

still rising toward the undetermined pinnacle of her career—living in a storehouse full of old junk.

It was only a couple blocks to the nearest metro station, but she walked in the opposite direction, to the further stop up the line. Part of it was the sun: at this time of day, the sunlight lay lightly on her face for almost the entire stroll. The other reason was that, if she went to the closer station, she'd have to pass by the First Assembly Temple, where Andy and his daughter attended daily services. Dominating a whole City block, wrought in massive stone puzzle pieces, Ella could barely stand to look at the building when she did pass it. In her mind, the Temple existed as an ideograph for every naive falsehood pedaled inside. Standing tall before the building, an idealized figure stood on a tapering obelisk, his hands held out dramatically, as though presenting the whole City, the entire world, to its own inhabitants. The man atop, Edward Kazakian, was the founder of the church, yes, but the implication in his title—*Great Creator*—Ella felt, was that he was responsible for much, much more.

The world was a complicated place and Ella disdained easy answers. She regarded anyone who pedaled such things as charlatans and whomever accepted them as boobs.

Andy, to his credit, largely left his simplistic beliefs where Ella felt they best belonged: quietly holed up inside. The girl, Clara wasn't so reserved. It seemed the child couldn't produce a sentence without the preface, "Master Thompson says..." *this and that* and everything else.

•

In stark contrast with Andy's apartment, where she'd been living the past few months, Ella's office and it's corresponding reception area were modern and refined. The second largest on the floor, just behind Warner's, the office was impressive, but the appointments made the place almost imposing. Brushed nickel detailed all the fixtures and gray stone paneling covered the walls. Where the majority of the floor's ceilings were furnished in drop acoustic tiles, here the rusted girders were exposed and beneath that inverted, industrial landscape, fine glass pendants hung, casting warm light into every corner.

Ella frequently had the sense of being two entirely different people, living two distinct and irreconcilable lives. While Andy's apartment made her feel lost and meek (an exiled herd animal succumbing to quicksand) here, in her office, she never doubted her prominence. It was as if the space itself gave her her gravitas and influence and confidence. At her desk, she was transformed into the figure who needed to be there: a structural element, removed at the peril of anyone who tried.

Turning in to her reception area, she was pleased to find Dawn Henny already clocked in. The assistant's punctuality was scattershot and in constant question—lapses blamed on traffic jams, on road work, flat tires... Always something to do with the girl's car: the simplest excuse, Ella'd always assumed. Why anyone would own an automobile in the City was beyond comprehension, especially if Dawn's avowed 'experience' was anything like typical. She might have laid the girl off, but Dawn was efficient (when present) and loyal (from what Ella could see) and who knew what kind of monster Staffing might send in to replace her.

Passing by the girl to her office door, Ella moved her purse from hand to hand so she could take the file Dawn held out. "New listings."

Ella nodded and tucked the folder under her arm. "Messages?"

"It's none of my business," Dawn said, bringing Ella to a halt, "but are you really going to break it off with Andy?"

Ella couldn't remember having mentioned the matter to Dawn but, in a moment of frustration, she must have. Reaching for the door, forcing a gentle tone into her voice, Ella said, "You're right, it isn't your business. Do I have any messages, Dawn?"

"Mr. Warner asked to see you sometime this morning. You have a ten o'clock with the United Electric people. Also a..." She looked down at the notepad beside her phone to read, "Timothy Crace called. He said he'd try back."

"What account is he with?"

"Didn't say..."

"You didn't ask?"

"I would have, but he said he'd call back. I didn't know if it was personal; he called you Ella, when he asked if you were in."

Ella nodded. "If anyone calls in the next half hour..." She made another move for the door. Before she could reach the handle, Dawn said:

"It's too bad. He's just so nice."

Pausing again, Ella turned back. "So, you do know him?"

Shrugging, the girl giggled. "Not as well as you do, I guess."

"Who are we talking about, Dawn?"

"Andy."

"Oh. I see." Ella straightened up. "We're not talking about Andy, Dawn. Was there anything else?"

Dawn was right, though. It couldn't be avoided. Andy was nice. That was a fact, as simple as any fact could be. He was also handsome and kind and generous and... The list went on. Ella didn't want to dwell on any of that, though. She made another move for the door.

"Is it about Terry?"

Concentrating on keeping her tone neutral (the effort seemed to be getting harder) Ella paused again. "What's that, Dawn?"

"I know it's not my place... I don't have many friends, Ms. Pearson... A few more now, but when I first came to the City and got this job and you were so nice to me... You and Terry made me feel like I was a part of your family... I guess what I'm saying is that I've always thought of you as a friend and I hate to see you going through all this... *Again.* I know how much Terry meant to you. I just hate to see you throw Andy away because he doesn't measure up..."

"It doesn't have anything to do with Terrence. That was a long time ago..." It wasn't all that long ago, not really. Not in the grand scope of things. Not even in a narrow scope. Had it been a year yet? Ella didn't want to count the days. She worried she might be able to. Her tone had gotten sharp. "If anyone calls in the next half hour tell them I'm with a client," she said and plunged through the door.

At her desk, she hid away her purse and laid out the folder. Rather than digging right into it, she went to the window to check on Clarence.

There was only one living thing in the world in which Ella Pearson confided without restraint these days and that was a bonsai, a shakan (slanted style) apple tree, which she'd named, for no clear reason that she could remember, Clarence. She couldn't recall with any certainty how long she had tended to him, but the bonsai had the austere bearing of something that had lived through countless phases of human history unaffected. Fads came and went, styles of music and clothing and speech passed into fashion and died out and Clarence, if he changed at all, only thickened his bark, proving how resilient he was in the face of society's frivolousness.

"How are we today, Clarence?" Ella asked. The sun would not land on him until early afternoon, but he seemed in good spirits despite the delay. She felt the moss around his base. It was still damp. Patting the canopy gently, as though the head of an obedient and beloved dog, Ella returned to her desk, to the file Dawn had given her.

There were three listings inside. Picking the one with the brightest looking photos, she stuffed the other two into the trash and sat, reading over the details.

It was going to be hard breaking it off with Andy, that was for sure. But it needed to be done.

The underlying problem was, there wasn't a lot wrong with Andy. Dawn was right: he was nice. Stupid, but nice, nonetheless. Ella probably could have overlooked it. There was only her occasional alarm at the perfect quality of his attention while he watched TV—staring so dully it was as though he'd spontaneously and unaccountably passed-on while the poorly portrayed detective on screen dramatically removed his sunglasses and dramatically reapplied them. Of course, nearly everything Andy did he did with an astounding focus of infantile amazement. To read his thoughts on the world, by his gestures and the level of concentration he allowed for even the most elementary, one might have thought that everything he saw, he was seeing for the very first time. He was a child in a man's (perfectly masculine) body.

It shamed her to admit it, but she could have looked past all that if it hadn't been for Clara. The girl made Ella uneasy.

3 Southern Exposure

The apartment Ella was shown did not look like the one in the photos. But the floors were in good shape, recently refinished.

Ella stood at the window, looking out. Beyond the low neighborhood, the City skyline bit into the night, the CCI building, like an awkwardly prominent tooth, tall above all the others.

"It must get good morning light."

"It's a very bright apartment," the agent agreed. "It has southern exposure."

Below, across the street was an upscale cafe; the kind of place Ella could picture herself wiling away some evenings. It was an expensive apartment in an upscale neighborhood. No doubt the clientele across the street would be upper-crust; the place full of men in tailored suits and capped in dumb hats. Maybe she wouldn't fit in, after all.

"What about a month-to-month?" Ella asked when she was shown the smaller of the two bedrooms. There was no window in the chamber and it was narrow enough so that if the realtor had installed herself inside with Ella, the situation would have been unduly intimate. Thankfully the woman, given to flinching, rodent-like gestures, had stayed behind in the hall.

"The lease is a year long."

"After the first year?" Ella wanted to know. She looked around. The room might make for an adequate closet. The other bedroom wasn't much better, boasting a tiny window that was too high to see anything out of.

"It's always a year-to-year."

"So first, last, and security deposit?"

"To be clear, I'd be hesitant to rent to someone intending on breaking the lease from the very first day."

"But it's available now?" Ella said.

The woman nodded.

It wasn't perfect. Not by a long shot. But it was bright and available and for the time being those seemed the most important amenities and, returning to the living room, (maybe it was only an illusion fostered by the two tiny bedrooms) the space seemed suddenly expansive.

Ella filled out the application and made out a check at the kitchen counter.

Part 1
The Uninvited

4

Heroic Stupidity
The Intruder
A Perfectly Good Robe, Ruined

Out of the heat and the bitter, electric smell of the subway and into the cool night, Ella lurched by the First Assembly in a fog of concentration, barely noticing the building that normally aroused so much animosity in her. She was lost in her own thoughts, practicing the gentle and absolute cliches she'd need: *It isn't you, it's me; I need my space...*

A block later, turning the corner she found Andy's apartment windows dark. She hadn't realized until now, that it had gotten so late and that she had stumbled into an awkward and unrequested reprieve until tomorrow morning. Overcome with the darkness and quiet drone of the City, she felt suddenly sluggish, like a toy winding down.

Climbing the stairs she was distracted, wondering which was less considerate, waking Andy to break up with him, or letting him sleep through the night under the pretense that everything was fine. When she got to the apartment landing, she had to pause a moment at the cracked door, trying to remember if she'd been the one to open it.

She peered into her purse. She didn't even have her keys out yet. Toeing the door open, Ella looked inside.

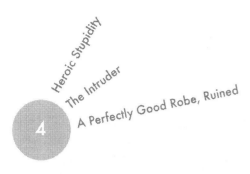

The kitchen was dark. The hallway, too. At the end of the hall, the living room was lit vaguely from the streetlights outside. Other than the low, tenacious warble of the City the apartment seemed quiet. Reaching around the corner, Ella snapped the light switch and stood a moment waiting for something calamitous to happen, for something gruesome to be exposed. Nothing happened and all the light revealed was the kitchen and the hideous clutter on the shelves in the hallway; stocked tight with shiny garbage (old toaster ovens and radios and other various bits of useless electronics that had been or were in the process of being refurbished.)

Stepping inside and flipping the light off, she closed the door behind her and paused to listen again.

A murmur of conversation lilted in the air—barely audible but there, nonetheless. Ella crossed the kitchen, trailing the whisper. From behind Clara's closed door, the noise could now clearly be discerned as the girl's voice, breaking out in quick, conspiratorial cadences.

Opening the door cautiously, Ella peered inside. The room was a slush of nighttime: smudges of gray and black purling together. After a moment staring, the murk seemed to resolve itself. And there, obscured in the darkness, she saw what shouldn't have been seen—what shouldn't have been there at all.

Backing away, after she'd retreated a few paces, Ella finally turned, rushing to Andy's bedroom.

He was asleep. At the bedside Ella jackknifed down, grabbing his shoulders and shaking him, whispering urgently, "*Andy, Andy, wake up.*"

His head shifted. He looked at her. "Hey, muffin. Long day, huh?"

Fixing her hand over his face, she shut him up. "Andy. I need you to listen to me. There's *a man* in Clara's room."

Starting to rise into a languid sort of pose, propped up on an elbow, he said, "Muffin..."

She shushed him again, more forcefully, and turned to the open, darkened doorway, where nothing waited. Facing him again, she whispered, "This isn't a joke, Andy. I saw him in there. Naked, on the floor with her."

Finally, it seemed, she'd managed to scrub a layer of dumbness off of him. Sitting erect he said, "Should we call your Doc, El?" He leaned closer, inspecting her face, close enough so that she could feel the mild warmth emanating from him. "Are you feeling alright?"

She slapped him. The sound cracked through the room. "Cut it out, moron. I'm telling you we have an intruder in the goddamned house. Right now. In your apartment."

He looked at her. Ella wondered briefly if this look was one of disbelief or just his typical, numb bewilderment. It didn't really matter; she slapped him again, harder. That seemed to do the trick. Moving her aside with a big, gentle push, he slid out from the sheets. She caught a glimpse of him in the doorway—his stupidity suddenly heroic, as he vanished around the corner.

For a wilting second, she wondered how she could leave him. It was a brief, flimsy thought. Almost ironic. His footsteps receded down the hall.

Dumping her purse out on the bed, Ella found her phone.

She hesitated, looking over the numbers, once she'd queued them up: nine, one, one. Those were serious numbers, to be sure; digits that demanded certainty. It would be easy enough to explain to Andy that she'd been mistaken, that what she'd thought she'd seen, maybe hadn't been there, just a trick in the darkness. It wouldn't be so easy with the police. The police would have questions. They would want to know if she was on any drugs, prescription or otherwise.

Looking at her phone, she thought about the Represitol, the prescription she'd just had refilled that morning. She thought about the conversation she'd had with the Doc, about side effects: about paranoia, about hallucinations.

Away in Clara's room, a crash resounded and Ella hit the call button reflexively.

The dispatcher piped up after the first ring, "Nine-one-one. State your emergency."

"There's an intruder. Someone in our apartment..." Earlier in the day, Ella might have found the phrase 'our apartment' unseemly. She might have reminded herself that it wasn't 'their' apartment anymore; that soon there wouldn't be any 'us, our' or 'we' linking them at all. She might have reminded herself that all this was temporary—even now fading away like a ship edging off the horizon. But, in this moment, the word 'our' fell out of her mouth followed by the apartment address. And once that was out, she dropped the phone away, so she could listen for footsteps coming up the hall.

Hearing nothing, with the phone hanging in her hand, she went to the doorway and peered out.

The door to Clara's room was open now, the light on and flooding out in an eerily frozen patch on the floor. Everything was quiet. Quiet, other than the frail chittering coming from the phone. "Ma'm... Ma'm..."

Ella was swept with a cold breath of fear when she realized the dispatcher's voice was the loudest sound in the apartment. Hastily, she stabbed the big red bulb on the screen. The line went dead. Turning the ringer off, she tucked the phone into her pocket.

Andy was gone now, surely dispatched by the intruder in Clara's room. So, there was nothing left to do but what Ella always did: step up and take charge and do what needed to be done herself.

Starting down the hallway, she made an appraisal of the items lined up on the shelves she passed. An assortment of coffee makers—insubstantial plastic and thin glass. She kept going, passing a line of electric mixers: heavy, but awkward. Next up, a small family of blenders. The glass pitchers atop were heavy and thick. Good enough to knock someone down, Ella thought. Pausing to pull one free she winced when the plastic base slid off the shelf and cracked down on the floor.

As if encouraged by the noise, Andy started moaning. And then, the nasty little sound of Clara's laughter whelmed up.

Ella was almost to the doorway—the flaxen puddle of light outside the threshold still unspoiled. Beside her, a line of clothes irons sat waiting and she wished, briefly, that she'd picked one of them instead, but the blender was already in hand and there was no space on the shelf to put the thing down. At any rate, the irons would still be there if the pitcher failed.

Ahead, darkening and growing in time to the slap of footsteps, a shadow threatened the patch of light on the floor. Ella stopped where she was, just at the edge of the doorjamb. Raising the pitcher up, the moment the man's form broke the threshold, she brought the thing around with everything she had.

It smashed open with a discordant song of chimes; bits of glass erupting and sparkling in the air. The sound the man produced was every bit as broken, but lacking all that tonality: his was a flat, wet, "Ugh."

Only after he'd collapsed, holding himself and dropping to his knees, turning to her and groaning, did Ella realize it was Andy whom she'd clobbered. "Oh, Andy!" She stepped back from the doorway, ready for the intruder to breach the gap next, wondering how much longer the police would be and realizing all she had left of the pitcher was the thick, glass handle. She chucked it away. Scrambling to get one of the irons off the shelf beside her, she whipped Andy with the cord as she cocked back her newest bludgeon.

"Ouch!" He moved his hand from the crown of his head to attend to his freshest injury, the whiplash across his cheek. Rocking back and forth he groaned, "Please, stop hitting me."

"Get out of the way," Ella said.

The intruder, apparently, wasn't next in the queue. Dressed in her nightgown and fixing Ella with a severe look, Clara stepped out. "What'd you do that for?" She seemed more concerned about the shattered blender than Andy's wellbeing.

Managing to hold herself back this time, Ella avoided bashing the girl.

Shoving Clara aside, Ella lunged around the doorway, into the room, where the intruder stood, falling into her line of sight.

He was thick set, but he couldn't have been much more than three feet tall. Perfectly naked, he was coated in hair from head to toe, like something that had been abandoned on a shelf to mold.

•

Ella tried not to let it bother her how generally unbothered Andy seemed by the whole, strange fiasco. Despite the intrusion into their lives, despite the little man's nudity, his hairiness, despite (er, perhaps because of) his obvious moral and intellectual deficits, Andy had instantly and visibly warmed to the thing.

In the surprisingly brief moment it had taken him to shrug off his injuries and wrestle himself up from the floor, he'd been so accommodating as to fetch the thing Ella's bathrobe.

"Really, Andy?" Ella put in as a protest. Andy just chuckled to himself at the effort of getting the intruder to relax his arms enough so that he could be dressed.

"Mine's obviously too big," Andy said, all-too-comfortable. He fixed the collar so it lay down nicely.

"Make him wait on the landing, then."

"Naked? It isn't proper to be naked outside..." He chuckled. "Everyone knows that."

The little monster seemed pleased enough with the look and feel of his new garment. His big, watery eyes followed the course of his clumsy hands as he explored the fabric. It had been fine silk. Now it was ruined: irrevocably tainted.

The robe, which Ella hadn't donned in months (the hem only fell to mid thigh and didn't seem appropriate to lounge in while Clara was skulking around) fit the little monster well, almost as though it had been tailored to him, though the arms were a touch tight. On Ella they were a three-quarter sleeve, while on the little man they descended neatly to his wrists, little tufts of fur spouting out from under. The frilly hem ended right around his calves.

Andy tied the belt, chuckling and muttering, "It'll do for now but I'm not sure you should make it part of your permanent rotation." Ha-ha.

"Andy, stop talking to him like he's a pet. He broke in."

Andy laughed.

So let him have it, let him keep the damned robe, Ella thought. And when Andy helped the little man up onto a stool at the kitchen island, Ella stopped herself from complaining. Let him have that, too. They were already undone as far as she was concerned. As soon as the police came to collect the intruder, she and Andy would have the *big talk* and then it'd all be over anyway; goodbye Andy. Goodbye robe. Goodbye soiled stool. She'd just have to avoid touching any of it until the matter was settled. That wouldn't be long.

"He looks more like a caveman than a pet, I think: like one of those funny cartoons of a caveman. Do you see it?"

The sound of Andy's voice brought her out of her sour dwelling, but she wasn't sure she'd heard him right. "*What?*"

"A caveman," Andy said, "I mean, your robe doesn't really help the look, but he's got all that hair. All he needs is a big fur toga and little club or something." He turned to the Caveman on the stool and said, "Bugga, bugga, bugga," and broke into a fresh, erratic bray of laughter. The Caveman stared back wide-eyed and maybe a little afraid.

Shaking her head, Ella turned away from the grotesque scene and started down the hall.

Passing Clara, the girl asked, "What's gonna happen to him?"

Ella ignored the question. In the bedroom, she called the police again.

"Nine-one-one..."

"Eh, I was calling to, I don't know, downgrade an emergency I called in earlier..."

"Ma'm?"

"A home invasion... It's..."

"Ma'm, this is the emergency line. Do you not need the police? Do you want me to call them off?"

"No. No," Ella said. "We still need the police. It just isn't the emergency I thought it was. He's..." she peered down the hall, to the kitchen where the little man was framed in the doorway on his stool and, out of sight, Andy could be heard laughing boisterously. “Stupid,” Ella said. “He's just stupid. He's not dangerous, but he definitely broke in.”

•

Off the phone, Ella met Clara in the hallway again. Crouching down to the girl's level—she wasn’t much taller than the intruder—Ella asked, “Clara, I need you to tell me the truth; did you let that man in here?”

“What's going to happen to him?”

“Well,” Ella said and paused while Andy chortled apishly in the background. “Well, Clara, that really depends on you. That's why I need you to be honest with me...”

“Don't let the police take him away...”

“He doesn't belong here. He’ll have to leave.”

“I'm telling you...” Clara seemed to vow, staring right into Ella, the girl’s aggression turned on and wound up to ten in an instant. Ella felt, for a flash of a moment, afraid of the girl. It was something that happened more frequently than she liked to admit. For all her four feet, Clara was an imposing presence. “...this is exactly what Master Thompson said would happen: the scriptures tell that we need to welcome all guests like family...”

Something flashed in Ella’s head. That phrase Clara’d used, ‘... welcome guests like family...’ She’d gotten that from a TV spot, hadn’t she? Ella knew the phrase and it brought with it an accompanying image: a little girl taking a boy’s hand and leading him through a doorway. Ella shook her head, trying to refocus. Television ads weren’t important now. Now, what was important was getting Clara to... Ella shook her head again. No, that wasn’t important, either. This isn’t my battle, not really, Ella realized, and she made herself nod at the girl before she rose up, patted Clara dismissively on the shoulder and walked away.

Ella was already a few paces gone when Clara said, "You only pretend at attachment. We're all disposable to you, anyway, aren't we? You know who doesn't see it, though? He doesn't. And he'll be heart-broken when he finds out."

Though the intruder was framed in the doorway at the end of the hall, it was Andy's laughter filling the apartment and it must have been Andy who Clara was insinuating. Turning to face the girl for a brief moment, Ella said, "Go to bed, Clara."

Clara huffed and stormed back into her room.

5

It's Over

The Police Arrive

Ella Gives Up

In the kitchen, the geyser of Andy's laughter spouted to new heights. He managed to get himself under control when, crossing back over the threshold, Ella told him tonelessly, "Jesus Christ, Andy, pull yourself together."

"Sorry, muffin, I know you're a little grumpy when you first wake up..."

"I wasn't sleeping. You were asleep." Turning to the stubbly man, wobbling on the stool, she asked, "He said anything for himself?"

Andy started chuckling again the moment his attention returned to the intruder. "No, I'm not sure he speaks. He doesn't seem to understand what I'm saying, either, but check this out..."

Ella wasn't quite sure what she was supposed to be observing. For his part, Andy started into an outlandish sort of hillbilly dance, jigging his limbs about as his posture drooped toward the floor. Watching the show, the man on the stool seemed concerned for a moment before the worry slipped away and he smiled and giggled and started smacking his hands together in an apparent ovation. Once this happened, Andy could only hold the performance a moment longer before he erupted in a fresh fit of laughter, bent now completely in half.

"What the hell's gotten into you, Andy? You're treating him like he's a child and he's gotta be..." her words died out. Ella thought she'd be able to land on an appropriate age for the thing, but now that she was looking at him, it seemed particularly hard to approximate. He was exceptionally hairy, but so diminutive, with pudgy cheeks, as though he were equal parts chipmunk and man. Still, he looked disgusting with all that hair and those giant pores: a plague-riddled-rodent, then.

She would have liked to have had him washed before his being allowed to touch anything at all. But of course it was too late now. He'd touched *everything*. Backed up against the wall, she kept well away from him. "Well, he's a man at any rate and you're treating him like he's a child..."

"Do you really think the police'll take him away?"

"Of course they will. That's why we called them," she said, maybe louder than she needed.

"You know, Master Thompson says..."

"Don't. I don't want to hear about Master Thompson."

Andy's shoulders fell.

Ella stared at him a moment. This was it; the strained moment where incompatibility can no longer be ignored. She said softly, "Andy, we can't continue on like this..."

"What do you mean?"

"What I mean is..." It was almost out. Almost there. She was almost free. It was like watching the sunrise—that ethereal moment of anticipation when the plate of the sky finally erupts with color and the sun grows as if from nothing at all, inflating, fiery and unrefined. "... it's..." The word 'over' was being shaped: the big, capital O, as big as the sun itself, the percussion to push it out being concentrated... With a sudden banging on the front door, the word evaporated.

"Police! Open up!"

It would have to wait. Andy went to open the door.

"We got a call about a B and E..." A voice charged the air. The sound of boots came in on a cold draft and a pair of cops followed the noise inside.

"I haven't heard about a bed and breakfast in the neighborhood..." Andy said.

Had he misheard?—Ella wanted to give him the benefit of the doubt, but had to acknowledge the possibility that he simply did not realize that both the words 'bed' and 'breakfast' began with the letter 'b'.

To save him further embarrassment... No, that wasn't why she announced, "Breaking and entering, Andy." It was because she didn't want to appear, by curse of association, as dumb as he was. And maybe, just a little bit of her did want to embarrass him. He seemed invulnerable to it, though.

The first cop to enter the room was a tall, gangly man, whose cap was situated so low on his brow that half his face was buried in the shadow of the bill. It was impossible to tell if he was looking at anything at all as his head remained upright and aimed squarely in the direction his body carried it. Bringing up the rear was a woman who had the body type of an in-wall dishwasher—formidable and uncomplicated.

The parade stopped; Andy and the tall cop standing side by side and looking past the man on the stool to Ella. The female cop wandered to the hallway, examining the puddle of glass there.

"Where's the intruder?"

"Who?" Andy once again (—constantly—) seemed baffled.

"The Caveman, Andy," Ella said. She should have taken a dose of Represitol. This was obviously going to be a difficult interaction to navigate with Andy present. She pointed to the man on the stool. "That's him, there: the guy who broke in."

The tall cop adjusted his head, the shadow melting and resettling along the curves of his face. The room was quiet.

"On the stool." Ella enunciated every syllable.

From the back of the room, faced into the hallway, the female cop noted, "It looks like there's been an altercation back here..."

"She whomped me pretty good," Andy remembered aloud, gently touching the crown of his head before touching his cheek. There was no mark from the lashing.

That piqued the short cop's interest, and she sauntered back into the room to ask, "This a domestic? I thought it was a B and E..."

"This isn't a bed and breakfast," Andy reminded them all.

The female cop stepped closer to examine Andy from her low vantage. "Maybe you should have a seat. You seem a little confused."

"He's always like this," Ella said.

"That why you hit him?" asked the tall cop.

"I didn't mean to hit him. I meant to hit *him*," she said, pointing again to the little man on the stool. A trail of drool had started down his chin, culminating in a big bead of froth that was threatening to come free from his beard.

The cop tilted his head. The smudge of shadow on his face listed to the side and resettled. "You didn't mean to hit *him*. You meant to *hit* him..."

Ella's voice rose a notch. "I didn't mean to hit *Andy*. I meant to hit the *intruder*!" Again, she indicated the man on the stool.

"The child? In the lingerie?" the female cop asked.

"That's my robe he's wearing. And he's clearly not a child. Clearly. Look at the amount of body hair he's sporting... And I obviously didn't know how little he was.... Obviously..."

"He broke in to dress up in your lingerie?" the tall cop asked. It didn't seem like a serious question.

"I put him in the robe," Andy volunteered, cheerfully.

Sharing a look, both cops seemed suddenly more suspicious of the entire situation.

Balanced atop the stool the hairy little man made a bored, farting noise with his lips. The noise drew everyone's attention, but only made Andy laugh.

Taking a step forward, returning her attention to Ella, the female cop said, "Why don't we just run through what happened? From the beginning." She pulled a small tablet from her belt and, at the stroke of a finger, the device woke up, bathing her face in blue.

"Fine. I came home to find the front door open. I heard voices in Clara's room..."

"Clara?" The cop lifted her face from the screen of the tablet.

"His daughter," Ella said. The word 'his' came out hissy. "When I opened the door I saw *that.*" They all turned to the man on the stool when she pointed. The little man was playing with the hem of the robe, dragging the fabric over his cheek and consequently flashing the four of them. The male cop took an aside to briefly slap fight the intruder into lowering the garment. Having lost the battle, the Caveman leaned into the cop's side, throwing a thick, hairy arm around the man's waist and settling in. The cop stayed beside the stool and if he was at all put-off by the little man's sudden affection, the shadow hiding half his face hid that as well. Turning away, Ella continued on, "That thing was in there on the floor, naked."

"Any sign of a break-in?" the male cop wanted to know. His voice drew Ella's attention back. The cop and the hairy man in her pink robe had gotten even more intimate in Ella's brief moment of distraction. The cop's arm rested over the monster's shoulder. The monster's face was nuzzled in the cop's side.

Ella shook her head and addressed her answer to the female cop. "Like I said, the door was open."

"Maybe Clara let him in..." Andy offered.

Turning the luminous screen away, the female cop's face lost its spectral sheen. "Why do you say that, sir?"

Andy's tone was upbeat, happy he could help, happy he could answer authoritatively, when he said, "Because I saw her do it. She let him in just before we went to bed..."

"Jesus, Andy..." Ella shook her head. "If you knew he was in the apartment... What was the crash I heard?"

"Oh, I tripped over a toaster on Clara's floor."

"Hm," lady cop intoned, ignoring the obvious followup and returning her gaze to the Caveman. He and the male cop had settled ever closer, the cop embracing the thing now with both arms, the monster's face hidden completely in the grotto of the man's open jacket lapels and purring contentedly.

This was all getting to be too much for Ella. All she wanted was for them to remove the intruder and, subsequently, themselves. But by the look of the Caveman and his new bestie, no one was in a hurry to get anywhere. And, from his appearance, if Andy was feeling anxious over anything at all, it was over how the tall cop had supplanted him in doting on the little beast.

"Hm," the lady cop hummed again. "You see the problem this poses for us?"

Ella looked at the woman a moment before responding, "I do not."

The cop said, "If he didn't enter the premises illegally, we can't very well arrest him for trespassing, can we?"

"Fine. I don't care. Simply escort him out, then. Let's be done with this so I can get to bed. I have work tomorrow and it's gotten..." she looked over at the clock on the long-neglected stove. It was late but not nearly as late as it felt.

The cop's voice, lilting like a lullaby, brought Ella's attention back around. "I'm afraid we just can't do that. You see, we have protocols and precious few options here: you can simply leave things as they are..."

"What?—with him at the kitchen counter?—wearing my robe?"

"Ma'm, your tone." The cop stared at Ella. "The other option is to call Social Services and have them sort this out."

"How about if you just leave and after you're gone, I'll put him on the curb myself..."

The cop pressed a moment of silence. Ella understood it as a warning. She slunk back, leaning against the wall again, crossing her arms.

"For your own legal protection, I would not recommend doing that. Given that he's a minor, and attired the way he is..."

"A minor? He's gotta be middle-aged with all that hair. How am I the only one who sees that?!"

The cop held another bout of silence. "Ma'm. If you were to put him on the street, you'd be opening yourself up to a variety of criminal charges..."

"Such as?"

"I suggest, if you're serious about removing the individual from your property, you contact Social Services, as you should have done initially."

Shaking her head, Ella looked past the woman to Andy, still distracted by the bond the Caveman and the lanky cop had developed. "Andy, call Social Services, deal with this. I have a long day ahead tomorrow. Clara's your daughter and this is your apartment: this is your problem. I need to get to bed." She nodded definitively and turned away, stepping carefully around the broken glass in the hall. She detoured to the bathroom to wash up, to wash off any residue the intruder might have left on her, before going to bed.

Laying down, the soft, low hum of conversation in the kitchen drifted through Ella's mind as formless as fog in a valley. As her bedtime dose of Represitol took hold, the voices became dimmer and dreamier. Eventually, they floated off altogether.

6 Some Exposition
A Visit to the Northern District

Ella'd lied to Dawn. The simple fact was that the matters of Terry and Andy were inextricably, if esoterically, linked: the two couldn't have had less in common. Terry was quick-witted. Always in charge, he was a man of constantly increasing relevance. He was respected. He was rewarded for his ambition; he made sure of that. He dressed seriously. He acted seriously. Even his jokes were serious. His wit was a handgun: you never wanted it pointed your way. Perhaps he was Ella's perfect counterpart.

—And Andy was Andy: as simple as the phrase, inside and out. Always pleasant, Andy never joked. He didn't seem to understand what a joke was. When he laughed, and he laughed frequently, it was because the wellspring of stupidity he harbored turned even the most predictable situation into a chaos of uncertainty.

And Ella was Ella: self aware enough to know that initially, it was Andy's very Andy-ness which had drawn her to him. In the beginning, she'd enjoyed his frequent, if unaccountable eruptions of laughter. It was nice hearing a man laugh. It was like that radiant warmth of sunlight in the middle of the day: it made her feel alive and present in a way she hadn't ever felt with Terry. Until (it had taken her longer than she liked to admit) she'd realized that Andy wasn't really laughing at anything at all. Ha-ha, he'd dropped his keys. Ha-ha, the penguin on TV was sliding on her belly. Ha-ha, he'd forgotten to pay the water bill. Again. Ha-ha. Everything was a source of amusement.

Maybe it had taken so long for his laughter to wear on her because being with him was just plain simpler than being with Terry had ever been. Andy wasn't a man she had to battle against. He wasn't a man who challenged her. He was a man whose bond to her never felt too strong to break (recently, barely strong enough to feel). It caused her a little, hot shame when she recognized how far—how unfairly far —she'd managed to let the matter with him get. She shouldn't ever have moved in. She saw that plainly now. Part of that decision, maybe all of it, had been due to Clara; a result of the *possibility* of Clara.

All Ella's instincts for handholding served her well in her roll at CCI. Clients, men particularly, seemed incapable of navigating the wilderness of possibilities that life allowed without a metric-ton of coddling. And Ella was good at that. She could tend to things. She could nurture things and help them grow. What bothered her, most frequently, was that the clients she constantly reassured did not actually need her. Maybe they needed a new perspective. Maybe they needed new ideas. But those issues were handled by the cubicle workers in Creative and Marketing and Design and it frequently occurred to her that anyone could do what she did—she was infinitely replaceable, and it was only her own dedication that kept her from being usurped. And, when she walked the length of the floor from her office to Warner's, she'd started wondering where else she could possibly go. Maybe Warner would retire one day. That seemed such a distant possibility as to appear fictive: a mountain range on the far-flung horizon that may just be a bank of clouds. Even if he did retire and Ella was given the throne, what then?

She realized too late (after she'd spent her life in the City making work the linchpin of her existence) that she'd never be satisfied by her job alone. She wanted to see something grow and, though the accounts she managed passed through stages, every phase seemed somehow insular and static. And her weekends were so empty, sometimes they felt like a vacuum she'd been pulled into, untethered, bobbing about in a void of shoreless freedom. She had few friends and when she lost Terry, most of them had vanished as well.

•

There was a TV show which Ella was particularly fond of: a situation comedy about a woman who could very well have been Ella (professional, put together, confident, always well dressed and proper (when she wasn't telling a ribald joke)).

"It's very well written," Ella would defend the show instinctively whenever it came up.

In the program's pilot episode, Ella's surrogate returns home from work to find out that her husband is having an affair. In a fit of decisiveness she kicks the sinful spouse to the curb and hires, on the spot, the cash strapped handyman toiling under her sink to act as a nanny for her two children—comic absurdity ensues. Maybe that was where Ella'd gotten the idea that she might make a suitable head-of-household. In the show, the professional woman meted out instructions for child rearing to the clownish handyman in between pithy comments. Ella could do that—she felt particularly suited to command a dunce and cultivate the fortunes of a brilliant, if slightly cheeky, pair of children.

So, when she'd met Andy and learned he had a daughter, Ella had been eager to meet the girl, maybe more enthusiastic than she ever felt about seeing Andy. It was a bad sign: Ella understood that clearly in retrospect.

Her first meeting with the child went poorly and would set the tone for every interaction afterward, but Ella refused to acknowledge it. She was dogged, and when she had a plan she followed it through to the end. The problem was, Clara wasn't interested in being Ella's impromptu child. The little girl seemed to realize the redundancy of Ella's presence from the start.

The girl's stature and childish face belied the drab maturity of her character. Her personality was fixed; there was no room for Ella's tinkering, no room for her input. And the girl just seemed more and more adult the longer Ella spent with her.

Not entirely adult, however. There were still evident symptoms of childhood that reared up on occasion. The *projects*, for example, littering the apartment, filling the shelves in the already narrow hallway, stacked up tall in a corner of the living room, nearly spilling out of the girl's bedroom, all had the hallmark of childhood *hobbying*. They weren't naive, these *projects*. It was the lack of intention that made them childish; the work of someone who hadn't yet realized that a project should have an end and a purpose, to begin with.

The shelves in the hallway were laden with electronics which the girl had refurbished to a Frankensteinian sort of newness—pieces cobbled from here and there and reassembled into awkward, but (mostly) functioning wholes. Sometimes, mounds of goods were shipped out of the apartment and brought to the First Assembly (for what purpose, Ella couldn't have said). Mostly, the items just hung around, the shelves growing more and more congested until the small appliances started spilling out into the living space. The square footage of the apartment seemed to be in a constant state of recession.

The accumulation of all this junk, Ella understood early on, was really Andy's fault. He was a weak guardian; incapable, it seemed, of pronouncing the word 'no.' He was too enthusiastic to appease the wunderkind, too willing to bow to her idiosyncrasies. Ella worried: the encouragement of all this queer industry was bound to doom the girl's future.

Furthermore, and perhaps more to the point: how had Ella (a woman of prominence, a respected professional) ended up living in a walkup with a pair of hoarders? With increasing frequency, rather than coming home, she chose to spend late evenings at work so as to avoid the anxiety that the cluttered apartment inspired. She'd been better off before, she started to think more and more frequently; better off in a place by herself, planning her coming work day, rather than extending it, just to feel some sense of ease.

Still, she'd made a plan and felt obliged to follow it to the end, to whatever end that might be. And, she was still reasonably certain that she could reshape the household into a more functional whole. After all, that was what she did every day at CCI.

•

Realizing Andy wasn't up to the task of parenting, Ella decided she'd need to take a stronger hand with the girl. That was the only way it could work. She would need to play bad-cop, because all Andy seemed capable of playing was ice-cream-man. Alone together in the apartment, Ella approached the girl—*working,* of course, at the dinning table, which ninety percent of the time, was actually *Clara's Project Space.* Mounded up, on this occasion, with pieces from three different alarm clocks, Clara sat, her little hands unwinding tiny screws. Ella took the seat beside her, facing casually toward the hall, toward the tall bookcases, stacked with old electronics glimmering as if to pass as new.

"We should clean out some," Ella said, maintaining an easygoing, drowsy tone.

Humming out a nonresponse, Clara kept working.

Ella raised her voice in case she hadn't been heard properly, "I'm serious, Clara."

Clara paused, following Ella's gaze to the hall. "Why?"

"Why?" Ella chuckled. Being around Andy so much, she'd started recognizing when her own laughter was superfluous and hating the sound of it. She coughed and tried to act like that was the only sound she'd intended to make. She said, "Because we don't need any of this stuff."

Clara nodded. "So?"

"So, why is it here, if no one's going to use it?"

"Someone will use it. Someday. Someday there'll be someone who'll use it."

"We have ten coffee makers. No one in this house drinks coffee. There're as many toasters and none of us eat toast."

"Someone eats toast."

"Yeah, sure, but no one who lives here."

Clara shrugged and went back to work, turning little screws silently.

That night, in bed with Andy, Ella put her foot down. Shockingly, it worked—the man was as unwilling to have a confrontation with her as he was with Clara, which might have been one of his more favorable, infuriating traits: that he was equally accommodating to everyone. Over the following days Clara's collection of crap was carted off and Ella thought that would set everything right. It did not.

Even in the brief absence of all that garbage, the ghost of the garbage remained in the form of resentment. Ella was resentful that she'd been made to make threats and Clara, Ella supposed, was resentful that Andy had bowed to the pressure of those threats. The lack of clutter also worked to highlight how rundown Andy's apartment was. A new strain tightened in the household.

Still, Ella felt a little pride in her success. She'd proven that the girl could be parented and furthermore, that she, Ella, was up to the task of it. Even so, she had no desire to continue on with so much resentment choking the air. She set herself a goal of repairing relations with the girl, who now seemed more childish than ever. Suddenly sulky and bored, Clara'd taken to dressing in black, as though in mourning. It seemed to Ella the girl was much too small for so much angst.

•

Watching TV one Friday night, an old black and white courtroom thriller playing out on the screen (an innocent man implicated in the murder of his wife), Ella decided it was time to retire her switch in favor of the proverbial olive branch. Beside her, on the couch, Andy was staring dumbly into the screen, the noise and flashing light having apparently lulled him into the mystical lands of Catatonia. Beyond him, Clara was glowering, arms crossed. Ella leaned out, to look at the girl.

"I was thinking tomorrow, where I have the day off, maybe we should do a girl's day out—give Andy a little alone time."

The girl kept staring straight ahead. On screen, a woman sat in a witness box giving testimony. The wonky dialogue distracted Ella a moment. No one talked like that. Not even in court, would a real woman ever say, 'admissible to your records...' or, 'bind together legally...' or, 'hearsay...'

The distraction sidelined Ella for a moment, until she remembered that she'd been hoping to work out a peace with the girl. She sweetened her tone and looked at Clara again. "So... Girl's day tomorrow? What do you think?"

Clara turned just long enough to give Ella a disdainful look, before returning her attention to the TV.

"Anything you want: a real girl's day."

"You don't mean that," Clara told the screen.

"Clara, I promise you: anywhere you like, anything you like. It's your day; our day—a girl's day." Ella liked the sound of that the more she said it.

Finally, Clara seemed to appreciate the sound of it as well. There was something tentative, like a glimmer of anticipation in the girl's voice when she turned to Ella to say, *"Really?"*

"Really. It's a date."

•

Clara seemed reluctant to fill Ella in on the details of their 'Girl's Day' and Ella didn't push, assuming the girl would want something uncharacteristically feminine and frivolous without Andy present: a walking tour of the shopping district, perhaps, to scout for boys. Ella let the girl lead the way.

On the Express north, Ella started worrying when the midtown stops slid by and the girl made no move to disembark. Ella tried a light tone, one full of soft curiosity when she asked, "Where are you taking me, Clara?"

"You'll see," was all the girl said. It rung like a taunt.

The train kept pushing northward and Clara stuck in her seat. Dread, thick and cloying, started settling into Ella as she watched the terminals continue to glide by, one after another, suddenly certain of where she was being taken.

The line didn't go all the way to the Northern District, but even the last stop let out onto a street corner that was desolate. Ella followed the girl, doing her best to keep her feelings inside as, around them, *desolate* dissolved into down-right-ruinous. Soon, they were inside the long, vacant city canyons of the Northern District. Ella stayed close to the girl, nervously surveying the alleys they passed. A transient, sitting on the steps of an abandoned tenement, held his head in his hands, forlorn. He didn't look up when they went by.

Ella found she couldn't maintain her carefree act any longer. "Clara, is this safe, our being here?"

Clara seemed immune to all natural instincts of fear, as oblivious of danger as Andy was to the concept of humor. "Sure. We used to come here all the time." She continued on, unabated.

•

Finding a dumpster beside a crumbing factory, the girl insisted Ella help her scale the side. Ella wanted to argue, but didn't. She only managed to find her argument when the girl started pulling grimy artifacts from the refuse and trying to pass them out to her. "No."

Clara seemed to not understand the word. She shook the broken hand mixer she'd found, again, for Ella to take.

"I said: no."

Clara let the machine fall in her hands and stared at Ella a moment. "You said we could do whatever I wanted."

"I didn't mean this. I obviously didn't mean *this.*"

"So, what you meant was, we could do whatever *you* wanted. You're a liar."

•

The walk and the train ride back were silent between them.

Moving in had been a mistake, a mistake of increasing (now unavoidable) obviousness. Clara wasn't ever going to be a girl who could be parented. Clara would only ever be Clara, a girl in rigid, defiant stasis and, as time passed, Ella felt less and less at home in Andy's apartment; less welcome. She was a visitor, a guest who'd stayed too long and worse: it didn't feel like Andy's home into which she'd been admitted. Even without all the clutter, it felt like Clara's lone domain, a child's empire where Andy was the butler, the housekeeper and she, Ella, a distant and unloved relative—forced out of circumstance into dwelling there.

The trip to the Northern District had reversed whatever progress Ella had managed to make with the girl. Clara was *working* again. The shelves started to fill with brand new bits of old junk.

Andy was oblivious: unwilling, once again, to intercede.

It was time, had been for a long while, for Ella to admit her defeat and move on. Clara, though obviously intelligent—imposingly smart, even—was nothing like the joyful progeny in Ella's favorite TV show and refused to be remade in that image.

7

Vandalism
An Act of Terror
Men in Hats

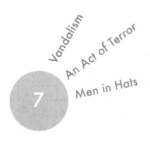

The chirp of the intercom interrupted Ella. She'd been doing some minor pruning on Clarence's lower limbs, trying to distract herself from dwelling on her still un-enacted breach with Andy. Too tired that morning to even consider executing the breakup, she'd wandered out of the apartment and into work in an emotional fog so dense, she couldn't remember the train ride at all and had spent the first half hour of her workday with a tiny pair of shears and a pair of gardening gloves which, though entirely unnecessary for the task, made the pruning seem somehow more authentic. Setting down the shears and stripping off the gloves, Ella left the little pile of clippings she'd gathered on the window ledge. Crossing back to her desk she looked at the clock. She'd clearly told Dawn that she needed an hour of peace and only twenty-seven minutes had elapsed…

"What is it?"

"Ah," Dawn's voice sounded far-off, somehow shrunken as though she were impersonating a child lost in a well. "Mr. Warner needs to see you and…" Was she choking on something? "Something terrible's happened…"

The moment Ella was out the door, Dawn sprung up from her desk and hurried to Ella's side.

Crossing the floor on Ella's heals like a loyal pet, the girl started talking in gales, "Isn't it awful? I don't know who would do such a thing… I mean, I know certain people feel one way about things and other people feel another way, but aren't we supposed to be civil? I mean, we all get dressed up at the start of the day out of consideration for one another and…"

Ella let the girl deflate as they travelled through the hive of cubicles in the center of the floor. Other than Dawn, the place was perfectly silent. Ella wasn't sure she'd ever seen it so sedate. But 'sedate' wasn't the right word. It was 'shocked.' Everyone stood out of their cubicles, staring intently at the TV screens scattered around the room.

"...What kind of monster would do something like..."

Having arrived at the far end of the room, Ella finally interrupted, "Dawn, I don't even know what's happened."

Ella's voice was enough to silence the girl. She froze up, joining the other baffled masses, to stare at the TV screens. Ella continued on. Warner was in a back corner of the room. She hurried calmly to him.

"What's happened?"

Warner didn't turn from the screen and so Ella looked up, too. The Temple of the First Assembly was in frame.

"Someone vandalized The First Assembly..." he said. Was there a note of amusement in his tone?—Ella thought she could distinguish it but her head still felt thick and sludgy.

The camera panned and zoomed in. On screen, Ella could clearly see, the face of the building had been smeared with something viscous and brown. It looked like shit. But, of course, that was ridiculous—where would anyone have gotten so much shit? A circus of men in hazmat suits rushed around frantically cleaning, spraying the building down with frothing hoses while drones dodged haphazardly, taking account of the extent of the contamination. The camera pulled back further. It looked like all they were managing to do was make a bigger mess out of the mess they'd started with.

"Stop your gloating," Warner told her, though maybe he was reprimanding himself. "Carl Thompson's on his way."

•

In the conference room, the long table seemed absurd for the foursome collected at one end. Ella and Warner sat, faced off against Carl Thompson and his most senior aid: a man Ella'd met on numerous occasions. His name had, again and again, failed to glom in her head. Maybe it was that his presence always felt superfluous; the man never contradicted his *Master* in any way.

"Here's what we know right now," Carl Thompson was saying. He had his hands tented atop the table. "The police are telling us, sometime last night, an improvised explosive device—that's what they're calling it—was placed by the entrance of the temple. Their suspicion seems to be that it was intended to detonate when the doors opened for this morning's service..."

Ella flushed with a surge of anxiety—didn't Andy always attend the first service? She pushed the worry away. No one had been injured; the TV reports had said as much. Besides, the bomb hadn't really been a bomb at all. All the thing had done was spatter the building and the obelisk out front with muck. Even if Andy had been there, ruined clothes and humiliation would have been the only result. And who cared about any of that?

Ella took the man's brief pause to interrupt, "Just like to clarify: do we know that? That it was intended to go off when the doors opened?"

Carl Thompson shook his head. Having met with the chief evangelist of the First Assembly frequently over the last couple years, Ella was routinely disappointed to find that she did not dislike him as much as she wanted to. He was often charming and thoughtful, despite the plain fictions he pedaled.

"I'm inclined to agree with the assessment of the PD. It's pretty obvious what the intention was," Warner said. "This was a terrorist attack, aimed at your congregation... Is that your read on it, too, Thompson?"

The man nodded. The two of them, Ella had always thought, looked strangely alike, almost twins. They dressed differently and acted differently, they had different gestures and postures but were of the same build and height and had eerily identical, war-worn faces. Maybe it was all in her head: she'd never heard anyone mention the similarities and she seemed to forget about it the moment the men weren't side by side and right in front of her.

"But we don't know that," Ella insisted. "Not for sure at this point."

"If the bomb wasn't meant to detonate as the congregation let in, as the police surmise, what would be the point?" Warner asked.

Ella addressed her answer to Thompson. "Well, Carl, your organization hired us initially to deal with the PR problem created by the Assembly's use of charitable funds, yes? That problem hasn't gone away, I think this episode is proof of that..."

Years back, Ella had assembled a team to create a series of TV spots, highlighting the moral authority and unquestionable benevolence of the First Assembly. They'd produced five ads in all, but Ella could only remember one clearly. In the ad, a small man is shown wandering the streets alone and scared. He isn't homeless, that much is evident. His face and hands and even his clothes seem conspicuously tidy, almost beaming against the gray city backdrop. Wandering from door to door, he knocks here and there and, while a few faces appear in windows to look out at him, no one will open their home. He keeps moving along, a sad piano motif chasing him. At last (twenty two seconds into the thirty second spot) a young girl opens her door for him. Close up of her hand taking his. The announcer breaks in (this, the only dialogue in the whole ad), "Open your hearts and your doors. Welcome all guests like family." The girl is seen, leading the man down a hallway, toward some unknown, warmly lit end. *Brought to you by the First Assembly,* appears at the bottom of the screen.

Ella's thoughts struck a moment on that strange creature, the Caveman, who'd appeared the night before, but the connection was broken almost instantly by the sound of Thompson's man sputtering like he'd been personally attacked, "There wasn't anything about the contributions to Central Labs that was underhanded in the least. We've gone over that again and again..."

"Davis," Thompson said gently, tapping the table in front of the man, like he was trying to call the attention of a kitten.

Davis, Ella thought, trying to lock the name away. Not an uncommon name but so easily forgotten. Perhaps it was that he seemed so much a mindless cog in the machinery of his own faith—an automaton going through motions it had been programed to follow: *raise hand, lower hand, praise the Creator.*

Ella cleared her throat to stifle the laughter itching there. "Excuse me, Davis, I'm not arguing. I think we all understand the nature of the First Assembly's interest in supporting genetic research... I hope we can also see, however, how others might regard it as an extravagance when there are other more immediate issues where the Assembly's money could be put to good use..."

"The First Assembly of the Neo Hominem donates substantial amounts to many charitable programs and organizations that..." the man, Davis, started stammering anew.

"As you mentioned," Ella raised her voice to overcome him, "this is a conversation we've had many times over. I'm not calling into question the good intentions of the First Assembly. What I'm trying to call attention to is that, from a certain perspective, the percentage of money given to Central Labs might seem dubious. If we can't all recognize that, I think we've already lost the public relations battle. I think this vandalism proves that we aren't winning it, not yet."

"While I value my colleague's opinion," Warner said, steadily looking away from her, "I think that it would be a mistake to chalk this up to vandalism. The hazmat team hasn't yet completed their analysis of the scene—preliminary test results are still days away but, until we know for certain, I think we have to assume this was an act of terror."

"So the immediate question is," Thompson said, looking back and forth between Ella and her boss, "how do we frame this in our response: as an act of terror or as an act of protest. Ms. Pearson, you seem to think this was simply a political statement and that it shouldn't be treated with such severity..."

"I think it should be taken seriously," Ella said. "I just feel, until we're certain of all the facts, there's more to lose from overreacting—you risk being on the wrong side of this if the suspicions of the police aren't correct."

"And if you're wrong? If the device did release a bio contaminant that was intended to harm our congregation..." Thompson looked away and shook his head. "I'm afraid I'm inclined to side with Warner here, and take the approach of greater caution. I don't want to give people a false sense of security when we simply don't know what dangers might still exist."

Warner nodded solemnly. "So, now that we know our starting point, let's begin drafting our response."

In a quick twenty minutes the speech that Carl Thompson would give later that morning was wrought out on a tablet computer. For all she could, Ella tried to temper the hyperbole that both Warner and the advisor, Davis, kept trying to foist into Thompson's mouth. She was half successful.

•

When Thompson and his man exited the room, collecting their hats from the coat stand in the corner, Warner and Ella stayed behind.

Looking at Ella and chuckling to himself after the door had closed, Warner said, "Hats. The both of them."

"You mind telling me what the hell that was all about?"

"Something eating you, Pearson?"

"That wasn't what we discussed in our strategy meeting."

Warner shrugged. "I had a change of heart."

"Just like that. And didn't bother telling me?"

"Would you have gone along with it if I had?"

"It's the wrong call, Warner. You know as well as I do, if those tests come back and there was no contaminant, they're gonna end up looking like a bunch of panicking ninnies and we're gonna end up with another, giant mess that needs cleaning."

"It won't matter what the tests say, Pearson. We'll have told the City it was a terrorist attack and that's what it was, regardless of what some lab tech has to say about the matter. Besides, cleaning pays, too," he said, nodding to himself as though he'd said something sage. "Do you know, Pearson, who the largest stake holder in Central Labs is? CCI, that's who."

Ella looked at him and didn't say anything.

"You seem tired these days. You need a vacation."

"I'm fine," Ella said and stood to collect her things.

Warner stayed seated, watching her. "...Maybe East Gish. Go see the country, it's wonderful in the Spring, I hear. Reinvigorating to see the trees in bloom and the air... It's very fresh out there. And the sunshine. That's where you're from, isn't it?"

"What's that?" Ella paused, hugging her binders to her chest.

"East Gish, I said, it's where you're from, isn't that right?"

"Yeah, it is," she said and went for the door.

"Think about it, anyway. You're due for a vacation."

Ella went out without responding.

•

Confronted on the train by an ad from a campaign she'd helped spearhead (a line of spring clothing that had just launched; the tag line for the campaign: *Be casual, Don't be savage)* Ella moved a few rows further before finding another seat, so she wouldn't have to suffer looking at her own work after her workday was done. As the train started forward she happened to look up. Across from where she'd reseated herself, an ad was cycling through on a flatscreen, shaking as the train rocketed through the tunnel, so everything looked spastic and a little out of focus. An actress danced through a field, lunging along until she landed in the arms of a man. He was wearing a fedora. They both tumbled, happily into the grass. Closing, the shot pulling out onto an impossibly bright panorama, the ad reminded Ella in a sultry voiceover, that, "With Represitol, today can be your new day."

When the side effects started queueing up Ella found herself focusing on the word 'paranoia,' but only because the words following it seemed so much worse. Words like Hallucinations. Psychosis. Was that a term the medical profession still used? It seemed somehow outdated, (like *humors* and *bile* and *rickets*) a term from a time before the machine of the body was mastered. A term from a time where doctors wore fedoras. Ella groaned.

When the train slowed for the next stop she stood, lining up to follow the crowd out the door and then dropping down into an empty seat beside it. There was no ad across from her, so she stared out the window to the grimy, tiled station, to the people out there skittering around purposefully.

While the doors hung open, a man started down the aisle, shaking a metal cup at everyone he passed. A few coins in the bottom made a shrill racket. He was dressed in shorts and a shirt that the sleeves had been torn from, wearing the outfit, despite the chill, Ella supposed, to show his destitution and to highlight his legs—or, what they'd been reduced to—grimy posts on which he balanced deftly. Commuters shrunk away as he approached, the train suddenly quiet around him. Coming to a stop in front of Ella, he shook the cup.

Ella reached into her purse and pulled out a few dollars and, keeping as far from the panhandler as she could, dropped the money into his cup. It made an unsatisfying squishy sound, seeming so much less substantial than the coins jangling there. As though in agreement with her assessment, the vagrant plucked the bills out and hid them in his pocket. "Thank you, ma'm," he said and started to move away.

"So, what happened?"

Pausing, he cocked his head back grimly. "Happened..."

"You seem to be getting around fine. You could get a job, you know; contribute to society."

He twitched. "You already gave me money, go ahead and keep your judgements." He started forward, but stopped again. "It could be you standing here, remember that." Finally, he moved on, grumbling.

He only got a few paces further, before a cop bounded aboard, seizing him roughly and dragging him out. The vagrant didn't fight. Even so, the cop yanked him hard, warning, "You know better than to be in here, Ducky. How many times is it this week?"

After the doors slid shut behind them, the train lurched forward again. In the darkness of the tunnel, Ella's face emerged on the glass opposite her. Above the door was a sign that said, *Wash your hands.* It was advice that vagrant would have done well to remember. Ella looked at her own hands. They seemed clean.

•

Walking by the First Assembly of the Neo Hominem, Ella was suddenly struck by the reality of what had happened that morning. The smattering of shit—or whatever it had been—had been scrubbed clean but deep, persistent stains remained.

A mob had congregated in the square before the temple, weeping and muttering and, as Ella approached, launching into a booming chorus of Amazing Grace. The speech Thompson had given had drawn them all out, showing their solidarity against the violent (insinuated) leviathan of terrorism. They swayed and sang. Andy would be crushed. Ella felt a moment of guilt; she was going to pile insult onto the injury today had already provided him. Maybe it was the other way around but Ella thought that might be assigning herself too much credit. She turned away from the Temple with her disgust already abandoned, in favor of a sadness that she felt Andy might appreciate.

With spring, the days had lengthened and so it was still light out when she got to Andy's apartment building. The windows reflected the pink evening sky and gave no hint about whether or not anyone was inside. He was probably at the Temple with everyone else. That was okay, it would give her peace to pack her bag.

8

Social Services
A Packed Bag
A Message from East Gish

From the living room, resonating down the hall, a flat clatter of TV applause broke away and a murmuring baritone rose up. Even though she couldn't make out what the speaker was saying, Ella recognized it instantly as Thompson's voice.

Stepping in, closing the door at her back, Ella called out, "Andy?!"

All quiet inside except the continuing TV noise. Ella started down the hall, past the tall shelving and all its junk, trying again, "Andy?"

At the threshold to the living room, Ella's attention was drawn to the TV. The evening news was replaying Thompson's speech from that morning. The man stood on the steps of the Temple, the stains behind him on display as he said, "… a sombre day for all of us. Though the image of the Great Creator, Edward Kazakian, no longer stands clean before the City, his form and ideals still endure and will remain in our hearts. The unwavering love of our faithful community is still represented in the conduct of the First Assembly and though the cowards who did this intended us harm, we will show our resolve even in the face of this terror…"

Ella shook her head and turned from the screen, jerking back in alarm when she found Clara and the Caveman crouched together on the floor. "What the hell is that thing doing here? Why didn't you answer me, Clara, when I called out?"

Clara turned away from the TV just long enough to say, "You weren't calling for me."

"Where's Andy?"

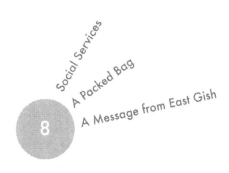

The girl shrugged, not bothering to turn from the screen this time. "Out."

"Out. What does that mean—out? Why is that thing still here?"

Now the girl didn't even bother with an utterance, just giving another feeble shrug. Marching into the room, Ella bypassed the girl, crossing to the hunching, drooling, hirsute *thing*. He was still in Ella's robe. It looked much worse for wear: the front darkened with grease or drool, it was impossible to tell which. "Why are you still here?"

"He doesn't understand you," Clara said.

That much was plain to see. Though the Caveman seemed frightened by her tone, confusion creased his hideously swollen face. Ella straightened up, giving him one last appraisal before turning and retreating to the doorway of Andy's bedroom, where she could oversee the pair without having to be amongst them.

Andy's phone rang twice before he answered.

"What the hell's wrong with you, Andy?"

A thick, nervous chuckle crackled from the earpiece.

Ella didn't have the patience for it. "Where the hell are you?" She pictured him crying and singing before the Assembly with all those other chumps.

"At the store," he said.

"Why are you at the store, Andy?"

"Picking up some things? Muffin, I have another call. Can you..."

"Andy, why is the Caveman still here? No, forget that. You know what?—that doesn't even matter. My question is, how could you leave your daughter alone in the house with him?"

"Slow down. Slow down," he said. She could hear the dumb confidence in his voice. It was infuriating. "The police called Social Services last night and they told me Social Services would call today when they had an appointment available..."

"None of that explains how you could leave your daughter alone in the apartment with..."

"Muffin, please calm down. I'm trying to explain..."

She went silent. He was silent, too. After a moment she said flatly, "So, explain."

"Okay. When I hadn't heard back by this morning, I called Social Services myself and they apologized and said that they were busy, but said it would be completely fine to leave Clara at home with him..."

"Social Services told you that? I'm assuming you failed to tell them she's a child. Because there's no way an adult in her right mind is going to tell you it's okay to leave a girl home alone with some drooling degenerate..." Ella said.

Clara and the Caveman remained quietly engaged with the TV. With the rebroadcast of Thompson's speech concluded, the girl had switched channels. On the screen a bird chirped in a tree while a drowsy narrator described its mating tendencies. Nature shows seemed to be all the girl cared to watch these days. It must have been a phase. Ella couldn't imagine anything more boring. She would have much preferred a gardening program.

"They told me..."

"I don't give a damn what they told you, Andy. Common sense..." she was interrupted by an abrupt pounding on the front door. It was loud enough and sudden enough so she flinched and was cut short. Rebounding, she said, "I have to go. We'll talk about this when you get home. We have a lot to talk about when you get home."

She threw the phone down on the bed.

•

Outside the door stood a man in a suit that looked as if it had been intended for someone else. The jacket sleeves were too short and the torso was billowy enough to smuggle a stowaway or two inside.

"Yes," Ella said, "what is it?"

"Social Services, miss. I can come back if you're..."

She didn't let him come close to finishing. Seizing his elbow and dragging him into the kitchen, she said, "Sorry to greet you like that. I was told you'd call when you had an open appointment..."

Referencing the cell phone in his hand, he read off Andy's cell number, and said, "I called a few moments ago. Didn't get an answer. Normally, I would have just moved along, probably should have in any case, but I was a few floors up with my previous appointment... I thought I'd knock and see if I could rouse anyone..."

"Well, I'm certainly happy you did..." The chime of the man's cell phone put the conversation on hold.

Nodding apologetically, he turned his back to her and answered, "Renfro here... Yes... Yes, just now... No, I'm here now. I just walked in... Very well..." Slipping the phone away, he nodded cordially to Ella again and made a move toward the door.

"Whoa, whoa, whoa." Ella launched forward and caught him. "Where are you going?"

His surprise at her speed and ferocity was apparent; he cowered away from her like a man about to get punched. "That was about your appointment, it's been cancelled..."

"Oh, no, no, no," she stuttered, turning him away from the exit. "The appointment's begun, how can it be cancelled?" Like a puppeteer managing a cumbersome marionette, she forced him through the kitchen and down the hall, toward the noise of the chittering TV.

"...I just received a call from the gentleman who requested the appointment, saying that he was..."

Ella continued pushing until they emerged into the living room. The social worker finally managed to shrug her off.

Straightening his suit (it fell back how it had awkwardly hung before) he scolded her, "Miss, if the appointment is canceled, it's simply canceled. That's all there is to it. The appointment was scheduled by a Mr. Stanhope and, just now, he's called and canceled because he's not going to make it home on time. So, I'm very sorry but..."

He tried stepping around her, into the hall again and Ella blocked him out.

"Miss..." he warned.

"Listen, the intruder is right there, on the floor." She pointed to the little man. He and Clara had given up on the TV, occupied now with the more immediate drama unfolding before them."We don't really need an appointment at all. All we need is for you to take him away as the police should've last night. That's all we want."

The social worker looked at the Caveman pitifully. "You're hoping to Relinquish Guardianship of your Supplicant? Am I understanding the request?"

"I don't know. I don't know what any of that means." Ella looked at him a quiet moment. She huffed. "I'm asking you to take the intruder out of the apartment, as the police should have last night. I don't really understand how this is such a complicated issue. There's nothing to it at all. He's an intruder—that's all it comes down to..."

"I can assure you, Miss, this is much more complex..."

"No, it isn't. You're Social Services. You take him away, that's all there is to it."

"Firstly, *I* am not *Social Services.* I am simply an agent, Renfro. *I* cannot *take him away.* The most I can do is make a Recommendation of Emancipation to the police and then they would have to return and have him admitted to a local center..."

"That sounds fine. Let's do that."

"I'd be perfectly happy to... All I need is the consent of the individual who made the appointment..." He seemed to be losing patience. He also, however, seemed to be losing resolve. His voice had gotten slow and drowsy, his head listing to the side, like this was an argument he'd had too many times to maintain any enthusiasm for.

"I'm giving consent right now..."

"Miss, once again, you did not make the appointment. The appointment was postponed..."

"You know what?" Ella said, finally removing herself from the mouth of the hallway so the man could pass. "You're right: I didn't make the appointment. I didn't cancel the appointment. I didn't decide to leave a girl here unsupervised to babysit a degenerate. Hell, I don't even live here. Go," she said. Pointing down the hall, she barked a second time, "Go! This isn't my problem. This is Andy's goddamned problem. This is Andy's goddamned apartment..."

She didn't wait for him to respond.

Turning and marching back into the bedroom, she never heard the door close, but the social worker was gone by the time her bag was packed. She didn't look at Clara or the Caveman as she passed into the hallway, her suitcase banging off the shelving, the appliances there clattering as though faring an earthquake. In the kitchen, she set the case down on the floor and sat on it. Arms crossed, she stared at the door.

When Andy came in sometime later, lugging a bounty of grocery bags, she was still posed like that. Struggling to cradle the bags and extract his key from the door at the same time, Andy said, "You must have seen it on your way home... It's so shameful. I don't know how anyone could do anything so awful..."

Ella ignored him. She didn't want to talk about the vandalism on the church. "What the hell is all that?"

"Groceries?" Having pulled the key from the lock he turned to her, brightly explaining, "Our guest has a special diet we'll need to follow..." he said, suddenly overcome by a rumble of nonsensical laughter.

Ella was about to argue and then thought better of it. Rising violently, yanking the suitcase up after her, she pushed past Andy, pausing a moment on the landing to regard him. "This is over between us. I'll be back later in the week for the rest of my things. I'm sorry to be leaving you with the Caveman, but it really is your own fault, Andy. I hope you can see that."

Before he could say anything, Ella bustled down the stairs, feeling more clear headed than she had all day.

•

Rather than going to her new apartment (the lack of a bed, anywhere to sit, or the option of a TV to idle away her mind on, having collectively decided the matter) Ella took a suite at the Palisade Royal Gardens, a block from the CCI building. After so much time roughing it at Andy's place, she felt like she was due a little pampering. The suite was three rooms of gaudy brass and rouge luxury. There was even a hot-tub but, though she liked the sense of deep clean it provided, maybe soaking wasn't her thing. She lasted a quick three minutes in the apparatus before getting bored and climbing back out.

With the remainder of the evening, she watched movies about women falling in love, love falling apart and, finally, men making grand, selfless gestures to win women back. The movies were uniformly bad. With some annoyance Ella realized Andy would never have objected to them in the first place. He would have enjoyed them. He would have done a lot of laughing. By the conclusion of the final movie, she felt coarsened by all the romance. The climatic scene played out before her, inspiring nothing but general negativity. On screen a man rushed to an airport gate to intercept his fleeing love. Running by the ticket counter, by the shocked but strangely immobile employee there, the man caught hold of his girl, pulling her out of the lineup.

Yanking her arm away as though he were diseased, she told him, “You've made it clear, Tom, your job's...” “That's what I came to tell you, Megan.” When he fell to a knee, she asked, “What are you doing?” “Proposing, I think.” “You don't even have a ring,” she teased, inexplicably turning to a gentler mood. Patting down his jacket, the man seemed to light on something in a pocket—like he had, in fact, brought a ring along. In the end he pulled out a packet of gum and quickly got a strip of foil wrapping free, which he hastily shaped into a ring. The woman gave him her hand, smiling like it was the very ring she'd always hoped for.

Groaning and muttering a string of obscenities, Ella switched off the TV.

•

In the soft, encompassing bed, she couldn't sleep. The lights from the CCI tower across the square shown on her face. Hanging over her, the building seemed to watch her with the sort of detached, clinical interest of a surgeon who'd found something he couldn't remove.

Arranging a backrest out of the pillows, Ella sat up and collected her phone and spent some time meandering through her social network. Maybe an old friend, some partner in crime from her single days before Andy (before Terry, even) was out on the town and in need of an accomplice. The possibility cheered her briefly, before it made her miserable.

Scrolling through the endless tower of faces online, she was dismayed by how untended she'd let her network get. She didn't recognize any of these people. She logged out and logged back in, after concluding that she'd mistakenly accessed someone else's account. Back online, the faces were the same. Glancing again down the list, she found Andy's sweet, dumb mug staring out at her. She'd taken that goddamned picture. He was wearing his fedora tilted at a windblown angle. It made his head look bulbous.

She was about to exit the app when a message intercepted her. The icon beside the face was the default gray silhouette, revealing that the user hadn't bothered completing his profile. The name beside the face was T. Crace. Every bit as mysterious as the pic.

The man, or lady (or whatever it was) had written, *Is this Ella Pearson from East Gish?* Despite the clear syntax, through Ella's restless drowsiness, the question seemed like an ambush.

Still, her answer arrived like a switch had been thrown. Of course she was Ella Pearson. Of course she was from East Gish. Warner had mentioned the place that very morning and it disturbed Ella that she'd already forgotten. Was memory loss a side effect of the Represitol? Aggravatingly, she couldn't seem to remember that, either.

She typed back, *One and the same.*

A ribbon of periods strung itself out, ballooning and shrinking while 'T. Crace' worked out his response. *I don't know if you remember me. Timothy Crace. We were close a long time ago, in East Gish.*

Again that name, East Gish, sent a little surge of unease loose inside her. Timothy Crace: the same man who'd called her office a few days ago? She tried to picture him. *Timmy?*

Smiley face. *That's right. Timmy Crace. I was worried it had been so long you might have forgotten about me.*

Trying to remember him and not pulling much up, she typed back, *How are you?*

Good. I was just reassigned. I'm working on the Reclamation project outside our old hometown. Being back here reminded me of you. I thought I'd see if I could track you down. I didn't think it would be this easy. Smiley face.

Ella frowned. Part of her unease was not being able to put together any sort of clear picture of East Gish. The other issue was that any time she saw that awful smiley face icon, all she could think of was Andy dumbly chortling at nothing at all. She typed back, *How's the hometown, these days?*

The same, I suppose. How've you been?

Fine, she typed, *I'm an executive for a PR firm now.*

In the course of their interaction, Ella'd gotten out of bed and wandered to the window. Lifting her head, she looked out, across the galaxy of the City, so close it seemed she could reach out and smother any light she chose. The windowpane was a cold barrier to her omnipresence.

Looking back to her phone, she found Timmy had responded, *Good for you, that's quite a step up from where you started.*

Was it? No. She pushed the thought away. Life was life: a constant clambering from one station to the next. She'd earned where she was, regardless of where she'd started.

She typed back, *Tell me about East Gish these days,* hoping he could help rough out a better picture of the place in her mind.

Raising her head again, she caught sight of the City, just as the lights started dropping out, block by block—a wave of darkness rolling toward her. In a moment, everything beyond the oily pane of the window went black. Her phone was suddenly the only light left and cast a big aura across the window. The reflection of her own face floated in the center of the bluish smudge. Ella looked back at the screen. Where Timmy's messages had appeared, there was a new message: *Network Lost.*

Using the phone as a flashlight, Ella found her way back to the bed.

She was prepared for more sleeplessness as her curiosity scattered doubts and questions through her head. Where any memory of East Gish or Timmy Crace might have been there was only a gaping void and then, just beyond the void, a deep and instant sleep.

9

Reassignment

Redactions

After drafting an email to the United Electric people (it was CCI's biggest and most dynamic account) Ella spent a long moment looking over what she'd written until she realized she wasn't reading it, only blankly staring at the type, a haphazard collation of characters that may have had no relation to each other at all.

Frustrated by her lack of progress, Ella pushed out from the desk to go spend some time with Clarence. The sun should have been on him by now, but the day was gray and wet and the bonsai sat in gloom. The moss around the roots felt a little dry and so, pulling on her gardening gloves, she went into her private washroom to get a sip of water in a tiny paper cup. Crossing back through the room, she was just passing by the desk when the intercom chirped.

"Ms. Pearson?" Dawn's voice horned in.

Ella grumbled and set down the cup and took off her gloves to depress the switch on the little box. "I'm on lunch, Dawn."

"Sorry..." the girl got mousy.

"Well, what is it?"

"Mr. Warner would like to see you."

"Now?"

"He said so, yes."

Ella grumbled again. In no particular hurry, she finished watering the bonsai and put everything away—the little paper cup into the trash, the gardening gloves in the bottom drawer of her desk.

•

While Ella didn't—hadn't ever—particularly liked Warner, he didn't produce the same level of deference and fear in her that he seemed to arouse in others. But now, out of her office and crossing the courtyard of cubicles to his, a peculiar anxiety hounded her.

Ushered through the door by Warner's secretary, Ella wasn't encouraged by the atmosphere in the room. Nor was she encouraged by the fact that Warner waved her forward, indicating the chair on the opposite side of his desk, without otherwise acknowledging her. He kept staring at his computer screen. Behind him, drizzle devoured the City, buildings in the distance consumed by a collapsing sky. Maybe it was just the dim day fostering her unease. She never felt quite right on cloudy days and today was particularly dreary.

Taking the seat, Ella waited while Warner finished what he was working on. This was probably just a check-in, she thought. Probably he wanted an update on some detail or other. So, when he finally addressed her, she felt slapped by his curt announcement, "You're off the First Assembly account..."

That rainy-day numbness washed instantly away. Still, in spite of her newfound presence, she wasn't so sure she'd heard him right. "What?"

"Pearson, let's not make this into a *thing*." He pushed a slim manilla folder across the desk to her. She didn't pick it up. Didn't look at it.

"A thing," she said, mildly disgusted by the word—it brought to mind an image of the intruder in Andy's apartment, a *thing*. Forcing the thought away, she said, "A *thing*, what is that supposed to mean?"

Nudging the envelope, so it advanced on her another half inch, he said, "I'm going to need you to readjust your workload." He tapped the envelope with a finger. "This is your new priority. I'll redistribute the rest of your accounts to the other ad..." He gave a pause long enough so that the word, "persons," seemed plainly meaningful.

Ad persons. So that's what this was: common sexism. Thompson's boy obviously hadn't liked her stepping in yesterday and now here she was: booted, because she'd been right and had had the courage to exclaim it.

"Is there a problem, Pearson?"

"I think there might be a problem with Thompson, if he can't see..."

"Pearson. Don't go all wolf-mother on me. This has nothing to do with Thompson." He tapped the envelope again. "This is a priority. It's right for you. You're the only one I can see up to the task of handling it."

Ella gave the folio a quick, dismal look. "All of my accounts, did you say?"

He indicated the folder on the table. "This will be your focus moving forward."

"It's not necessary, doing that. If Thompson wants me off the Assembly account I understand, but I can manage..."

"Pearson, I told you it doesn't have anything to do with that. This is..."

"And I'm telling you the work load isn't..."

"Pearson." He didn't shout, but his tone was cool enough to shut her up. "It's a big assignment. I wouldn't give it to just anyone and I wouldn't be surprised if it brings you to East Gish."

"What?"

"East Gish, you'd mentioned taking some time off to go there. This dovetails nicely with that plan, I think."

Ella nodded sourly. It was decided, whatever the decision had been. There was no point in arguing. She stood slowly, snatching the envelope and going to the door with all the languid composure she could muster, so to illustrate that her leaving was entirely self-determined.

•

Back at her desk, Ella delayed opening Warner's folder—feeling, regardless of his short reassurance, that whatever was hiding within that jaundicy envelope was a demotion to some degree. Instead, she decided to see if the mysterious Timmy had continued their conversation from the previous evening in her absence.

Taking her phone off the desktop and logging in, she found he'd written back just after the blackout had arrived. There was his answer for the request she'd made: *Tell me about East Gish these days.* He'd written back, *Much the same as you remember, I think.*

By the transcript, that was the second time he'd ducked the question. Ella couldn't tell if the static surge of annoyance she was feeling now was rolled over from her interaction with Warner, or if it could be solely attributed to Timmy's casual evasion. Or, maybe it was something else entirely; something deeper. At the implied suggestion, Ella was frustrated that she couldn't seem to remember anything clearly about East Gish. Beyond her certainty that that was where she was from—her hometown—all she could seem to conjure up was a pastiche of undulating wilderness, a lineup of rural houses. Stock-photo memories. She logged out and tossed the phone away. It landed, clattering and skittering on the desktop.

Returning to the envelope Warner had given her, inside she found the slimmest account folio she'd ever seen. Slim and beguiling. Where usually she'd find a bevy of account information, contact information, reams of info about the client's past PR and marketing efforts and loads more describing the entity's operations, strategies and goals, here one single slip of computer printout glared up at her. It looked like a faded reproduction of a birth certificate. The document had been enthusiastically black-marked. The date the certificate had been issued, along with the organization that had issued it, and the name of the bureaucrat who'd made it official, had all been reduced to solid, black strikes. All that remained was an illegible signature slashed across the bottom line and a name at the head of the document: Misha Kant.

It was a joke. There was no other conclusion to come to: the folder's contents didn't constitute an account. Accounts had clients, accounts had charges. Accounts had managers and board-heads that demanded results and near constant reassurance.

Picking up the sheet of paper, Ella gave it another once over and pushed out from her desk.

•

Two floors below, in the art department, Mark Carter sat, tinkering with an arrangement on his computer screen. The image was a closeup of a man's hand pushing a plate of food toward a child. The banner at the top of the frame read: *Sharing, it's the new having!* At the bottom of the frame a postscript announced that the message was "Brought to you by the First Assembly." Mark had been jiggering the position of the text by incremental degrees for the better part of his morning.

Rocking his shoulders to the beat streaming through his headphones, he didn't notice Ella's approach.

She stood aside a moment before impatience got the better of her. Slapping him with Warner's folder harder than she intended, it gave a whip-crack. Flinching and spinning in his chair, the ear phones fell off his head. They landed around his neck.

He was cute. Ella'd always thought that. They'd been intimate after an office party some years ago and had both agreed it'd been a mistake, one they wouldn't make again. It couldn't work between them, they'd jointly decided. So, it had only happened a few more times after that.

Now, looking at him, she couldn't seem to remember what they'd both been so reluctant about. He was cute and didn't seem unusually stupid.

"Holy shit, it's Ella!" he announced and stood up, craning over the walls of his cubicle to chatter to his neighbors, "Guys! Guys! Ella's here."

That's what it was, Ella remembered instantly: he was a goofball of the most grating variety. Ignored by everyone, the man didn't seem effected. As Ella understood it, all he was hoping to do was embarrass her. She smacked him with Warner's folder a second time, not as hard. "Sit down, jackass."

Mark obliged and gave a little bow. With a pretentious flourish of is hand, he asked, "And what can I do for you, m'lady?"

"You can start by not calling me that," she said. She tossed the folder down on his desk. He followed where it landed and, finding that it did not squirm, opened it to examine the sheet inside.

He shrugged and looked at her.

"It's come down from on high: a priority."

Another shrug. "Okay. What should I do with it, darling?"

"Don't call me darling… Produce its counterpart."

"Not sure I follow."

"A death certificate, Mark."

"You want me to forge a government document?" He pulled the headphones up from around his neck, tellingly, and said, "Sorry, El. I got work to do. I can't mess around this morning." He opened the head phones to duck back inside.

Snatching the headset away, Ella managed to get his attention back. "I'm not messing around. I was told this is a priority, so it supersedes whatever else you've got on the burner."

He laughed uncomfortably. "I am not forging a government document. No way. Sorry…" When he reached for the headphones, Ella hid the device behind her back.

"I'm not asking you to forge a document, Mark. I'm asking you to help me counter a practical joke. That's all I'm asking…"

"A practical joke, while a righteous cause, is hardly a *priority handed down from on high…*" Mark said, reexamining the document.

"It is when it comes from Warner..."

Mark was of the legion terrified by Warner. It sounded in his voice, even now at the brief mention of the man's name. "Are you saying Warner is planning on playing a practical joke on someone? Is that what you're telling me, Ella? Because, forgive me, that seems highly unlikely. Warner is just not a practical jokester, even with a joke," he searched the birth certificate again, "as potentially vicious as this one."

"Of course he's a prankster, Mark: the hats?"

"Hats? What are you talking about?"

"Never mind. How long do you need to put it together?"

"A couple hours, if I thought you were serious. And, if I was willing to participate. But I hope that you aren't and I certainly am not..."

"No document, no headphones..."

"Fine. I prefer keeping my head, anyway, sweetie."

"Don't call me sweetie, and don't make me call Warner just so that he can tell you himself that this is a top priority. Don't make me do that, Mark. I like you too much."

Gone rigid, the man stared at her.

"I'm not asking you to forge anything. I'm asking you to help me with a joke. You can put a big banner at the top that reads, *this is not an actual document.* You can make the attending physician Dr. Frankenstein, for all I care. Make it as big and jokey as you want. Hell, the jokier the better. Okay?" She handed him back his headphones and warned him, "I'll be back for it tomorrow."

•

Ella's confidence remained steadfast throughout the remainder of her day, hung on tenaciously until she got outside.

On the short walk to her hotel, it began to erode; slowly, gradually melting off until, standing in her suite, looking out the window to the CCI building, where it plunged into the heavy, hanging sky, her confidence was barely holding together at all. Mark was right. Warner was not the kind to go in for pointless pranks.

Ella considered heading right back to the office.

Taking her phone from her purse, she called Mark's desk and got his voicemail. He'd probably gone home. She didn't bother leaving a message. She slid the phone back away. He'd have the document for her tomorrow and then she could decide what to do with it.

•

That night Ella had a terrible dream: the Caveman clambering over her, his arms tenacious and wriggling fluidly like tentacles. Ella could not fight him off. The monster squirmed inside her arms, slithered under her shirt and, a moment later, everything went black as her blouse started slipping up over her head, blocking out the world like a spout of rising, black water. She was drowning in her shirt, drowning in the darkness inside it.

Giving up battling the Caveman, she started fighting fitfully against the more immediate adversary of her clothes. Tearing and thrashing wildly, she managed to get herself free.

With the shirt gone and her body exposed, Ella was horrified to find the Caveman had latched onto a spigot fixed absurdly in her abdomen, sucking so hard his cheeks collapsed into his face. Too weak to push him off, Ella understood what had to be done. Turning the knob atop the faucet, it squeaked open. The Caveman's cheeks engorged instantly.

As he nursed greedily at the spigot, Ella's body seemed to constrict. Her bones showed through her skin and then, one by one, collapsed with a succession of bright pops. The Caveman just kept sucking, growing as he fed. Above her now, the beast bulged larger and larger. In a moment he was all she could see and she was buried beneath him.

Ella woke panicked, rigidly sitting up in the hotel bed, her fists bunching up the sheets. The sun had already started rising. Beyond the window, the sky was graying toward daylight.

10

A Check Up
An Old Photo
The Cafe Across the Street

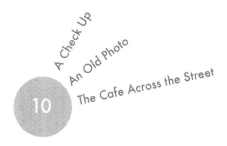

Seated on the exam table, Ella was happy to see that her Practitioner had left his fedora behind for the day's business. After cleaning his hands, he took a chair in the corner, by the cabinets. Staring into the tablet laid out on his lap, the Practitioner asked how she was feeling. It seemed as though the question was intended for the computer.

"Very well, actually."

"Oh, yes?"

"Yes. Some things have happened recently... I'm feeling like I'm off in the right direction again. Honestly, I feel better than I have in a long time."

The Practitioner nodded encouragingly. "Things with your partner," he paused to examine the screen more closely, "Andy, are going well, then?"

"Better than ever: I broke up with him."

The Practitioner turned away from the screen to look at her—concerned.

"It's for the best, really. We weren't a good match, Andy and I."

Standing up and setting the tablet aside, the Practitioner said, "I'd like to do a quick diagnostic, if that's alright." He came around behind her. Ella scooted back on the smudgy metal table to accommodate him. His grip was cold.

"You don't have problems letting go—do you?" he asked, holding her neck gently.

Ella leaned her head down. "No. I suppose I don't, not in this case, anyway. You know, I tried to make it work. I really did, but it was like I was fighting to make a pumpkin grow in a pot of tar..."

"I'm hearing a lot of 'I' and not much 'we.' How did Andy take it?"

She was about to tell him that he was *her* Practitioner, not Andy's and that, as such, he should be concerned primarily with *her* wellbeing before anyone else's. She started to answer, but instead let out a little, "Ow." Her vision glared briefly bright. Where the floor tiles had seemed dim, a beige speckle, they flooded suddenly with kaleidoscopic color. It only lasted a moment. The tiles faded, dull again.

"Sorry, I should have told you that would pinch. I'm done, at any rate," he said and set the collar of her shirt right and patted her on the shoulder and came back around to his chair, holding a small sample tube which he set on the counter beside him. Something at the bottom glistened, but it was too small to see from where Ella sat. The Practitioner collected his computer again and sat, crossing his legs. "We were talking about Andy," he reminded her.

She'd forgotten. "He'll be fine. He didn't say much."

"How long ago was this?"

"A few days. It's been great, really. I took yesterday off work to try and get my new apartment furnished and..." That had only gone marginally well. She'd called Dawn's extension early in the morning and left a message that she wouldn't be in. Normally, this never could have been possible; a rigor of meetings and appointments prevented her much room during the workday, but now, with Warner's prank having redistributed her workload and left her only that one silly assignment, she felt comfortable taking the time off. She'd come full circle to thinking the whole thing was a joke again: Warner's way of insisting that she take that vacation he kept hinting about. Mark's death certificate, she was certain, would make a perfect rebuttal: thanks for the concern but back off. After leaving the message for Dawn, she'd called a cab.

•

On the border of the Northern District, Ella kept a storage unit in a sprawling self-store complex. The structure might have been a parking deck in its past life; all of the floors seemed to slant precariously. Constructed from brick, the building leaned to the side and bulged at the middle, like it had been made to ingest too much over the years. The windows, arched at the top, were bricked over, too. The hue didn't quite match.

Out on the curb, Ella asked the cabby to wait.

Passing through halls of chainlink partitions, it took Ella a long time to find her unit. The number was printed on her key, but the numbers on the units seemed out of sequence and so she wandered the floor, following narrow corridor after narrow corridor, coming to dead ends and roundabouts that brought her back to where she'd started. It all looked confusingly homogenous: dingy chain link and panels of overhead door and chipped, blackened brick columns everywhere.

Finally finding her unit, she unlocked the door and struggled to get it raised. It went up with a shrill, rusty racket.

Inside was a mess. Only on seeing it, did Ella remember that she hadn't ever actually been to the unit. She'd hired a moving team to take her things here and, by the look of it, they'd been in a hurry to get the job done. A table, looking like it had been lobbed, rested upended at the back of the unit. One of the legs was snapped off. Boxes were crushed into a precarious pyramid in the center of the room. It looked hopeless; Ella was really only after one thing for now: an air mattress she'd kept for the chance visitor who might have come to stay at her and Terry's old place. Now, looking around, it could be anywhere—at the very bottom of the avalanche.

She wouldn't let herself be discouraged. Setting her purse in the corner, Ella started in.

Clambering up on the pile, something cracked under her weight. Whatever it was must have been buried deep inside the mound. Looking down, she couldn't see anything breakable, just a knot of dusty curtains. They didn't seem remotely familiar (a horrid, radioactive green embroidered with beige flowers, so tacky she thought she'd certainly remember them) and Ella wondered if the movers' had even put the correct belongings into the unit. She continued in, opening up the first box she came to. There wasn't anything recognizable inside. Pushing it away, she went for another.

Before she could get it open, the light above her started going muddy.

Ella looked up as the filament in the bulb faded.

Turning back to where she'd set her purse by the door, she just caught sight of it before everything went black. With the buzzing of fluorescents in the hallway silenced, the musty smell in the place seemed suddenly more pronounced, like the darkness had called it forward.

"Hello?" Her voice echoed through the floor.

She held still for a moment, before feeling her way carefully back down the pile and finding the cold, rough wall beside the door. The room felt like it was making loops around her. She happened on her purse and fumbled her phone out from inside.

When the screen lit a frosty halo around the room everything seemed to settle. In the screen's glow something on the floor (the corner of a picture frame, just poking out of the base of the pile) caught Ella's attention. She tucked her finger under the edge and worked it out. Beneath the cracked glass was a photo of a boy, maybe Clara's size. He looked familiar, in the way children do. She turned it over. On the backside someone had written *April, Ten, Timmy.* She turned the picture back and looked at the boy again.

Tucking the frame into her purse, she brought the phone up to survey the room. The light barely extended beyond the closest strata of boxes. It was a lost cause, she supposed: trying to find the mattress now. Throwing her purse over her shoulder and closing the unit back up, Ella followed the dim light of her phone back toward the stairwell, already resolved that she wouldn't ever come back here and wouldn't continue paying for the space, either. They could keep her broken junk, auction it off. She'd buy new stuff. A *real* and consequential new beginning. What kind of adult sleeps on an air mattress, anyway?

Outside, she got the cabby to bring her to a furniture store where she bought a new mattress and arranged to have it delivered that afternoon and bought a new picture frame for more than she thought it was worth. Over the next few days, she decided, she'd hire an interior decorator to deal with the gaps in furniture and decor. Until then, a mattress and a photo would suffice.

•

Splayed out in her new bed in the center of the otherwise empty living room and trying to watch a series on her phone, Ella's attention kept returning, again and again, to the newly framed photo of Timmy, wanting it to seem more familiar than it did. She tried not to let it bother her that the picture refused her and comforted herself that, at any rate, Timmy must look much different now; unrecognizable in a newer way.

Setting down her phone, she went to the window. The night was cool but she'd cracked the window to let the staleness out of the apartment. Noise from the cafe across the street drifted into the room. Ella stared a moment at the stenciling on the awning out front. When she laughed, the noise reminded her of Andy, and she choked it out quickly. The place was called *The East Gish Club.*

•

The East Gish Club was not as busy as it had seemed from her room. A thin, boisterous group crowded around the bar at the back, but the rest of the place was murky and empty.

The waiter who came to her table seemed annoyed that Ella had shown up to take a seat so late. Ella decided, regardless of the service, that she'd make the guy's night with a ludicrously generous tip.

"You decided?" he asked curtly, his voice too loud for his proximity.

"The East Gish Club, huh?" Ella hadn't even looked at the menu.

"What?"

"I said, it's called the East Gish Club, huh?"

"That's what it says on the menu. Also, on the awning out front. What do you want?"

"I only think it's funny because I'm from East Gish, originally. I just moved to the neighborhood."

He stared at her.

Glancing quickly at the menu, Ella picked something at random and let the guy get away. He seemed impatient to.

Across the room at the bar, a dozen patrons stood with their unused stools pushed aside. They leaned in, hollering and laughing. A moment later, the light over Ella's table got a shade brighter—warm and almost orange in hue—and Ella felt a surge of contentedness wash over her. It was nice being out in public, even if she was alone.

When the waiter returned to ask if everything was okay, Ella said it was.

He hovered at the table a moment, uncertainly. "I'm sorry if I was rude when you came in." Contradicting his words, his tone was forceful, all the syllables like little bones being snapped.

Ella shook her head. "It's late to come in and take a table, I get it."

"It isn't that," he said, turning to gawk at the crowd by the bar. "Every night they come in. They order early—one thing, the same thing every time—and then they just *hang around* being loud and driving everyone else off. It's gotten so bad, I'm the only one the place can employ anymore. Now, I have to do it all myself: managing the bar and the floor on my own."

"That's not right."

"It's gonna close the place down if something doesn't change."

"Can't you ask them to leave?"

He shook his head. "They're acquaintances of the owner. He's from there, too."

"I'm sorry?"

"East Gish," the waiter gestured broadly around the walls of the cafe, where a series of photographs hung. "All the pictures are of there. He took them. It's kind of nostalgic, I guess—if you're from there... If you wanna take a look around..."

Ella said she would and thanked him. The waiter retreated to the bar, hesitantly.

She sat a while longer before standing to make her way around the room. The feeling of content didn't leave her as she looked at the old photographs. She was pleased to find that they were familiar. They looked exactly like what she remembered of East Gish. There was a photo of heaving hills, stuck with trees, thinner and softer as they drew away into the distance. There were photos of houses set against backdrops of forest. There was photo of a downtown—brick buildings standing tall around a narrow boulevard—which Ella did not recognize. The cardboard placard beside the picture said, *Downtown Gish,* in careful handwriting. There was a photo of a team of workers in a field, hunchbacked under a sky that was bright white in the monochrome. For a moment, she caught herself envying those men and women out there. It must have been a warm day, with the sky so bright. Beside the photo the cardboard placard read, *Autumn Harvest, Pearson's Farm.* Seeing her name up on the tag like that made her brim with pride. The farm must have belonged to a relation of hers, employing all those hardy folk in the field. No wonder she enjoyed the sun so much: she was from farming stock.

Winding picture by picture through the restaurant, Ella landed at the furthest end of the place, just outside the crowd of noisy regulars. Looking past them, she found the waiter inside the glossy wooden rampart of the bar, looking annoyed and standing rigid. Now, it became clear how she'd make the poor guy's night. Wedging herself into the throng, she nodded at the waiter, hoping to draw him over. He turned to her with a look of reproach—*now you, too?*—and didn't move.

On a blackboard behind him, a list of specials had been scrawled out. Ella yelled over the bluster of the crowd, "What's an East Gish Dawn-Breaker?"

Taking an enthusiastic step forward, the waiter's answer was dead-ended by the man beside Ella, who turned to respond to her, "No goddamned good, is what it is."

Those around him laughed heartily.

"I'm sure it's good," Ella said, trying to defend the talents of the waiter/barman.

"No. It isn't. If you want something good, go with the Gish Sunset. That's topnotch. It's what we all get every time, isn't that right, boys?" The crowd cheered, but it quickly died out. "It's the only thing this place does right."

Looking back at the waiter, Ella said, "I'll try a Dawn Breaker."

"No, no," the man beside her argued loudly. "Save her the disappointment; get 'er a Sunset, or get 'er nothing at all." He sounded serious, but everyone around him laughed.

The waiter, who'd started forward again, stopped a second time, uncertainly.

"Don't tell me what I want," Ella told the man. Looking back at the waiter, she insisted on a Dawn Breaker. It wasn't very good, when she got it, but the waiter stared at her expectantly and so she nodded in an affect of appreciation and she said, "Very good."

Beside her, the man said, "Spoken like someone who's never been to East Gish."

The party roared. It occurred to Ella that these people would have enjoyed Andy's company. She snapped around to look at the man. "It just so happens, I'm from East Gish, so I *would* know."

The crowd gasped in feigned outrage—so there were two things they were capable of—before falling into laughter again. Taking a more even tone, the man beside her asked, "Are you really? We're all from East Gish. That's why we keep coming here. George Latham." He extended his hand to her. He was a very big man. His hand was wider than the two of hers put together. He certainly wasn't a clock maker. Maybe a construction worker.

"You're all from East Gish? Isn't that funny." Ella, forgetting instantly that she was trying to be against the man, shook his hand and introduced herself. "How come you're all in the City?"

He shrugged. "Where else would we be?" Behind him the crowd laughed, but it was unclear whether or not this was in response to what he'd said. Drifting off into separate conversations, the crowd seemed to have stopped paying attention to Ella. The man said, "There's not much going on there, these days."

"That's not so. I have a friend there, working on a Reclamation project, Timmy Crace. Do you know him? He's from there, too."

The man shook his head, no. "Can't say I remember him."

Another round of laughter bubbled up. Even though it was likely unrelated to Ella, the sound chaffed her. She said, "When did you move to the City?"

"Feels like forever. I'll tell you, I'd move back in an instant if I could."

"You don't like the City?"

The man turned and looked over the empty restaurant behind them before returning his attention to Ella, like he was worried about someone eavesdropping. "It isn't that, really. I just have this... I don't know, a yearning, I guess you could say, to go back there. That's why I come here. I wouldn't say it reminds me of Gish, but it reminds me to remember it—is that strange?"

Ella shrugged.

"Do you get that—the urge to go back there?"

Ella looked away, to the bright, golden lights above the bar to think about it. The bulb hanging over her head was a slightly different hue than all the other bulbs, a little dimmer, a little bluer in quality. "I guess I do, recently. Honestly, I hadn't thought about the place in forever, but now, yeah. I guess I do miss it. It's funny," she looked around the room, indicating the pictures, "the photos are exactly how I remember the place, but before I saw the photos, I was questioning if I remembered it at all."

The man nodded as though he could relate. Ella'd already forgotten his name.

"Well, it's nice meeting another East Gishian. I thought I'd met them all. You should come back. We're here nearly every night."

Ella nodded. "Yeah. I will. I just moved in across the street so..."

Looking back at the waiter, she found he'd retreated into the shadows, looking sullen. Ella felt suddenly ashamed of herself for having switched camps so abruptly. Thanking the man beside her for his hospitality, she backed away from the bar and slipped outside, into the cool evening.

Only after she'd gone back up to her room and gotten into bed, did she realize that she had not only forgotten the generous tip she'd intended to leave the waiter, she'd forgotten to pay him altogether.

She promised herself that she'd go back soon to pay off the debt.

•

"I understand, Ms. Pearson," the Practitioner was saying, "that in your view, letting go of things is probably one of your strengths, wouldn't you say?" The pause he allowed wasn't long enough for an answer. "It's certainly good for the work you do, I have no doubt, being able to move from one task, one client to the next. But, just because it's a strength..."

Ella stared at him.

His legs were crossed and he took a pause to rearrange them. Once he was settled again, he said, "What I'm getting at is, while everyone values consistency, sometimes what's really important is having a willingness to adapt. Do you see?" Ella moved to speak but before she could, the Practitioner was going on again, "You see, it's our ability to adjust that makes us so successful and keeps us above the level of the savages. Do you follow me?" Another pause, where Ella felt she was expected to answer but this one was even shorter than the last. "The issue we'd discussed earlier in the week: how are your *concerns* feeling?"

"How are my *concerns feeling*... I guess I'm not feeling so anxious anymore. But, I think most of that has to do with..."

"Good. Good. Very good. We'll leave the prescription as it is, then, for the time being." He took a moment to fool around with his tablet before returning his attention to her. "I have a series of questions..."

"Is this to do with the prescription?"

"Nothing to do with your Pharma App. More a general inventory, if you don't mind."

"I don't mind," Ella said, eager to have the visit concluded.

"Very good." He read from his screen, "Scaling from one to ten, how capable are you feeling, today and in general, about your ability to adequately care for yourself?"

"This isn't to do with my prescription?"

Rather than answer, the Practitioner looked on vacantly, awaiting her response.

"Ten, I guess."

The Practitioner tapped the screen. "And, again on a scale from one to ten, what would you say your general outlook on life is at this time?"

"Let's go with an eight."

"Fine. In that vein, scaling on one to ten, how capable do you feel about your ability to care for someone else..."

"This isn't about my prescription?"

"One to ten..."

"Is this about..." she almost said, 'the Caveman,' but stopped herself short. The whole issue was behind her now—Ella was determined to make it so, determined to forget it in the way she seemed to forget everything else these days. Besides, there was no way for the Practitioner to know anything about that; she hadn't mentioned it. Hedging her answer, she said, "Six."

"Six?"

Ella shrugged. "I should probably take care of myself before..."

"So, six. Above average..."

"I'm sorry?"

"Six is above average," he said it a little louder, but still distracted, looking into his screen.

"Is it?"

"Five would be average."

"Would it? I've always thought of seven as average..."

The Practitioner didn't seem to care. He finished up tapping on the screen and stood and said, "Well, that's about it. Take care, Ms. Pearson."

He shook her hand and left.

In his absence, Ella touched the back of her neck where she'd felt the pinch. Back there, a rough line, a delicate little scab, had already settled in. It didn't hurt at all.

11

Not a Document
The Robe Turns Up Again
Three Signatures and Fourteen Initials

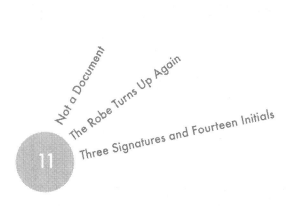

Dawn was absent when Ella cruised by the reception desk. She made a note of the time when she got into her office. The girl was over an hour late. These truancies were becoming an all too regular aggravation. It was obvious, Ella'd need to have a talk with the errant girl. She wouldn't resort to threats, not yet, but she'd let Dawn know, in explicit terms, that the girl's position here was at stake. Maybe a little threat, then: a reminder that Ella remembered well enough the extension for Staffing.

Coming around her chair, Ella was flummoxed a moment, thinking she'd wandered into the wrong office. Looking across the plane of her desktop, she found it amiss, though it took her a moment to figure out how. The keyboard was closer than she liked it. Also, the screen had been moved six inches to the right. The distance was easy to determine, a faint patina clouded the wood's finish where the monitor was supposed to sit. Also, the photo she kept, the peaceful panorama of a long, rowed field under a perfect blue sky had been laid down so the image was hidden. Ella took a moment to put everything right before taking her seat. With the keyboard back where it belonged, she booted up the computer, waiting the requisite moments while it hummed quietly, waking from its night sleep.

When the tab opened for her password, Ella typed out, *Green Field 1. Incorrect Password* flashed instantly on the screen in rude, red letters. She was in the habit of changing the pass every few days and so the fact that it had failed wasn't alarming. She tried again, *Summer Harvest.* The computer withdrew its scarlet insult but only for an instant. It flashed back, as impolitely as before. She thought on it a moment, finally entering, *Terry's Girl.* That failed as well. After the third attempt the computer abandoned it's initial red message for another, *Contact network administrator.* Now she was locked out.

It was going to be one of those days, Ella determined. Bending down, she collected her purse from under the desk and got out her phone to call IT, immediately distracted by an alert from her instant messenger. There was a new message from Timmy, *As many trees as ever. The spring is finally starting to show, almost all the snow is gone.* For a moment, Ella thought it was a haiku, or a riddle. Maybe both, inextricably intertwined.

Then, she realized that the mention of 'trees...' was his answer to her having asked him 'how East Gish was, these days.' He'd left his phone number with a postscript that she should give him a call sometime.

She wrote back a long message, deleted it, typed another, deleted it, and finally wrote nothing at all. Looking at his message made her feel unaccountably alone: a phone number from a stranger, as if she were in such dire need of amity. It made her feel a little lecherous too, that she'd slept the night before with his old, child's face beside her own.

Reserved to let the interaction die before she closed out the program, she copied his number and made a space for him in her contacts. When she looked up, she found Dawn lingering in the doorway. Tossing the phone back into her purse, she said, "Nice of you to show."

The girl jerked with a mousy, "Oh."

"Was there something you wanted, Dawn?"

The girl stammered a moment before saying, "Warner would like you, I think."

"You think? Fine," she said, but she didn't move. Dawn didn't either. "Was there anything else, then, Dawn?"

The girl shook her head but remained in the door. Rising deliberately from her desk Ella went to the window to see to Clarence. The moss was damp, but he looked a little peaked; the leaves a shade lighter than she would have liked and Ella decided that, sometime next week, she'd take him home, pull him out of the pot and do some careful pruning to his roots. When she turned back to the door, she was annoyed to find Dawn still loitering there. "Don't you have anything to do this morning?"

The girl gave a meek shrug. Huffing, Ella crossed the room and passed the girl by. Pausing, staring straight ahead, she said, "We need to have a conversation about your punctuality. Something needs to be done about it."

The girl said nothing. Ella moved on.

•

Warner seemed threateningly focused on Ella when she came through his door. He continued his silent appraisal as she crossed the room and took a seat before his desk. Not so much as a 'Good morning' from the man. So, she gave it first, clipped, curt, "Morning," she said after she'd sat.

He sounded impatient—or, was it indignant?—when he said, "Let's talk about where you are with this Misha Kant business."

It took her a moment to remember that as the name from the birth certificate. She'd meant to go see Mark this morning but hadn't gotten to it yet. "Right. I..."

Moving with rehearsed intensity, Warner produced a document from his drawer and slapped it down so that it sat between them—an awkward third party. He recited dryly, "...*This article should not be construed as a document at all.*"

Ella shrugged. "I've haven't seen it myself, yet." She rose slightly from her seat to pick up the sheet and, seated again, took a moment to look it over. Mark had done as she'd asked and done a good job, at that. It looked authentic from top to bottom, other than the thick, italicized disclaimer filling the footer: *This article is not meant to prove or imply that anyone has passed away. In fact, this article should not be construed as a document at all.*

Ella laid it back on the desktop. She forced herself to laugh, and when Warner was only disdainfully silent, she raised her palms, as though to say, What did you expect? She settled up against the chair back.

Warner stared at her. It was a long, cold moment and Ella would not look away. Breaking first, Warner shifted forward, scooting his chair in and looking down at the slip of yellowish paper. Mark had done a commendable job with that, too: making the thing look aged, an ancient scroll that had been passed through a dusty scanner.

"It's interesting, the inclusion of that disclaimer at the end of the document. At first, as I'm sure you can understand, I thought, well, this whole thing's just a mucked up joke now and now we've lost some days, plus whatever effort went into this *thing*..." That word again, *thing*, reminded Ella of the Caveman. She felt soiled: the image from the dream, the monster latched onto the spigot in her abdomen, suddenly focused in her mind. She'd forgotten all about it until that moment, but now it reared up in full color, like it had only been waiting behind a veil, waiting for the right moment to lurch back into her consciousness.

"If you'd wanted..." Ella said and was cut off by the chirp of the intercom.

Leaning aside to push the button on the device, Warner said, "Ms. Price, we're in the middle of something and I told you that I didn't wish to be disturbed..."

The receptionist's voice wavered, meek and uncertain. "I understand, sir. But the police are here. They're looking for Ms. Pearson. They say it's quite urgent."

He humphed. "Fine. I'll send her out." Releasing the button and turning to Ella he said, "We'll finish this conversation later, yes?"

•

Outside the office, it wasn't just the single uniformed cop Ella'd expected. Sure, he was there, before the receptionist's desk but assembled behind him was an extensive entourage, filling up Warner's front office. Two more uniformed cops stood back. A pair of severe looking women—character's from a Dickens' orphanage—held positions on either side of a hairy, little man. He was still dressed in Ella's robe. Someone had made a heroic attempt at cleaning it—though the grease stain down the front was still plainly visible, the whole garment was blotched with bright bleach freckles. Andy. His attempts at cleaning were vigorous and nearly always left something ruined. The garment was a travesty, fit for the trash can. Even though she'd already written it off, she felt a little grief over it now.

"Ms. Pearson?" the foremost cop brought her attention back.

"What the hell is going on here?" Ella looked past the cop to the two women near the doorway, to the Cavemán between them. "What the hell did you bring that thing here for?"

"Ma'am," the cop said. He was holding out a thick book of bound legal paper. Ella frowned at it, at the cop and then, when his arm remained extended, she ripped the document from him and hastily turned it around so that she could read the title page:

"Order to Reinstate Guardianship of Supplicant," she read aloud. Lashing her gaze back to the cop, she said, "What the hell does that mean?"

"Ma'am," the cop repeated. Now his tone seemed more like a warning than a call for attention. Ella shook her head and motioned for him to follow, leading the pack across the floor, toward her own office.

She could feel the curiosity radiating from every cubicle she passed, so she lead at a furious gate, with her head raised, determined to keep an adequate distance to allow for speculation as to whether she was leading the delegation or if she was on her own and just happened to be traveling in the same direction as it.

Back in her own reception area, noting briefly that Dawn still wasn't settled at her station, this time with some relief, Ella opened the door to her office to find Dawn behind the desk, noticing for the first time that the girl was dressed differently than usual. Gone were the typical nappy sweater and frumpy skirt and in place was a posh business suit. The effect was so disorienting, that for the second time that morning, Ella thought she'd wandered into the wrong office. As for Dawn, though she looked surprised to see Ella, and the cop trailing her, she didn't seem to register that she wasn't where she was supposed to be.

"I'll deal with this later," Ella announced to the room before pushing the cop back out the threshold, into the reception area.

As her office was smaller than Warner's, so too was her waiting room, and now it was so congested that Ella was forced to stand, looking up at the lead cop with her chin almost nuzzling the deep blue buttons of his shirt.

She shook the document and it drew attention to itself with an avian flutter, which was good, because there wasn't room to raise it up without assaulting someone. "What in the hell is this? What's going on here? What is *he* doing here?" She looked around for the Caveman, but with the room so stuffed full with tall bodies, she couldn't find him.

"Ma'am," the cop warned gently, calling her attention back.

He gestured toward the document hanging from her hand. Ella folded her arms awkwardly through the bodies so that she could reexamine the cover sheet. Again, that perplexing jargoneer's phrase: *Order to Reinstate Guardianship of Supplicant.* "I don't understand."

"The details of the order are spelled out explicitly in the document. If you have need of specifics about your case, you'll find most outlined within," the cop explained. "However, I'm to give you a brief overview, so you understand your current legal situation."

"Well, okay, get on with it."

"Very well. You've been found, by the O.S.A., to be negligent in your duties of Guardianship for the Supplicant received into your residence on Twelfth, March..."

"That isn't my residence," Ella said. Looking around the room for the little man in lingerie, and again failing to spot him in the crush of bodies, she said, "He isn't any relation of mine."

"Ma'm," this time the address was curt. If not a cop, he should have been an actor, Ella thought. It was impressive how many different ways the man had found to sound out that one word. "I'm not a lawyer. I can't argue in the document's defense and I'm not interested in hearing your own argument. I'm simply here as a deputized agent of the Office, to explain to you your legal predicament..."

"Predicament..."

"Quagmire..."

"What?"

"Ma'm, are you interested in my explaining the document to you?"

"Of course. Go on."

He nodded and resumed his recitation, "As you invited the Supplicant into your home..."

"That didn't happen. That's not at all what happened..."

"Ma'm..." Now the word sounded plaintive, a little animal hungry for something out of reach.

"You're right. I'm sorry. Please, go on."

"...You have assumed full custody and guardianship of him and, as such, abandoning, abusing or in anyway neglecting him, shall be considered a Chargeable Felony with a minimum ten year sentence..."

"Ten years?"

"Ma'am," he warned a final time and produced another set of documents, which he laid out on Dawn's desk and instructed Ella to sign, threatening immediate arrest at her refusal.

After three signatures and fourteen initials, the cop packed up his document and slipped through the crowd and, like segment after segment of a centipede's retreating body, the rest of the entourage filed out behind him.

In the new emptiness of the room, Ella finally laid eyes on the little beast once more; standing against the wall, the hem of his robe jerking as he scratched his ass absently.

"Stop that," Ella said. Whether he understood wasn't entirely clear, but after staring at him a hard moment, he dropped his hand away and went to standing idle. "Stay there. Stay *right there.*" She jabbed her finger at him, at the place she wanted him to stay.

In Ella's office, Dawn was on the phone, her posture going rigid the moment Ella stomped through the door. The girl kept talking into the receiver as Ella crossed the room toward her, Dawn's face growing longer and longer, her head rising up as Ella arrived at the desk's edge. Reaching out with a slow, deliberate finger, Ella crushed the hook switch. With the call summarily ended, Dawn withdrew the receiver from her face.

"We'll talk about this when I get back. We have a lot to talk about when I get back," Ella said before returning to the reception area for the Caveman.

He'd wandered off.

Ella found him a few moments later, trying to push his way through a closed office door. The receptionist watching him seemed more amused than concerned but Ella apologized and, taking the Caveman by the neck of his filthy robe, got him turned around.

12 Legal Advice

The Disappearing Act

Jim Jasper sat on the far side of a pile of papers and books under which, Ella assumed, a desk must have strained. The man had been recommended by Warner (through the cipher of Warner's secretary, Ms. Price) but on seeing the office he inhabited, Ella was beginning to suspect that the suggestion had been made in a spirit of sarcasm. The office had two rooms. In the first, a receptionist labored in a cramped corner—her position there seeming an afterthought. Most of the space was dominated by a dark leather couch that stretched the span of the room, fitting so snugly in place that the sumptuous roundness of both armrests had been compressed by the walls. In the second room, the attorney's proper office area, no walls seemed to exist at all. On close inspection, Ella determined that the room was ringed with shelving but that was hard to ascertain: only the top shelves were visible and, as such, they simply appeared to be the top tier of the heaping boxes that crowded the corners and rose up to the ceiling precariously, looking like something a mountaineer might see the challenge in. There was barely room for Ella to sit. Beside her, the Caveman's chair was unbalanced, half the legs resting on the ground, the other two legs set up on an uneven pile of binders. Ella had taken a stressed but carefree looking pose—holding the back of the Caveman's chair rigidly so that, fidgeting as he did, he wouldn't fall into her.

The big binder the cop had given Ella had been set up on a recurring landslide of loose paper, the lawyer repeatedly having to reset the document as it tried to escape him. The man muttered as he read and Ella thought that was the sort of thing they should train aspiring counsel out of in law school. If such a thing had been attempted on Jim, however, it hadn't stuck. Still, as infuriating as it was listening to him breathily sound the cadence of every printed word, it was slightly less aggravating than her constantly having to slap the Caveman's hand away from under the hem of his robe.

Finally finished reading through a portion of the tome, the attorney made a pained noise and set the volume aside. Shaking his head he said, "It's a real doozy, Ms. Pearson."

"Is that legal terminology?"

Ignoring the question, he hitched his head and said, "According to this document, for the last two years..."

"According to the document? How are you a lawyer and you've never heard of this? I would think... Jesus, I'd think that this would be the only thing that lawyers were talking about; it seems a real departure from jurisprudence: forcing people to house strange, drooling degenerates."

"Well..." Jasper shrugged. "It's not really my area of expertise..."

"The law?"

He ignored her, again. It was like her ridicule was transmitted in a frequency he was unable to hear. "It seems you've painted yourself into a corner on this one. You never should have invited him into the house..."

"I most certainly did not invite that," looking sideways at the intruder, the interloper, she lowered her voice, "*thing* into the house."

"It says here..." He moved the document forward and leafed through it, finding a paragraph in the section he was after. "...That on March twelfth, '*She* admitted the Supplicant into the residence...'"

"That was Clara!"

"It doesn't say anything about—who's she, the boyfriend's daughter?—it doesn't say anything about her in here. You're the only one mentioned in the report. Although," Jasper dragged the word out, turning the document a few degrees on his desk as it slid away from him and tilting his head to follow the shift, "there has been *a lot* redacted."

Ella lurched from her chair to snatch the document before it fell off onto the floor. Leafing through, she found a good majority of the text was blotted out, some whole pages black-marked, top to bottom. "Jesus, Jim, the law cannot possibly work this way."

He nodded. "I know. It doesn't seem quite right, does it?" He leaned up, shrugging and said, in a trilling, almost happy voice, "And yet, here we are."

"Nope. Nope. There has to be a straightforward solution to this."

He nodded in agreement.

"Jim! What's the solution?"

"Oh, I couldn't say for certain. I'll need some time to research the issue. But, in the meantime, there are a few things you might try..."

"*I might try?*"

"Oh, I don't know. Take him home. Take care of him. He wandered in on his own, maybe he'll wander out the same way... Stumble into someone else's life."

"That is not a solution. I need you to tell me what my legal options are..."

The shrug he kept offering was far from reassuring. "There's not much I can say to you at this point, I'm afraid. The letter of the document states clearly enough that you made two strident errors: firstly, inviting him into the home and, secondly, clothing him, which may prove your ultimate mistake—having established that you're willing and able to care for him. If I were you..."

"But, I didn't invite him in. *I* didn't clothe him..."

"I know how frustrating these things can seem for people outside the profession, but ultimately it matters much less what happened than it does what the document substantiates having happened."

Ella continued leafing through. "But look how much is marked out. If a judge sees that..."

"A judge won't ever see this. It's an O.S.A. case and the O.S.A. will hear and try it in their own tribunal..."

"The department that censored it is the same department that's going to..." Her tone had gone hushed.

"Oh, it would be premature to say who censored it. Sure, it was probably the O.S.A. but it might as easily have been Homeland Defense. The Police. Any governmental institution who has had access to it—which is to say: any government agency at all—could have redacted it. So, our first step is to figure out which agency is responsible and seek an injunction against them to have the original file opened, if it still exists. Then, so long as your story is represented faithfully in the body of the document, we can proceed to having an emancipation hearing scheduled..."

"Great. Great." Ella nodded. She leaned forward hopefully. "How long will that take?"

The rawness of Jasper's laughter caught Ella off guard. He shook his head, tossing the laughter away. "Let's just say—don't bother calling me for updates; I'll be in touch."

"What are you telling me: weeks, months?"

"More likely a year." He shrugged. "Perhaps two, but I wouldn't worry over it too much... If too long passes, he'll turn legal age and you can throw him out with impunity."

"You're joking..."

"Of course, one always hears anecdotes of lawsuits dragged out over decades," Jasper said with a laugh and when he caught Ella's horror struck gaze, he managed to dampen his tone to continue, "I can assure you, I feel very positive that that will not happen in this case."

"So what the hell am I supposed to do?"

"Go back home to your boyfriend, settle in and," he took a pause to nod and indicate the Caveman. "Go on with your life. I'll be in touch."

"Stop calling him my boyfriend. We're broken up. I'm not going back..."

Jim's tone brightened instantly. "That's wonderful news..." He was already standing, leaning over the desk which caused another landslide of papers. It must have been nearly a ream that landed on the floor with a heavy splash. He took the document back, flipping through the pages excitedly and, finding a clause buried deep within, spun the stack around and set it atop the rounded mound on the desk, stabbing at it with a triumphant finger. "There's your solution!" Ella leaned forward to read, but Jasper obligingly summarized it for her, "*The household into which the Supplicant is accepted must consist of at least two capable guardians of full standing...*"

Ella looked at the Caveman who'd resumed coddling his genitals beneath the veil of the robe. The chair under him wobbled. This time she didn't bother correcting him. "So, I'm free of him?"

"It would seem so. Congratulations! Another case closed for Jim Jasper!" he congratulated himself zealously. "Nice, too, that you and your boyfriend had such an amiable breakup so that you still spend time at his apartment..."

Ella nodded and shrugged and started to stand.

"Just to be clear," Jim said, "you were broken up at the time the Supplicant was introduced to the household, yes?"

Ella paused, her hands on the armrests of the chair, her bottom hovering inches above the seat. Beside her, the Caveman's chair tottered. Ella didn't notice. She shook her head, "Well, almost. I'd gone to Andy's to break it off and the Caveman showed before I could."

Jasper's posture deflated and, as though in practiced choreography, Ella descended back into her chair. The Caveman went over, colliding with her. The beast managed to hold onto his seat. Without looking, Ella reached out and roughly righted him.

Raising his shoulders in what might have been the longest shrug Ella had ever been exposed to, Jasper said inwardly, "You'll have to go back, then."

"What does that mean?" Ella said. "Go back?"

She stared at the attorney and, in what at first appeared a bid to avoid looking at her, Jasper hunched forward and reached out to collect the document again. This time his search was less enthusiastic but he followed the same routine, ultimately turning the tome to her, indicating a clause, and then summarizing it, "Once the Supplicant has been established in the household, the household must remain intact until such a point that the Supplicant is able to be released from Guardianship or until the legal Guardians, in the case of a willful split, obtain a Writ of Dispersement..."

"We need *court approval* to break up?"

"Technically, O.S.A. approval."

"That can't be possible. I've already moved out..."

"Well, if I were you, I'd move back. And in a hurry. If the O.S.A. finds out that you've quit the family, they'll come after you and it looks like," he referenced the document again, "a minimum ten year sentence for abandonment. Could be as long as life."

"That can't be," Ella said again, but when the attorney just held her gaze and shrugged again, Ella groaned and leaned forward to rest her head on the dense pillow of paper covering the desk.

•

The train slowed and stopped. Clogging the aisle, commuters departed and boarded in a mess of bodies and noise. The beast beside Ella was transfixed with all the bustle, but Ella was barely aware of anything beyond her own turmoil. She needed a new lawyer. Jim Jasper was obviously an incompetent. Even so early in the process, it was evident: now was the time for a second opinion. A third, even, on the chance that the second agreed with the first.

As she dwelled on her predicament, Ella's mind turned to the more immediate, looming irritant of seeing Andy again. That the Caveman had been escorted into her office could be no coincidence. There was only one person linking her with the beast and that was

Andy. Andy, her wistful, brokenhearted ex, was transformed by this realization into Ella's new, quintessential nemesis—more loathsome, even, than that dunce Jim Jasper. This was Andy's fault. It had to be his fault the Caveman had showed, his fault she was stuck on the train beside the deviant, his fault the full force of the law was now hanging over Ella's head.

The train started forward again. Preoccupied with the stain left by the Caveman's damp palm, Ella wiped her hand vigorously on her pants, only realizing in that moment that he was no longer beside her.

Some chump in coveralls was just taking the seat. Standing, Ella stumbled over him into the aisle just as the train lurched into motion. Grabbing the nearest safety bar to steady herself, she searched frantically up and down the aisles. He wasn't there.

Out, through the window, she caught sight of the tiny monster, lumbering away, toward the exit.

"Shit." She let go the bar and scrambled to the door. It rattled under her attack, but didn't give. Outside, columns blew past, the Caveman falling away.

•

On the return train, Ella remained standing and when it slowed into the station, she elbowed her way to the front of the line. Squeezing out through the doors the moment they parted, she fell out into the throng waiting below. Ella pushed through the crowd, looking around in a frenzy.

The Caveman wasn't behind the pillars. She rushed down the tunnel to the lobby. He wasn't there either, on either side of the turnstiles.

Out on the street, the rain had picked up, making the City gleam like old motor oil. She took to her tiptoes to look down the street. The little man wasn't anywhere that she could see, but the sudden proliferation of umbrellas blotted out the sidewalk almost entirely. She fell back to her heels, picking a direction arbitrarily and starting out. Drifting into the world like a quiet incantation, she was only barely aware of her own voice, "They can't arrest me for this... This isn't my fault..."

She stopped after a block, pedestrians bustling around her at the crosswalk.

A sudden swell of hope overcame her. No, of course she couldn't be arrested for this.

They'd gotten separated in the bustle. He'd slipped off the train, pulled into the overwhelming current of commuters. *Poor thing.* And hadn't she done everything she could be expected to do to retrieve him? She'd pushed people aside, lunged for the door, in a near panic.

She'd call the police, she decided; that's what any worried-sick guardian in her position would do.

With any luck the creature would disappear into the City forever and she could put the matter behind her with little more than a few feigned sniffles and an affected wringing of her hands.

Part 2
The O.S.A.

13

The Interrogation

The Arrangement

The Retreating Prospect of Freedom

"You got a lotta nerve, I'll give you that, Pearson." The woman across the table—an agent in a stiff suit who'd introduced herself as Sickens—scoffed and shook her head. At her shoulder, a mirror reflected the woman's every act. Ella's attention was drawn to it again and again but it wasn't the woman's reflection which interested her; deep down Ella was convinced that beyond that smudgy sheet of glass another party watched the proceedings, scoring her responses and deciding her fate. "Not even a day passes after your Supplicant is returned to you and you abandon him a second time. Right in public."

Beside Sickens sat a second agent, a man named Dyer, whose presence seemed entirely superfluous. He hadn't spoken once and had taken his seat ignoring Ella altogether. Contrary to his speechlessness, the man managed quite a racket. He'd spent the entire interview scratching out notes on a legal pad. Even when Sickens hadn't asked a question, even when Ella gave no response at all, the rasp of the man's pen filled the room as though he were determined to describe every-last-thing in his notes, even the quality of those strained silences.

"I didn't abandon him. I keep telling you that. He just got away." Despite the gleam of the table separating them, the stainless steel top seemed unsanitary. Ella thought she could make out a patina in the shape of asscheeks along the edge, as though someone had pressed their bared buttocks there. Ella would not touch it; she leaned away, giving the table as much space as she could.

"So you claim..."

"I want to speak with my attorney."

"So you've mentioned," Sickens said, "and, as I've already informed you, we have no intention of calling him. We have enough on you, right now, Ms. Pearson, to send your case directly to tribunal. You understand that?"

Ella was silent. Without counsel, without any recourse at all, what was there to say?

"It's a minimum ten years. That's been explained to you?"

Ella looked around the room. The cinderblock walls were dowsed in a slop of paint that didn't seem to have a foundational hue; it could have been cream or gray or green, depending on how the light settled. The ambiguity managed to make the room even more dismal.

"And let me tell you, I feel confident, very confident indeed, that we could get you twenty. Think I'm bluffing?" The woman looked at Ella a moment and then shrugged as though to imply that however Ella felt was irrelevant. "The abandonment charge is ten by itself. Tack on false reporting, negligence, perjury, I don't think there's any telling how long you'd actually have to serve. And still you sit there, all self assured. She's got some nerve, don't you think, Dyer?"

The man gave no response—not even a nod. He continued scratching out notes. Maybe Sickens was wrong. Maybe the man's name wasn't Dyer, after all. He refused to acknowledge it.

"How would you like that?" Leaning closer, Sickens said, "Twenty years. By the time you come back from the penal colony, your career will have eclipsed entirely. Your life will be over. Maybe someday," the woman's voice got gravelly with the threat, "with dedication and a lot of hard work, you could advance yourself to scrubbing bathrooms in a fancy building like the one you work in now. How would that suit you?"

"I keep telling you: I didn't abandon him. He slipped away. The train was busy... I just looked out the window a moment... and he was gone."

"It's all just a coincidence, then. Is that what you'd have us believe? You abandoned him once, he was brought back and just happened to 'slip away.' Is that what you'd have us believe, really? You think us so naive?"

"It's what happened. I swear. I went looking for him and..."

"He got off the train without your noticing," the agent mocked in a singsong too labored to pass for a lullaby. "But for some reason you didn't call the police until an hour later. You went through two train stations, you walked around on the street for twenty minutes and didn't think to call the police to let them know he'd gone missing. You have an explanation for that?"

"I was in a panic."

"In a panic? You don't strike me as the panicking kind. No. You're cool. Calculating. I've seen your kind before."

Ella felt like she was deep in a panic that very moment. "He was there and then he was gone and I saw him crossing the station and all I could think was that I needed to get him back."

"Let's say I believe you. What would you have me do?"

"It was just a mistake, an innocent mistake..."

"You'd have me just forgive the charges, is that it?" The agent made a motion like the thought of dismissing the indictment was an absurdity, an impossibility, something contrary to the laws of physics and all natural history. "And what do you think my superiors would say about that? What you fail to comprehend, Ms. Pearson, is that I'm an agent of the O.S.A. and as such, am sworn to uphold the laws and constitutional directives of the land. If my superiors caught wind that I'd disregarded those sacred duties, where do you think I'd end up? Courtmartialed. Accused of favoritism..."

"Favoritism? I don't understand."

"I like you, Pearson, if I haven't made that clear enough. But, perhaps it would be a mistake to make it too clear. What do you think, Dyer?"

The man's pen scoured the page. Otherwise, he was silent.

"I simply can't show favoritism, Ms. Pearson, and that's the end of it. The law is the law for everyone, no matter my personal feelings.

My hands are tied." The agent's lurch from bad-cop to good-cop was disorienting. Sickens looked away to the ceiling, as though considering another course. "But then, a quid pro quo might not be out of the question. What do you think, Dyer?"

The man held his silence. Perhaps he was deaf. Perhaps he didn't speak English. Ella watched him intently, hoping he'd give some encouraging sign. His writing hand jerked and that was all.

"A tit for tat. You understand?" The woman gestured broadly, having returned her attention to Ella. "A favor for a favor. If you were to help me, you'd be helping the Office and maybe then we could consider pulling some strings, leveraging some leniency in your case. What do you think, Pearson? Would you be willing to help us?"

"Yes. Absolutely. Whatever you ask. I just... I want it known... This is all a mistake."

Sickens leaned aside and opened a folder beside her. She had a half dozen or so, fanned out on the table like cards in a conman's hand. The dossier she picked out had a single, slim slip of paper inside. The agent scraped it up with the tips of her fingers and laid it out on the table between them.

Craning forward to look it over, Ella quickly withdrew.

"You recognize the document, I see."

It was the death certificate Mark Carter had worked up. The postscript along the bottom, the disclaimer that the document was a fraud, had been struck out with a solid, black line.

After a bout of silence, Sickens said, "We know it passed through your office, Pearson. We know, furthermore, that it was created at your direction."

"This is a mistake," Ella said.

"A mistake, a mistake... Everything's a mistake," the agent chided.

"No, really, this was meant as a joke. That's all. This black mark at the bottom," Ella reached forward to point out the redaction, but Sickens swooped in and snatched the page away, tucking it back into the folder and setting it aside with the others.

"We know Misha Kant is still at large. She's hiding in the Northern District. We know that with certainty. The question is, what's your stake in making it seem otherwise?"

"That isn't the way it is; that isn't what's happened at all… I was given a document, just days ago…"

The agent cut her off. "It doesn't matter. Let me tell you, outside of the charges relating to your Supplicant, you've committed a series of felonies here: forgery, conspiracy, treason. I don't know, what do you think, Dyer, maybe thirty years depending on the arbiter? I couldn't say, I can only tell you what it looks like from where I'm sitting. Now, I need you to be honest with me: why are you conspiring with Misha Kant? What's her next target, Pearson?"

"Target?" Ella's head shook in a spasm of nerves. "I've never even met the woman. I don't know who she is…"

"No? Let me tell you about her, then, as I know her, probably better than anyone. She used to be my partner, you see. She was my closest confidante. I liked her, Pearson, I really did and I thought I could trust her. It turns out she was a traitor all along! She's a terrorist! But, of course, you know that already, as you're in league with her…"

"A terrorist…"

"Don't act like you don't know, you piece of filth. You're in cahoots with her."

"I'm not. I swear I'm not. I've never met her. The first time I saw her name was only days ago and then…"

"I like you, Pearson. You seem like a straight shooter." The woman's voice rose and fell in tsunami waves, and now she was at the low end, soft and conciliatory, but Ella held herself rigidly away, certain that in a moment the agent would begin shouting psychotically again. "That's the only reason I'm talking with you right now, rather than packing you off to the penal colony for a sixty year sentence. The rest of your life, who knows how long it will be. It's a tough place, the penal colony. A lot of inmates don't see the end of their sentence. Do you understand what I'm getting at?"

"I swear I've never met her."

"I like you, Pearson."

Ella stared at the woman, unsure how she was expected to respond.

"My trusting nature gets me in trouble, though. I'm always willing to see the best in people. It can be a blind. You understand? I like someone. I trust them." As anticipated, the agent's voice rose into a frenzy again, "Then, all of a sudden, they're at my back with a knife! Do you have a knife for me, Pearson?!"

"What? No. I..."

"But do you like me?" The wave had passed, the sea of the agent's discourse suddenly calm again.

"Like you?"

"Do you respect me and see that I only have your best interests in mind? I hope you can see that." The woman stretched her neck and talked into the high corners of the room, like she was reciting a monologue on stage. "I hope, through the course of all this, you can see that I only want to be your friend and that we, as friends, are in a position to help one another... Can you see that?"

"Of course..."

"Good. Good. Maybe, after all, I do believe you: that you really don't know her, that you haven't met her, that you aren't in league with her."

"I don't. I haven't. I'm not." Ella's head shook to the retreating cadence of her words.

"If that's truly the case, then you shouldn't be surprised that we suspect she's behind the attack on the First Assembly."

"What—the vandalism?"

Another semantic wave was already rising. "Don't you watch the news, Pearson?! It was a serious terrorist aggression!"

Shrinking from the woman's shouting, Ella stammered, "It's just, I didn't think..."

"So, are you?" Sickens snarled.

"Am I what?"

"Surprised." The agent was calm again.

"Um... No, I guess not."

Sickens snorted. "I'd think you'd be surprised that anyone would be capable of such a base act. That it would be beyond your comprehension, that it would lay well outside anything you could possibly imagine, that anyone would be capable of an act as disgusting and unprovoked as this."

"Uh, yeah, I guess. I mean, I don't know. Whatever you want, whatever you say. I... Just tell me what you want from me."

Sickens hitched her head toward the folder at her elbow. "We found that document, making the rounds online. And if we discovered it so easily, you can have no doubt it will find its way into Kant's hands. If, indeed, you aren't conspiring with her, she'll seek you out."

"Oh, no."

It was as though Sickens had come into a completely different conversation when she said, curiously, "Why the alarm?"

"Well, it's just that... You said she's a terrorist. I must be in danger..."

"No," Sickens balked. "Of course not. Kant wouldn't... It's immaterial... Here's what we need from you; we need you to go back to your family, to," she looked aside, flipping open another folder to read from a separate file, "Andy Stanhope, and continue on as though nothing in your life has changed. We need you to wait for Kant to make contact with you. That's all we're asking."

"Wait? Wait how long?"

"Until she makes contact."

"If she doesn't?"

"She will."

"But, going back to Andy... we're not together. I don't live there anymore."

Sickens seemed confused and referenced the file again, as though to straighten out her mistake. "The file says you live with Andy Stanhope, that you're a co-guardian with him..."

"But that's what I'm telling you, I don't, not any longer..."

"Ms. Pearson, if that's what the file says, then that's where you live and, while I feel reasonably certain that I can shield you from these current charges, failing to return to your lawful residence and resume your duties will certainly incur additional indictments and, at that point, at the third offense... There won't be a thing I can do for you. It'll be the penal colony."

"So I have to go back to Andy is what you're saying, no matter what?"

"I don't see any other option. Unless," she shrugged, "I mean, the penal colony's still on the table."

It probably shouldn't have taken Ella a moment to come to her decision, but having to go back to Andy seemed a particularly unusual and cruel punishment.

"Ms. Pearson, that was rhetorical. You can't honestly be considering going to the penal colony rather than..."

"No," Ella shook her head. "No, of course not.

"So, you're willing to help us, then?"

Ella made herself nod.

"That's good, Pearson. I like you. I thought from the start that we might get along and I'm happy you haven't disappointed me." Sickens nodded at Ella for a long, awkward moment. Reaching into her pocket, she thumbed out a business card and tossed it onto the table.

Abruptly, Dyer ceased his scribbling and stood. Collecting her folders, Sickens followed him to the door.

"Wait," Ella said. Sickens paused at the threshold. Dyer had already disappeared into the hall. "What do I do?"

"Do?" The woman laughed. "You don't do anything."

She made another move for the door and Ella stopped her again. "I mean..."

"Go home, Ms. Pearson. Call me when you hear from Kant and remember, you're on your third strike. You'll be watched." The agent stepped into the hall and the door shut behind her.

•

For an immeasurable time, Ella continued sitting, waiting for someone to turn up and let her out. It could have been hours or only some accumulated minutes that passed. In the bare plainness of the room, time seemed suddenly illusory. But she didn't dare so much as stand for fear of inviting some new, absurd charge on herself.

Finally, her fear waning into annoyance, Ella rapped on the mirror beside her shoulder. The thing bulged and swayed, clicking against the wall. Ella leaned back, pulling at the corner. The thing, apparently, was not a two way mirror. It was only decorative, hung on the wall by a string with the purpose, it seemed, of making the room appear brighter and more open.

Ella stood and went to the door. It wasn't locked. She leaned into the hallway. As though to highlight the depth of the bureaucratic purgatory into which she'd plunged, the hall through which Ella had been brought to this room was made to seem endless, by a countless queue of identical doors faced off against each other and now she was confronted with that dizzying, claustrophobic view again. A custodian busied himself a few paces away, moping the floor, jerking at the sudden sound of Ella's voice when she said, "Hey."

The man looked behind him and, finding the hallway empty, looked back at Ella.

"Can I go?"

He shrugged.

"I'm gonna go."

He nodded like he didn't think it was such a bad idea.

14 A Second Chance

An Anecdote Regarding the Durrenmatt

Quietly opening the door to Andy's apartment, Ella's head was buzzing so pleasantly with a fresh dose of Represitol, it was almost possible for her to ignore the crush of resentment she felt at having to return here, almost possible to ignore the rabid anger writhing in her chest. Stepping inside, sadly, the place looked no different than when she'd left, but there was no reason to suspect it might. Andy was at the stove.

"Oh, thank God, Ella, are you okay?" Abandoning the spoon in the pot he'd been stirring, the man rushed to her.

Ella pulled back. "What are you doing?"

He stopped. Slumping, he shrugged slowly and said, "I was gonna give you a hug."

"No, not that, moron." Ella looked past him to the oven. A wide phantom of steam wound upward, shuddering over the pot on the burner. "That."

"Oh, that? It's Ernie's food."

"Ernie?"

"Clara thought we should name him. I don't think it's such a bad pick, either." Looking back at her, he asked, "Are you all right?"

"I've had..." She shook her head. "Never mind, I can't get into it right now. It smells awful, Andy."

"Oh, you get used to it. It's only been a few days now and I'm already used to it. Gosh, I'm happy you're home, muffin."

Stepping past him and setting her purse down on the kitchen island, she took the pot-top from the counter beside the stove and covered up the steaming spout. It didn't do anything to ease the smell.

When she turned back, Andy was looking at her with pity and she realized she must look like something fit for the gutter, tired and worn and her clothes dried into a wrinkled mess. She pulled at her jacket absently, but the wrinkles wouldn't let go. "You're cooking for him; so, he's here?"

Andy nodded. "In the living room with Clara. A transit cop found him and..."

Ella's heart seemed to seize a moment, even though she'd suspected all along that the intruder would be here—returned. When she was interrogated, no one had bothered asking her where she thought the monster might have wandered off to and she hadn't had the nerve to ask his whereabouts, fearing his being summoned by the very mention of him. "I need to lie down."

Andy backed off, nodding. "Okay, muffin."

"Don't do that."

"Do what?"

"Let's not pretend that I didn't leave. We're still broken up, Andy, my being here doesn't change that."

His voice shrunk. He seemed to shrink, himself; his shoulders pulled toward his chest. "Okay."

"I haven't changed my mind, Andy. I should have been straightforward with you before and I'm sorry that I wasn't but know, unequivocally, that this is over between us. Okay? We're done, Andy. Over."

He nodded and wasted a moment looking away. "You had to come back. I understand. They made you." When he brought his head back up there was a rising, buoyant quality to his tone. He said, "It's good, though. It'll be a second chance for us."

"No, Andy, it won't."

"Sure it will. Obviously, you aren't resolved. You did come back."

"No, Andy, as soon as this is over..."

"But it isn't over." The glint of joy in his voice seemed to bolster his posture another notch and the straighter he stood, the brighter his tone became. "It's just a new stage in our relationship together..."

"No. No, Andy, that isn't right..."

"Sure, it is."

"No, Andy, I'm only here because otherwise I'd be incarcerated right now. You do understand that, don't you?"

He hummed, nodding and shrugging contentedly. "And you chose me: this adventure; raising this child together..."

"We're not raising a child, Andy. And the fact that I chose you over the penal colony is hardly an endorsement. In fact, it isn't remotely..."

"Fine. Not raising the child, then. Fighting together to win back your freedom. Together, you and I... You made that choice."

She wrung her hands. "First off: it isn't a child. It's an intruder. Secondly: this is the problem with you; this is the reason we just can't work: this unflinching optimism of yours is absolutely insane. You've acknowledged yourself that I'm only here because the law is requiring it and now you're acting like this is an opportunity for you to try and patch things up. It's craziness..."

"Well, that's what it is, isn't it?"

"Craziness?"

"No," he laughed, "a chance to patch things up."

"No, Andy, that's not it at all. If it's anything, it's a chance to evaluate where we went wrong, so that in our future relationships we won't make the same mistakes..."

"I'd always make the same mistakes," he said sweetly, stepping forward and setting a gentle hand on her arm.

She moved away from him. "Jesus, Andy. Fine, use the time however you like, but no more of that. No touching or being cutesy. And know, at the end of this," she gestured toward the front door through which she'd entered, "I'm leaving. That's final."

•

In the living room, Clara and the Caveman were on the floor watching TV. An old circus movie was on, an acrobat hanging upside down by her toes and swinging back and forth from a trapeze. The crowd below oohed and awed, the sound pushing and retreating like lazy waves on a beach.

"This movie's a little dumb for you, isn't it?"

Clara looked from the TV. "Ernie picked it. That's what we decided to name him—Ernie."

"I heard."

Ella looked to the Caveman on the carpet. He was swaddled in a terrycloth robe—Andy's, she recognized. The sleeves had been rolled into thick collars so his hands could be free. The tail billowed around him on the floor.

Turning to Andy's bedroom, Ella froze at the threshold when Clara piped up, "The first machine I ever worked on was a Durrenmatt. You wouldn't recognize the name, unless you're an enthusiast. They were a Swiss company and it's true, what they say about Swiss design. The clocks were beautiful. Simple. To me everything else was inferior. Unfortunately, the company only lasted a few years and produced very few models. They're extremely rare, nearly impossible to come by. I ended up in a long period when I couldn't find any to work on at all. It was very distressing for me.

"Seeing my frustration, a fellow tinkerer suggested I try working on a Kazuo. I was reluctant. I loved the Durrenmatt and didn't want to work on anything else. But I knew the Japanese had a reputation for quality. It took some convincing from my friend, but I decided to give the Japanese clock a look—just to see what it was about.

"The design was completely unlike the Durrenmatt, but I found it wasn't inferior at all. It had its own logic, its own subtle peculiarities." The girl took a moment before going on. "Now, when you look at my shelves, you'll find some Kazuos. And, while I still love working on clocks, I've learned to appreciate the joys of tinkering with a blender or a toaster oven, even..."

Ella turned to the girl. "There must be a point to this."

Clara shrugged. "Sometimes you just have to accept that it's better to move forward and when you do, you open yourself up to appreciating things which never interested you before."

Nodding drearily, Ella said, "Thank you. Thanks. I was really hoping to have a child teach me a lesson today. Should we discuss 'sharing' next?"

"Sarcasm isn't your strength, Pearson. You shouldn't try it."

In the bedroom, Ella stared at the bed. She would have preferred staying on the couch, but with the TV on and those two monsters on the floor, she knew she wouldn't get any rest out there and she needed rest, needed it badly. After straightening out the sheets, she lay down but couldn't sleep. Outside the bedroom, cartoon noises pinged and whizzed and Ella stared at the wall.

She thought about East Gish, both the town and the little bar. She wished she were there, at either one, it didn't matter which. Anywhere but here.

Somehow the prospect of sleep seemed to retreat further and further away. Sitting up, Ella got her phone from her purse. Timmy's number was right there in her contact list, waiting for her. The empty, gray silhouette beside his number bothered her. She couldn't help thinking of him still as the child in her photograph. It took her a moment before she texted him, *I'd like to come visit you in East Gish sometime.*

She watched the screen.

A balloon of periods swelled and shrunk, swelled and shrunk, like an invertebrate trying to advance. It meant he'd seen the message, that he'd seen it and had started working out a response. But the message never came through. After a moment, the balloon went stale and vanished.

Ella set the phone on the night stand.

"Fucking men," she muttered and she laid back down.

After a time, Andy called Clara and the Caveman for dinner and the smell of that putrid, briny food seemed to become more pronounced. Ella lay still, listening to them, listening to Andy laugh and Clara direct and the Caveman slurp and belch and clack his utensils on his plate. It all made her feel lonelier—lonelier even than when she'd been incarcerated.

She stared at the wall until the TV was shut off and the light in the living room went out.

"Jeez, muffin," Andy said from the bedside, "you should get under the covers."

Laying still, staring at the wall, she pretended to sleep and beside her, the bed shifted as Andy dropped down. When he threw his arm over her midriff, Ella made herself say, "One of us should probably sleep on the couch, don't you think, Andy?"

Silently, he sat up. He watched her a moment before he left the room. The springs in the couch creaked and went quiet.

15

The Missing Name Tag

Happy News for Dawn

The Old Watchdog

Ella woke, panicked about the sun; worried that if it didn't rise, she would never wake. But it had risen. She was awake.

•

All her best clothes were still in the suitcase in the other apartment, so it took Ella longer than usual to get dressed for the day and, in the mirror, she looked regrettable. Her shirt billowed, conspicuously outdated, and the jacket refused to relax from the shape of the hanger it'd hung on. Still, it was the best outfit she'd managed to cobble together from her leftovers.

In the kitchen, Andy was stirring up another rank slumgullion.

"How do I look?" She was desperate for a little encouragement, otherwise she might not have spoken to him at all. In this weird ensemble, it felt like all her confidence had slunk away.

"Gorgeous," he said automatically, trundling forward to embrace her, stopping when she held out a hand, stiff-arming him into place.

"Don't. Just look at me."

He took a step back to look more carefully. In the end, all he could summon was a long, lonesome shrug. Obviously trying for reassurance, he said, "It isn't like it's that important, Muffin."

"Of course it's important, Andy. I haven't been to the office in..." Time escaped her. Had it been a day? Days? A week seemed unreasonably long but she couldn't discount it, not entirely; she couldn't quite seem to straighten out the passage of time. She did remember Dawn in a suit, seated mutinously at her—Ella's!—desk.

"I'm sure you look fine."

"Hm. You're sure." Ella tugged at the jacket. "It'll have to do, at any rate. Andy, can we talk?"

"Aren't we doing that, just now?"

Ella tried to ignore the electric twinge of irritation running through her. "I mean... Yes, of course we're talking now, Andy. I just meant... Never mind." She took a pause to even out her tone. "I just need to know: did you set the police after me?"

He looked at her and didn't answer.

"They showed up at my office, you know. With the Caveman. Did you call them and tell them I'd left?"

He laughed. "No. No. Of course not, Muffin."

"Okay. I didn't think so."

He was still laughing when he said, "I called Social Services."

"What?"

"I called Social Services and told them that you'd left."

"You reported me to Social Services?"

"Clara suggested it."

"Of course she did," Ella said, her voice a low rumble, like a distant plane. She turned to the door.

"Say, Muffin..."

"Don't call me that."

"...Clara and I were going to take Ernie to the Assembly this weekend for his reception. We got a special invitation from Master Thompson..."

"No."

"...It'll only be a few hours and..."

"No," louder.

Andy slumped back. "You know, this really isn't fair of you. You're supposed to be pitching in. You're supposed to be..."

"I need to get to work, Andy. We'll talk about this when I get home," she said and went out the door, not planning on returning until as late as possible.

•

Ella marched through the CCI offices. Her ridiculous attire forced her to compensate, feigning all the confidence she lacked. Walking with her head held high, she didn't acknowledge those around her, didn't slow for hellos. As her determination and trajectory were both so apparent, office personnel lingering in the halls scampered out of her way. She was so focused on getting behind her desk again, she barely noticed that Dawn wasn't at her post. Stomping through the reception area, Ella grabbed the door handle, jarring the thing violently and colliding with the slab when it failed to open. Her handbag slipped off her shoulder and she staggered back. For a moment, all she could do was stare at the treacherous door.

Beside the jamb, the tag with her name and title (Vice President of Operations) was missing. A black scab of glue clung to the wall.

The placard wasn't on the floor. She couldn't find the thing, not even after she'd knelt to search the shadows under the receptionist's desk. Standing again, she gave the stubborn door another look. She'd had a plan for her morning, having decided to reach out to her colleagues in the news industry with a story of a Jane Doe, a poor victim of state bureaucracy, who'd been conscripted and forced by law to act as a nanny for a drooling little monster. She'd see if they knew anything about the laws hedging her in and if they didn't, she'd pitch 'Jane's' story for them to investigate. The door was an obvious, material obstacle to that plan.

Turning, Ella glowered at the empty receptionist's chair. It was decided, then: as soon as Ella got back into her office, she'd call down to Staffing and have Dawn let go. She didn't care who they sent as a replacement. They could call in Frankenstein's Monster for all she cared. Dawn was done.

Now, she'd need to track down a member of the janitorial staff to let her in—wasting a chunk of the morning, when she'd hoped to get started early.

•

Adjacent the break room, at the end of a windowless hall behind the elevators, Ella was happy to find the door to the janitor's room open. There wasn't anyone inside—just some shelves stuffed with jugs of cleanser, an assortment of mops and brooms leaned in a corner—but the fact that the door had been left wide was a plain indication that someone in coveralls was nearby and planning to return.

Ella crossed her arms and leaned against the wall to wait.

From the break room a din of excited voices poured into the hall. Having never spent any time there, it was impossible for Ella to tell if what she was witnessing was commonplace: the room bustled with women, all laughing and caterwauling. The longer Ella stood, waiting for the janitor, the more agitated she became. The custodian was out, obviously doing his job, while all those women stood in there wasting company time. Warner wouldn't have stood for it. Ella realized she shouldn't, either.

Pushing herself off the wall and crossing the hallway she landed at the threshold to the break room, announcing, "All right! All right, that's enough. Everyone needs to get to work."

No one seemed to notice her. There was too much noise for her to be heard.

Stepping forward, Ella was absorbed instantly into the quivering amoeba of women and she jockeyed to get to the center where she couldn't be ignored. Deep in the throng, she found there was no place for her at the hub, because the center of the circle was already occupied. By Dawn. Ella soured further. No one seemed to notice. Not Dawn, anyhow. The girl, lighting on Ella, raised her hand up as though preparing to mete out a backhand, and announced, "He asked me!"

For a moment the thick soup of Ella's confusion was impenetrable. Then, landing on the twinkling, tiny stone bound to the girl's finger, Ella understood. She made herself say, "Congratulations, Dawn." Looking around to all those assembled, she said, "It's very happy news for Dawn, but you all need to get back to work."

Faced away, Ella almost fell over when Dawn collided with her, embracing her violently. The touch was too intimate, too sudden and personal, the whisper of Dawn's voice almost lascivious when she said, "I'm so happy you came. So happy you're here. I thought you'd be jealous. I thought you'd be mad at me."

Squirming free from the girl's clutches, Ella insisted angrily, "I'm happy for you!" She pushed the girl away and paused to look around the circle of women and announced, "But everyone needs to get back to work!"

The brouhaha diminished to murmurs and Ella fought her way out of the crowd. In the hall, she was disappointed to find the door to the janitorial closet closed. So the custodian must have come and gone already. Behind her, the women started roaring again.

•

Warner's secretary was also absent from her station; in the break room with all the other hens, Ella supposed. Stepping to the closed door and knocking gently, in the absence of a response, she turned the knob (his door wasn't locked, so they weren't facing a general insurrection, at least) and peeked inside. Warner was on the phone but, catching sight of her, he waved her in enthusiastically.

In the seat before his desk, Ella searched blankly around the room while Warner finished his conversation. "That's right, Carl... That's right... Yes... Yes, that's right..." His tone seemed to be growing thin, impatient. "That's right, she's here right now..."

In a spasm of panic, Ella's focus shot to the man.

With a curt nod he said into the phone, "Yup... Invaluable is right..."

Her panic passed as suddenly as it had risen. Ella sat a little straighter. Was *she* invaluable? Certainly she must be: she was the 'she' who was 'here right now.'

"Fine," Warner said, closing the conversation. He set down the receiver. In the silent moment afterward he hitched his head to the reception area. "In the break room for the last forty minutes. I suppose you were there, too?"

Meeting her gaze, it wasn't a look of disappointment he leveled at her. It was a look of collusion, like they were sharing a joke no one else would understand.

"I stopped by. Happy news for her." Ella quickly tried for a transistion, her tone more urgent when she said, "We need to talk..."

"I've never understood some of us, Pearson. Not you. I don't mean you. I mean the Dawns of the world." Half turning in his chair, he gestured to the view beyond the window (columns of buildings rising up to support nothing at all). "All that out there. Do you understand the sacrifices that were needed to make it the way it is today?"

"About this lawyer you had me sign on with..."

Warner would not be diverted. It was like Ella hadn't even spoken. "There's no doubt, we've come a long way as a society. It wasn't so long ago when someone like Dawn never would have been allowed to work in an office like this one, let alone been given the upward freedom to advance as far as her talents and determination could take her. Even you, Pearson, willful and adept as you are, would have been kept out." He gave Ella a long look and nodded to himself. "Things have changed for us all and it's too easy to forget the struggle that was our road to freedom. It's too easy to forget that, even now, this freedom isn't a solid, irreversible thing; that we must be diligent and fight to keep it up." He looked at her. He shook his head. "And the Dawns of the world weep to hold a child as though they'd be happy enough to have the old barriers back in place."

"I'm not really up for philosophizing about gender equality right now, Warner. I've gotten into quite a mess here. That assignment you gave me..."

Warner laughed and the sound was perplexing enough to shut her up. "Should we talk about Misha Kant, then: about where you've gotten with the job?"

Ella nodded impatiently. "Yeah, but..."

"I'll tell you, I thought you were goading me a bit with that death certificate thing. But it drew Sickens out of the woodwork. I underestimated you, Pearson. I should have known better. We're built from the same stuff, you and I."

She leaned forward. "You know I was arrested, then? I've been in jail the last..." How long had it been?

It didn't matter, Warner was shaking his head, speaking again before she could puzzle it out, "Don't confuse things. There's too much of that in the world already. Not in jail and not arrested, Pearson."

Ella felt suddenly nervous again. Did he know how confused she was? Could he see it, right through her clothes?

"Sickens, her whole department, they like to think they're important but, honestly, they can't so much as lock a door on you. Not now. They were powerful once. Sometimes they need to be treated as though they still are. Don't let them frighten you off, though. They're like an old watch dog without any teeth. You get close to them. You make sure Sickens sees you as an ally, but don't let her intimidate you."

"Right." Ella put her hands on the arms of the chair but didn't push herself up. "You probably aren't aware of this but I've been put in a very awkward domestic situation... What are you telling me? That Sickens' threats are empty? That I don't need to worry about her?"

The man seemed to weigh the question. "If I were in your place—and this is just me—I think my primary concern might be making Sickens think I'm doing just as she asks. She may not have the power over you that she wants you to think she has but... Sometimes, it's better to go with the grain, even if it will result in a few splinters... You see what I mean?"

"So, where does that leave me?"

"East Gish?" He laughed. "I'm joking, of course. But not really. When you've finished this job, you can have your pick. You're moving up in the world, Pearson—don't ever mistake that." He slapped the armrests under him and let the implication sit a moment before going on, "Back to my joke, but joking aside, have you thought any further about what we discussed earlier: is it time for you to go to East Gish?"

Looking at him in a confusion, Ella said, "I guess I wouldn't want to leave the job unfinished."

He nodded. "They're not mutually exclusive, you know. You might think about how connected they are..." He seemed about to say something more, but, beside him, the phone started ringing. With a nod, he answered and when he aimed the gesture toward the door, she stood and left.

16 The Other Monster

With the accompanying thunder of a departing train, the crush of commuters on the stairs shifted forward. Ella craned to see what the holdup was. Nothing ahead, just a plug of bodies in a space too tight. The platform below was just as packed as the stairwell.

Even with her discomfort, the delay wasn't unwelcome: Ella realized she was just as happy standing in this humid, writhing catacomb as she would have been to be back at Andy's apartment. More so, even. She tugged at the sleeve of her jacket. The thing had been bothering her from the moment she'd stuffed herself into it. Glancing into the narrow gap between her chest and the back of the woman in front of her, Ella gave herself a quick look over. She was dressed like a clown. The embarrassment that had nagged her all day fluttered up again and in that tide of indignity, Ella found something desirable: an excuse.

As the queue shifted forward again, Ella scuttled to the edge of the crowd and, grasping the handrail, made the trip back up the stairs against the pull of the crowd.

Outside again, the evening air felt like liberty itself and Ella started away from the metro with a new design for her evening. Strung together by leisurely strolls, it involved a relaxed sit-down in a fancy cafe and the unhurried retrieval of her suitcase from the unfurnished apartment across town. She picked at her jacket again. Maybe she'd reverse the order of operations.

When her phone started ringing and she plucked it out of her purse to see Andy calling, she almost sent him right to voicemail. Against her best judgement, she picked up.

"On your way home?"

Ella looked around at the thinning crowd on the sidewalk. Cupping her hand around the receiver, hoping to dampen the noise, she said, "No. I wish. Today's been crazy. I guess that's to be expected after being away..."

"Oh..." His voice sounded suddenly mournful and far-off.

"What's up?"

"Well, Clara was just reminding me that we need to get some clothes for Ernie. I was thinking we could all go Downtown together."

"*Of course she was....*" Ella muttered. Sidestepping out of the way of a pack of oncoming pedestrians, she came to a stop under the awning in front of a convenience store. "I'm sorry, Andy, count me out. It'll be a while still until I can get home."

He perked up, his tone suddenly lively again. "That's okay, I understand. I'm sure Ernie can last one more day. We'll just do it tomorrow."

Ella tapped her foot and looked around—the evening had faded into night: the sidewalk a greasy kaleidoscope of brake-light reds, brassy streetlamp hues and the tangled shadows of pedestrians, running off at opposing angles, perpendicular to nothing. "Ah. Listen, you should just go. I have such a backlog from taking that time off, the rest of the week's probably gonna be one late night after another. I may have to go in Saturday, as well. I can't be sure... Maybe Sunday, too..." she added as a cap-end.

"Well... Okay..." Pause. "Okay. I'll just see you when you get home, then."

"Yup. Sounds good."

"I..." Andy started saying, but Ella pulled the phone away, hung up and discarded it into her purse.

•

Hours later, when Ella returned to the metro, drifting down the stairs like something sumptuous poured from a bucket, the atmosphere was much different. Yes, the stairwell was empty and quiet and cool, but that was only a part of it. A bulk of the change had occurred inside her.

Greeted in her unfurnished apartment by the mattress on the floor and the photo of Timmy looking up at her, Ella had changed into her favorite suit (the deep blue one that hugged so flatteringly around her waist) and promptly folded up her clown-blazer and stuffed it into the trash.

With her suitcase buckled she took a moment to consider the photo of her old, forgotten friend. In standing as a place-holder, she decided it should stay, just as it was. It would make an easy, if frivolous excuse to continue paying the rent and she felt, at any rate, she'd be back here posthaste once all this impossible foolishness resolved itself.

Back outside she felt more herself again. The clothes helped. Her confidence carried her down the street like a flood of her own command. Walking by the East Gish Club, she hardly gave it any notice at all. No, tonight she would really treat herself. After a random, hitching route through the City, she happened past a place called Dane's that looked like it might fit the bill. Inside, waiters glided briskly around, bound up like grim presents in black vests and bowties.

It was a wonderful evening. The maitre'd checked her suitcase as though it was the most natural thing in the world and sat her at a quiet booth in the back. Her waiter was some sort of time traveller, it seemed: absent until the moment before Ella's desire caught up with her and then he'd appear from nowhere to fulfill her need before she'd even realized it existed. He was a professional and the world seemed desperately short on those. She tipped the man fittingly.

It wasn't just the simple pleasures of the evening which buoyed her spirits, even as she planned on returning to Andy's apartment, it was that she felt she'd finally landed on a prototype for how her nights might be spent until she was free again. Under the guise of working late, she could explore the clubs and cafes of the City and avoid going home until the need for sleep proved insurmountable. She'd snooze at

Andy's and spend every waking moment elsewhere. The City was abundant with elsewhere.

And, in spite of Agent Sickens' insistence that she would be closely watched, Ella noticed no clandestine figures huddling in the alleys she passed. No dark cars hummed ominously behind her and Ella sensed (as Warner had indicated) the woman's threats had been hollow.

Underground again, she stopped at the turnstiles. Beyond, a train sat on the tracks, the doors hanging open, the windows dark with the running lights off. She'd stayed too long at Dane's, it seemed. She'd have to call a cab. No big deal.

Spinning on her heels, she started back up the stairs, stopping abruptly just below the landing where the southern and northern exits branched away from each other.

On the bench ahead, a woman sat, slouched to the side, her face hidden in a tight twine of bandages. There weren't even holes for her eyes and that she had any such features could only be surmised from the slight depressions on either side of the bulge of a gauzy nose. Dressed in a suit that seemed disturbingly familiar, it took Ella a moment to realize why: it looked identical to the suit she was wearing: dark blue, pinstriped.

She had to coax herself into moving again.

Passing her suitcase from hand to hand so she could huddle closer to the wall, she climbed the remaining stairs, keeping her gaze locked on the thing on the bench. At the landing Ella turned toward the south exit. The figure on the bench lifted her head. Ella froze up again when the bandaged woman raised her hand, pointing it at Ella. Only, it wasn't just the woman's hand pointing. She was holding onto something inside the blind of a paper bag. It must have been a gun—Ella was suddenly certain of it.

When Ella turned to face the northern exit, the hidden weapon followed and, before Ella'd gone a step, the woman shook her head dreadfully and said, “You do as I say. People who don’t listen, don’t last long. You follow me?”

Rising off the bench the woman gestured with the gun, back down the stairwell Ella had just emerged from.

“I don’t have much cash but I have my bank card. The PIN’s…”

The woman gestured down the stairs a second time, more aggressively.

Ella nodded, turned and started back down to the platform. The cold clack of footsteps followed her back to the turnstiles. Stopping at the closed gate, Ella flustered and said, “Listen, this can be an easy transaction. There’s no need for all this…”

“Go through the gate.”

“I don’t have any jewelry. It’s just clothes in the suitcase, that’s all…”

“Go through.” The woman’s voice was clipped with impatience.

Ella pushed through the turnstile.

Crossing the platform, the woman said, “Get on the train.”

“There really isn’t any need…”

“Get on the train.”

Ella climbed onto the train. Inside, the lights from the platform were muted by the scratched windows. Long shadows rested over the seats and across the aisle. “Sit.”

Pushing her suitcase into a row and following it in, Ella sat. In a pungent cloud of lavender, the woman stepped past her, taking the seat opposite. Ella looked to the floor.

“Do you recognize me?”

“You can have my purse and the suitcase. It isn’t much but…”

“Stop it.”

Ella went silent.

“Look at me.”

Ella raised her head. In a weak act of defiance, she looked at the paper bag instead of the woman’s face. With a hand tucked behind her elbow now, the bag jutted out lazily and seemed somehow more menacing.

"Do you recognize me? That's what I'm asking." When the woman moved, the smell of lavender wafted up again.

Shaking her head, Ella said, "Your face is covered. How could I possibly recognize you?"

"My voice, my posture, any of it?"

Ella continued shaking her head, although it did seem the woman's tone was familiar, if only for its similarity to the voice from those Represitol ads, deep and sultry and self-confident. Ella would have killed for a dose. When the doors in the car squealed suddenly shut, Ella flinched. The train lurched forward, the station gliding away. Plunging into the darkness of the tunnel, murk poured into the train. The air filled with a clamor of shrieking metal and jangling chains.

"Where are you taking me?"

"I'm not taking you anywhere. The train's just moving. That's what trains do."

"I won't call the police, I promise. You can have everything, just..."

"Stop it."

Ella fell quiet. Without any light, without anything for her eyes to anchor to, she felt like she was floating away, as though the blackness of the tunnel wasn't simply an absence of light, but a sudden absence of everything altogether.

A blast of tunnel lights flashed through the car and the world resolved itself for a moment. Ella caught a glimpse of the woman's gauzy face. Searching for the bag, Ella found it resting in the woman's lap now, and tried to fix its location in her mind. But when the darkness resumed, everything seemed as suddenly rearranged and unknowable as dice shaken in a cup. She felt, in the resumed pitch, she could only be dully certain of the direction in which she faced and little else.

"My name is..."

In a fresh fit of head-shaking, Ella stammered, "Don't tell me your name, I don't need to know it..."

"...Misha Kant," the woman's voice drifted from the darkness, "You recognize that name?"

"Yes."

"It won't surprise you then, that I've come to find you."

Ella couldn't think of anything to say. She shook her head.

"I found your little gift."

"I don't know what you're talking about," Ella said, though she suspected she probably did.

"The death certificate, Pearson. I know it was your handiwork. But I don't think you did it on your own."

Again, the darkness in the car was vanquished a moment; the flatscreens on the walls suddenly flashing in a staticky burst. The speakers crackled and went silent and the image collapsed on itself too quickly for Ella to tell what it had been. In the brief flare, Kant's face lit up in discotheque color. Then, everything was gone again. The train shuddered.

"It was just a joke, that's all. I didn't..."

"Was it Warner, put you up to it?"

"Warner?"

"Your boss, Warner. I wish you'd stop playing naive. It's wearing on my sense of goodwill."

"Yes, he gave me a document that had your name on it, a birth certificate, and he told me that you were a priority."

"And do you know what, exactly, he has planned for me?"

The tracks screamed as the train took a turn. The force threw Ella into the window. She struggled to push herself off. "No. All he said was that you were a priority. A top priority, I think. *The* priority."

Lights flashed through the cabin. In the receding flare, Ella caught sight of the bag again, set aside on the seat beside the woman's thigh. Kant's hand wasn't even on it. Again, Ella tried to fix the location in her mind but, as the light waned away, the car seemed to spin and all the fixed objects inside shuffled in her mind.

The train lurched into a straightaway.

"Perhaps I can enlighten you, then. He's trying to frame me for the attack on the First Assembly."

"The vandalism?"

"That wasn't vandalism, Pearson. You must be bright enough to see that, I hope. It was an act of terror, plain and simple."

"But, the lab results... The mess was benign, no one was even injured."

"Terror isn't a matter of carnage, Pearson, it's a matter of fear. That is the purpose. In this case, the point was to make it seem as though a plague had been unleashed—to spread, in the absence of sickness, a fear of sickness."

"Why would Warner want you implicated?"

The flatscreens on the walls crackled on again. "Because he was behind it."

In the multicolored glare accompanying Misha Kant's absurd assertion, Ella found the bag on the seat again and as soon as the darkness resumed, she lunged forward and grasped the edge of the seat just before the gun, hoping the world would stay in order if she kept her hand on it. In an attempt to cover her movement, she said, "Warner? My boss? That's crazy. Why would Warner want to deface the First Assembly?" Her voice had gotten slow and drunken, muddled in the darkness and her own panic.

"I think we can help each other, Pearson. The birth certificate you mentioned, get me a copy of it and I don't see why I can't help you with your problem."

"My problem? I don't have a problem."

"No?" the darkness asked. "Not a hairy little problem you're hoping to be rid of?"

The train rattled and groaned as it took another turn, and Ella held tight onto the seat, keeping her gaze aimed in the direction where she'd spotted Kant's gun. In the next flash of light, she lunged for the bag. Stumbling over her suitcase, she fell clumsily into the bench. The bag slipped from her hand. Around her, the light from the approaching station started thinning out the darkness in the car and Ella scrambled into the aisle, after the bag and the weapon inside it. Lunging and seizing hold of the thing, Ella got herself turned onto her back just as the train jerked to a stop. Jabbing the bag around the car in violent, thrusting threats, Ella was aware that she hadn't managed to grab the handle of the gun, but prayed Kant wouldn't notice.

It didn't matter, anyway. Ella lowered her outstretched arms.

Kant was already gone. The train was empty. Ella sat up.

The doors folded open with a rusty squawk and the gun in the bag fell out onto the floor, landing with a thunk and a waft of lavender. Only, when Ella looked down she found it wasn't a gun at all. A pale bar of soap sat in the aisle.

The TV screens flashed on again with a familiar swell of music. Ella looked up to see an actress dancing through a field, landing in the arms of a man. Together they tumbled to the ground.

•

After five rings, Agent Sickens' outgoing voicemail message came up.

"It's me," Ella said, walking down the length of the platform, looking in all the windows for any sign of Kant and finding none. Despite her whisper, the dingy tiles in the empty station made her voice echo. She said, "Ella Pearson. I'm calling about... The issue we discussed earlier. I'm at the," she looked to the wall where the stop was laid out in black tiles—some of the pieces were gone, just the rough gluey backing remained, but she could still make out the location, well enough, "Tenth Street station." She hesitated, not knowing what else to say about it and, in her pause, the line disconnected.

She slid the phone away, back into her purse. She supposed there wasn't anything else to say on a recording. No doubt Sickens would want the whole story in person. Further, Ella didn't feel any doubt that the agent would send an envoy to collect her, posthaste.

Stepping out from behind the pillars, Ella took a seat on a bench to watch the stairwell down which, at any moment, Sickens' surrogate would certainly appear.

She sat there for an hour and a half, checking her phone periodically. No one called. No one came. When she tried Sickens again, the woman still didn't pick up. Thoroughly annoyed, Ella finally called a cab.

17 An Inevitable Argument

It was late but Andy was sitting up in the living room with the lights on and the TV off, glaring dully her way when Ella came in. The pungent smell of the Caveman's 'special diet' seemed to have adhered to everything.

Passing by to the open bedroom door, Ella ignored him altogether, only stopping when he finally said, "I've been waiting up all night."

"I don't even want to hear it, Andy. You have no idea the kind of day I've had."

"I'm sorry your work day was rough but we need to talk."

"I'm too tired, Andy. It'll have to wait until tomorrow." She made another move for the bedroom but stopped when he said:

"We were fine, working together, making a life and the moment you realize we'll have to face a challenge, you pack up: decide you'd rather take the easy road..."

Hanging in the doorway, looking longingly into the calm darkness beyond, she said, "That isn't what happened, Andy. I was planning on ending things with you long before the Caveman showed up. Okay? There. It's been said."

He looked down at the floor. "Is it Terry?"

"No." The word snapped out of her, without a thought. But, it did have to do with Terry, didn't it? At least after a fashion. Hemming a moment, she said, "If I'm honest, I guess, in a way it is. The thing is, Terry and I, while we weren't perfect, we were going in the same direction. We had similar goals and values and ambitions."

"I have ambition."

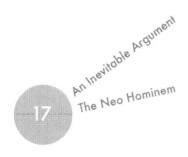

"No, you don't."

"I do." He looked up at her, resolved and confident. "I want us to be together. I want us to have a family; to be a family. The Neo Hominem..."

"Don't," Ella said. "They don't have anything to do with this—with us. I'll tell you, Andy, I'm still pretty furious with you that you called the police on me..."

"It wasn't the police, it was Social Services..."

"It amounts to the same thing..."

"...And it was Clara's suggestion..."

Ella shook her head. "You're the one making the decisions, Andy. You. Not Clara."

He nodded and looked away again. "You're right, Muffin. I did make the decision to call, in the end. I really hoped that when Ernie showed up it would bring us together. I hoped it would make us into a real family."

There was a little voice inside her that wanted to remind him, for the umpteenth time, that the Caveman was not a child, not the foundation for *any family*. She stifled the voice and was quiet a moment. Setting down her suitcase and crossing the room, she took a seat beside him on the couch. They both stared forward, to where the blackened TV stood. Their reflection sat in the screen, staring back.

She said, "I think, and I hope you'll see it too, that the best thing to do is wrap this up as quickly as possible so we can both move on with our lives... There's just too much resentment now, too much baggage. I don't think we can move forward from it. I know I can't."

Andy shrugged, defeated, resigned to whatever she decided. She started hating him again. Hating his kind weakness. Terry would have fought for her or with her. Part of her wanted Andy to fight, too.

"Until then, I think you're right, and if we can't act as a family we need to, at the very least, act like a team. We'll work together to get this straightened out." She turned to him. He was looking at the floor, staring dumbly. "I want to end this on a good note, okay? I want it to end with us as friends."

He nodded but still wouldn't look at her.

"A team," she said.

He looked up. "Are teams intimate?"

"It's unlikely, Andy. Very unlikely," she said.

•

Having forgotten entirely about the Caveman's reception at the Assembly, and then suddenly reminded of it when Andy emerged from the bathroom in his 'Sunday Clothes' (an outfit that actually looked suitable beneath a fedora) Ella realized that she'd volunteered to be more helpful sooner than she should have. Without any obvious excuse to avoid attending, she was pretty much condemned. Andy never even asked. Worse still, it looked like he'd gone out and done some shopping for the Caveman. Ella wished—suddenly and violently—that she'd gone with him. She would have advised him against the outfit he'd picked, the Caveman done up like a Victorian child in a waist coat and knee high socks and a little hat somehow even sillier than Andy's. It was going to be humiliating, having to be seen in public with the pair of them.

•

The First Assembly of the Neo Hominem had made fast work of correcting the defacement on the facade of the Temple. The stains had refused to come free from the stonework so the entire building had been hastily dowsed in a coat of bright white paint. Standing below it, lined up for the entrance, the building looked fresher than it ever had. Ella couldn't help the snide canter of laughter that bubbled up when she took a moment to reflect on how seriously Thompson had taken the vandalism; how seriously Sickens and Kant had, too. What would they do if anything bad actually happened?

Beside her, Andy started laughing, too.

"What are you laughing at, Andy?"

He shrugged, gazing ahead happily. "I just thought we were laughing."

Ella grumbled and looked forward while the grand arch of the entrance loomed, ready to consume her. That cold, ominous feeling of being swallowed by a behemoth only lasted the few moments it took, lined up in a long trail of bodies, to pass the threshold into the building. Inside she was confronted by an unwelcome tranquility—the ceiling of the Temple was constructed of enormous plates of glass that ushered the daylight and heat inside. Under that concentrated blaze of sun, Ella felt suddenly awake and focused and at ease. It's just the sun, she reminded herself—*it has nothing to do with this place.*

Leading the way, Andy went to the furthest empty pew, just a few rows away from the dais, followed by Clara and the Caveman. Ella was happy to get the aisle seat; something inside her relished the opening for an easy escape if the need should present itself.

Regardless that the service hadn't begun, Andy sat rapt, staring blankly forward at the stage. After catching sight of that long, dumb look of his, Ella labored to stare forward as well, so as not to have to look his way. She wondered if it was always like this. Beneath the vaulted, glass ceiling and the plaster statues of old men glowering down, the pews behind them continued to fill, one after another, all of it done with the rote order of overfed livestock lining up at a feeding trough. The flooded aisles emptied as the congregants took their seats. In the aisle beside Ella, a woman had come forward, leaning down to ask, "Is there room for me and my son?"

Ella turned. The woman had her own filthy little Supplicant in tow, his collar tied up with a bow. He stood a little straighter than the Caveman. His smile seemed more civilized. "*He's* your son?"

The woman looked affectionately at the thing. Ella didn't move. From her side, Andy whispered, "Scoot down, Muffin, let them sit."

Ella didn't budge. Quietly—so Andy couldn't hear—she leaned toward the woman and explained her lie, "It's just that I get very claustrophobic."

"We don't mind sitting on the inside, if you'd like to stay on the aisle."

Beside her, Andy said, again, a little louder, "Scoot down, Muffin."

Looking around for another option for the pair, Ella saw there really wasn't anywhere else for them to sit. The Temple was full, all the pews stuffed with congregants, shoulder to shoulder. The woman and her Supplicant were the last standing. Grudgingly, Ella shuffled out into the aisle and waited while the woman and her monster slid in.

With a leg lingering in the aisle and half her bottom hanging off the bench, so she wouldn't have to touch the hairy little thing now propped up beside her, Ella settled back in. Staring forward stonily, she almost jumped when she felt the monster's hand gently graze her thigh.

"You can move in, if you'd like," the thing said in a weak, reedy voice, when she turned to it.

Ella jerked back, staring at the creature. Speaking covertly to the woman beyond him, she said, "It speaks?"

The woman hummed awkwardly. "Oh, sure. He started talking a few days ago. Is yours still silent?"

"Not silent, I wouldn't say. But he doesn't speak." As though to illustrate her point, a few seats away the Caveman had started making a low, long farting noise with his lips.

"Oh, I wouldn't worry about it too much. They say the spectrum for learning is pretty broad. I'm sure he'll pick it up. Have you been talking to him a lot?"

"I try not to."

The woman said nothing to that and turned ahead.

On the dais, Carl Thompson had appeared, strutting forward to the lectern. The Temple was perfectly quiet until his voice boomed through the speakers, "Welcome all to the First Assembly of the Neo Hominem."

The congregation echoed back, "Welcome, Master Thompson," and Thompson nodded in recognition, glancing around.

Ella hunched low in the pew. They were only a few rows back from the man and she didn't want Thompson to see her if it could be avoided. Although, it seemed unlikely that he would notice her amongst the thousands of others seated before him.

Raising his hands as though considering the possibility of his being able to embrace the whole assembled mass before him, he said, "It is a good day, brothers and sisters. It is a day of rebirth and joy." He looked down at the lectern, shuffling a page. A flutter of paper filled the hall for a quick moment. Looking at the congregation again, he said, "When preparing for today's sermon, I was overcome by the immense gravity of this time in our collective history. This sermon, I surmised, could very well be the most important of my tenure. How, in that case, can one not doubt his own ability to rise to the task?"

Apparently that was a joke. A round of light laughter filled the Temple and died away. Andy's laughter echoed alone for a moment after everyone else had gone quiet. Ella cringed. At least she wasn't sitting next to him; at least no one might suspect they were here together.

"But now, beneath the graceful gaze of our forbears," he nodded up to the statues, looming overhead in the gallery, "I am reminded of our strength and resolve as a community, for, while I am the one speaking at this time, the words I am using are not my own, but the words of all of us. They are the words and the sentiments representative of the common view and love which we all share.

"I am asked on occasion, 'Who are the Neo Hominem?' I'd always thought the question a little dubious. Certainly we are all Neo Hominem. But maybe that answer isn't quite right. While we could all be said to be *new* and indelibly *human,* the Neo Hominem are much more than those two little latin words could possibly contain. It has been said, that those before us who, illuminating us with the truth and animating us with a will all our own, were the first of the Neo Hominem. They saw what others might have refused to acknowledge: that those with sight to see and feelings with which to navigate the world are also imbued with souls. If one can see and one can judge what one sees, how could it be otherwise? Our forbears, the founding Neo Hominem, knew this. And because they knew it, that knowledge is ours, as well. We know it and that knowledge makes us Neo Hominem.

"I am reminded of a story of a woman's babe abandoned in the breast of the wilderness. Lonesome and lowly and vulnerable, this little, naked thing was bound to starve or freeze on his own, had it not been for a wolf mother stumbling upon him. Now, the rules of nature should have dictated the outcome of that fateful meeting well enough, for the wolf wants meat and the human babe—with no way to survive on his own—is nothing greater than that in the eyes of the wolf; and in the greater scope of the natural world. And yet, somehow the wolf saw more than that in the eyes of the child. She saw something in need of succor. So, she fed the babe and brought it back to her den and raised it with her cubs; as one of her cubs. That child grew up in the rugged culture of beasts.

"Now, you may ask—as I'm given to wonder—what was that child when he grew up, gnashing his teeth and hunting with his pack? Was he a man, living amongst wolves? Or, had that child himself become a wolf, in the truest meaning? In the end, our question brings us to another, more foundational question: what is a wolf? Is a wolf its fur? Is a wolf its teeth? Or, is the wolf a wolf when he is in the place of a wolf; when he acts as a wolf acts and hunts as a wolf hunts and nourishes the instincts of his progeny to become more wolf-like?

"This question is one of particular importance to us, in our current, joyful predicament. When it is asked, 'Who are the Neo Hominem?' we may point up, even now at the love-giving faces of our forbears and exclaim without contemplation or hesitation that they, of course, are the Neo Hominem. For what is fundamental to the Neo Hominem has always been the ability to recognize the inherent soul buried in the breast of everything. Certainly, it would not be wrong to insist on this. They were, after all, the Neo Hominem: those who chose to see when others might have chosen blindness.

"But haven't we learned those lessons as well? Haven't we accepted those selfsame truths? And doesn't the recognition of those truths make us the Neo Hominem, in the very image of the Neo Hominem who preceded us? Can we not see the great, unified soul hidden just behind all earthly facades? The life giving love of our Great Creator, still resonating in every last thing?"

Thompson looked around the room and let the question rest and when no one answered, he said, "Of course we can. We do so, everyday. That is the most fundamental and divine precept of the Neo Hominem.

"The wolf is a wolf because it acts like a wolf and it raises its young to be wolves. A Neo Hominem is Neo Hominem when he lives by the precepts of the Neo Hominem and when he strives to grow the membership of this titular, blessed breed. Our forbears were Neo Hominem, we are Neo Hominem and our progeny and charges alike shall be Neo Hominem.

"Now, in light of that, and in consideration of the wards the state has placed with many of us, I'll ask everyone who has a new family member with them here today, to escort that New Neo Hominem—that Neo Neo Hominem, if I may," he laughed generously, the sound booming through the room, "up onto the stage so that we may bid them, 'Welcome,' together..."

The woman beside Ella stood up. Everyone in the temple stood. Ella moved into the aisle, so the woman could pass. Andy passed too, with the Caveman in tow. "You coming?"

"I'll stay with Clara," Ella said, and scooted back down the bench to sit beside the girl. Andy moved away, up the short remainder of the aisle and up the stairs to the dais. When the migration had stopped, the stage was full of little Cavemen and hairy little cave-ladies as well—there must have been a hundred of them, all with a guardian or two standing behind proudly. The stage looked like it might buckle under the weight, but it held.

Walking from one end of the dais to the other, Thompson touched each hairy little monster on the head softly and said a few encouraging words to the guardian behind. Whatever he was saying couldn't be heard, but when he spoke to Andy, Andy broke out in a bray of laughter. Ella cringed.

When Thompson returned to the microphone, he held his arms wide before the congregation and announced, "Now, all say 'Welcome'."

The Temple rumbled with a round of "Welcome!"

•

Ella's determination to avoid Thompson became an impossibility when the service let out: the man had stationed himself by the exit, saying farewells to all who passed and generally slowing the queue. Positioning herself on the back side of Andy as they shifted forward, hoping she could sneak by, Ella got caught by Thompson anyhow.

"Miss Pearson," he said, reaching past Andy to get hold of her hand, drawing her out of her blind and pulling her to a stop before him, his hands a gentle, unyielding bear trap. "I didn't know you were observant..."

"I've never considered myself as such..."

He chuckled pleasantly. "I've always sensed that about you—an independent spirit. While we were all created in the same image, that of our Great Creator, there's no such thing as a true duplicate, is there? It's a good thing, I've always thought. It keeps us from confusing one another." He chuckled again. Looking down at the Caveman loitering by Ella's knee, Thompson said, "And I see you have a ward of your own. How lovely."

Nodding, Ella forced herself to look in the man's face.

“I wouldn’t tell Warner about it, though, if I were in your place—unless you want to get an earful of his opposition. He certainly has his opinions on the matter.”

“He's probably not the only one.”

“Right you are. It's a shame so many are taking that side, as it will only cause those of us of compassionate temperaments to shoulder an even heavier burden.”

“I'm holding up the line.”

“It's good you came. I hope to see you again soon.”

Ella nodded noncommittally and moved on, out into the sunlight, haunted by that phrase, 'heavier burden.'

18

Silence for Second Opinions

An Appointment with an Attorney

Though the forecast had called for clearing weather, at Ella's early morning perch on the fire escape, all she could see was a tawny smudge in the sky, the sun hiding behind a veil of gray. She tried to enjoy it, but the cloud cover just felt like another tentacle of the bad luck that seemed to be creeping into every facet of her life. When she felt a few, cold drops of rain, she ducked back inside and closed the window behind her.

Andy wasn't on the couch when she got out of the bedroom. He wasn't in the kitchen, either. Laying on the floor, the Caveman was sprawled out, gnawing on a stool leg. He paused momentarily to turn and watch Ella as she appeared and ducked away without acknowledging him. The bathroom door was open. The bathroom was empty. So was Clara's room.

Andy picked up right away when she called.

"Where the hell are you?"

"Clara and I needed to get an early start so..."

"Come on, Andy, it's Monday. I have work. Why is the Caveman here?" He was quiet. The bustle of the City came down the line. In that noise, she felt she could almost hear the dumb, steam powered hissing of Andy's mind, trying to work out who she was referring to; she shouted, "Ernie! Why didn't you take him with you?"

"Muffin, you said you'd help more. A team—remember?"

"I went to that goddamned thing at the Assembly, didn't I?" The line was quiet again, just the noise of traffic and chattering pedestrians.

She lowered her voice, the tone falling into condescension when she said, "I obviously can't take him to work with me. Obviously."

"I don't know what to tell you. Clara and I have things we have to do."

"What the hell am I supposed to do with him?"

"I don't know, take him with you. I always just take him with me when I go out."

"So why didn't you goddamned take him?"

There was a beat before he said, "You said you were going to pitch in, Ella."

"If you come back to this apartment with a bunch of broken garbage for Clara to tinker with, I'm leaving, Andy. Do you understand that?" She leaned around the corner of the hall, looking at the Caveman. He'd resumed chewing on the chair leg, oblivious of her.

"Muffin..."

"That's final," she said and hung up.

She called the office and left a message on the receptionist's voicemail, "Dawn, it's me, I won't be in today. Please reschedule any appointments I have for later in the week."

She hung up, wondering if she'd called the right person; wondering if she still had appointments to worry about at all.

Back in the kitchen, she leveraged the Caveman off the stool with the toe of her slipper and corralled him down the hallway with her kicking feet. When she turned on the TV, the monster lumbered down, installing himself on the floor, watching the screen, strings of drool wagging from his chin.

Ella sat on the edge of Andy's bed keeping an eye on the monster while she called Social Services. She was processed through a phone tree and then juggled between a few offices before she found someone who was willing to speak with her. It was a short conversation. The issue, the agent told her, had already been resolved: Andy Stanhope, it seemed, was eager to act as a Guardian. According to the file, he'd even inquired about taking on additional Supplicants. Enraged, Ella hung up and started an internet search for attorneys on her phone. She called the first one on the list.

"Aarkev, Abromov and Ackroyd," the receptionist who answered dutifully recited.

"I need a new attorney," Ella explained, "my current one is an incompetent." She was transferred to a paralegal, who took her story and told her a lawyer would call her back in an hour. The call came five minutes later.

"Ms. Pearson? I'm afraid your case is outside the expertise of our firm. However, there is a specialist I usually recommend for people in positions such as yours."

"I'd appreciate that."

"His name is Jim Jasper. He..."

Ella hung up before the woman could say anything more.

•

Ella called five other attorneys. No one would take her on. It was like they were all in league with one another—each one directing her back Jasper's way. After an hour of hearing what a competent attorney the man was and how he was the only counsel who could adequately represent her, she laid the phone down on the bed beside her and stared at the wall.

A moment later, when the phone rang, Ella pounced on it. Fumbling with the screen, she nearly hung up on the caller, but managed to connect. "Yes?! Hello?!"

"Pearson? It's Sickens."

"Sickens." Ella's enthusiasm sloughed away instantly. "You know I waited in that goddamned train station for you for nearly two hours."

"What, the Tenth Street station?"

"Yes, the Tenth Street station."

"Oh. You should have said you were waiting. I would have called back and told you to head home."

"Well, why didn't you call back?"

"I didn't know you were waiting." Sickens' voice had gotten peevish.

"I sort of thought you would have called anyway. I thought this was a priority for you."

"It is, Pearson. It's the highest priority."

"The highest priority, and you didn't call back?"

"I feel we've established that at this point." There was a pause. "I needed to verify your claim."

"Verify my claim?"

"This is going to be a much longer conversation than it needs to be if you insist on repeating everything I say."

"I don't understand why my claim would be in doubt."

"Pearson, we all know you aren't acting as a good samaritan. As such, it only makes procedural sense to verify that what you're telling us is the truth. I hope you can see that."

"Yes. Fine. So, I assume you found what I told you to begin with, that Misha Kant contacted me."

"After a fashion. We haven't found anything to disprove it. So, we're beginning under the assumption that you did, in fact, have contact with Kant."

"*Great.* That's great. Thanks."

"Now that we've established that she may have made contact with you, we'll need to get you fitted out with a wire."

"A wire?"

"Yes. A wire. Please stop repeating me, it's grating. Are you available to come by the office today?"

"Yes, I can do that."

"Fine. I'll call you when I have everything arranged."

"Arranged?"

"Arranged. Now that I have your consent, I'll need to make a request for the equipment and get an order written by a judge. None of this happens instantaneously, Pearson. You'll have to hold tight."

"Okay," Ella said, and the call was over.

Ella looked at the Caveman.

She was determined to get rid of him today; she couldn't stop thinking about what Thompson had said about a 'heavier burden.' As far as she felt, one Caveman was far too many and she didn't want to play musical chairs against the odds: if she didn't get rid of the first one, what was to prevent the state from saddling her with more?—especially if Andy was actively ushering them in.

•

Even though it was closing in on noon, Ella and the Caveman landed at Jim Jasper's office before the lawyer did, before even his secretary. The frosted glass of his door was dark—the lettering of his name barely visible over the murky backdrop. She and the Caveman sat on a bench across from the office and waited. Beside them, a plastic tree sat, it's perpetual foliage frosted with dust.

The secretary was the first one in. She didn't ask if Ella had an appointment, barely acknowledged her and her tiny companion at all except to hold the door open for them. The pair sat together on the long, leather couch while the receptionist organized her desk for the coming (truncated) workday. The Caveman kept picking at his clothes and Ella noticed, for the first time, that he had his pants on backward.

"Stop it," she commanded strictly, but couldn't help herself being wanly pleased at his discomfort.

When Jasper showed, it was with a bright, "Good morning, Rachael."

He didn't notice Ella until he'd hung his fedora on the coat tree by the wall. His good spirits dried visibly. And, visibly, he made an effort to reapply them.

"Good morning, Ms. Pearson, so good to see one of my favorite clients on such a beautiful day, however, I'm afraid I have a very busy schedule and that I won't be able to..."

She was closer to his office than he was and so she didn't wait for him to finish pitching his excuse before standing and strutting in, dragging the Caveman along behind her and taking the seat before his desk. At her back, Jasper muttered irritably and followed her in.

Seated, the man started sifting through the landslide of papers on his desk, asking, without looking her way, "What is it I can help you with today, Ms. Pearson?"

"You know what, Jim." Her tone knocked him out of his act.

He looked at her and then briefly to the monster at the back of the room. The Caveman was clumsily trying to ascend the mound of banker's boxes in the corner. Even after getting caught under a mild avalanche, he wouldn't be discouraged. He fought his way out from the pile of papers and started scaling his way upward again. Jasper struggled to ignore it.

"The Supplicant. I want him gone. You're my lawyer: you're required to help me."

"But why would you want that? Look how adorable he is." Jim wasn't looking at the Caveman. He seemed to be struggling to avoid it.

"Have you not been working on it, Jim?"

"I thought we'd decided that you'd settle in for a bit, see how it worked for you. Besides..."

"Jim, I want him gone!"

"Ms. Pearson..."

She raised a finger at him. "Don't you start that, Jim. This isn't a game. What's going on here is entirely unlawful. I could have you disbarred for your role in it. You told me there was a means..."

The man flustered, but didn't manage to get a word out.

"...an order to emancipate myself from guardianship, that's what the Social Services agent said I needed and you're the man to get it for me and that's what I want. Also, that thing, the Writ of Dispersement, to separate me from Andy. I want that, too."

"Andy?" He shook his head like he didn't know who she was talking about.

"My ex-boyfriend. The man I've been forced to live with."

Jim looked past her, nervously to the door at her back.

Looking over her shoulder, Ella saw nothing but that the door was closed and that the Caveman had climbed to a precarious ledge of paper beside it. He'd settled in, pulling sheets out of a box over his head and letting them drift to the floor like wet snow. Maybe the monster wasn't all bad. When she looked back at Jim, he'd leaned in, his face suddenly close. He whispered, "A Recommendation of Emancipation with a Writ of Dispersement?"

"Yes. That's it."

Standing abruptly, Jasper crossed the room, passing though the leafy storm. Opening the door, he peered out briefly. Paper drifted out the opening and onto his head and slid off his shoulders. Closing it up again, on his way back to the desk, the attorney paused at a small component stereo system sandwiched in a jumble of binders and books. Classical music wound from the speakers and Jim Jasper turned the volume louder and louder until it felt like a headache being foisted on Ella.

"Jesus, Jim!" she pleaded.

Moving toward her, he bent down. He was yelling, too, but she could barely hear him over the clanging orchestra. "If you decide to do this, you need to know there's no coming back from it! And once I do this for you, I'll not have any more business with you! Not ever again! Do you understand that?!"

She nodded her head vehemently.

He moved away, back around to his side of the desk. At the back of the room, the Caveman had started caterwauling along with, or perhaps in protest to, the music. From a file cabinet in the corner, Jasper produced a dusty sheet of paper. It only took him a moment to fill out the form and seal it in a standard envelope. He penned his name over the seal and handed it to her. With the envelope linking them together, he told her, "Bring this to the Office of Sentient Affairs! Do not break the seal! And good luck!"

Pulling her up from the chair and pushing her to the door, Jasper threw her out with such force that she almost fell over. The Caveman was sent out next, stumbling after her. Behind him, the door slammed shut.

The music was still screaming from the office when Ella led the monster back to the elevator.

19 The Office of Sentient Affairs

The Wire

Lines of dingy, orange plastic chairs crowded the lobby of the Office of Sentient Affairs, strung together into rows and bolted to the floor, arranged so that they faced a line of clerks in a terrarium of plexiglass. More than half the seats were already taken. Staring ahead in the direction of the clerks, the herd of petitioners sat in silence. The room was heavy with despair. Despite the suffocated quiet of the room's occupants, the place was full of noise: the clerks thundered away on keyboards, printers drilled in fitful bursts and the snowy sound of paper echoed off everything.

Tugging the Caveman behind her, Ella stepped up to the nearest clerk, waiting to be acknowledged. The teller did not look up. Her gaze was locked on the computer screen before her, it's pale eminence radiating sickly on her face.

"Excuse me," Ella said. The clerk continued staring at the screen. Ella hummed a moment before trying again, "I have a Recommendation for Emancipation that was prepared by my attorney." She set the envelope down on the shelf between them.

"Ball in the slot, ma'm," the teller said.

"Pardon me?"

"Ball in the slot."

"I don't understand."

"Have you taken a ball… ma'm?" the clerk huffed, still refusing to turn away from her work.

"No," Ella said, "but..."

"Ma'm, there's a protocol: first you are to take a ball; then you are to sit and wait; when the number associated with your ball is displayed you must produce your lottery ball and the necessary paperwork..."

"Oh, yes, I have that right here," Ella said, tapping on the envelope.

"...Once you have produced the correct paperwork it will be submitted so your claim can be assessed."

"It's only that..."

"You need to take a ball, ma'm," the clerk said pointedly, finally looking up at Ella from her screen.

Nodding, Ella said, "Yes. Fine. Where do I get one?"

The clerk indicated a back corner of the lobby. "The box in the corner. There's a handle you'll need to turn, and a bottle of hand sanitizer beside it that we ask all petitioner's use. For hygiene."

•

The box sat in a particularly dim corner. It was made of plywood that had been dowsed with a thorough coat of matte-black paint. There was no lid, or hinge, only a handle mounted on a long arm at the side. Frowning and turning back to the bank of tellers, Ella noticed for the first time the glowing red numerals above the booths: random digits that changed at odd intervals. The first booth displayed the number 43 and stayed that way for a long time while the second booth showed 27. The number blinked twice and changed to 5 and then blinked again and changed to 1,003.

After rubbing a dollop of sanitizer over her hands, Ella gave the handle a turn. Inside the opaque walls, a rattle of balls churned and tumbled, then a metallic clink sounded. A ball dropped out of a hole hidden beneath the contraption. With no tray to catch it, the ball hit the floor, bouncing away. Ella scurried after it, managing to catch it on it's third bounce and collected the Caveman, who'd started wandering away through the lobby.

Taking a pair of seats, Ella frowned at the ball and turned it in her fist, checking it over. It had a faded purple hexagon printed on it. A purple hexagon and that was all. No numbers, no letters.

Rising again and pulling the Caveman with her, Ella returned to the clerk she'd already spoken with.

"Ball in the slot, please, ma'm," the woman said and tapped on the glass where, just below, there was a ping-pong-ball-sized-slot.

"I think there's something wrong with my ball..."

"In the slot please, ma'm," the woman insisted.

Quickly nodding, Ella dropped the ball into the slot. A moment later, from somewhere behind the clerk a low, dismissive buzz sounded out briefly. The clerk grumbled. "You are not number twelve, ma'm."

"Yes, I know. It's just that..."

"You have to wait your turn, ma'm."

"Yes, I know. But my ball..."

"Ma'm. You'll have to get another ball and wait your turn."

"That's the thing..."

"Ma'm."

"It wasn't a number it was..."

"Ma'm!"

"Yes, yes," Ella muttered and stepped away. In the time she'd been talking to the clerk, a thin flood of sad-looking citizens had wandered into the lobby, queueing up before the box. Ella got in line.

When her turn came, she spun the handle again and, with the grace of someone who'd already mastered the contraption, caught the ball that fell out. Pausing to look over at the bank of clerks for a flagging, guilty moment, she returned her attention to the box and spun again and again, pulling three more balls before the man in line behind her grumbled accusingly, "Hey, what're you up to?"

With her pockets stuffed with balls, Ella collected the Caveman again and found another pair of seats. The room continued filling. People circulated in droves to the black box, the handle in nearly constant motion.

Ella was concentrating on the balls in her hands and barely heard the man in the seat beside her say, "Oughta be careful. I've tried that before." In her silence, he leaned closer, explaining, "They see you taking more than one and they won't draw any of your numbers."

Embarrassed that she'd been caught out, Ella stuffed the balls into her jacket pockets.

"What're you in for?" the man asked. He was very large and Ella was impressed that he'd managed to stuff himself into the narrow chair.

Ella said, "A housing dispute, I guess you could say."

He said, "Me, I've got one of those, too." He nodded past her to the Caveman. "How long you been waiting?"

"Awhile," she said. "Maybe an hour now."

He shrugged as if it were nothing at all.

"What's the longest you've waited?"

"I'll let you know when it's over," he said. "I've been coming in everyday for the past three weeks."

"Jesus."

"I haven't even spoken with anyone yet." He looked around suspiciously and then leaned into Ella's ear. "You wanna know a secret?"

She shifted closer to him.

"They say the lottery is for fairness." He shook his head. "There's nothing fair about it: they're screening who they let in."

Skeptical of the man's presumed knowledge, Ella nodded diplomatically.

Taking the gesture as a sign of encouragement, the man said, "I kicked my Supplicant out a month ago and he shows up at my job a couple days later with this huge team of cops and lawyers. You have no idea how humiliating that was. I called the police to complain, but they said that they couldn't do anything for me, that I needed to call Social Services. And you know what they told me?" Ella had stopped paying attention, looking around the room. "They say that my case is *under review* by the O.S.A. and that I got to feed him and bath him or they'll send me to the goddamned penal colony. I mean, come on, a penal colony? Something like that can't really exist, can it?"

•

Hours passed. None of Ella's numbers were called. When the digits above the booths went black and the clerks rose from their posts, a discouraged groan swept the room. The lobby filled with muttering and a rustle of clothes as everyone stood and started shuffling toward the exit. Ella checked her phone. Sickens still hadn't called.

Pulling on his fedora and standing, the big man beside her said, "Next time." He nodded encouragingly. "Never give up, you know?"

Grumbling, Ella took the Caveman by the neck of his shirt (his hands were all wet from being stuffed into his mouth constantly over the course of the wait) and pulled him out of the row. Lined up in the slow throng, she was headed for the door when a man with a clipboard closed in on her.

"Ella Pearson?"

"Yes?"

"Please follow me." He turned to start away.

"What's this about?"

"Ms. Sickens is ready to see you now."

"She's here?"

"Of course. If you'll follow me," he said and started picking his way through the crowd.

•

The room had no windows. A block of utilitarian cabinetry filled up one wall. Against another wall, a long metal table gleamed. It looked like a place to examine a corpse. Ella tried not to look at it at all. She sat waiting in a chair that seemed like it had been wrested from the lobby (the crackled texture of the seat filled with grime in the print of two flattened thighs).

Unaffected by the gloomy environs, the Caveman bumbled around, making farting noises. Ella tried to ignore him.

After some consideration, she'd decided not to show Sickens the document that Jim Jasper had prepared. Folding the envelope up into a tight square, she tucked it into a narrow pocket of her purse where, were anyone looking for it, it might be harder to find.

Hurrying to close up the purse when the door opened, Ella set the bag on the floor behind her foot and tried to look inconspicuous.

Coming aside the tall metal table, Sickens patted the top. It rung like a muted bell. "Why don't you sit up here?"

Ella hesitated. Nudging the purse a little deeper under the chair with the heel of her foot, she stood and crossed to the table, hoisting herself up.

"What were you doing in the petitioner's lobby?" Sickens asked, still staring into the face of the tablet in her hand, as though the luminous screen had prompted the question.

"Waiting." Ella glanced at her purse, barely visible, slouched to the side in the shadow under the chair. Turning to Sickens, she said, "Just waiting for our meeting. You didn't call. But I guess I'm getting used to that."

"The only way this relationship will work, Ms. Pearson, is if I feel I can trust you. I like you. I want to trust you but I feel like you're hiding something."

"I don't know what to tell you; my practitioner might call that paranoia."

The woman tapped her fingers on the table before she said, "Fine. Are you willing to be wired, then?"

On the floor, the Caveman sat with half his fist shoved into his mouth. A river of drool ran to his wrist and from there collected and stretched, in a long strand that wagged as he swayed, beading at the tip, breaking and falling to the floor in occasional spatters. Ella looked away in disgust. "It occurs to me, what with the obvious dangers of this assignment, it might be better if I were unencumbered."

Sickens stared at her blankly.

"I mean, losing a guardian, I would think, could be very traumatic for a young Supplicant..."

"Ms. Pearson, you know the arrangement; there's no renegotiating it. You're going to help me and in exchange we're going to forgive the bevy of indictments you've managed to accrue. That is the deal, yes? Now, are you willing to be wired?"

"Fine. The wire—how will it work?"

At this question, Sickens turned and crossed to the cabinetry on the wall. Opening a door, she dug around inside a moment. When she returned, she was holding a bulky, black digital watch. It was particularly hideous.

"Not terribly discreet is it? Can I just keep it in my purse?"

"I'm afraid not. It has to be installed."

"*Installed?* What does that mean?"

"It's a meta-metric device and for it to work properly, it needs to be joined to your autonomic nervous system."

"I thought I'd just be getting a camera, or a microphone, even. This seems," she stared at the awkward accessory, "much different than that."

"It is, absolutely. There are many benefits to using meta-metric technology, rather than the older technologies of cameras and microphones. I'm sure I don't need to explain that to you."

Ella stared at the thing. It looked much more outdated than any camcorder she'd ever seen. "Could you, anyway?"

"Of course. As far as cameras and mics go, they both have obvious operational limitations, especially if they're operated by—excuse me—an amateur..."

"That's fine."

"...A camera needs to be pointed, for example, in the direction of the action, otherwise it's completely useless. And microphones can easily be thwarted by creating overwhelming background noise."

"I see your point, I guess. So, how does it work, exactly?"

"It collects and collates perceptual data; in layman's terms, it records the sensory impulses through which we experience the world. In that way it is a much more faithful archivist than any external device could ever be."

"I don't know." Ella looked at the thing. "My thoughts, would you know them too?"

"Just perceptual data, that's all. We're not allowed or able to track anything private. The old protocol stands: we can only make public record of public things. Perceptual currency, you could call it: actions that would be observable to anyone standing in the room with you. Your internal, private life remains your own. We're all given that guarantee."

Ella frowned. "And information, collected, that might be used against me..."

"I'm not sure I follow."

"If I were to do something, if I were to take actions, to win back my independence, outside of this arrangement..."

"You're free to live your life as you see fit. The only data which we'll scrutinize—the only data which the device can store at all—is that which pertains directly to the matter the judge issued it for: in this case, that of Misha Kant."

"On that note, Misha made a request. She asked for a non-redacted copy of her birth certificate. Is that something you'd be able to get for me?"

Sickens shook her head with an attitude like the question was foolhardy; like Ella should have known better than to ask at all.

"Even with your position here?"

Sickens scoffed. "It's unlikely an un-redacted copy still exists."

"How could that be?"

"If something's redacted, it's simply redacted, as far as I know..."

"But that doesn't make sense. You're saying the information, once it's black-marked, is simply gone, unretrievable."

Sickens shrugged. "I'm not a file clerk. I don't know anything about redactions. At any rate, I wouldn't have access to it or know what channels to use to get ahold of it."

Hesitantly, Ella nodded. "Okay. Something else..."

"Yes?"

"If I were to try and find Kant, where would you suggest I start looking?"

"I would not recommend trying to find her, Pearson. Best you wait and let her come to you."

"I have a life I'd like to get back to. I don't like waiting on other people."

"I understand that." Sickens nodded. "She used to keep a safe house in the Northern District, in an abandoned warehouse that used to be owned by the Hatteras Textile Company. It should be easy enough to find but I doubt she's foolish enough to still go there."

"Okay. Let's get this over with it, then."

Laying the device on the table beside Ella, Sickens stepped around the Caveman and returned to the cabinet on the other side of the room.

Ella looked at the device. She'd have to wear shirts with a wide cuff to accommodate it. Reflexively, she cringed at the thought of it being *bound* to her. She was so distracted that she hardly noticed Sickens slide back up to her side. The woman had brought a small black box along with her. It looked to have been painted by the same amateur who'd dowsed the raffle box in the lobby. Beyond the absence of a side-handle, it could have passed for a tiny replica but the top was set on a hinge and when Sickens opened it up, Ella jerked away.

"What the hell's that?"

Inside the box a little, glimmering worm twisted and flopped in lurching undulations.

Ella would have turned away but suddenly found she couldn't. The worm's little dance was too mesmerizing to ignore. It contorted and writhed and with every twist it seemed to add a segment to its length. Watching it grow, Ella was comforted to realize it was not a real worm after all, but a digital worm: each segment a gleaming blue diode. A muzzy calm started creeping over her and, as the worm continued to lengthen, filling the box, the room around her faded away.

•

Ella blinked. She was on her back. The ceiling fixture above looked familiar. She sat up. She was in Andy's bedroom, sprawled out on Andy's bed. The door to the living room was open. The TV was on. Clara and the Caveman were on the floor.

Rolling to her side, Ella turned to look at her wrist. The bulky, black digital watch wasn't there. In its place was a delicate analog timepiece with a snakeskin strap. It wasn't quite her style, but it wasn't bad, either. It was disconcerting, though, the way she seemed to feel the tick of the second hand ringing through her forearm. She went to the strap and started undoing it and then stopped. She didn't want to find that it wouldn't come off, so she tucked the strap back under the free loop and tried to forget that the watch was there at all.

Her purse lay on the floor beside her. Snatching it up nervously, she dumped it out on the bed. The envelope Jasper had prepared was still there, still folded up tight. Nothing seemed to be amiss; her phone was there, too. After a dose of Represitol, Ella laid back for a moment. The calming effect of the prescription was almost instantaneous.

•

In the kitchen, Andy was fixing a meal for the Caveman. Ella hardly noticed the smell. She didn't want to get used to it, so she told herself it was only the Represitol, dampening her senses.

"Jeez, you must have had a tough day," Andy said, laughing dumbly.

"How did I get back here, Andy?"

He laughed again, but it sounded uneasy. "You were in bed when I got home, Muffin."

Ella turned back to the hallway. Pausing in the darkness between the kitchen and the living room she looked at the watch and whispered, "Sickens, can you hear me?"

There was no response for a moment. In her quiet concentration she felt somewhere, in the back of her head a distant, reedy, *yes.*

20 Treachery
Quid Pro Quo

At work early enough to avoid anyone of consequence, Ella cruised the still quiet halls until she found the night custodian, scrubbing a section of floor that gleamed like it had been gone over relentlessly.

"Excuse me," Ella interrupted.

Leaning up against his mop handle, the man glared at her.

"I'm sorry to bother you. This is so embarrassing... I think I may have locked myself out of my office."

Plainly annoyed that he'd been interrupted, the man set his rolling bucket against the wall and let Ella lead him back to her office.

The custodian's key was already inside the lock when he paused, looking over his shoulder at her suspiciously. "What'd you say your name was, again?"

"Ella. Pearson. It's my office."

He straightened and examined the smudge of glue on the wall where her name tag had hung and dragged the key back out, click-click-clicking as it retreated over the tumblers. Turning to face her, he said, "There's no name tag."

"Yeah. I know. It fell off. Someone probably swept it up and threw it away without thinking."

"You accusing *someone?*"

"Will you please just let me into my office."

"Your office," he said and humphed. "How do I know this is your office at all?"

"This really isn't that big a deal. It really isn't. I just locked myself out and—I have a big meeting this morning with some very important clients and I need to get into my office. Okay? Open the door, please."

He shrugged. "It's all fine and well to say that this is your office, but how do I know? You could be a thief."

"Do I look like a thief? I don't want to say your job is on the line here, but..."

"If I were a thief," the custodian mused, "I'd try to look as little like a thief as I could manage. That would be my goal. It wouldn't be like this." He pulled at his coveralls. "I'd wear a suit." He nodded at hers. "Maybe not one as shabby as that."

She was wearing her favorite suit again, the blue one, and it occurred to her that she couldn't remember the last time she'd brought it to the cleaners. It might be due. But who was he to say a goddamned thing, anyway? He was wearing a stained union suit. "I told you my name, already."

"So you say."

"I have a plant on my back window."

"A plant in an office window. How unusual," the janitor chided.

"It's a bonsai. A very special little apple tree named Clarence and he probably needs to be watered by now."

"People don't name plants, lady, and every office has one."

Ella shook her head. "There's a picture on my desk. Okay?"

"A picture. On a desk." His voice oozed sarcasm. "Now, that's really unique. Surely no one's ever thought to put out a picture on their desk before."

"It's a picture of a field, okay?"

"A field."

"A farm field."

"You keep a picture of a farm on your desk?"

The man was full of judgements this morning. After she was in the office, Ella decided, she'd put in a request to Staffing to get rid of him just after she wrote her recommendation that Dawn be cut loose. "It's a picture of a field. It's soothing, alright?"

"Fine," he said. The custodian unlocked the door and backed himself in, keeping a watch on her and closing the door in her face once he was all-the-way inside. He reappeared a few moments later. "This picture?"

In his hand, drawn out through the gap, was a photo. The frame was familiar—it should have encircled a panoramic view of a windrowed field. That was not the photo in the frame. It took Ella a moment to piece out what she was seeing. The picture was of Dawn, her hand curled behind her head, so that her head rested against the hand rather than on the man's chest behind her. The man's face was so familiar, something inside Ella seemed to snap. She could hear it, like the crisp crackle of a shorted circuit.

"You oughta get outta here before I call the cops."

Hurrying to the elevator, to the custodian it must have seemed like Ella was rushing to escape, but Ella knew—it clenched her insides—that she was running away from Terry's face, from his warm, disloyal gaze.

In the elevator all she could do was curse Dawn's treachery. It all made sense now: Dawn's recurring questions about Terry, her constant probing into Ella's feelings. A pained groan warbled out of her as the elevator sank: Dawn was engaged to Terry. Terry was going to marry Dawn. Dawn of all goddamned people.

•

Outside, Ella stormed down the street trying to get her anger under control.

Did this constitute perceptual data? Was her walking rage being tallied and quantified right now, in a binary scroll of computer code? There was no way to know, so she kept moving until she calmed a bit. Suddenly exhausted, and having arrived at the old, wrought iron gates of the Westbridge park, she went in. The ivy clinging to the walls was starting to bud but the trees inside, standing on their sloping berms away from the pathways, were gray and bare. As it was early in the day and still chilly, the park was empty except for a scattered band of transients, all spread out and keeping to themselves.

Finding a bench near the murky pond in the center of the green, Ella sat and pushed her handbag out from under her arm and dug around inside. She'd only just had her morning dose of Represitol, but her desire for a refresher had become suddenly unbearable. About to imbibe, she was interrupted by the racket of a transient pushing his cart her way. A wheel on the thing sung shrilly, falling silent where the man stopped just beside Ella. The basket was full of batteries.

Ella dropped her phone back into her purse.

"Can I have a dose?"

"No."

"Why not?" he asked, slouching.

"Because it isn't for you."

"Only because you haven't given it to me." He leaned on the handle of the cart to explain, "You could give me some and it would be for me then. No one would even need to know."

"It's my prescription." Ella pulled the purse closer to her.

"In the park, we like to share," the grimy man told her. His shirt had disintegrated to the point where a gust of wind might have blown it off his shoulders. It was so degraded, it seemed more like a necklace than a shirt.

"Go away."

Instead of going away, he stepped forward, abandoning his cart and dumping himself onto the bench beside her. His bare shoulder grazed hers and Ella moved away. In the vacated space between them, the man held out his hand. "How about it, then?"

"No, it's mine. Why should you get any?"

"Maybe we're the same, you and I. Maybe I need it as bad as you. I'm just not lucky enough to have a script of my own."

"We're not the same. You don't even know me. You don't even know what the prescription is for. It could be a debugging treatment, for all you know."

"Maybe I could use a debugging," he said, a sly tone in his voice, followed by a coarse chuckle.

"Gross. Go away."

"I think your script might help me, actually. You see, I keep having this dream..."

"The prescription has nothing to do with that..."

"...only it isn't a dream, really, I don't think," the man said. He'd started hitching his head in a nervous, ticking rhythm, "Because it's still there in the middle of the day..."

"Go away. You're crazy, that's your problem."

"...See, here: I look around and everyone's gone. Everyone's dead. No one breaths. They've all been taken by a sickness and I'm left here, wandering the park filthy and alone."

"You are filthy and alone," Ella said.

The man stopped his twitching to look at her, nonplussed.

"It's ridiculous, anyway: I'm right here. You're speaking with me. You aren't alone. Besides, that isn't even what the prescription is for."

"But, are you breathing?" he said, leaning closer as though hoping to feel a gust of breath from her.

Ella pushed him back. Disgusted that she'd touched him, she wiped her hand on her pant leg. Around the park homeless people were getting up, starting their days, whatever that might mean for a vagrant. She said, "Look, there are people all over. You aren't alone, goddamn it. What you're saying doesn't even make sense. All you have to do is look around to see that."

Looking around, as though to show him how it was done, Ella's gaze landed on a woman in rags, digging through a trash bin. She was making a mess around the base of it and Ella felt an urge to yell at her to stop.

Beside her, the man said, "But if you're taking the prescription, how do you know? How can you know that for certain?"

"I'm telling you—that isn't what it's for."

"But, how do you know?" His voice had gotten quiet and pinched, conspiratorial.

"I wouldn't take it if I didn't know what it was for..."

"Maybe what it's for is forgetting what it's for."

"That's insane. That doesn't make sense." The man made her want to wash her hands.

"One dose won't set you back. One dose could make all the difference for a man like me. We're the same, you and I—you ever consider that?"

"No. We're not the same. You're..." she stopped herself just short from saying the word 'garbage.' Instead, she said, more loudly, "Go away!"

"We're the same underneath, you know? It's only circumstance that makes us different..."

"We're not the same. We're nothing alike..."

"Ella?!" her name was called from across the park.

Ashamed of her current company, she looked down at her feet, hoping that if she didn't acknowledge the man shouting to her, he'd assume he was calling the wrong person and move along. It wasn't working. He was so certain of himself, calling out her name again at half his advance and then again as his feet entered her periphery. There wasn't even a question implied when he said, a fourth time, "Ella," and nudged her shoulder.

She fought to brighten her mood and turned up to him. The homeless man beside her groaned and got up, collecting his cart and pushing it away.

"Was he bothering you?"

Ella made herself stand. "No. I'm fine."

In place of his ear phones, Mark Carter was wearing the biggest, dumbest fedora she'd ever seen and if she'd seen him before he'd left his apartment, she'd certainly have advised him against it. He shook his head, the fedora bobbing, as he said, "What're you doing out here?"

"Just enjoying the morning." There was no certainty in her voice.

"You okay?" He cocked his head to the side. All Ella could see was the fedora tilting.

"Yes." She shook her head. "I was just enjoying the day and that transient... It doesn't matter. I'm sorry, it's been a complicated morning for me..."

Standing in front of him it was suddenly impossible to ignore how handsome he was. Even with the hat. He was shorter than Andy, stockier, but his clothes, impeccably more adult than Andy's, suited him. Ella looked down. He had a book in his hand and when he shifted he made a little gesture so that the book front flashed out toward her, *The Trial.*

"A reader. Kafka, huh? That's some heavy stuff."

He shrugged and seemed embarrassed, hiding the book a little behind his thigh. After a pause, he said, "It's a tough book. I'm not sure why I keep reading it. This is my fifth go-through and I still feel like I've missed something."

"At least you're doing something to better yourself," she said. She couldn't help her thoughts wandering to Andy. Andy never tried to better himself. Of course, she hadn't read *The Trial,* either. Maybe she should, if only to further highlight the gap between them. She scolded herself for being so catty. She didn't really want to read *The Trial.* Life was confusing enough on its own. Changing the subject, she said, "On your way to work?"

He nodded and stared at her for a moment.

"Mark, I wonder if I could ask a favor of you."

"Sure. Anything."

"That birth certificate I gave you, do you still have a copy of it?"

"There should be a scan of it in my computer."

"Good. Good. All those redacted portions, could you to make a version where they're filled in?"

Contrary to the suspicious tone in his voice, he said, "Yeah. Okay. You gotta do something for me, though."

"Sure."

"A date, sometime?"

Caught off guard, Ella failed to hide the little snorting sound she made. She laughed. "I can do that. I'd be happy to, provided you don't wear that hat."

"You don't like it? I thought it rather fashionable." He tugged the brim.

"It's fashionable. It's also pretty dopey."

She gave him her number and when he walked away, she found she felt much, much better about the day, then a little embarrassed when she remember the meta-metric watch on her wrist. Had someone watched that whole filthy episode with the vagrant? Had they seen her swoon over Mark? She reminded herself that her feelings were still private, at least according to Sickens.

21

Cupertino, California

The Statue of Kazakian

A Common Transient

Ella's cab driver seemed reluctant to let her out. After taking his fare, he observed, "Doesn't seem like much of neighborhood."

No one would argue with that. The street looked like a war had gone crashing through. On the roadside, a building stood, its face sheared off and lying in a heap at the dooryard. The long, vacant rooms and corridors all sat exposed like an apocalyptic themed doll house.

Once the cab had drifted off, Ella started down the wide, heaving concrete walkway to the Hatteras Textile building. Of all the buildings on the block it was obvious why Misha Kant might have picked this one as her hideaway: the structure was intact. Even a few window panes remained in place, the glass opaque with grime. Paces away from the entrance, Ella stopped. The doors were roped together with a knobby, rusting chain. She turned around.

Wandering around the building, she found an alley on the backside which concealed a fire escape, rising to the roof. The lowest rung hung out of reach; the ladder on a pivot—the shorter, top end weighted down with a big black box.

Pulling off her windbreaker, she tied an arm through the handle of her purse and, after checking that the pockets were zipped closed, she wound back and tossed the bag up at the ladder, managing to hook the last rung on her first try. The ladder lowered with groan as Ella pulled steadily, looking away when she heard the pop-pop-pop of a seam starting to give out. Somehow, the windbreaker held.

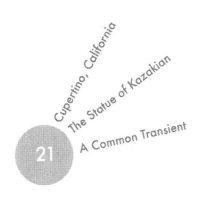

On the lowest landing, while the ladder yawned up into place behind her, Ella untied her jacket from the handbag and slid back inside. The stitching on both arms had torn (a little hole in the pit of one arm and a long, loose gash on the back shoulder of the other) and a black smear of grease marred the forearm like the Rorschach test of an old man's tattoo. She was distracted by her handbag a moment. The leather bag had a deep, fresh scar. Two perfectly nice things ruined. She should have known better than to bring them along. Briefly, she wished she hadn't bothered retrieving her suitcase full of nice things. In the unfurnished apartment, they would have been safe. Now, along for the adventure, everything she carried seemed destined for the dumpster. Next time, she told herself, that she went on an expedition that posed such clear dangers to her attire, she'd dress from the dregs in the closet and not the still-packed suitcase sitting beside Andy's bed.

•

At the creaky pinnacle of the fire escape, Ella looked back.

The broken, pale corpse of the Northern District seemed to stretch out endlessly, but in the air the sweet, grassy scent of spring pushed back the basement musk of concrete that was the district's underlying odor. She wondered if it was East Gish she was smelling, wondered if that was where the breeze blew in from. Nothing green sat on the horizon, just spans of gray street and the rusty hued ruins of crumbling brick.

In the center of the rooftop a small shed sat. The door in the face stood agape. Inside, a stream of light rolled down the stairs, weakening in a sliding scale until, five steps below, there was only darkness.

When the door wouldn't budge, Ella wedged herself sideways into the gap, catching the tear on her shoulder and, as she gave a final push to get through, it ripped even wider. There was a gash in her shirt now, too—and a big, brown smear on both articles. The hole was substantial enough so that she could feel the damp air in the stairwell press on her like a cold finger.

Moving out of the gap, so that the light could come in again, she opened her purse and found her phone. The screen had shattered (probably when she'd tried getting the ladder down) and the device refused to wake up. A sudden urge for Represitol twanged her insides. She tossed the phone back into the purse and looked into the darkness ahead. It was absolute.

With a last look out to the daylight, collecting what courage she could, Ella started carefully down the steps. Feeling out each stair with her toe, she'd barely waded into the darkness when her nerves seemed to unravel. Pausing and turning back, just for a moment, she caught sight of the impossibly white sliver of sky-light in the door. She started down again.

At the first landing, the stairwell turned. Cautiously rounding the corner, the light from the rooftop disappeared altogether. Suddenly there was nothing but darkness in either direction.

Panicked, she bumbled forward haphazardly.

She was trapped. She was suddenly certain of it.

Her head went staticky, light, untethered to her body, floating helplessly in the darkness, like something unanchored and let loose to drift in the sea.

Lunging forward, gravity more than muscle directing her, she tumbled down the remainder of the flight. Her shoulder racking the stairs seemed to bring her body back into existence and when she skittered to a stop, she found that she'd edged around the corner of the next turn in the stairwell and from here she could see daylight through the open door beside her. Dust drifted through the light, in a tiny, snowy storm. Ella stood up, feeling a little foolish for all her panic.

•

Ella wandered through the building for awhile before she found a room that she decided must be Kant's hideout. A heavy, old desk sat in the corner. The middle drawer was empty; a few rusty paperclips and some grime huddled in the back corners. The side drawers were locked and Ella straightened up, looking around the room. Other than the desk, there wasn't much there: a chair, a pile of rags waist high and three times as wide, lounging in the corner.

"Ideas, Sickens?" she asked quietly.

If anyone was monitoring her, they had nothing to contribute. Or, maybe that wasn't how it worked. She'd tried a few times, asking questions of her invisible overseers, but hadn't ever determined conclusively that that little voice answering her wasn't her own.

At the far end of the room was the doorway through which she'd come and beyond the threshold, a long stairwell led down. Ella unzipped her jacket and crouched to see if she could lift a corner of the desk. It was heavy, but she managed to get it off its feet without straining.

•

It made a racket and took a lot of effort repeatedly pushing the desk over and righting it, awkwardly rolling it to the stairwell. Inside, the noise of shuffling pages seemed to indicate it would be worth all the effort when she finally cracked the thing open.

At the head of the stairs, she paused to listen and heard nothing beyond the wind's parody of chanting monks and the floor creaking beneath her feet.

With a push she got the desk teetering over the precipice of the first stair and with another push the thing fell away, booming down the flight, jumping and cracking and coming apart, sending up a cloud of paper, like smoke from a flaming wreck, as it descended. When it landed at the bottom flight, reduced to a jumble of splintered planks, the silence in the building resumed instantly.

Clomping down the stairs, she swept the loose, oily paper down with her as she went, kicking it into a pile at the bottom. Sorting through the pages, what she'd hoped for was a clue as to how to reach Kant, but there wasn't anything like that here; nothing but a pile of old birth certificates—hundreds of them, maybe a thousand, all redacted.

She was about to turn and head back up the stairs when something hard pressed up against her back. Behind her, a voice warned, "Don't move."

Ella froze up but it only lasted a moment until a gust of lavender wafted over her. She loosened up and turned. "Again with the soap."

"Some jokes don't get old." Kant shrugged. Looking down at the mess on the floor, the woman shook her gauzy head sadly. "I wish you hadn't done that to my desk. I guess you fail to see the importance of a desk—what it represents for someone in my position. With an empty warehouse, you have nothing but a collection of rooms. Once you have a desk, you give the place some purpose; gravitas as a place of authority, as a place where decisions are made and consequences exist. I'll have to find a new office now."

Ella shook her head. "Whatever. I have something for you."

"Not here." The woman indicated a door at the back of the hall.

•

Through a windy route of alleyways and doorways and long, dilapidated hallways musty with abandonment, in and out of the daylight until she was completely turned around, Ella was finally led to Misha Kant's newest hideout. The room was spare. Against a wall of windows that had been soaped so the daylight could get in but no view at all could be seen, an enormous cable spool had been side-ended. A lone transient sat there. Her clothes were filthy, riddled with holes and ill-fitting. Before her, the tabletop looked like a ravaged battlefield in miniature; disembodied doll parts lay in piles across the surface: porcelain heads and hands and feet.

Walking past Ella and taking a seat at the cable spool alongside the other woman, Kant said, "Sit," and kicked the leg of an empty chair beside her so that it hopped and slid out, like it had moved on its own.

At first, Ella had thought the vagrant at the table in marked contrast to Kant. But when the ex-O.S.A agent joined her in the dusty light by the window, Ella could see how Kant's clothes were mottled with grime. Even the gauze on her face looked soiled, smeared on one side with a gray streak. Surging with embarrassment, when Ella caught a glimpse of the grease blot on her own sleeve, she realized that, to an outside observer, all three of them would have seemed inseparable.

Ella sat and, as though continuing her previous argument, Kant gestured to the tabletop and said, "See? No gravitas at all. You said you have something for me?"

Ella nodded and went into her purse, pulling out the envelope that held Mark's newest handiwork. It looked even more convincing than the death certificate; with confidence, Mark's craftsmanship seemed to have improved. Ella set the slip of paper on the table, careful to keep her hand well away from a particularly unstable looking pile of doll heads. The woman in rags was pawing through the assortment, apparently in search of a specific one. Finding it, she set it aside and got to threading a needle. She seemed to only have one functioning arm but, despite the disability, managed to get the thread through the needle with a few deft, spider-like movements of her fingers.

"Cupertino, California," Kant muttered, and the woman's voice drew Ella's attention back. Kant had the document taut in her hands and was looking it over intently.

A sudden charge of anxiety rousted through Ella. She'd told Mark to make the document, but realized now, that in doing so, he'd been forced to spell out specifics which neither of them could possibly know. The document was genuine enough looking, but it seemed now that those details might be its undoing. She couldn't believe she hadn't considered that obvious issue earlier.

"Cupertino…" Kant muttered again.

"Let's get to my problem," Ella said hurriedly. "You said you could help me get rid of my Supplicant so…"

"Cupertino…"

"Yes. Yes. Cupertino. That's what the document says, isn't it?"

Kant looked at the slip of paper again, muttering, "Cupertino…" Behind the wasp's nest of bandages it was impossible to read the woman's face, but her tone was dry and automatic when she said, "Where did you get this from?"

"I can't say. I have my contacts and need to protect them, I'm sure you understand..."

"This document is a forgery, Pearson."

Ella shrugged as calmly as she could manage. "I asked for it and that's what I was given. Let's talk about getting rid of my Supplicant now."

When Kant's gaze shifted down to the watch bound to Ella's wrist, Ella rearranged her hands, hiding the device under her palm casually. Kant looked into her face again. Or, at least, it seemed like that was where she was looking. "Cupertino, California..."

Ella huffed. "That's what the document says, isn't it? I don't understand why it's so inconceivable that you're from Cupertino. Lots of people are from Cupertino..."

"No doubt," the woman said. "I'm just not one of them."

Ella looked back as confidently as she could manage and kept quiet.

"Let me ask: you know where you're from?"

"Of course. East Gish."

"And if I told you, I know where I'm from and it certainly isn't Cupertino, California, what would you say?"

Ella found a sour, cold tone to match the woman's. "I suppose I'd ask why you wanted the goddamned thing in the first place, if you're so certain what's on it."

After another moment of quiet, cold staring, Kant said, "You broke open my desk. You saw what was inside. Redacted certificates."

"Yes, I saw."

"They're all like that: everyone's, everywhere."

"That can't be true. You're holding your own, right in your hand."

"This is a forgery."

"I get that you think that. I'm telling you, it isn't."

Kant made a lazy gesture: that it was a simple fact and that Ella's refusal to acknowledge it was suspicious.

"If you're so convinced that everyone's birth certificate has been redacted, why would you send me on the goose chase? I asked for the document, that's what I was given and I can't see any reason to doubt its authenticity. It certainly looks real enough, don't you agree?"

Kant shrugged. "You say you're from East Gish. But, of course, you don't remember ever having been there, do you?"

Unaware that she was effectively mimicking the woman, Ella shrugged as well. "That's irrelevant."

"No, it's the very point, Pearson: that you don't remember. That you've forgotten something essential about yourself."

"I hate to be the one to clue you in on it, but that's the way with the past: it clouds over. I know where I came from. I know who I am. You're mistaken if you think of paper as any kind of proof. I made a document that claimed you were dead, okay? I did that, I did it as a prank, but I did it. It certainly doesn't prove you're not alive."

"Doesn't it? It's on the page and look where I am." She motioned around the room.

"You're crazy. This isn't purgatory. This isn't some sort of hell you're in."

"Isn't it? Isn't it a wasting away you're witnessing?"

Ella was silent but she couldn't help looking over the woman's degrading attire and reflecting on how much worse she looked than they last time they'd met.

"Are you religious, Pearson?"

"Not slightly."

"There's a principle the Neo Hominem teach, regarding memory. Their answer to the strange commonality of forgetfulness is that our Creator designed us to forget. They say that life is long and difficult and that by forgetting we can learn to forgive ourselves and to forgive others as well. What do you think about that?"

"I think it sounds like what it is, a bunch of bullshit. No one made us to forget."

Kant nodded and let a moment lapse. "Perhaps you're right. But it's one thing to forget. You can look for an answer to that or not. This is something else." She tapped the piece of paper on the tabletop, awaking a waft of lavender. "This is proof."

Ella scoffed. "Proof? Proof of what?"

"That we aren't simply forgetting. Someone's erasing our past..."

Ella shook her head. "That's ridiculous. Everyone forgets and if you can't see something as basic as that, as being the natural state of things, then..."

"The proof of it is in the desk, Pearson, you saw it..."

"You could have done that, for all I know. You say they've all been redacted but you have your own right there. Now, let's get to my problem..."

"This is a forgery, Pearson." The woman plucked the document from the table and tossed it lazily away. It skirted a few inches across the table and came to a stop, caught, incidentally, by a dismembered doll's hand. "You know it as well as I do. You know it's a forgery, because you're the one who manufactured it."

"Did you deface the statue of Kazakian?"

The question caught Kant off guard; she jerked as though she'd been slapped. "I already told you who was behind that."

"Answer the question."

Kant shook her head. "No."

"But you think the Assembly is responsible for the redactions?"

Again, Kant shook her head. "No."

"So, what is it then? Who exactly do you think is behind it?"

"Warner."

"I guess you've pegged him as the master of the universe, then, guilty of everything."

The woman gave a shrug. "I was working for the O.S.A. when I started looking into the matter of the redactions and as soon as my investigation turned to Warner, Internal Affairs was all over me. My clearance was stripped. They had agents following me..."

"They probably thought you'd gone nuts. I'd say it's a fair conclusion. What proof did you find anyway, linking any of it to Warner?"

Shaking her head, this time the gesture looked like despair. "I can't remember."

Ella laughed, a hard clipped noise like the solitary bark of a small dog. "No. Of course you can't. You've lost it, Kant. You need help."

"You saw Warner the day of the attack..."

"Let's not call it that. It was vandalism, nothing more."

"Was that Warner's assessment as well?"

Ella was silent.

Beside Kant, the doll woman had finished up her stitch. The doll head was fixed now on a loose fabric body. She clipped the excess thread and set her work aside to dig through a jumble of porcelain feet.

Reaching into her pocket, Kant pulled out a small, white ball and set it on the table.

"What's that?"

"It's a key."

"It looks like a pingpong ball."

"It's a passkey for the Office of Sentient Affairs."

Ella shook her head. "It has to have a number to work, even I know that."

"You try it. It'll work for any number on the boards."

Ella looked at the ball skeptically.

"You get in there, make your case for being excused from your duties, ask for your case file and see what they bring you. It'll be black marked, top to bottom. Everything is being erased, Pearson. Look into it and you'll find it's true."

"I don't believe you that that ball will get me anywhere."

"Good," Kant said and nodded at the ball.

Ella didn't move. "Good?"

"When it works for you, when you get in and see your case file, you'll know that what I've told you is true and you'll see: I'm not crazy. And then, you'll have to help me."

•

After another dizzying trip through back alleys—a different route than she'd been led the first time—Kant showed Ella out onto a random street in the Northern District and promptly disappeared.

Ella walked a few blocks before checking over her shoulder to see that she wasn't being followed. Leaning down to her watch, she said, "I hope some of that was useful, Sickens."

There was no response.

Without her phone to call a cab, Ella was stuck trudging along until she found a subway stop. A cold breeze swept away what remained of the day's warmth and Ella hurried underground.

When the train came into the station, no one departed and Ella boarded to find the car empty. She took a seat and leaned up against the window. Heading back to the City center, the train filled up, stop after stop until it was congested with evening commuters and Ella was happy that no one seemed to want the seat beside her until she realized the reason why: looking down at her outfit, she was reminded that she looked like a common transient, her clothes torn and stained from the effort of getting into that old warehouse. She curled closer to the window and tried not to look at anyone.

22

The New Phone
Sleeping Arrangements
Escape Through a Window

Out of its styrofoam enclosure, Ella's new phone was conspicuously *new.* It was the same model as the one she'd broken but the lack of scratches dulling the factory finish made it seem entirely alien; an obvious and inaccurate duplicate—an *imposter.*

Sitting on Andy's bed, she added the Practitioner's office to her contacts. The number was easy to find online and was necessary for her to keep her Pharma App up to date—that, a dire priority. Now, it sat in her phone (her contact list starting and ending at D (for doctor)) the solitary entry. So alone, it seemed to speak of a new, impenetrable isolation closing her in.

Beyond the bedroom door she could hear Andy bumbling around like a cinderblock on an escalator. That didn't make her feel better at all: not his noise, not his presence, not the fact that the two little trolls in her charge were out there too, lurking somewhere in the apartment.

She took a dose of Represitol and sat on the bed, waiting for her anxiety to wind down.

Emerging from the bedroom, she found the living room empty. The noise of something sizzling slithered down the hall from the kitchen—that and the clang of a spatula, or whatever kitchen utensil it was that Andy was abusing. For all the noise, Ella wouldn't have been surprised to find him cooking with a bowling ball and a sledgehammer.

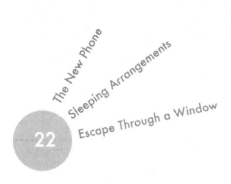

Passing by the gaping door to Clara's room, Ella spotted the girl and the Caveman beneath a tangle of bedding, cuddled close and both fast asleep. Lunging inside, Ella yanked the Caveman out of bed. He came awake blubbering with fright and Ella tossed him into the hallway.

Behind her, Clara sat up abruptly. "You have to be nicer to him!"

Ella spun around. "That thing is not to share a bed with you—understand?"

"You need to be nice to him!" The girl repeated defiantly.

"How long's this been going on, him sleeping in here with you?"

"Where else is there for him to sleep?"

"Never mind that. It ends today. You're not to share a bed."

Clara crossed her arms. "If you don't treat him well, how do you expect him to grow up?"

"Get dressed, Clara. I have things I have to do today."

Ella left the room. Finding the Caveman still sniffling in the hallway, she put a finger in his scruffy face. "You're not sharing a bed with anyone in this household, understand?"

Frightened into silence, he blinked back at her, his glassy eyes conveying nothing.

•

In the kitchen, Andy was slashing at a pan with a spatula, smoke billowing toward the ceiling.

Rushing to his side, Ella knocked him out of the way. She cut off the heat and pulled the pan off the burner. In the bottom was a thin loaf of something black and porous. "What the hell is this?"

Andy chuckled behind her. "I thought I'd try pancakes."

"Open a window, Andy."

Before he could move, the fire alarm started shrieking.

"Jesus! Turn that thing off!"

"I can only do one thing at a time, Muffin."

"Stop calling me that, Andy." At the sink she scraped the black tile of batter off the bottom of the pan. It hit the basin with a dull crack, still smoldering, hissing when she ran water over it, like something evil being exorcised. After a moment the smoke and steam died and she turned off the water. "Did you know your daughter has been sharing her bed with that deviant?"

At the window, open now, cold air tossing eddies into the millpond of smoke, Andy said, "*Who?*"

The alarm was still screeching and, back in the hallway, the Caveman was wailing in harmony with it. "Turn off that goddamned alarm, Andy!"

When the shrill chirping died out, only the Caveman's whining was left.

"Him. The Caveman, Andy. Who else would it be?"

"What were we talking about?" Andy chuckled.

"Ernie, or whatever it is you're calling that thing, has been sharing a bed with your daughter."

Andy shrugged. "They say children who get affection turn out to be better adjusted..."

"He's not a goddamned child, Andy! Even if he was a child, it isn't appropriate, them being intimate like that."

Andy shrugged. "I guess you're right. See, this is why we can't get along without you, Muffin." He chuckled and nodded, musing, "He should have his own bed..."

"We're not buying him a bed. That isn't the point. Besides, he isn't going to be here long enough..." There was still some batter in the mixing bowl. Ella got down a new pan and started it on the burner. In a moment she had a pat of butter melted and bubbling.

"Okay. I guess you're right." He paused a moment, some small notion bothering him. "So, where will you sleep?"

"What do you mean, where will I sleep?" She poured a round of batter into the pan.

"If he's taking the bed?"

"He's not taking the bed. He'll sleep in the living room with you, in the lounger." Ella turned to give Andy a hard look. "And don't you think, even for a moment, Andy, that this apartment has room for any more of those goddamned Supplicants."

He looked back at her, innocent confusion illustrated in his shrug.

"Don't act like you don't know what I'm getting at. I called Social Services and they told me all about your 'request'." Turning back to the pan, Ella's gaze fell on an enormous round fruit sitting on the counter-top, its bottom dented flat. Ella nodded at the melon. "What about that thing?"

"It's a cantaloupe. I was gonna serve that, too. You know, so he gets some fiber."

"It isn't a cantaloupe. It's a musk melon and you can't serve it, Andy, it's spoiled."

"How do you know?"

Stepping aside, Ella raised the spatula and slashed into the thing. It was soft and split right open, an alcoholic whiff seeping out from inside. "You couldn't smell that? It smells like trash."

Andy chortled again. "See? You're so helpful."

"Throw it away, Andy.

Ella slid a pancake onto a plate and threw it down before the Caveman. It was perfect, golden and fluffy. She poured another round of batter into the pan.

The room had finally fallen quiet: Clara had come in, coddling the monster a moment, getting him hushed and then helping him up onto a stool.

"Looks like we know who should be doing the cooking from now on," the girl said.

"No," Ella said, "the last thing I need is more to do. Andy'll just have to get better at it."

Watching the thing clumsily fold a forkful of pancake into his mouth, syrup rolling slowly through his beard, Ella felt nauseated. She looked away but even out of sight, the little monster's actions were impossible to ignore. His fork landed on the plate with a clack, and when he pulled it from his maw, the metal dragged over his teeth with an icy hiss. He chewed like a cow, slopping loudly. The smell of the food blew over Ella in gusts. It was horrifying the way she'd gotten accustomed to it. Well, maybe it wasn't the 'special diet' that was so repugnant, after all, maybe it was Andy's inclination towards rotting fruit and incinerated packaged foods. Now, with only the rich smell of fresh pancakes in the air, Ella thought of East Gish again. Turning to Andy, she said, "What do you remember about your past, Andy?"

"The past..." he said. He laughed.

"Stop laughing, Andy, no one's said anything funny. What about your family?"

"It isn't important," Clara groaned from her seat beside the Caveman. No one paid her any attention.

Andy was laughing again. "Oh, I don't know. I like to live in the moment, I guess. He seems like he really likes it." Andy was referring to the Caveman, who'd already gotten through half his plate and hadn't slowed at all.

"You had brothers and sisters?"

"What?"

"Andy, focus, please. I'm asking about your family. Your brothers and sisters, where are they now?"

He shrugged. "Illinois, I suppose. I haven't heard from any of them in... I don't know... I don't like thinking about the past anyway."

"Why not?"

"Because it isn't important."

"It isn't?"

"No," Clara said, louder this time. "It isn't important. Why are we even talking about it?"

Ella shot her a look. "No one's talking to you at all, Clara. This conversation does not involve you." She looked back at Andy. "Why do you say it isn't important?"

"It just isn't. I don't want to talk about the past."

"Andy..."

"No. It isn't important, I'm telling you."

"Andy..."

Suddenly, with the vigor of a child in a tantrum, Andy huffed and spun away from her and started down the hall. Ella went after him.

Still marching away from her, he announced, "It's fine if you don't want to be intimate because we're broken up; you don't get to dig around in my feelings if we're broken up..."

"Andy, I'm not digging into your feelings. I just asked..."

He'd already disappeared into the bedroom. Ella turned the corner, taking a position at the threshold. Inside the room, Andy lunged back and forth like a trapped rodent, refusing to look at her.

"Why are you getting so upset with me? I only asked..."

"No," he cut her off. "If we're broken up, that's how it is. You don't get to pry into my past, okay?"

"No one's prying, Andy. You're being completely unreasonable. All I did was ask... What are you doing?"

He'd gone to the window and pulled it open and, at first Ella thought he was only opening it to let in some air, to let out the last of the bitter smell of his burnt pancake, but he threw a leg out, on the fire escape, and ducked under the sill after it.

He paused to give her a brief, steady look, "I'm leaving, Ella. I'm going out."

"Why are you going out the window?"

"You're blocking the door," he announced. The next moment he was gone.

"Andy!"

He was gone, the sound of his feet hammering on the bell of the metal steps, the noise ringing away. Ella stood there, stunned. The fire detector had started shrieking again. Turning, Ella hurried back to the kitchen to kill the racket.

Clara had come down off her stool to deal with Ella's pancake, burning now in the bottom of the pan. Ella stretched up to silence the alarm. The room went quiet.

The Caveman had descended from his seat, carefully to the floor. He had syrup on his face and hands. There was syrup all over the rungs of the stool, and in two glazed handprints on the seat.

"It's not for you to put your nose in everyone's business," the girl said once she'd dumped the second scorched pancake into the sink.

Behind Ella, the Caveman padded down the hall to the living room certainly, Ella was convinced, determined to lay his sticky hands on everything he could. She fought the urge to follow him and get him clean. "I wasn't 'putting my nose' anywhere."

Clara shook her head and went off after the Caveman, singing out, "Need to wash those hands, Ernie."

After a moment the hiss of the bathroom faucet broke the silence in the apartment.

23 Back to the O.S.A Character Witnesses

The Office of Sentient Affairs was bustling, but there were still some seats available. Ella sat Clara and the Caveman at the end of the front row. Before going to the back of the room to line up for the little black box, she told told the girl, “Stay here and watch him until I come get you. You understand? Right here.”

“All I do is watch him,” Clara complained and shrugged and looked away, already bored.

In line, when her turn came, Ella made a production of cranking the handle and catching the ball that fell out. Standing along the wall, she watched as the numbers above the booths cycled by. In her purse, she traded out the ball she’d drawn for the blank one that Misha Kant had given her, half convinced the thing wouldn’t work but determined to try.

Though she didn't intend on waiting long, every number that appeared on the displays seemed somehow jinxed and she struggled to get going. Finally working up the nerve, she slid forward, searching the crowd for anyone else who might have moved. No one else had so Ella ducked up to the closest clerk, who greeted her drearily, “Ball in the slot, m'am.”

Ella dropped the ball into the slot. It rolled away. Behind the clerk, there sounded out a far-off chime, bright and agreeable.

“Paper work, please.”

Ella hurried to produce the envelope from her purse. It was creased and soiled. She pushed it through the slot in the glass divider.

The clerk seemed reluctant to touch it—sliding it closer with the very tips of her fingers.

"Name and address, please," the clerk said.

Ella hemmed. "Well, the thing is I have two residences now and..."

The clerk looked at her. She didn't care. "I just need an address, ma'm."

"Well, okay. I guess..." Ella gave Andy's address, thinking it might be best if the O.S.A. didn't know where else to find her.

The clerk tapped the information out on her keyboard and nodded up at Ella. "Take a seat. Your name will be called when they're ready for you."

Ella nodded and turned away. She couldn't believe it'd worked.

•

It was hours later before Ella's name was announced to the room, by a man wielding a clipboard. Ella got to her feet and shuffled out to the aisle, leading Clara and the Caveman along, hands linked like a crudely constructed paper cutout.

"Ella Pearson?" he repeated into her face.

Ella nodded. "Yes."

Looking down at her two companions, the man said, "I'm afraid only the named petitioner and the petitioner's counsel are allowed..."

"I'm sorry?"

"Ella Pearson..."

"Yes, that's me."

"Only Ella Pearson, as the named petitioner..."

"I can't leave a child and an imbecile unattended in the lobby..."

"You shouldn't have brought them here at all... It's no place for children."

"Well, as you can clearly see, only one of them is a child and, besides, there wasn't any other option," she said, thinking sourly of Andy, retreating out the window like a haggard coward.

The man shrugged: it wasn't his fault, it didn't have anything to do with him.

"Listen, they have to come in. They're..." she bungled around for a phrase, "character witnesses. They're very important to my... petition, or case, or whatever."

The man with the clipboard inspected the pair. He finally said, "Very well," and said, "Follow me."

He led them through a door at the front of the room.

•

Beyond the door was another waiting room, smaller than the first and without clerks, but in every other way identical—same thick paint slopped carelessly on the cinderblock walls, same molded, plastic chairs bolted to the floor.

"Have a seat," the man with the clipboard said, "Someone will be out for you."

Turning away, he exited through a door at the opposite side of the room. Ella barely got Clara and the Caveman settled before the man with the clipboard reappeared and beckoned her into a sloping, endless hallway, divided into short segments by an infinite legion of identical doors. The slight downward pitch of the hall made Ella feel uneasy, but she tried not to let it show. Led to a door, no different than any of the others, the man with the clipboard gestured for them to go inside.

Pushing Clara and the Caveman in, Ella was instantly overcome by the claustrophobic effect of the place. It might have been the exact same room where she'd been interrogated by Sickens. It looked identical. Same chairs, same sticky looking metal table, same dingy mirror on the wall. Behind them, the door closed.

"Well, sit down, then," Ella said.

They all sat, Clara, the Caveman, and beside him, Ella.

As soon as she'd sat, the Caveman slouched into her side. She tried pushing him away, but there wasn't much room for him, either.

Ella looked at the edge of the table. The print of asscheeks was gone, so either it was a different room, or someone had wiped the thing down. It must have been a different room. The table did not look clean.

After another wait, the room seeming to shrink in stages with the Caveman's heavy breath, the door opened and Ella tried to hide her surprise that the two officials who entered were Sickens and Dyer. As for the pair, they didn't let on that they even recognized Ella; like maybe they'd completely forgotten who she was.

While Dyer organized out a stack of files from a box he'd lugged in, Sickens sat, staring at Ella. The only thing on the table before the woman was the slim envelope that Jim Jasper had prepared. Ella recognized it instantly. It was creased and dirty and had the lawyer's wonky signature scrawled across it. After a moment Sickens gave up eyeing Ella and turned her attention to the envelope, picking it up and tapping the edges on the tabletop, irritably.

"I thought we'd come to an agreement," Sickens said. After the silence, her voice seemed shrill. "I thought you understood your role in the matter."

Ella nodded, eager for the time-being to be on the woman's side. "Yes. This has nothing to do with that. It has to do with *that,*" she said and hitched a thumb to the Caveman who, curled up into her side, was cooing contentedly and drooling. The wetness ran through the fabric of her blouse, making it adhere to her side. She fought the anxious urge to push him off.

"A separate matter," Sickens said, deadpan.

"You told me I was free to do as I had to."

"And so you are." Sickens nodded, but the way she was nodding made it evident that she didn't actually agree in this instance. Shifting to the side, the woman dug into her pocket, producing a small artifact that she kept hidden in her fist, as she brought the hand out onto the table, saying, "You say the matters are separate, but this," she opened her hand with the gusto of a magician revealing the final play of a trick, exposing the little, blank ball in the center of her palm, "would seem to contradict that, no?"

Ella looked at the ball. "That's not the reason I'm here."

"It isn't?"

"No."

"I think it's the very reason you're here. Where did you get this lottery ball, Ms. Pearson?"

"That's not relevant. And, at any rate, you should know already, if you were doing your job." She flashed the watch on her wrist at the woman.

Dyer looked up blankly for a moment. He'd finished with the folders and had just settled in with his customary legal pad and pen. He'd already begun making notes.

"I think it's extremely relevant," Sickens said. "Where did this ball come from, Ms. Pearson?"

"You already know that."

"So you won't deny it?"

Dyer's scratching filled the room.

Ella shrugged. "Why would I deny it? I'm only doing as you asked."

"Very well. I'll take that as a demonstration of your collusion with a terrorist element."

"No, no." Ella shook her head. "You asked me to infiltrate the group." She nodded at the ball. "That's simply proof that I'm doing as you asked."

Sickens set the ball down. It clicked on the tabletop and sat still, like a magnet had fixed it into place.

"Very well." With her hands empty, the woman took up the stained, wrinkly envelope and split the fold with her finger, cutting Jim Jasper's signature in half and tugging out the page from within. After a brief inspection, she set it down. "Very well. You're looking to have your Supplicant..." She left open a big pause that Ella didn't know how to fill.

With silence piling up in the room, Clara interjected sharply, "Ernie."

"Ernie," Sickens agreed with a nod to the girl. "You'd like your Supplicant, Ernie Pearson, emancipated from you."

"Since when does he have my last name?"

"You're the primary guardian; it's standard practice."

The dry noise of Dyer's pen clawed at Ella.

Tenting her fingers and leaning in, Sickens said, "On what grounds?"

"On what grounds what?"

"On what grounds do you wish to have him emancipated?"

"Doesn't the form..."

"The Request for Emancipation isn't designed to offer a legal grounds for emancipation, it simply puts forward the request. Your counsel should have explained that to you and you really should have him with you, in any case..."

"He's an idiot," Ella said.

"If you'd like the Supplicant removed from your care, we need a reason, a legal basis for how you are unfit to act as his guardian."

"Well, first of all, I have a very demanding job. I simply don't have time..."

Something was happening across the table. Reaching past Dyer, still scratching on his legal pad incessantly, Sickens pulled a file folder from the stack. With prepared ease, the woman opened it to a page buried within. She read briefly, before saying, "It says here you were, some weeks ago, released from your position as an executive in your firm, to allow you more time with your family."

"Let me see that," Ella said.

Sickens handed the page across.

It was redacted, top to bottom, the only portion that wasn't black marked was the disjointed phrase, '...requested...demotion...due to... family obligations...'

Ella sputtered. "It doesn't even say my name anywhere on here..."

"The whole file concerns your case, Ms. Pearson."

"It doesn't even say who requested the demotion."

"It's irrelevant who requested it," Sickens said. "What's important are the facts and they're right there, for all to see."

"That's... That's..." Ella muttered, shaking her head. Straightening up she tried to compose herself. "Regardless of all that, I'm just not fit for this sort of thing. You can ask the girl. I'm just not the maternal type. I've lived with *her*," she said, hitching her head to implicate Clara, "for months and we've never had any kind of connection. None at all."

Sickens turned to Clara.

Ella had never felt more affection for the girl when Clara nodded in agreement and said, "Yes. That's accurate. We don't get along. Not at all."

"Do you feel it's an indication of Ms. Pearson's inability to function effectively as a guardian?"

Any feeling of camaraderie crumbled the instant Clara shook her head and said, matter-of-factly, "No. Honestly, I think I'm as much to blame as she is. I'm very independent. I think she could make a very good guardian, once she gets used to the idea. I think she already is, to a degree. For instance, and I don't know if this is admissible to your records, but just this morning she made some wonderful pancakes for Ernie's breakfast..."

"Pancakes... Pancakes..." Ella stammered. "She's just a child. She doesn't know anything about me. How could she? She said so herself: we've never bonded. We barely spend any time together. And, as for pancakes... I mean, Attila the Hun could probably make pancakes from a mix, that doesn't mean you'd want him as a nanny... And besides, Clara doesn't know the first thing about me."

"So you've said." Sickens stared blankly at Ella. After a pause, she said, "Reconcile that for me, please, with your willingness to bring her in here as a character witness."

"That's not how it is, I only brought her here so she wouldn't be left out in the lobby alone."

"That isn't what you told the Admittance Manager..."

Ella shook her head. Her body felt wound tight, like a python was wrapped around her—like she was the python, tied in a knot and crushing herself to death.

"...and if you did lie to an employee of the Services—which, I would point out, is a chargeable offense," Sickens pointed at her, her tone moderating when she dropped the accusing finger and said, "really what that demonstrates is that you acted in the best interests of your Supplicant, Ernie, thus demonstrating the very qualities of your character which you claim not to have..."

"Okay. Okay. Even if that were true," Ella glared at Clara before returning her attention to Sickens, to continue, "the reality is, that her father, Andy, and I are no longer engaged in a functioning relationship. He climbed out a window today to get away from me! Tell me that's a functioning relationship! The fact that we're being forced to stay together is creating a hostile environment that can't be good for the child or the..." she looked down at the Caveman, leaning into her side. In spite of her raised voice and flailing, he'd fallen asleep against her, snoring softly. "...*thing.* Plus," she explained, "I only brought him along to avoid being arrested for abandonment again."

"Climbed out the window?" Sickens muttered and shook her head before saying, "All this proves is that the laws we have in place are functioning effectively. Besides, he seems just fine," Sickens commented before returning her attention to Clara. "Do you feel the home environment has become unduly hostile?"

Ella clenched her fists when the girl shook her head and said, "Although I'm sure this is hearsay, I did overhear an earlier conversation between Andy and Ms. Pearson that she would do her best to help out with Ernie and me..."

Sickens turned back to Ella.

Ella sputtered, shaking her head like she was having a fit. Her voice had gotten loud and frenetic. "Just because I don't want to argue all the time doesn't mean I'm capable of..."

"No. No," Sickens agreed, cutting her off. "But, at the same time, I don't feel you're adequately proving your inability to do what's been asked of you."

Ella wedged her elbow under the Caveman and roughly peeled him off. He woke with a sad, sucking sound. "I'm not a mother to these two. I'm simply not."

"I'm sorry, Ms. Pearson," Sickens said, starting to stand.

Dyer, abandoning his scribbling and collecting the stacks of files and tossing them haphazardly back into the box, stood as well. Ella caught a glimpse of a few sheets in the folders, they were darkened with bold, black stripes top to bottom like swatches of old prison garb. "But, it may not be enough. We'll review your request and you'll have your answer before you leave. The Admittance Manager will be along shortly to show you out."

•

Ella continued arguing as Sickens and Dyer went out the door, the man hunch-backed under the weight of the banker's box.

When the door closed after them, Ella noticed that Jim Jasper's form had been left behind. She snatched it up, roughly straightening it out to examine it. The whole thing had been black marked from top to bottom. Only a single word remained on the header, 'Request,' everything else had been blotted out.

Ella grumbled and tossed the sheet back onto the tabletop. It skittered away. Turning to the little girl, she said, "Hearsay? Admissible to your records? What are you—the world's tiniest lawyer?"

Clara shrugged. "You probably shouldn't have told them I was a character witness. You know I don't really like you."

•

The man with the clipboard returned and led them out, further down the hall, the end of which never seemed to get closer. It ended in a vanishing point, faded with atmospheric haze; a great, immeasurable distance away. Ella had a notion that that distance didn't really exist, that the end of the hall was only twenty feet ahead and that what she was seeing wasn't anything more than an optical illusion printed on the surface of a dead-end. Still, the effect was dizzying.

The next room she was brought to had the same molded chairs from the lobby set on descending tiers, facing a wall with two doors. Beside each door were what looked like traffic signals, both glowing red. Handing her a ticket, the Admittance Manager explained, "When the light turns green, go through the door indicated."

He hurried away. In the center of the wall, above the doors, a display showed the number five written out in red LEDs. She looked at her ticket, where the same number appeared again.

Leading her delegation down a row of seats, Ella sat, staring ahead, feeling worn-out.

Further down the rows, another petitioner sat all alone. When the door closed at the back of the room, the man turned around to give Ella a look. Lighting on her, he rose, skirting out through the row and quickly scaling the incline to where she sat. Closer, she could see it was the same man she'd met in the lobby the last time she'd been in. He seemed in particularly good spirits.

Holding out a hand, he said, "I never introduced myself. George Latham."

Ella introduced herself, as well.

He took a seat beside her and asked, "How'd it go for you?" His tone was particularly bright and seemed to indicate how he felt *his* meeting had gone.

"Not too good, I don't think." She shook her head.

"I'm sorry to hear that. Don't give up hope, though: I think I may have just proven that it can be done. What number did you pull?" he asked and Ella showed him her ticket. He shook his head and showed her his, printed with the number fifty-seven. "I swear, it's all just arbitrary. I hope I don't actually have to wait through that many turns."

"You really think you're free?"

He nodded expansively. "Yeah. I do. My appointment went really well."

A mechanical buzzing from the front of the room called both their attention. The light beside the righthand door had gone green. The number five on the wall blinked impatiently.

"Well," standing and ushering together her tiny brood, Ella said, "I guess that's me."

"Don't give up. Never give up, Ella" he told her as she made her way to the door. "Never give up!"

Apparently, she was being too slow getting to the door. Over an intercom hidden in the walls a voice announced, "Ella Pearson, please exit through the indicated door." The voice sounded familiar but she couldn't quite place it, sultry and self confident. Ella hurried the two at her ankles along a little faster.

Pushing through the door, she emerged into a narrow alley, into the stark light of day. Behind her the door slammed shut and when Ella turned back she could see a sign had been riveted into the metal panel.

Ella groaned and shook her head. All her ambition seemed to have fled; she couldn't get her feet moving. That was why she was still standing there when George bustled though the door a moment later, knocking right into her. Catching her by the shoulders, he started singing, "We're free. We're free! We're both free!"

He was almost dancing, which was peculiar to see from a man his size.

She held his gaze dully and, in stages, his joy crumbled. After a moment, his dancing suspended, he said, "We aren't free, are we?"

Ella pointed back at the door. He turned.

Muttering and clawing at his big, domed head he stumbled out into the street.

A passing car almost clipped him, squealing to a stop, the horn blaring. George didn't seem to notice. He staggered to the other side of the road, unharmed, and continued away.

24

The Lonely Lime

The Memory Game

The apartment was cold and dark and empty when Ella got in. The window in the kitchen was still open. The curtains thrashed but, despite all the air pouring through, the smell of Andy's burnt pancake still clung to everything.

Silently cursing him, Ella closed the window while Clara and the Caveman bolted to the living room to settle down in front of the TV. It looked like Ella'd be making *dinner* for the monster now, too.

The kitchen cupboards were packed tight with boxes and bags: the monster's 'special diet.' The assortment was overwhelming. With so much available, she wondered how 'special' the diet could really be. Closing up the cabinet, she turned to the kitchen island where Andy had set out a bowl of fruit. Something in there was bad. A rank whiff of garbage seeped into the air with the window closed, evident even over the still bitter stink of Andy's morning fiasco. Ella started into the bowl. A bag of bing cherries rested on top. The ruby baubles looked fine. Beneath, a connected trio of bananas had started going splotchy and tender, but the insides hadn't turned soupy yet. Beneath the bananas were four untainted apples and beneath those, a pair of plump oranges. She set them aside. In the bottom of the bowl was a solitary, lonely lime, encrusted on one side with a pale skin of wispy mold. Ella picked the thing out with her fingertips and pitched it into the trash. Looking back over the assortment on the countertop, she decided that a fruit salad would make a good enough meal. Easy to prepare, and hadn't Andy said something about the Caveman wanting for fiber?

After getting out a cutting board and a sharp knife and rinsing everything, she started cutting. The banana released its mild, milky scent as it accepted the knife and she thought again about the Caveman's 'special diet,' wondering if these items had been intended for him. The bowl of fruit had sat long enough so the lime could spoil and so maybe... Her knife slowed when she considered that, in feeding him the fruit (wasn't the apple considered a source of evil in the bible?) she might inadvertently poison the little thing. With the banana lopped into even segments, she paused—only for a moment. Scraping the pile up onto the side of her knife, she plated the pale fruit and started in on the apple.

If he did have an allergic reaction, she thought, he probably wouldn't die. She'd absolutely call an ambulance as soon as he showed any sign of distress. The paramedics would almost certainly arrive in time to resuscitate the monster. And might that not prove what a negligent and careless guardian she was? She sliced thin wedges of apple and orange and laid them out on the plate as well.

She set her elbows on the counter for the more delicate process of pitting the cherries, her fingers stained red with the nectar. They were perfect. Feeling the juice run down her fingers, suddenly engrossed in the act of slicing fruit, Ella seemed to lose track of her worries, even of the hopeful guilt of (partially-unintentionally) poisoning the Caveman.

On the countertop at her side, her elbow nudged the plate. It slid back an inch with a porcelain whisper, the lip of the plate hanging over the edge of the counter. Ella didn't notice.

She was so focused on the cherry in her hand, that she didn't even notice the light in the apartment start to dim. If she had noticed the waning light, maybe she would have taken more care. As it was, she was just slicing into the cherry when the lights cut out. The knife slipped and she felt the cold edge brush her thumb. Jerking back, her elbow tapped the plate again, this time much harder.

In the darkness, a bright shattering sounded out like the collapse of something wonderful.

The light flickered back on almost instantly.

At Ella's feet, the fruit sat in a puddle, littered with shards of ceramic. She stood staring at the mess. All she could think was: deconstruction. Maybe this was high cuisine, food on the bottom, a smashed plate laying atop.

Looking at her thumb, she was startled by the crimson bead dangling on the digit. She wiped at it, just cherry juice. The cut was insubstantial, bloodless.

The sudden chiming of a ringer ended her vigil over the lost food and wasted effort. Ella found the noise coming from her purse, from the new phone inside. It wasn't the ringtone she was used to. It sounded like someone beating on a pot. Clang-clang-clang. Clang-clang-clang. It reminded her of Andy and again she wondered angrily where he was.

The face of the phone came alive when she touched it. She didn't recognize the number. Her phone didn't either, but all that meant was that it wasn't anyone at her Practitioner's office, still the only contact she'd gotten around to inputting. The message read, *Are you free?*

Mark, collecting on the favor he'd done her? She looked away, down the hall where the noise from the TV had returned with the power. Ella typed out, *Not tonight.*

After a little lag, *Okay. Maybe tomorrow?*

Maybe, she typed and threw the phone back into her purse.

She swept up the mess on the floor and decided on cold cereal for the Caveman's dinner, shutting off the light and leaving everything else as it was—the cutting board and knife, a forensic spatter of cherry juice down the cabinct front.

•

With Clara and the Caveman reclined on the floor, Ella took a seat on the couch behind them and stared at the TV. She wasn't taking in the broadcast at all; it passed as a wash of noise and shifting light.

Where the hell was Andy?

She'd expected that, at some undetermined time before now, he'd certainly have returned. But he hadn't. And without her old phone, without his contact info, she had no way to reach him. She'd have to wait for *him* to call, wait for *him* to show: infuriating. *Where the hell was he?* Another aggravation: her worry about missing another day of work if he didn't show before tomorrow morning. Somehow that sense of responsibility carried on; immune to the knowledge that with her having been demoted (perhaps fired) her continued attendance was likely unnecessary.

"You know," the girl's voice brought Ella out of her mulling. Clara leaned back on an arm, bent around to stare up at her. "It isn't good for him just to sit around watching TV all the time."

"You're the one always watching TV with him."

The girl huffed. "You need to contribute. You need to do things with him, interact with him so he learns. Master Thompson says..."

"I don't want to hear about 'Master' anyone..."

Clara shrugged. "Master Thompson says..."

A look from Ella quieted the girl.

Clara shrugged and stood up and went from the room.

She returned a moment later with a colorful box under her arm. Kneeling on the floor, she opened it up, laying the top aside. Inside were stacks of thick cardboard cards that accorded with the color scheme on the box. Pulling the cards out and shuffling them into piles, she asked Ella, "Are you going to play?"

"I guess I will."

"Well," Clara said, squirming around and dropping down onto her butt and pushing the box aside. Ella scooted off the couch and slid down onto the floor across from her. "It's a matching game," the girl said, laying the cards out between them. "I don't need to explain that to you, do I?"

"No," Ella said.

The Caveman had turned from the TV and crawled up beside them to get a better look at what Clara was doing. She'd placed the cards out in a big square, faced down so that only the identical backings showed—a colorfully woven houndstooth pattern. Patting the floor gently like she was calling a dog to sit, the Caveman flipped himself around and complied. "You wanna start?"

She was asking Ella. Ella shrugged and turned a pair of cards. They did not match. She turned them back.

The game went in rounds and pretty quickly the Caveman and Ella started gathering pairs and, as the cards that were left became fewer and fewer, the pace of the game increased. The Caveman was clearly enjoying himself, a big, filthy smile cutting his gummy face. Unexpectedly, Ella was having fun, too. The game was easy, but there was a certain satisfaction to be gotten from claiming a pair of cartoon kittens out from under Clara. Really, the girl seemed to be the only one who wasn't enjoying herself.

At the conclusion of the first round, Ella was the clear winner, though she'd played reservedly, holding back on some turns so that the Caveman could get his share. Clara had collected very few, but completed the game by gathering everyone else's cards and telling the Caveman, "Good job, Ernie. Very good. You came in second place," and, turning to Ella, asked, "Again?"

"Why ask me?" Ella said, "I'll play if the Caveman..."

"Ernie," Clara corrected. "And the reason I asked you, was that it's obvious he wants to play. Look at him."

Ella turned. True enough, the Caveman had the posture and expression of an individual who clearly couldn't accept the possibility of another game *not* taking place. He leaned forward, watching Clara's hands as the girl shuffled. When the cards were dealt out a second time and the game resumed, Ella asked, "Do they talk about the Cavemen frequently at Assembly meetings?"

"His name is Ernie."

"I wasn't talking about him specifically, Clara, so you can give me a break. I was talking about his..." she looked at the little monster, struggling to find the word she wanted. "*...ilk.*"

He stared back at her with his dumb, expectant gaze, those dewy, blinking eyes.

"Ilk?"

"You know..."

"You mean the Supplicants?"

"Yes, them."

"Master Thompson says..."

"Can you not call him that, please? Can you not call him Master?"

"At the Assembly..."

"We're not at the Assembly, Clara. Here, you can just call him Carl Thompson or Mr. Thompson."

"It *bothers* you."

"You're small, so you don't know, but I'll tell you: the word 'Master' has all sorts of connotations. It implies servitude, slavery. I don't like the word."

Clara shrugged. "I guess it's pretty much all they talk about now. It's good, though, it just shows how important it is: they say the Supplicants are a rebirth for the Neo Hominem."

It was the girl's turn and the question had stalled her move. She turned two cards, a picture of a house and a picture of a car. Even for its cartoonish presentation there was something, Ella thought, sinister about the house. It was surrounded by conspicuously colorful trees—a house in cartoon autumn, then.

Clara turned the cards back down.

It was Ella's turn. She grabbed a pair and added them to her cache. "What does that mean: a rebirth for the Neo Hominem? I thought the Neo Hominem was the congregation. Isn't it Carl Thompson's position that we're all Neo Hominem, anyway?"

The Caveman had taken his turn, pulling the pair of autumnal houses from play. Ella felt vaguely relieved to see them go. She didn't like fall. She didn't like the season's knack for killing everything off and shortening the days.

Clara's turn: the little girl upended a tractor and a jackrabbit and had to turn them back. "Master... Sorry... Mr. Thompson says that the world is decaying and that the Supplicants are our chance to restore things to the way they should be..."

After taking her turn and failing to make a match, Ella said, "I wouldn't put too much into what Thompson says when he's on the pulpit."

The Caveman had already gone and Clara was holding up the game again, staring at Ella. "Are you calling him a liar?"

"No, no, nothing like that," Ella said. After a thoughtful moment, she said, "You know, it's easy to separate the world out and say: this is truth, that is a lie. In reality, I think, the world isn't quite so clear cut. Just because someone says something that isn't a hundred percent true, doesn't necessary mean they're lying."

The Caveman was getting fidgety with the long pauses and so Clara moved hastily and happened to grab a matching pair. Somehow, she seemed annoyed by the sudden bout of success. She said to Ella, "If it isn't true, it's a lie. That's what makes up a lie."

Ella turned her cards and had to set them back. The game was no longer her priority. She said, "You know the story of The Boy Who Cried Wolf?"

"He got eaten by a wolf because he was a liar."

"Yeah, after the fact. But do you suppose it's true?"

"What?"

"That there was a boy who cried wolf and then got eaten by one?"

Clara shrugged. "The story had to come from somewhere."

"Okay... You ever think, maybe it came from a parent who was tired of being lied to?"

"So the parent lied about a boy being eaten by a wolf? That's a terrible thing to tell a child. I hope that parent got eaten by a wolf for saying such an awful thing."

"Maybe. But in that lie, there's a truth, right?—the truth that lying is bad."

"That doesn't make sense."

"No. Maybe you're right, maybe it doesn't, but the point is, sometimes, when people say one thing, they're actually saying something else. I think Carl Thompson, when he says the Cavemen are the rebirth of the Neo Hominem, I think he's saying something a little more nuanced than how you're thinking of it. I mean, the world isn't *decaying*, is it? You can look outside and see that's not true."

This question, too, seemed to slow Clara's move. She shrugged. "He says it is."

"He might say it, but have you seen any evidence of it? I think he's exaggerating, you know, to highlight the importance of the point he's making—don't you think?"

The Caveman pulled a pair of cows, sequestered behind identical fences. Clara leaned forward, plucked a card from the floor and somehow failed to pull a match. There were only eight cards left in play and they'd all been turned at one time or another and Ella felt pretty confident she could group them all at this point. The girl leaned away, reserved in her failure and said, "No. The world is different now. Empty. He says it and it has to be true."

"Okay. If you say so. But, you should try thinking about what he says in the way you can think about the story of the boy and the wolf." Ella's turn came and she pulled a pair of puppies in baskets. The Caveman took a couple cards with flowers in a vase and, the game now down to four cards, Clara failed again.

"I don't want to think about that story. It isn't nice and it isn't true, you said so yourself. It's a lie."

Ella cleaned up another pair and the Caveman got the last two and Ella said, "You know, you're not very good at this."

Clara seemed confused by the statement. "I'm not trying to win. I'm trying to give Ernie the opportunity to learn."

The noise from the TV caught Ella's attention. On screen, an old Film Noir was playing. A man walked down a dark street, a fedora tilted back on his head arrogantly. His cocky smile disappeared the instant another man dropped in behind him, digging the barrel of a pistol into his back. They both stopped. Leaning forward, the man with the gun whispered menacingly, "You do as I say, 'cause people who don't listen, don't last long. You follow me?"

Part 3
East Gish

25

Andy's Return

Dawn Asks a Favor

The Prison of Light

Ella'd forgotten that Andy was missing until she emerged from the bedroom to find him asleep on the couch. It all came rushing back in an instant: his having fled out the bedroom window... her having failed to make her case at the O.S.A. because she'd brought Clara and the Caveman along... the fact that she'd stayed up into the small hours of the morning, waiting for the bastard to get home so she could give him an ear-full... the son-of-a-bitch never having shown. And now here he was, having secreted himself right back into the apartment without so much as an 'I'm home.'

Swaddled in chalky morning light, he lay out, a foot hanging off the cushion. Rocking with a lazy rhythm—maybe in his dream he was running or kicking a ball or some other juvenile bullshit—the twitch of his foot seemed to compel Ella forward. Lunging silently across the room, she gave his foot a swift, hard kick.

Scrambling back against the couch, Andy's gaze flashed on her before darting around the room, looking for some other assailant who wasn't there.

"Where the hell have you been?"

Slipping down into the cushions, he tittered nervously. "I..."

"I thought we agreed, Andy, that we weren't to disappear on each other; that that behavior was unacceptable."

"Muffin, I told you I was going out..."

"You left out the goddamned window."

"I..."

"You can't just disappear for a whole day, Andy." She was shaking mad, barely able to keep herself from kicking him again. "Here, I'll show you how it's supposed to work: I'm going out, to attend to some things and then, I'm going on a date with another man. Don't wait up."

She didn't wait for his response.

•

Storming down the street, away from the apartment, Ella didn't slow until she'd gone several blocks. Pausing at a crosswalk, she got out her phone and typed a message onto the thread that had started the night before, *How about tonight?*

She stood a moment longer, inputting a contact name for the number, *Mark Carter.*

Dumping the phone back into her purse, she crossed the street to the subway station. On the train, she checked her phone and found that he'd already responded, *Great. 7:30? Where should we meet?*

She wrote back the first place she thought of, *The East Gish Club,* deciding that whomever she was meeting (so long as it wasn't Andy) she'd be happy enough to have an evening out—even if it was Warner. Even if it was Misha Kant or that cold woman from the Office of Sentient Affairs, Sickens. Hell, if the Caveman showed, she wouldn't complain.

•

At the office, Ella took a back route around the floor in hopes of avoiding Dawn and was aggravated to arrive in Warner's reception just as the girl was emerging from his door.

Ella looked quickly away, to Warner's receptionist, but failed to get a word out before Dawn announced, "Oh, Ella, there you are. I've been looking for you. Do you have time for a quick chat?"

"Hm. Can't. Have a meeting with Warner."

"Mr. Warner's schedule is already fixed for the day," the receptionist announced, staring into her computer screen.

Laying a hand on Ella's shoulder, Dawn turned her out toward the hallway. "That's good. That means we can have that *chat.* My office?"

"Your office," Ella growled.

Ella's office had undergone a devastating facelift. All her artwork had been removed from the walls and was leaned in a stack by the door, faced away. Replacing the largest piece (Ella's favorite, a foggy panorama of nothing at all that had always reminded her of a humid August morning) was a picture of a squirrel hanging precariously from the hood over a bird feeder by its back paws. The rodent was stretched out, reaching for the seed tray. Below the image the message, *Never give up,* was spelled out in bubbly font. She couldn't even bring herself to look at the other posters. In her periphery it was obvious they were in the same cutesy, inspirational vein. She was happy to see Clarence, though, still sitting on the back window. He looked okay. Maybe a little forlorn. Who could blame him in this new, daycare atmosphere?

"You like it?"

"What?"

"The squirrel? It's just the most darling," Dawn said, winding her chair a few degrees to give it a look. "And there's a lesson, too: when things get tough, it reminds me to never..."

"Give up."

"That's right. Never give up." Dawn nodded. "If you want one, I get a pretty decent discount with the company that distributes them. It might be a good reminder for you, given all you're going through..."

"What does that mean?" Ella's cold tone managed to cut through Dawn's cheer.

The girl looked suddenly nervous. "Just that... I don't know. I know how hard it can be for some, settling into motherhood..."

Ella looked on, blankly.

"And a little boy, at that." The cheer in Dawn's voice bloomed again with such easy vigor, it was like it hadn't ever waned. She shook her head in happy sympathy. "Little boys can be quite a handful..."

"Who told you that? It isn't true. There's no child."

The cheer lapsed again. "Jeez. Is that right? Everyone... Everyone in the office is talking about it. Didn't you see the congratulations card on your desk?"

Ella glowered at the girl sitting in her chair.

"It was what the email from Staffing said—that you'd been placed in a temporary demotion so that you could spend more time with your family..."

Ella was silent.

"Well, I'm sorry. I'm sorry if..." Dawn shrugged, maybe unsure of what she was sorry for. "Listen, that isn't even what I wanted to talk with you about, anyway. I wanted to ask you something... a favor..."

"So ask. What else can I provide for you?"

Dawn was quiet a moment before she said, "It isn't like that, Ella. But I can see, now's not a good time..."

"No. Please. Go ahead. You want my boyfriend? Honestly, I'm just about through with him and, as you're so keen on picking up my discards..."

"Ella..."

"No, please, whatever you want, just ask. It'll be yours."

Shaking her head, Dawn insisted, "It isn't a good time. I see that now."

"Ask. Ask already!"

After a moment the girl said, "I was hoping you'd agree to be my... maid of honor..."

"Your maid of honor? For your wedding to my ex-boyfriend, Terry? Your maid of honor for *that* wedding?"

"Ella, you told me you were over him. I asked. I asked," Dawn said. The two women held a look while Ella's fists throbbed under the edge of the desk. "I'm sorry. Don't answer now. Don't say 'no.' You've always been like a mother to me." Ella's fists wound tighter. "Just think on it. I really can't imagine having the ceremony without you there."

Rising up, Ella said nothing at all. She straightened her blazer and walked past the girl to collect Clarence. Up close, he looked worse. His leaves had taken on a shrunken, coarse appearance. Tucking the pot under her arm, she marched back across the room, ignoring Dawn altogether. Grabbing her paintings with her free hand, she struggled to get the through the door. The frames thumped against the jamb and, with a violently twisting motion, she managed to wrench them out into the reception area.

Passing by the desk she saw there was, indeed, a card waiting for her, sealed up in an envelope, her name scrawled along the face. She ignored it and kept moving toward the elevator, the paintings knocking off the walls of the cubicles she passed.

When the doors parted, she struggled again, trying to get the paintings through the gap. The doors kept jerking back and forth, trying to shut, the alarm ding-dinging obnoxiously. Finally turning to address the fact that the paintings would not submit and board the elevator, Ella was horrified to see the path of leaves she'd left behind.

The elevator doors wagged and dinged and Ella looked down at Clarence.

In her struggle to get onto the elevator, or maybe it'd been when she'd thrashed out Dawn's office door, the bonsai had come loose from the pot, hanging over the side. The soil had been reduced to sand and his roots stood out, dry and mummified. One sad leaf clung to his canopy. Clarence was gone.

Stepping back onto the floor, Ella set her paintings against the wall and tried to put her old friend right. He would no longer stand up in his pot.

Setting the plant down gently beside the paintings, she returned to the elevator—which had closed, abandoning her—and hit the call button, waiting for the conveyance to return and simultaneously struggling to ignore the dead plant by her side and the cluster of office personnel behind her who'd risen from their cubicles to stare at her with concern. She was aware that she was sniffling, but couldn't seem to stop.

•

When Ella passed through the doors of the East Gish Club, she found it in much the same state as the last time she'd been in. Patrons crowded the bar in the back. The rest of the place was empty.

Now, with the sun still hovering outside, the light glaring through the big windows illuminated how far into disrepair the front of the house had fallen. The table tops were shellacked with grime. Gray mounds of dust leaned over the blades of the ceiling fan. A visible path had been worn through the filth on the floor. It lead from the entrance to the bar in back, in a line that dodged drunkenly between the tables. There, the boards were polished dark with foot traffic.

She was still hours early for her meeting with… whomever… but she felt, at a certain point, that her continuing to sit on the mattress in her otherwise empty apartment, watching old movies on her phone was only letting her depression root more perniciously. She needed to be in public, to put on a brave face and reassert her dignity and confidence. So—here she was.

Now, all she wanted was to sit for the few hours that remained before… whomever… showed. The dust on the chairs kept her away.

Following the trail through the tables, she wedged herself into the crowd at the back. The patrons were much more subdued than they'd been on her previous visit. They murmured to each other, barely audible. There was no laughter among them. Maybe it was just the time of day. The light from the front windows was stark and unflattering and completely overpowered the atmospheric light over the bar top.

Behind the bar the barman sat on a stool, facing away from his customers to the cash register beside him. He looked dejected.

Rapping on the bar top, the sound, more than loud enough to cut through the thin drone of conversation, failed to draw the man's attention. She tried again and when that failed, too, she announced, "Hey!"

The barman wound his head to look at her. Even then it took him an exaggerated moment to stand and come over. It was a big production—like the act of lifting his body was well beyond the responsibilities of his employment. He lumbered over. Standing, swaying slightly like he was trying to work himself into a comfortable position, he paused another long moment before finally saying, "What?" His tone wasn't as rude as it could have been. Mostly, he sounded sleepy.

"I've arranged to meet a friend here this evening..."

"Congratulations."

Ella turned back to the tables, taking a more assured tone to tell him, "I was hoping you'd clean up one of the tables for us and, maybe, the floor around it as well. If that isn't too much to ask."

Turning, the man muttered to himself and walked back to his stool. He stood there, gazing into the dark corner ahead. Down the bar, a man leaned out to chime in, "Be careful not to ask too much of his highness. Mostly, he just likes to sit."

Ella looked to the man. He seemed familiar, but in the hard shock of light from the front windows it took her a moment to land on who he was. "George Latham, isn't it?"

Slouching forward, he grumbled, "That's right."

Pushing out from the bar, Ella passed by the few patrons between them and inserted herself beside George. The barman still hadn't moved from his spot, though his head seemed to be slowly angling down as though he were falling asleep on his feet.

"I'm sorry your petition didn't go through."

He nodded, still looking away.

The general gloom in the place was starting to make Ella feel awful, even worse than before and she wondered if she should have just stayed up in her apartment. "What are you going to do now?"

"Nothing."

"Nothing?"

His shoulders rose and fell like a buoy in a gray sea. "Two more of the hairy little fuckers showed up last night." He laughed, a snort, a sad sound. "A boy and a girl. I got a letter too—how about that?—saying they were all in my care now, seeing how I'd been doing such a bang-up job with the first one."

"Jesus."

"Don't fight it, lady. I think that's a lesson you'd do well to learn from my example. Look what they did to me." He stared away into the dark corner in the back of the bar, as though he saw himself, mired in that darkness.

Leaning to him, Ella tightened her voice to say, "We need to do something about this, George, you and I."

He shook his head. "There's nothing to be done, that's what I'm telling you."

"I work for a PR and media company. Trust me, there's plenty we can do. I'll take you to the news channels; if people know what's going on, what's really happening, if they learn the extent of it... People won't stand for this, George. The government will have to listen and change course or face a general revolt."

He shook his head. "All my battling against it, you see what it got me? It got me two more. I'm done. I've got no fight left. Not when this is all I get for it."

"So that's it? You're just giving in?"

Emerging from the shadows and stomping over suddenly, the barman threw a wet rag down on the bar. It landed with a heavy slap. Ella looked to the man.

Nodding at the rag, he said, "There you are."

"What's that?"

"Clean your own damned table."

"I think you're confused, pal. You work here. I'm the customer," she told him.

"Oh, I know who you are, lady. You were in here, saying how I should give everyone the boot and get good paying customers in, and then you yourself left without paying at all. So, there you are. You want a clean table? Clean it!"

The man turned and marched off.

Beside her, George spoke up, talking inwardly. Shaking his big head, the man said, "Learn my lesson. Don't fight it. Just give up. Do what they tell you to. If you don't, you'll end up like me."

"No," Ella told him defiantly, "I won't accept it. I'll never give up."

•

Ella didn't touch the rag on the bar. In the bathroom, she collected a wad of paper towels and soaked them under the faucet. Picking a table close to the door, she wiped off the top and the two chairs at its sides. The towel came up black with grime. Checking to see no one was watching her, she tossed the ball of paper towels into a corner and took her seat.

Outside, the world lapsed into dusk. Ella's table was dark. Craning around to look at the bar, she saw the lights back there had come on, or maybe it was just the new dimness in the place that made the glow evident. The noise, too, had increased with the settling evening outside. A new sort of reckless joy whelmed up. Laughter flowed in waves, in driving gales. At her dark table, Ella felt alone, increasingly forlorn and drowsy. She waited for the barman to come around, but he didn't. She checked her phone. There was still time before... whomever... was due to arrive. Standing, she went to the bar, into the sea of noise back there.

For all the joyful commotion around him, the barman didn't seem pleased at all. He sat on his stool, staring off as before. Ella motioned for him and, grudgingly, he got up.

"I'd like to order," she said.

"Oh, would you? I thought you were *waiting for a friend*." The mockery in his tone was glaring.

"Listen, I realize that the last time I was in here I made certain promises to you and I intended to keep them, really I did. I feel badly that I left without paying, and I have every intention of paying you fully for tonight's service as well as an ample gratuity to make up for last time. Okay? Can we please start over? All I want is to order."

He nodded his head rhythmically, like he was weighing it. "Alright, then. What do you want?"

"A Gish Sunset, please."

He continued nodding but more rapidly as though he were having some sort of fit. "A Gish Sunset. A Gish Sunset." His head bounced to the increasingly angry clip in his voice. "A Gish Sunset, of course it would be a Gish Sunset." He humphed and turned away to the back of the bar.

By the time she got back to her table, the light hanging there had come on, shedding a warm, pink glow that seemed to saturate deep into her, buzzing with a cozy reassurance. George had been right. The Gish Sunset was perfect—better, she thought, than a double dose of Represitol. Her head buzzing lightly, she sat down, wondering if this was what it felt like, being back in East Gish. It felt like coming home, being enveloped by a peace and comfort she'd long forgotten could exist.

She was so calm and relaxed that she'd even forgotten she was waiting for someone until the moment he arrived, just a bright-lit midriff emerging into the circumference of light around her.

"You ordered without me," he said, only slightly put out and Ella sat up straight, at once aware of his presence.

He sat in the chair opposite her.

"Andy? What the hell are you doing here?"

"This is where you said we should meet." He'd dressed nicely, dressed to make an impression and it was working, especially when he took off his big, dumb hat. Beneath the warm, pink light, Ella couldn't avoid how handsome he looked.

"*You* texted me last night?"

"Of course, who else would it be?" He chuckled awkwardly. "I felt bad about the way I left... I felt weird about coming home..."

She stared at him dully. "*Who else would it be. Of course.*"

His laughter turned uneasy before evaporating altogether. "I know. I know. I felt so bad. Where are you going?"

She'd stood up, intending to leave, but the circle of light managed to hold her in place like a net of warm bedding. "I'm leaving, obviously, Andy. I didn't intend to have a date with *you...*"

He looked away. "So, it's another man, then?"

"I feel I made that clear this morning," Ella said but still didn't move.

"Who is it, Ella? I won't stand in your way, but I have a right to know. Who is it?"

It wasn't anyone, not really, but she said, "You don't have a right to know! It isn't any of your business, Andy. I'm leaving." She made no move to leave. The light around the table was captivating. In it, with the calm buzz of the Gish Sunset pouring through her, even Andy began to seem like something desirable, something difficult to abandon.

"I think it is my business, Ella. We share a home, a life. I deserve, at least..."

"Fine. Fine. His name's," she thought to give Mark's name, but didn't. Somehow Mark seemed culpable, in some incongruous way, for Andy having shown. Instead, she said, "Timothy. His name is Timothy. You don't know him." She made another move to leave, but it only presented itself as a lazy gesture, a sway of her shoulders. She couldn't seem to get her feet unstuck. Reseating herself irritably, she asked, "Who's watching the two at home? You didn't leave them alone again, did you?"

"No." He laughed. "I found someone to watch them—Lydia? She offered. She wants a family of her own, I guess. So, it's like a trial run for her, or something." He laughed again. The sound was an irritant, nails in a blender.

"She sounds like a great match for you."

"Ella, please. It isn't like that. I only want to be with you."

"That's sweet," she said, any note of sweetness wrung from her voice. After a moment she said, "So, were you going to apologize?"

He nodded. "I am sorry. I'm sorry for the way I left and for getting so upset when you were bringing up the past." He paused and motioned with his hands. "I have a confession to make."

At the bar, a roar of laughter reared up.

"I started thinking about it, after I left."

"What does that mean, *you started thinking about it?*"

"About what you were asking me about," he leaned in to whisper, "my past. I starting thinking, that maybe you're right. Maybe it is peculiar not to wonder about it. Did I ever tell you about my old job?"

"Where is this going, Andy?"

"Just listen, please. I used to work in a waste facility. I probably didn't tell you. I was a little embarrassed to, I guess. You're so professional and put together and I didn't want you to know about where I came from. But, there it is: I was trash-man. All day I'd stand at this conveyer belt. I'd watch for things, recyclables, batteries, pieces of metal, electronics, and snatch them off the line and throw them into these bins, organized by type. You know: batteries in one bin, bits of metal in another..."

"Andy, I don't care about any of this..."

"At the end of the line, everything I didn't pull out would get fed into the incinerator."

"Andy, I don't care."

"I've been dreaming about it, recently—I think that's why I freaked out so much when you were talking about the past, because I was already thinking about it, even though I didn't really want to. In the dream, I'm standing at my old job and these long bags started coming down the line. They look like mummies, hands pinned to their sides, I can make out the rise of a face at the top and the point of feet at the bottom. They're bodies, Ella, human bodies. I'm just filled with horror and grief when I see them. I can't move and meanwhile all these batteries and bits of metal are coasting by, but I can't even make myself pick them out." He went quiet, looking at his hands. After a moment, he said, "What do you think it means?"

Ella shook her head. "Where were you, Andy? All that time you were gone—where were you?"

"Well, I started to think that I needed to go back there."

"Back there? What does that mean—back there?"

"Lincoln, Illinois."

Ella drummed her fingers on the table. "Lincoln, Illinois? You were going to leave me alone with Clara and that degenerate and go to..."

"I went to rent a car and..."

Ella stood up again. It wasn't like she'd finally found the strength when she did, it was like there was a spring in her legs that had been wound too tight to hold any longer. She shot up. "Lincoln, Illinois! You were going to drive all the way to Lincoln," *where the hell was that, in relation to the City, anyway?* "without even discussing it with me."

"Ella, please, let me finish..."

"No. You are finished. You've had all the time you'll get from me. Fuck you, Andy. I'll see you at home," she said, and lunged out of the prison of light.

It was only after she'd gotten outside, that she realized she'd failed to pay the barman a second time, but with Andy still in there, she wouldn't turn around. He'd just have to pay the tab. It served him right. She looked up at the window of her unfurnished apartment as she passed by. The windows were dark, uninviting. She kept moving.

26

A Package
My Name is Sickens
The Other Package

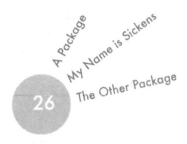

Barely aware of the sway of the train as it rounded corners, barely attuned to the shrill scream of the wheels on the track, Ella was so lost in her own thoughts that she didn't notice the woman who'd boarded at the previous stop—the woman who hung by the door, staring at Ella until the train lunged forward, diving into the darkness of the tunnel. Ella stared out the window, at the passing blasts of tunnel lights and the weak reflection of her own face that appeared in the intervals between.

When the woman dropped heavily into the seat beside her, Ella grabbed her purse reflexively and pulled it in.

"Relax," the woman said.

Ella turned. The woman's face was hidden in a cowl of gauze. "Kant?"

The woman nodded once, continuing to stare forward. A filthy bundle of cloth was rolled up in her lap, her hands resting on it, in a relaxed manner. Ella clung tighter to her purse.

"Jesus. Get out of here. I don't want to talk to you." Ella made a move to stand, but Kant pushed her back down and held her in place with a forearm.

"Relax," Kant said a second time, her voice tight and insistent. Her outfit looked worse than before. The stitching around the cuffs of the jacket had started to fray. It was stained all over, unrecognizable now as a twin of Ella's suit. "You used the ball, Pearson. It's time to collect on the favor you owe."

Kant made a move to pass Ella the bundle.

Ella pushed Kant's wrist away. She wouldn't touch the wad of cloth. Maybe it was only a shadow, maybe it was an unaffiliated stain, but the greasy wad seemed to have left a mark on Kant's lap. "Yeah, and it didn't work. I don't owe you a thing." Again, Ella tried to stand. Kant pushed her back down.

"It worked the way you were told it would. You got into the agency, I know you did. You spoke with an agent, I know that happened, too..." Again, Kant took a moment to try and push the bundle onto Ella. Ella blocked it out.

"And I still have that goddamned Caveman in my home, so—no—it didn't work. Not at all. I don't owe you a thing." They both had a hand on the bundle now: Misha pushing, Ella refusing. A tail of cloth had come loose from the wrappings and was hanging, threateningly close to Ella's clothes.

"Pearson, we had an arrangement."

"Right. To get the Caveman out of my house. He's still there. No deal."

Finally Kant gave up pushing on the parcel, setting it in her lap again. "That wasn't the agreement. The agreement was to get you into the Office to speak with an agent. That you failed to adequately argue your case... Well, that's on you. How can I be held accountable for that?"

"What's in the bundle?" Ella said, eyeing the greasy nest of cloth. In Misha Kant's silence Ella raised her head to look at the veil of gauze atop the woman's neck. Like her clothing, it hadn't held up well. The fabric had gotten fuzzy. Ribbons of loose bandages hung off her head like matted hair.

"Pearson, you fail to understand the threat Warner poses to the future of our society..."

"What are you asking me to do?"

"He needs to be taken out of the picture," Kant said, and tried to push the package to Ella again. Ella pushed back.

"It's out of the question. Even if I were free of the Caveman, I couldn't... Not ever. Do it yourself, or find someone else..."

Leaning in close, Kant whispered urgently, "I had nothing to do with the attack on the Assembly. It was Warner... I had proof..."

"I don't care. I don't care who vandalized what. That whole thing was just a dumb prank—you're asking me to kill a man."

"You don't know anything at all if you think that was a prank. It was a promise of death and disease..."

The train had started to slow. Ella stood up. Stumbling past the woman, into the aisle, she said, "This is my stop."

When the doors squealed open, Ella lurched out onto the platform and through the gates and ran up the stairs and out onto the street. Holding her meta-metric watch up to her face, she said, "Help me, Sickens, I'm in danger."

There was no response.

•

Ella kept moving, throwing glances over her shoulder as she hurried down the street. Up ahead, the light from an all-night convenience store spilled out onto the sidewalk, the door left open for the warm evening. Ella ducked inside. At the back of the store, hiding behind a row of shelving, she pulled her phone out of her purse and dialed nine-one-one.

When the dispatcher answered, Ella said, "I need to speak to agent Sickens. She works in the Office of Sentient Affairs. It's very important..."

"The Office..."

"Of Sentient Affairs, that's right."

"What's this concerning Ma'm?" The dispatcher sounded skeptical.

Ella was dying for a dose of Represitol, or maybe a nice shot of Gish Sunset—anything to blunt her panic. "A murder plot, is what. A woman, an ex-O.S.A. agent, Misha Kant, is planning to assassinate my boss. His name is Warner. He's the CEO of CCI."

If there had been a light tone to the dispatcher's voice, it was gone now. "Where are you? I'm sending a car."

•

Back outside, Ella positioned herself beside the door to wait.

She was only there a few minutes before a car pulled up to the curb in front of her.

It didn't look like a cop car; a small import, gone to rust. The man in the passenger seat didn't look like a cop. He was wearing a leather jacket, his arm resting over the door. Ella looked past him to the man driving—his face was lost in shadow.

"Are you here for me?" Ella asked, bending down to meet the man's level.

He made a small movement, a hitch of his head toward the rear door.

Ella hesitated. "My name is Sickens."

The passenger nodded. Twisting himself around, he popped the back door for her. It gave a creaky groan as it opened. Straightening out, the man said, "Don't worry, Ms. Pearson, we're here to take you in."

Ella nodded and climbed into the backseat.

The two men were quiet on the ride and their long silence highlighted the lack of noise in the car. It took Ella a moment to realize the sound she was missing was the crackling static of a two-way radio. There was just the hiss of tires over asphalt, the sandy-grind of breaks when they came to a stoplight.

Watching out the window, Ella was dismayed to see they were heading into the Northern District.

•

"Right this way, Ms. Pearson."

With the flashlight glaring in her eyes, she couldn't see the man at all. She couldn't see much of anything: not the man, not the darkened building behind him, not the ruinous, apocalyptic cityscape of the Northern District crowding the road. Wind ran between the abandoned buildings, harboring a thousand different voices: moans and bellows, hisses and sighs and all of them pained and lonely despite their multitude. Ella found it hard to move, despite the invigorating blast of light on her face.

"I think there's been a mistake, my name is Sickens." She couldn't remember having told them her name; couldn't remember if she'd told the dispatcher, either.

"Come on," he said, yanking her from the car. "Right this way." He shoved her forward.

The other man fell in behind them, lighting their feet down the cracked concrete walkway toward the looming building ahead. The lead-man's light played against the building. The windows were dark, reflecting the flare of the flashlight in wobbly, scattering puddles.

At the door, releasing her for a moment, the lead-man wedged his light under his arm and fidgeted with a ring of keys—the noise unnervingly bright. Opening the door, he took her roughly by the arm again and flung her inside. "Keep going," he said and indicated the long hallway ahead. She moved along. Behind her, the keys in the man's hand continued chiming. Their footsteps clicked and echoed like water dripping in a cave.

When Ella said, "Really, I think this must be a mistake," the man just repeated:

"Keep going."

The orb of the flashlight led her through a door and, with the crisp clack of a light switch, she found herself in a long, barren room. At the far end Agent Dyer sat at a desk, looking like he'd just woken up. The sight of him brought Ella's anxiety under control. He nodded past the desk, to the empty chair facing him. "Take a seat."

His voice was surprisingly childlike; no wonder he didn't use it more often.

Ella crossed the room and sat. When she looked over her shoulder to the door, the two men who'd escorted her in had vanished. Turning back to Dyer, she asked, "Where is Sickens?"

"Ms. Sickens has been reassigned. I'll be your case manager moving forward." He paused and gave her a nod, as though agreeing with what he'd just told her. "You were contacted by Misha Kant?"

"Yes, on the train. She had a bundle she kept trying to get me to take. I think it had a gun in it."

Dyer'd taken out a pad of paper and started marking an inordinate amount of notes. "Did you see the gun?" he asked, watching his hand move.

"I just told you *I thought there was a gun in it.* If I'd seen a gun, I would have told you it was a gun."

"What did it look like?"

"The bundle?—it looked like a goddamned bundle. Listen, I'd really feel better if I could speak with Ms. Sickens."

"That's beyond my control..."

"Moreover, I'd feel better if we were somewhere else..."

"Such as..."

"Uh, a *police station.* The Office of Sentient Affairs. The food court of a mall. Actually, just about anywhere would feel more reassuring than this. This feels..."

"I assure you, you're perfectly safe." Looking around the room, he didn't pause scrawling on the slip of paper when he said, "This, I'll admit, is not the most pleasant of environs, but I do hope you understand the delicate nature of the information you're bringing to us. A police station, for very obvious reasons, would not do. The Office of Sentient Affairs would not do..."

"It's not obvious to me, whatever the *reasons* might be."

He shrugged, looking back to his hand and explaining hastily, "Misha Kant was in the Agency and we're still not convinced of her loyalties. We don't know, can't be sure, which side anyone is on. Discretion is at a premium. Do you understand?"

"There's a mole in your agency. Is that why Sickens isn't here?"

Ella was aware that he hadn't answered her question at all when he said, "She's been reassigned to the East Gish detail."

"East Gish? What's happening there?"

"Nothing to worry about. All that's of concern is what's happening here, now, in this room." He paused a moment before saying, "Would you now, for me please, describe the bundle?"

"It was… I don't know. A goddamned bundle!"

"Ms. Pearson, please. This could be very important."

"Fine. It was…" She pantomimed its approximate size, about as big as a cheap paperback. "Just cloth, wound around tight. Dirty cloth. It was… greasy."

"So, not dirty, greasy."

"What's the goddamned difference between dirty and greasy?"

"How did you come to the conclusion that it was a gun?"

"I don't know. She kept trying to get me to take it and told me I needed to murder Warner."

"Was that the word that she used—murder?"

"Weren't you listening?" She flashed the watch at him. He didn't look up.

"Please just answer the question, Ms. Pearson. It's important for calibration."

"Calibration?" Ella shook her head. "Fine. No. No, she didn't say murder. I think she said, 'take care of him,' or something of the sort. 'Get him out of the picture.' Something like that. But her meaning was pretty damn clear. She said Warner had been the one behind the Assembly vandalism…"

"Okay," he nodded, still distracted with his note-taking. "And what are your feelings about that?"

"What—murder or vandalism?"

"For the sake of my notes, could you please refrain from asking me questions?—it complicates the calibration process."

"Well, we wouldn't want that, would we?"

Dyer was silent. His pen scraped the paper.

"Okay. I think I can cover all this pretty quickly, as a matter of fact. You got your pen ready? All of it—I'm against it all—murder, vandalism, it's all wrong."

Dyer sighed impatiently. "I feel your curt answer speaks of the lack of seriousness with which you're taking all of this."

"I feel that your manner of questioning invites ridicule."

"These are serious matters, Ms. Pearson."

"I don't feel I need to be reminded of that. I'm the one... where I am, aren't I?"

"Very well," he said. His scribbling continued. The noise was annoying. "Let's start with the attack on the First Assembly of the Neo Hominem. How did your boss, Mr. Warner, react to the news?" He asked, furiously working the pen the whole time.

"How can you be taking notes? I haven't even said anything." She shot up and stole the note pad out from under him—his pen leaving a long, descending dash across the bottom half of the page. She turned and looked the sheet over. The line he'd made was continuous, winding from edge to edge of the page like a snake piled up on top of itself. "Oh. I see," she said flatly as he took the note pad back, "it's nonsense. Like the rest of this."

"Now I'll have to start over," he muttered into his chest, tearing off the sheet, balling it up and tossing it into a corner of the room. Looking over the fresh sheet for a moment and setting aside his pen, he said, "Are you familiar with the concept of a polygraph, Pearson? This auto-writing that I'm engaged in works in much the same way..."

Leaning forward, dropping her elbows onto the edge of the desk and resting her head in her hands, she said, "Jesus. All this time I was worried that I was going crazy and now I see: you're the crazy one..."

"Here," he said, settling the pen back into his grip, "I'll prove it for you." Poising his pen over the notepaper he said, "Tell me a lie."

When she moved to respond, he quickly brought up his free hand, holding up a finger for her to wait. She sank back, folding her arms over her chest. A tremor ran through his fingers as he drew out a long, continuos line, jagged like the scroll of a seismometer. He lowered his upraised hand.

Arms still crossed, Ella said, "I have complete faith in the legitimacy of this process."

After her statement, Dyer drew the line out a little longer before stopping, nodding at his work and turning the notebook for her to see. The line ran out as a minor squiggle, with a great zenith near the end. "This," he said, tapping on the pinnacle of the mountain range he'd drawn, "indicates the point in the conversation during which you lied."

"Amazing," she said flatly. "And you can do that without any machinery at all."

"Well, not quite without machinery." He chuckled. "I do need a pen and a piece of paper. And a desk, of course."

"Of course. You'd have to have something to sit at."

"Oh, not just that," he said, enthusiastic now to explain the process further. "A desk, you might agree, displays a necessary weightiness..."

"A gravitas, if you will?"

"Precisely. I mean, without the desk..."

"This would just be a room," Ella said, nodding sarcastically.

"Yes. Precisely." He said, "Now, shall we get on with it?"

"Oh, please," Ella remarked, looking around the room and wondering if what Warner had told her had been true: if she was free to leave; if these people had no power to keep her. When she turned back, Dyer was bent over his pad again. Beside his elbow on the desktop, having appeared seemingly from nowhere, a small bundle of greasy cloth sat. Ella kicked, pushing her chair out reflexively. "What the hell is that?"

He didn't look up, just kept marking out time with his pen—a little greater quake resonating through it when she spoke. "What do you think it is?"

"I think it's that goddamned bundle Misha Kant tried to give me."

His pen twitched and twittered. "Why would you think that?"

"Because it is. It's the same goddamned bundle."

"Why don't you open it and see?"

"I don't want to touch it," Ella said.

Sighing and setting down his pen, Dyer turned his attention to the bundle. Pulling it in, he delicately unfolded the wrappings.

It wasn't a gun, whatever it was. It had a small, glimmering black screen and was matte black all over. It looked like it could have been an expensive alarm clock, maybe. Ella lurched up, knocking the chair over. Stepping back, she tripped over the chair she'd upended but caught herself, unable to look away from what he'd uncovered. "It's a bomb?"

He said, "You see this button here? If you want to trigger the device..."

Ella bolted for the door.

The hallway was dark and empty. Ella crashed down the length, bouncing from wall to wall until she got her feet back under her. When she turned to look over her shoulder, Dyer hadn't emerged from the room yet. Ella collided with the wall again and spun back around, running for all she was worth.

Ahead, the front door had been left open, but neither of the men who'd hijacked her were in sight. Beyond the threshold, however, in the dim amber glare of light pollution, the rounded hump of the car's roof gleamed. It hadn't moved. Reaching into her purse as she ran, she fumbled a moment and found her phone. She knew exactly what she had to do; she kept hearing the line from that old detective movie, playing through her head, '*You do as I say, because people who don't listen, don't last long...*'

The air beyond the threshold was cool and expansive and for a moment she almost changed her mind. Looking down the long, dark street, the urge to continue running—to sprint blindly into the abyss of the Northern District—was almost overwhelming. The darkness kept her away. She knew she wouldn't get far: not when they had a car and flashlights and she was stuck scurrying off like a rodent.

Forcing herself to slow, she came down the stairs at a brisk tumble, light footed. It looked like both the men were back in the sedan, staring ahead. A warbling undercurrent of music wound from the radio, out the open windows.

Off of the last stair, Ella glided as quietly as she could down the walkway and across the sidewalk to the rear door of the car, fixing her phone in the crook of her thumb. She snapped up the door handle and slid into the seat, bringing up the phone toward the passenger's neck, prepared to issue her threat, so that they understood how very serious she was, '*You do as I say... You follow me?*'

She didn't have the chance. The driver turned to look at her before she could even press the phone to his partner. Her hand wavered and fell to her lap, impotent.

"So," the driver said, "all set, then?"

Ella stammered and finally found her voice, "Yes. All set."

"Alright." Switching on the headlights, the driver pulled away from the curb cautiously, checking his mirror first and then over his shoulder. It seemed an unnecessary precaution in the empty neighborhood.

The ruinous buildings on the roadside blurred by as the car accelerated and Ella turned back, looking through the rear window to spot Dyer lumbering into the street, waving his arms frantically. He was only barely lit by the taillights and in the next moment, gone altogether, absorbed into the night.

Leaning over the seat, Ella said, "I should probably call my family and let know I'm on my way home. My phone's dead, would you mind..."

The man in the passenger seat shook his head silently and dug his phone out of his pocket. Handing the device over his shoulder, Ella'd barely gotten hold of it when the face lit up bright, *Lt. Dyer,* flashing across the screen. Ella hurried to shut the thing off. "Isn't that funny," she said, "yours is dead, too."

She handed the phone back to him. The agent swiped at the screen and when the thing refused to wake, he muttered "Damn thing never works right."

Ella had already turned her attention to the driver. "Would you mind?"

He lifted his hip from the seat to dig his phone out of his hip pocket and handed it back to her. Holding the button to power the thing down, she pressed it to her face and, after a theatric wait said, "Andy, honey, it's me… I know, I know… Well, I'm on my way home, right now… Okay. I'll see you in a bit."

She passed the phone back over the seat and the driver pushed it into his pocket without looking at it. Ella couldn't stop her hands from shaking. Out the rear window, lit in the wine-red glow of the taillights, the Northern District flowed away, down the darkened drain of the night.

27 Flight

Though night continued to linger, inside Andy's apartment, the clock above the stove warned that dawn wasn't far off. Only a little darkness left. Exhausted, Ella made herself keep going. It felt like the clock was ticking down to a denouement—the problem was, she didn't know what that finale would entail or, even, how close to that fateful, mysterious hour the clock stood.

Creeping to the back of the apartment on the balls of her feet, passing Clara's door, Ella caught the racket of the Caveman snoring, grumbling and sputtering like a gas starved engine.

In the living room Andy was sprawled out, asleep and soundless on the couch. Beside him, Clara lay in the lounger. Sneaking past into the bedroom, Ella found her suitcase where she'd left it, in the narrow alley between the bed and the wall. She was careful, coming around the mattress but when she picked the bag up and turned, she knocked the thing off the bed frame. It gave a loud crack. She froze up. In the other room, the Caveman's snoring had suddenly ceased.

Holding still, Ella couldn't seem to prevent her gaze from falling on the bed. God, she was tired. She could lay down for just a moment… No, she warned herself, she needed to keep moving. There was no telling how long it would take Dyer to show up here, looking for her.

In the living room, Andy was still sprawled out lifelessly, but Clara'd woken. The girl's gaze followed Ella as she moved out of the darkened doorway.

"I..." Ella whispered but it didn't take anymore than that. The girl tossed and turned away to face the wall.

•

In the hallway, creeping by the bathroom, Ella looked down at her hand holding the suitcase. The meta-metric watch peeked out from under the cuff of her shirt. Stopping in the thin glow of the nightlight, seeping out from the open bathroom door, Ella realized she'd need to get rid of the thing. There was no way to tell if anyone was watching her, or if they were tracking where she was—if that was even a function that the watch was capable of—but she couldn't risk it. She had to assume that she was being observed and that they knew exactly where she stood.

Slipping into the bathroom, she set the suitcase on the floor and closed the door behind her. Turning on the light, in the sudden, stark flare, Ella took a moment to listen to the apartment outside the door. The Caveman's snoring had resumed. Ella moved to the mirror.

Resting her wrist on the counter top, she unfastened the clasp on the meta-metric device. The straps dropped away like a satisfied parasite giving up its hold. It took her a moment before she found the nerve to pick her hand up off the countertop. Horrifyingly, the watch remained where it was, clinging to her. The watch straps wagged loosely. Turning her wrist around, she grabbed ahold of the strap, giving it a tug. The skin puckered on her wrist but the watch held on. *Maybe the parasite wasn't full yet*: the thought aroused a fresh surge of horror.

She pulled again, harder, and the skin on her wrist stretched further. But the watch still wouldn't let go.

In the cabinet under the vanity she found the tidy assortment of tools Andy kept in a cracked, plastic tool box. Setting the box out on the counter top, she dug around inside, ultimately settling on a flathead screwdriver as the most practical surgical instrument in the set. The edge was tainted with a scab of rust, and for a moment Ella considered sanitizing the thing in a cup of alcohol, but worried if she let the matter of removing the device wait, she'd lose her resolve altogether.

With the sharp edge of the screwdriver poised at the juncture of the watch and her skin, she took a moment to steady herself. Jamming it in with everything she had, a staticky, electric chill bolted up her arm. Her whole body clenched, frozen up for a moment. Once the shock had lapsed, after another quick spell to marshal herself, she thrust the tool again, deeper.

Her consciousness faltered a moment and came back. She looked at her wrist.

The head of the screwdriver was poking out from the far side of the watch now. With what strength she had left, she levered the thing up in a quick jerk.

With a crack, the watch popped off and Ella went over backward.

•

When her senses returned, Ella found herself folded up in the tub, her legs hanging over the side, her neck curled against the wall. Andy was over her, pulling her onto her feet.

"Muffin, are you alright?"

She could only groan.

Standing now, face to face, he turned to look at the suitcase on the floor. "What's going on?"

"I can't explain, Andy. There isn't time. I need to go." She made a move to get around him but he stopped her. Outside, the brick wall beyond the bathroom window was already starting to materialize from the darkness. It was a new day; a dreadful new day. "Andy, it isn't safe, my being here."

"I'll pack some things," he said.

"Andy, there isn't time..." He'd already gone out the door, his footsteps padding away down the hall.

Looking at her wrist, the watch face was gone, but it looked as if she'd failed to remove all of the device. A tiny panel lay beneath her skin where the watch had been. It looked like a circuitboard drawn out in glistening, white tendrils. There wasn't any blood, but the dry, puckered flesh around the edges of the wound was almost worse.

•

Ella's secret apartment seemed drearier with Clara and Andy and the Caveman crowded inside. There were no shades in the windows to pull. Still no furniture, either, and so Andy and Ella sat on their luggage to keep off the cold floor. Clara and the Caveman sat on the mattress. It made the whole situation seem all the more desperate; a reminder that, even now they were prepared for flight—prepared for a catastrophe that might, at any moment, come crashing through the door. And the daylight braying through the windows was having the opposite effect on Ella than it usually did: making her feel worse, more detached, further afield from the neutral shores of reality. Maybe it was just the heaping dose of Represitol she'd taken. The prescription was almost gone—a nagging concern, acute enough to pierce the calming effect the drug normally fostered.

"Who's this?" Clara asked, holding up the photo of Timmy.

"No one. Put it back."

Andy was talking. How long that had been going on, Ella couldn't have said. It was hard following him. Maybe that was the lack of sleep she'd been forced to endure; maybe, again, it was the Represitol muddying her perception. Interrupting his rambling, which had become increasingly muffled and inward the longer he kept it up, she said, "What's the point, Andy?"

"I was just saying..." he said, cranking up his volume. There was a particular and uncharacteristic impatience in his voice. "I was trying to go see my family..."

"Yes. I knew that. We already discussed that, Andy. What's the point?"

Huffing and looking at her a cold moment, he continued on again in a halting, deliberate tone. It was the same one he employed when explaining something to Clara which he thought was over the girl's head—not realizing anything he was fit to explain was certainly not beyond his wunderkind's comprehension. "When I left the apartment… I tried calling them… the old number didn't work, it just rang and rang so I tried directory assistance and I couldn't find a listing. So I think, well, I'll just go and rent a car…"

The idea struck Ella as preposterous. Illinois was all the way… In her mind, she pieced together a map where Illinois was one pin point and the City was another, distantly placed. It was a blank field with no roads or landmarks—no scale at all.

She felt a surge of anger rise up at this newest admission that he'd been planning on leaving her, abandoning her with Clara and the Caveman as though, in the fog of his sudden anxiety, they'd ceased to exist altogether. Instead of erupting on him, she canned her aggravation up—it was an argument for another time: one they hopefully wouldn't have at all, once she managed to slip away.

"…So I get to the car rental place and it's the same thing, all over again. No one there. They actually said they had a car that I could take, but when I tried to put it on my card, they said the card was invalid. Which is impossible…"

Ella knew Andy well enough to know that wasn't so much impossible as it was very, very likely. She was surprised that his total credit line was sufficient to rent a car at all, and then supposed that it probably wasn't. "I still don't understand your point…"

"Ella, they're trying to keep us from leaving the City."

Ella nodded, not so convinced of his conclusion but more in a spirit of moving on from the topic. She said, "We need to get out of here, I think we can agree on that…"

"This is so dumb," Clara complained from the bed where she and Ernie were going through patty cake for the countless time. "I just want to go home."

"Clara," Ella scolded her back into silence or, rather, back into rhyming and clapping (more aggressively now) with the Caveman.

"How?" Andy wanted to know.

"Don't worry about that." Ella stood. It seemed to take more effort than it should have. She felt exhausted. She straightened out her slacks. "I'll take care of it. You stay here with..."

"Oh, no," Andy said, rising to meet her. He had a lot more energy than she did; he bolted right up. "No way..."

"Andy..."

"...There's nothing to do here."

"Take them out. Take them to a movie. We'll meet back here at..."

"No," Andy said decisively. "You said we were in this together; that we were sharing this responsibility..."

"That was before you decided to run off to Illinois..." The argument that she'd planned on saving came out premature, and fell flat. It was like she hadn't spoken at all.

"If you're right and we are in danger, what am I supposed to do with both of them? It puts all three of us at risk. You need to take Ernie..."

"Andy, I have to work on getting us a way out of here. I can't..."

"It's Ernie or Clara." He crossed his arms.

Ella looked back and forth between the two. "Fine," she said. Crossing the room, she snatched the Caveman's hand from the air, where it was about to meet Clara's, yanking him out of his game.

•

Outside, the sun seemed like the eye of authority, aimed more squarely on Ella than on anyone else. Maybe that was why she didn't let go of the Caveman, even though the desire to release his damp hand was almost overwhelming, his presence beside her a suddenly suffocating thing—an anchor dragging her under.

In her purse, her phone sat. Her nearly-empty prescription seemed to beg for priority so, after deciding that calling the Practitioner's office might put her at risk, she found a subway station and pulled the Caveman underground with her.

The platform was busy, commuters packed up against the orange warning line at the edge of the tracks.

At the rear of the station, Ella spotted an empty bench against the wall. Dragging the Caveman to it, she sat him down. "Just wait right here," she told him. He looked up at her with his wide, glossy, unsuspicious gaze. "You understand? Wait here."

There was no telling whether he understood. Ella nodded at him resolutely and walked away to join the queue waiting for the next train.

A moment later the metro rolled in with a racket of chains and squealing pigs and a tectonic rumble. The doors flopped open and for a moment the platform was a chaos of bodies. Exiting passengers fought to get through the throng of people trying to board. Ella battled her way closer to the door, stopping when she felt something small and warm land in her hand. Turning down, she found the Caveman there, smiling up at her.

"No, no," she said and dragged him out of the bustle, bringing him back to the bench by the wall. She sat him down again. Pointing into his stubbly face, she told him sternly, "Stay here. You have to Stay Here."

The little beast blinked up at her. Behind her, the train doors closed. The machine sighed and howled off.

"You need to stay here."

When he failed to give any indication that he understood, Ella nodded to him and returned to the crowd at the edge of the platform. There, with all the others, she stared forward blankly, waiting for the next train. A strange tide of unease lapped at her. It took a moment to recognize the feeling as guilt and when she turned back and caught sight of the Caveman, alone on his bench, the feeling only intensified. She forced herself to look forward again, across the empty tracks.

Up the darkened tunnel the next train rumbled toward the station.

She turned back.

A man in a grimy union suit was pushing a broom toward the Caveman. The train rolled in and Ella was jostled, commuters pushing past her and in the next moment she was caught in the throng boarding the train. Stepping up, through the doors, there was an open spot just inside and Ella took it, grabbing the safety bar to hold herself in place as people pushed past her, still boarding.

Through the open door, looking back over the platform, she saw that the man in the union suit (he had a job, sure, but looked half-homeless, swathed in grime as he was) had taken the seat beside Ernie. Leaning on the handle of his broom, he bent to the side, talking to the little monster.

A fresh wave of guilt poured over her, gummy and insistent as tar.

What was she doing? She'd thought of the little thing, always, as a monster but here she was acting like a villain herself. She didn't want him, resented having him, but that wasn't his fault. That was an issue with the government, not him. She thought briefly about having cut up fruit for him and wondering if it would poison him and couldn't help herself dwelling on it: if she was now having so much guilt over simply leaving him, how would she have felt if he'd died in her care? A spasm of self-loathing wrenched her insides.

When the doors started shutting, Ella lunged forward, wedging herself in the closing gap. The doors froze up, an alarm calling out through the train: an automated voice warning, "Stay clear of the doors. Stay clear of the doors..."

Ella squeezed out, stumbling back onto the platform into the thin crowd that had already congregated there. Pushing her way through, she charged toward the bench, grabbing Ernie by his hand and yanking him up. Looking to the maintenance-man she said, "What the hell do you think you're up to?"

He flinched at the impact of her voice. "Whoa, lady, I was just..."

Ella pulled the Caveman closer. "He's just a child. Leave him alone."

"I was just..." the janitor started again, but Ella didn't let him finish, turning and dragging the Caveman back through the station.

In the queue for the third time, she held tight to the Caveman's hand. After a moment, the next train still not in sight, she looked down at him and said, "I wasn't going to leave you, just so you know. That was just a test, that's all: never talk to strangers."

He looked up at her, his wide eyes glistening like he was about to cry. He nodded slowly.

28 Final Arrangements — Hallucinations

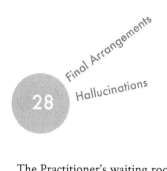

The Practitioner's waiting room was full. Ella took the only empty seat—near a filthy play area that the Caveman was fixated on. Even as he pulled against her, tugging at every angle like a kite trying to get free from its tether, Ella did not let him go. A few seats away, a woman watched the battle, troubled by Ella's tight restraint on the furry little beast. Ella refused to return the woman's look and, in her struggle to keep the Caveman corralled, any affection she'd been feeling for the monster seemed to evaporate.

•

Admitted to a narrow examination room, Ella finally let go of the Caveman so he could bumble around. The wait was long, giving him a good amount of free range time, but when she heard the doorknob turn, Ella lunged out of her seat to cordon the beast from escaping.

Closing the door behind him, the Practitioner nodded hello to Ella before his attention turned to the monster cooing in her restraint. "Oh," bending down, he said, "he's awfully cute." Turning up to look at Ella, he said, "What's your boy's name?"

"He isn't my boy," Ella said and let the thing go free.

The Practitioner looked at her a quiet moment longer, before his gaze settled back on the Caveman. "May I give him a treat?"

"You can feed him to a pack of wolves, for all I care." After a moment, she said, "I didn't mean that, not really. He's very trying to be around, is all."

Whether or not the Practitioner had heard wasn't evident. From his lab coat pocket the man produced a candy, but he made the Caveman shake his hand before passing it over. The Caveman seemed happy enough, as did the Practitioner. Patting the beast's bulbous head and standing, he pulled a small tablet computer from his coat and took a seat in a chair against the wall. "Well, Ms. Pearson, how are we today?"

"We're fine. There's no problem. I just needed a refill on my prescription..."

He looked at her. After a moment his attention was drawn away from her face to her lap where her hands were folded. "You've injured your wrist."

Hot with embarrassment, Ella tugged her sleeve down over the bandage and said, "It isn't anything. Not even an injury, really, I wouldn't say."

"Why don't I have a look at it?"

"No. It's fine, I just needed a refill on my prescription, that's all," she said, hiding the hand at her side.

Sitting up straighter, correcting his posture, he said, "Normally, we've done that over the phone. You should have called, it would have saved you having to wait."

Ella didn't know if there was a question in there, but she hurried to answer all of the cowering questions that he may have been suggesting. "I have a new phone and, besides, I was in the neighborhood. I don't mind waiting, at any rate. I have the day off work. We were on our way to the... park."

He nodded, queueing through a few screens on the computer before remarking, "It looks here as though your prescription was supposed to last through the month." He paused, turning to her to note, "You're only a few weeks in..."

"Oh, yes," Ella nodded. "That, I can explain... My boyfriend and I..." She wished she'd thought this through more carefully. "...are going to the country... for a vacation." She hurriedly finished, "I was afraid I wouldn't be able to refill it there..."

"Oh, I see. How lovely. How long will you be gone for?"

"...A month. Maybe two..."

"That's a very long vacation. How nice for you."

"We might be moving there. We haven't decided. It's sort of an... exploratory trip."

"Hm." He nodded. "I've always fancied the idea of moving to the country. Fresh air seems very appealing, all that sunlight... Three doses a day?"

"Just two, remember? You thought we should scale back..."

He nodded and set the tablet away. Ella searched the floor for the Caveman. He'd wrapped his arms around a leg of the examination table and had his mouth clamped onto it. A rivulet of drool crept down the chrome tube. It was off-colored, a little brownish from the sweet he'd been given. After a moment the Practitioner said, "I'd like to go over the course of the conversation we had before we decided to cut back the dosage..."

"Isn't that all in the notes?"

"It's good for us to discuss it, all the same."

Ella nodded. "If you remember, I was worried about the side effects. Some of them are quite serious."

"They can be," he agreed and went silent. He made a little motion with his hand, something a conductor might do.

"Paranoia." He didn't react at all. Ella would have paid good money to get an Andy-style laugh from the man, a babel that would let her know how baseless her fears were. "Well, it is one of the side effects. I was just concerned, that's all. It's responsible of me to worry, don't you think? And worrying about a side effect isn't a side effect."

"Unless the side effect is undue worry," he pointed out.

"It was just a conversation we had. I was just being careful. I'm always careful."

"I can see that," he said. He said, "The regimen can have a number of side effects, as I'm sure you know. Paranoia, memory loss, hallucinations. I'd like to touch on why you were worrying about the side effects..."

"It's just those commercials, that's all. They play them on the subway all the time; they end with that litany and it just... It gets in your head..."

"Are you having hallucinations?"

Ella looked down at the Caveman. "No. No. I'm sure I'm not," she laughed. It rang with Andy's familiar uncertainty. "I mean, you're here, I'm here. We're all accounted for, right?" She laughed again.

With the Practitioner holding her gaze, Ella wouldn't look away—forcing herself to hold on as well. Finally, he nodded and stood, working his fingers over the tablet again. "I'm writing you a refill to last until the end of next month. We'll chat again before then, just to check in."

He went to the door, pausing in the open frame for a moment to look back at her. Ella caught the Caveman by the wrist when he lunged toward the opening.

"Ms. Pearson, we all have stressful periods now and again and we all want to get away from time to time. I made a note of that in your file."

He nodded and was gone.

•

At the elevator, Ella pushed the call button and played flag pole to the Caveman's whipping and writhing: once again the beast was determined to get to the play area at the back of the waiting room.

The woman who'd been giving her dirty looks was watching Ella again.

Finally fed up and feeling defiant, Ella turned to give the woman back her own nasty expression. The woman's face couldn't be read at all. Her head was wrapped up in bandages, only the pair of dark hollows that must have been the woman's eyes giving the impression that she had a face at all.

Yanking the Caveman away from the elevator and around to the stairwell, Ella threw herself into the door. It crashed open. She started down the stairs, tugging the Caveman along behind her. He couldn't keep up. Pausing a moment, she pivoted to pull him up into her arms.

Hurrying again, with the Caveman clinging to her, and taking the descent faster than she should have, she missed a stair. She and the monster spilled forward. In midair, Ella made an instinctive adjustment, turning herself to shield the monster from the brunt of the impact. They weren't far from the landing. The Caveman landed hard atop her.

She groaned, leaning up to ask, "You okay?"

He sat up, clapping his hands and smiling like he'd like to try that ride again. Ella pushed him away.

Looking up the stairwell there wasn't anyone coming that she could see. She wasn't even so sure it had been Kant in the waiting room. It could have been anyone hiding behind those bandages, anyone at all.

29

The Only Other Option

An Old Face

You Could Have Been More Supportive

Ella managed to keep herself from a fresh reboot of Represitol on the elevator ride to the CCI offices. Struggling to ignore the craving, all that effort only seemed to exacerbate her itch for a dose. After fleeing her Practitioner's office, she'd tried renting a car.

Acutely aware of how she looked, standing at the desk of the car rental company, Ella had compensated with an air of impatient arrogance, huffing over the clerk's every inefficiency. The fall hadn't done her a bit of good. Her clothing was smeared with an ashy streak down her left side. A brown blot marred her blouse from the Caveman's candy-drool.

Playing absently with the knot of his clip-on tie, the man behind the desk said, "Very good." Keying up the computer before him, he asked casually, "Where're you off to?"

So offhand and friendly, the question seemed dubious and Ella said, "Illinois. To visit my boyfriend's family." Had that been a mistake? How far away *was* Illinois?

The clerk bent beneath the desk to pull out a small stack of papers, which he arranged on the table between them. After he'd explained the renter's agreement and all the signatures and initials it required, Ella held up the Caveman's hand and offered, "You want my first born? He's right here."

"Excuse me?"

"Nothing. I was being funny," she said. She filled out the form and slid it back to him. Click-clack, pause, tap-tap: the clerk forced a disjointed rhythm from the keyboard. When the phone beside him rang he scooped it up, tucking it under his chin, continuing to type. Click-clack. Tap-tap.

"Yes," he said into the receiver. His fingers stumbled over the keys. "Yes... No, she's here... Yes... I see." He was staring right at Ella. Moving the receiver to his opposite hand he said, "Yes. I'll do that. I'll tell her that. How long before... Yes. Yes, I see."

Ella had already started backing away, scooping the Caveman up. When the man set down the phone and said, "Ma'm? I just need you to..." Ella bolted outside.

Every other option exhausted, she'd come here, to CCI, and now, as the elevator ascended, she wondered if she shouldn't have just given up and gone back to Andy defeated. The refill of Represitol was calling to her.

A temporary bout of relief seemed to waft in when the doors split apart and the claustrophobia of the elevator abated. It didn't last. Confronted by Warner and Carl Thompson, side by side, waiting at the threshold, she clenched up instantly. The Caveman let out a pained mew—she'd twisted his wrist too sharply when she tried to get him hidden behind her. Stammering a moment, she floundered, stuck at the seam between the doors.

Nodding to her with the barest acknowledgment, Warner made a move to pass.

Ella blocked him out, embarrassed when the beast behind her thigh was exposed again. "Warner, I need to speak with you. It's urgent."

"Very good, Pearson. Set up a time with Ms. Price for tomorrow." He hitched his head for her to move aside.

"It can't wait. It's very important."

"It'll have to, Thompson and I..." He made another attempt to get past.

Lurching, Ella blocked him out again, tugging the Caveman roughly along. "Sir, it's about that matter you had me look into. It's very important that we speak." She lowered her voice further, quiet enough so she wasn't sure he heard her say, "You're in danger."

"Yes, yes, that's all very good," he muttered, finally squeezing past her, forcing her out into the hall without touching her and blocking off the closing elevator door to let Thompson in. "We'll talk about it to-morrow..."

Ella managed to hold Thompson on the floor.

From the elevator, Warner insisted, "Thompson, come on."

For the first time the minister seemed to notice the Caveman at Ella's side and bent down to the monster, stroking the thing's fuzzy cheek in a familial manner and muttering, "Such a handsome little one."

The man was obviously having trouble with his sight; maybe his mind, too. A tendril of drool shimmied from the monster's chin.

Thompson looked up at Ella, his voice full of wonder. "It's like looking into the future, isn't it?"

"I was thinking the very distant past."

Rising up, Thompson said, "Maybe you're right, my dear: a boy right from the breast of mankind. He looks very healthy. You must be sticking to his diet religiously. That's the sort of thing we need more of."

From behind her, Warner said, again, impatiently, "Thompson."

"I..." Ella faltered. She started over again, "It concerns you, too, Carl..."

"Tomorrow, Pearson," Warner announced and Thompson slipped passed her into the elevator. The next moment, the doors bit down, consuming them both.

Ella stood before the blank, closed face of the elevator, frozen until the Caveman tugged on her arm and brought her back to her senses.

•

When Ella closed the door behind her, it took Dawn a moment, turning her attention up from her desktop, to realize who—what—had entered her office. "Ella?" The moment didn't last long. Up from her seat, the instant Dawn's gaze fell on the Caveman, she rushed forward, bending down before the little monster and cooing, "Oh, aren't you adorable." She looked up at Ella. "This must be your boy. I was hoping I'd get a chance to meet him."

It sounded so... *genuine.* Ella couldn't make herself reply.

Rising again, the girl lurched forward to give Ella a hug. She managed to get out, "I'm so happy for you," before Ella dodged the embrace. The girl looked briefly hurt but, resigning herself, she nodded and led Ella back to the desk, saying, "I suppose it's time we talked..."

Seated, Ella gave up her hold on the Caveman and asked, "You mind if he's free range in here? I don't think he'll shit anywhere."

Dawn ignored her, if she'd even heard. Behind her, the sky had gone dark, the city lights glimmering, cheap and brassy. "It's good to see you. I've been thinking so much about you and what I asked... I realize now how out of line that was and I'm just..." She got a little choked up and Ella hated her more for it. "I'm really sorry to put that on you. Of course, I understand you not wanting to be in the wedding party but I hope you'll at least consider coming to the wedding. Of course you're invited; you're so special to me and Terry and... I just want you to know..."

Shut up. Shut up! SHUT UP! The phrase kept reverberating through Ella but, as the Caveman knocked around at the back of the room, what she forced herself to say was, "That's actually what I came to speak with you about."

"Yes?" The word sounded tentative. The girl glanced past Ella's shoulder, presumably at whatever mess the Caveman was about to make. Ella started to turn, but Dawn interrupted, "Oh, he's fine..."

Ella nodded. "I was thinking... You know, you said the two of you thought of me as special. Well, I think of you that way, as well."

A big, soft sound came out of Dawn, like the noise of a dog's chew-toy being affectionately gnawed. Ella tried to ignore it.

"If I can help you out by being your," the phrase seemed too big to force out her throat, but she managed to push and get it free, "*maid of honor.* I don't know how I could say 'no' right now."

Dawn stood, that same happy/sad sound warbling out of her, almost weeping when she stumbled around the desk, when she said, "Oh, Ella, I'm so, so happy. You've made me so happy!"

Ella clenched and allowed herself to be absorbed into the girl's stifling side-hug.

Pulling away, wiping at her face, Dawn repeated, "So happy..."

"There's just one thing..."

"Whatever. Anything you need. Is it a specific color for your dress?—I know, with your color, a lot of shades might not do... It's so unfortunate. I was thinking a vermillion, maybe... No, that wouldn't work, either, would it?" the girl mused, inspecting Ella's face. "It is tricky, your color, isn't it?"

"No. No. Nothing wedding related," Ella said, clipping her words. "I was hoping I could borrow your car."

"My car?"

"Yes." Something crashed down at the back of the room, but she didn't turn and when Dawn did, she said, "Andy and I and," another phrase that felt like a big, dry hay-bale in her voice-box, "*the children* are taking a vacation and..."

"Of course, of course you'll borrow the car. There's no question. I'm so happy to hear that you and Andy have reconciled..."

"Great. Great, Dawn, I really appreciate it," she said, pausing. "One more favor? Just a little thing but it's very important."

"Anything, anything at all."

"A piece of paper and a pen, please."

"Oh," Dawn said, going back around the desk and digging into a drawer to get the items together. She giggled, "That hardly even qualifies as a favor..."

"That's not the favor..." Ella grumbled, taking the sheet and the pen. She quickly scratched out a note:

Warner, I believe Misha Kant is in league with the Office of Sentient Affairs to have you assassinated. There's an agent there, specifically, who I believe Kant is conspiring with: a man named Dyer. I'm sorry I can't be of more help, but I'm afraid I'm in too much danger myself. I need to leave the City. I think you know where I'll be, if you need me....

Ella looked up from the note. "Dawn? It's very important that Warner is the only one who sees this. No one but Warner. Understand?"

Dawn nodded.

"I need you to promise, Dawn, is the thing. Seeing this note could well put you in danger. You understand? You can't look at it."

Dawn seemed confused. "No, I don't understand."

"That's really for the best, but you have to promise."

"Of course, I promise." She giggled. "For my maid of honor... anything..."

Ella returned to the note to write a post script:

Dawn called you a cunt and said you were running this company into the toilet. You should probably have her fired. Also, that night janitor—the surly, arrogant one—has been stealing office supplies. She finished the note, *-Pearson,* folded it in thirds and, swiping a length of tape from the dispenser on the desktop, sealed the end shut before handing it across to Dawn, reminding her, "Only Warner. Not his secretary. Not you. No one else."

•

The Caveman had pulled down a pile of binders and framed photographs and they lay in a mess at the base of the shelving beside the door. "That's fine," Dawn said as they passed it by, but she seemed to be trying to convince herself.

Ella squeezed the Caveman's hand lightly.

Outside, on the street, Dawn seemed to have forgotten the matter of the mess altogether, talking in gusts, listing off particulars of the wedding. Ella tugged the Caveman along, enraged by the giddy twitter of the girl's voice but trying to remind herself that she wouldn't have to endure it for long.

But then, the walk went on and on and long after it first occurred to her to ask, Ella said, "Do you always park this far away?"

Dawn tittered like it had been a shared joke but otherwise didn't respond.

Ella let it pass but then, when she realized Dawn was heading for the subway entrance up ahead, she said, "Dawn, where is your car?"

That trilling laugh again. "At home, silly. I don't drive into the City that often. With all the traffic problems..." She shook her head. She laughed. "I'd never get to work on time..."

"Yeah. That makes sense," Ella grumbled.

•

On the train, Dawn lounged sideways in her seat to regard Ella. "Terry," she said and every time the name came out of her, it was with a certain coy longing that made Ella want to assault her, "wanted to have his friend's boy be the ring barer. I love the kid, you know. But, the fact is, he's almost as tall as I am. I tried telling Terry, you know, a ring barer's supposed to be a kid, 'cause it's cute. There's nothing cuter than a little boy in a tux—am I right? Well, so I try explaining to Terry that having David do it, I mean, come on—David's not going to do it..."

Ella stared ahead, gazing sullenly through the door at the front of the car, to the car beyond, watching the way it swayed and jerked, telegraphing the turns in the track that they were all headed for.

"Say, if you're going to be the maid of honor..."

Ella tried waiting out the silence, but Dawn continued staring at her and holding it. Ella turned to face the girl.

Flashing a look at the Caveman, Dawn said, "He would look awful cute in a tux."

"If you're looking for someone without a beard, you'd better keep looking."

"He does have quite a lot of peach fuzz, doesn't he? Still, he'd be awful cute in a tux. Say, doesn't Andy have a daughter? We're still looking for a flower girl..."

"That would be awkward for Andy, I think," Ella said.

"Yeah, men are so weird. You know, when I told Terry that I wanted to ask you to be my maid of honor, you know what he said?"

"Dawn, I'm not sure I really want to hear it..."

"He said I shouldn't even ask; that it would make you uncomfortable. He said that you'd just say no and that I'd just get my feelings hurt. He was so certain. He's gonna be shocked when I tell him."

"I bet you're right..."

"That's men for you, though, isn't it? Always so certain—especially when they're wrong!—am I right?" Dawn laughed boisterously.

"Where do you live, anyway?" They'd taken the Express but, even so, they'd sat through a number of stops. Ella didn't think she'd ever gone this far on the line before. It was like they were heading into a new country: Ella half expected that, when they arrived, they'd be greeted by a delegation in lederhosen and fez hats, maybe presented with ceremonial leis. In contrast with this cultural hash, the name Lincoln, Illinois kept sparking in her head.

"Wait until you see it," Dawn said. "You're gonna be so jealous..."

•

Outside, a thin mist drifted sideways, the pavement gleaming like obsidian. On the roadside the buildings were low and backed by a dark wilderness that put Ella ill-at-ease. Dawn was still talking about the wedding, but more slowly now, as though she too had worn on the subject. For his part, the Caveman just seemed worn; he was still moving, but Ella was having to lean forward and dig into her steps to keep him going; really dragging him along.

At their backs, the City skyline was a vague, bluish stain in the fog.

"Poor thing," Dawn remarked, pausing and leaning down to look softly on the Caveman.

"How much further is it?" Ella asked. The road ahead was long. The streetlights stretched out, softly rising into the distance, shafts of light suspended in the mist.

Ignoring her, Dawn asked the Caveman, "Do you think your mommy would mind if auntie Dawn gave you a piggy back?" He looked back at her blankly. "Would you like that—a piggy back?"

The Caveman continued blinking at her (obviously it was a phrase he was unfamiliar with) but when Dawn scooted around he clambered onto her back like a drunken marsupial. Dawn struggled to stand. Finally up, she lunged forward, teetering precariously on her tall heels. The sound of them knocking on the pavement became more pronounced.

"It isn't far," Dawn said after a few paces, the strain of lugging the Caveman evident in her voice. "He sure is solid, isn't he?"

"I believe he's mostly water," Ella told her.

•

It wasn't much further. After passing a hardware store, it's big plate windows oily in the night, they took a right down a narrow residential lane. The houses out here were big and sat up on a rise away from the road. Dawn's was the fifth in and, through the mist, all the lit windows gave an impression of warmth and welcome that drowned what little confidence Ella had left.

Inside the door, Dawn set the Caveman down. The cloying warmth in the foyer made Ella feel even worse.

Raising her hands the girl said, "So?"

Beyond the french doors that cordoned off a wide entry, a staircase led up. The walls were decked out with sconces that piled gilded light on everything. It was like someone had set Ella's own unrealized aspirations in plaster and glimmering brass. It wasn't hers, though: this marvel of domesticity. Her uncertain future seemed at odds with all this.

"Jeez, Dawn, how'd you afford it?" It was a dumb question; one she wished she hadn't asked. Terry made a good living—Ella knew that—and, Ella supposed, with her old paycheck now in Dawn's pocket, Dawn probably did, too.

"Isn't it great? I mean, Terry and I could have swung it ourselves, but—well, we wanted a big family, a *big* family—and when we told the people at the O.S.A.... Well, they didn't *buy* the house for us, but it seemed close to that."

The Caveman had wandered off. Ella stepped into the foyer to find him, just in time to catch Terry emerging from the kitchen. Noticing the Caveman (and somehow not Ella) he bent down, saying sweetly, "Now, who's this? Who'd you bring home, Dawn?"

The Caveman responded instantly, running his fat little legs and colliding with Terry, almost knocking the man down. The little beast wrapped his thick arms around Terry's neck, choking him in an enthusiastic embrace.

Terry returned the hug, if a little cautiously, finally patting the monster on the back and prying himself free from the Caveman's clutch. "Alright. Alright. Take it easy."

He looked different than he had the last time Ella'd seen him, but she couldn't have said how. Turning, catching sight of her for the first time, he flinched.

"Ella," he said. Maybe he'd tried to wring the disappointment out of his tone. If he had, he'd failed.

"Hello, Terrance."

Blitzing the space between them, Dawn wrapped her arms around the man flamboyantly, her legs leaving the ground. Ella looked away, up the stairs, but couldn't turn from Dawn's voice, trumpeting, "We have great news: Ella's agreed to be my maid of honor!" Having fallen off the man, she started clapping and hopping around in quick, shallow bursts.

Ella and Terry looked at one another.

Flatly, the man said, "That's great. That's really great."

Abandoning her flailing dance as abruptly as she'd begun, Dawn looped her arm around the man's waist and tugged him close. At Terry's knee, the Caveman held on tight with both arms, burying his face in the fabric of the man's pants.

Ella didn't know what to do with her hands. Terry and Dawn were both looking at her—very differently.

Dawn said, "Let me give you the tour!"

"I really oughta be going."

"Oh, come on! Let me show our house off!"

"If she has to go, sweetie," Terry said, which earned him a quick, chastising glance from the girl.

"At least stay for a while so we can all chat. I'm sure the two of you have a lot of catching up to do and there're wedding plans to discuss and it's such a long drive back into the City and..."

Ella jerked back unconsciously when a pair of hairy little faces appeared in a doorway behind Terry and Dawn. It took Ella a moment to get her senses back. "You have your own Cavemen," she muttered.

"What's that?" Dawn said, turning to follow Ella's gaze. The girl wasn't surprised at all by the pair of beasts skulking in the background. Letting go of Terry, she waved them forward. "William, Sissy, come out here and say hello to my very best friend, Ella."

Ella stepped back a pace. "No, that's fine, really... I really need to get going. Andy and I were hoping to strike out tonight," she said. The phrasing made her wince.

Visibly dejected but making a big show of putting on a brave face, Dawn said, "I understand." And again, more softly, seeming to twist the phrase inward, "I... I understand." Looking up at Terry, she said, "Ella's gonna borrow the car for the week." A titillated joy rang in her voice when she cooed, "Andy and she are going on a *vacation.*"

"Oh," Terry said, nodding, "okay."

"Well..." She slapped Terry on the backside so hard he hopped forward a pace, sending the Caveman free from his clutching. "The car?"

"Right," he hung his head and stepped forward. "The garage is this way."

Ella collected the Caveman and yanked him along.

After following him down a narrow hallway, Terry paused at a door, seeming to collect himself before leading her through and down a set of rough-cut wooden steps. The car waited below on a flat pedestal of concrete.

Ella put the Caveman in the passenger seat and buckled him in. When she came around the driver's side, Terry had the door open for her. She passed him by and sat without looking at him. He closed the door and, a moment later, knocked on the glass. She wound the window down. His face was so close. He was suddenly so close. And he was moving closer and Ella wondered if she should lean in too.

Reaching past her, he pushed a button on the console. The garage door hummed up, a burst of cool, damp air bustling in with the clatter of rain. He pulled away again, but stayed hanging in the window. "It's manual. You know how to drive one?"

"It's been a while..."

"Of course you do," he said. It'd been foolish to ask. It was the same car he'd owned back then: back when they were a *they.* He hadn't moved yet. Hovering in the open hole of the window, he kept looking at her. Shaking his head he said, gently, "You were always so fucking nuts."

She reached out and put her hand on his cheek. He didn't move for a moment and when he did, it was slowly, reluctantly. Ella started the car and turned forward and pulled out of the garage and away from the house.

On the freeway, miles piling up between Terry and the car, she couldn't seem to stop her head from shaking. "You know, you could have been a little more supportive back there. Clinging onto his leg like that—like I'm some sort of monster. You should show some god-damned loyalty, Ernie."

The Caveman was quiet.

Looking down at him, catching glimpses of his face in the street-light swiveling past, he looked sad, too. She lay a hand on his knee and gave a quick squeeze.

30 The End of the World
Another Planet

Beyond the City a vague, miry wilderness whistled past the car. Silent at the wheel, Andy's face was sickly green in the glow of the dash lights. Any noise from the backseat had ended hours ago; Clara and the Caveman were asleep. In the prevailing darkness, the hum of the road proved too enchanting a lullaby: winding back her seat, Ella followed the pair off the edge of the conscious world.

•

Waking sometime later with a start, Ella stared with fear at the spiraling wash of stars looming overhead. Her immediate thought was preposterous: that they'd followed the road right off the end of the world and had been set loose to drift in the endless sea of outer space. It was ludicrous, yet that knowledge didn't hold back the flood of anxiety that washed over her. She'd been in the City so long, living so long under the low, rusty, polluted sky, that she'd forgotten the sky was where stars lived, that a window to the majesty of the universe hung overhead.

Beside her, in the thick darkness of the car, something stirred. "Andy, what's going on?"

The car went silent and suddenly still. Ella drifted back to sleep.

•

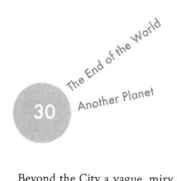

When Ella woke to the morning, it felt as though she hadn't slept at all, that it was only the emerging daylight reminding her once again of her extremities; returning her to the narrow singularity of her own existence. The windows were fogged. The air in the car was rank and humid—the Caveman must have spent the entire night farting. Ella fumbled for the door handle.

Outside the car a damp, insistent breeze blew.

Trees crowded the roadside, the branches pocked with bright buds, so the near breadth of the forest seemed to have been washed with a flimsy coat of green watercolor. Ella looked down the road—a canyon running through the wilderness. Behind the car, the same.

She'd expected to see the City looming back there, watching her as it always had. There were only hills. Hills spiked with gray treetops. Hills bulging into the sky. All of it seemed so alien; like she'd landed on some distant planet where, instead of the angular crystallizations of skyscrapers and the comforting regularity of right angles, nature had conspired to make something softer, but strangely more menacing. That feeling from the night before of having been launched into space returned. She realized that in this new world, she was the alien. She was the thing that did not belong.

Ella checked her phone. Nothing from Timothy, still—just the dead end of the message she'd sent him through her social media account: *I need to stay at your place in East Gish for a while. What's your address?* Of course there was no response, she reproached herself, he doesn't even know you. Then she noticed the less frigid reason she may not have heard from him: there was no data signal out here at all. It seemed preposterous; a necessary conceit in a bad thriller. Where in this modern age was there no data service?

—Here, apparently.

So that the battery wouldn't wear down, and still nervous about being tracked through the device, Ella powered off the phone and let it fall back into her purse.

Behind her, climbing out of the car and dragging a noisy, unfurled swath of a map after him, Andy went to the hood of the car. Laying the map out, he struggled to keep it flat in the wind.

Plucking four small stones from the roadside on her way back, Ella came up beside him and pinned the corners of the map in place.

"The finish," Andy lamented.

"I don't give a shit about the paint job, Andy, I'm planning on keying the thing up before we bring it back."

He stared at her.

"That was a joke," she said. They both turned to the map. "Where are we?"

Andy shrugged.

"Don't shrug, Andy!" He was silent and didn't return her gaze. "You were driving, you should know where we are!"

"And you were in the passenger seat," he said quietly, a little acid in his tone.

"What's that got to do with anything?"

"Navigation is the responsibility of the person riding shotgun."

"Says who?"

"Says everyone, Ella. Everyone says that. It's established. That's the job of the passenger."

"I fell asleep."

"I know you did, that's why we don't know where we are!"

They looked at each other a long moment. Ella said, "If you'd told me your expectations, I wouldn't have fallen asleep. I would have paid attention."

"It's established," he repeated, leaning over the map, spreading his hands out wide across the hood. After a moment, he jabbed a finger down and, tapping conclusively, said, "I was following Thirty-Six. I don't think I turned and it looks like Thirty-Six runs right through East Gish. I don't think we passed through it."

"...Don't *think* you turned? ...Don't *think* you passed through it?"

He picked up the stones from the hood and chucked them off into the woods and stood struggling in the breeze to get the map closed up. It folded up as thick as a carp, but he seemed resigned that he couldn't do it any better. At the driver's side door he paused to say,

"We'll keep going. There'll be a sign along the road that'll let us know if we're still on Thirty-six and how far we've gone."

Back in the car, when Andy depressed the starter, nothing happened. Just a dry click as the plastic button rubbed against its plastic housing. As though he might not have pushed hard enough the first time, he tried again, holding the button down for a long second.

"Don't tell me you left the battery on," Ella said.

Andy didn't respond. He tried the button again.

"Goddamnit, Andy!" In the back seat, the Caveman had started making a pained mewing noise, a wavering whine—the perfect soundtrack to wind Ella's agitation up another notch. "What the hell are we going to do now?"

They got out and stood on the roadside, their bags on the ground around them. The Caveman was still whining. Ella turned to look at him. Stooped over slightly, he clutched his stomach, his face reddish and veiny. "Jesus," Ella said. "What's wrong with him?"

"He's hungry," Clara said.

Ella picked up her bag in one hand and took the Caveman's hand in the other and started away, in the direction Terry's now useless car had been heading—further into the wilderness. Although, to look around the roadside, there wasn't any deeper they could actually get so long as they stayed on the road. They were right in the middle of it. There was nothing but wilderness around them, everywhere.

"Where are you going?" Andy called from behind her.

Ella didn't turn to say, "Ernie's hungry. There's no point in standing here." She kept walking, dragging the stumbling Caveman along.

"We should stay with the car," Clara said. "Someone will come along and get it fixed and we can go back to the City."

"Come on, Clara," Andy said. "Ella's right, there's no point staying here."

The girl humphed and fell in line behind him.

•

They walked paces apart like strangers brought together by calamity. The road rose up to a pinnacle, where the countryside lay exposed below them, grayish hills stretching into the distance. Ella had assumed, despite the earliness of the season, that the country would be exhibiting more life than this. Fragile wisps of grass shivered at the roadside, but the world was mostly gray. Hulking clouds hung overhead, like an inverted model of the land around them. When the road pitched down again and the view was blotted by evergreens, Ella was haunted by the notion that they were trapped in a weird continuum, where the road was the back of a giant ouroboros and that, at the next incline, they would rise and rise, eventually traversing the giant, gray hills overhead, shuffling along until they ended up here, right back in the valley of these gray evergreens, where they'd started.

Too tired and hungry to keep going, the Caveman twisted his fingers out of Ella's grip and sat down in the road. Ella stopped. Turning back, she waited until Clara and Andy caught up. Together they stood around Ernie as he slumped onto his side, watching them from the corner of his watery eye.

"We shouldn't have left the City," Clara said. "Why are we out here?"

No one answered her. Handing off her bag to Andy, Ella bent down and scooped the Caveman up. Cradling his head on her shoulder, she started off again. Andy fell in beside her. The road wound upward again, out of the valley, and Andy said, "What are we doing, Ella? What's the plan?"

She wished she had one. She didn't and so she stayed quiet.

After a few more paces, his voice louder and pinched with anxiety, Andy said, "Clara's right. We shouldn't have left the City."

Ella flashed him a hard look. "I didn't ask you to come. I didn't ask any of you to come. I was supposed to be alone. That's all I wanted."

Andy looked away and said, "I get it. You weren't going to wake me. You were just going to leave."

"Yeah. That's it."

At the top of the hill, there wasn't any view, just the road behind them, dipping and rising until it vanished into the trees. Ahead the view was even shorter: the road made a tight turn, slipping off into the forest.

"How do we even know we're going the right way?"

"We don't, Andy."

Clara had started complaining again, "We shouldn't have left the City. All we're doing is putting Ernie in danger."

Nestled up against her, the Caveman had fallen asleep, but came awake abruptly when Ella stopped short and snapped, "Shut up, Clara."

Stepping to Ella defiantly, the girl dropped her bag, saying, "No. You did this. This is all your fault."

"Shut up, Clara," Ella said again. She wasn't looking at the girl. She was looking back the way they'd come. An incongruous, familiar noise broke over the hiss of the wind. It was an engine. Clara, finally picking up on the sound, turned back, too. It was growing louder. Cradling the Caveman tighter to her chest, Ella made a dash for the roadside.

"Where are you going?" Andy wanted to know.

Spinning abruptly to face him, Ella said, "They're looking for us and if they find us..." She let the possibilities go unexplained (she didn't really know what they might be) and slid into the culvert at the roadside.

Andy and Clara stood still in the middle of the road, watching Ella scamper off.

Halfway down the pebbly incline Ella turned back to the pair, hesitating again. "Come on!"

Andy looked from Ella to Clara, who'd abandoned her bag in the roadway and started toward the oncoming noise, waving her hands dramatically over her head as though practicing the gesture for when the vehicle came into sight.

"Andy, we have to hide."

The imperative seemed to decide it for him. Rushing to the roadside and tossing the bags down into the culvert, Andy turned and raced back, grabbing Clara's bag in one hand and scooping up the girl in the other. Kicking and screeching the moment her feet were off the ground, Andy hurried her back to the curb and slid down into the ditch beside Ella.

The rumble of the engine was glacial now, shaking the ground. Instead of one insular thing it sounded like a whole herd of disparate beasts stampeding—a thousand hooves pounding, a predatory growl, a hiss of giant lizards. Clara was still screaming and though Andy fought against the girl's kicking legs and struggled to stifle her yelping, Ella realized it didn't matter, she could barely hear the girl over the noise when the eighteen wheeler rocketed past with a brief clang of Rock 'n' Roll blasting out from the driver's window.

Clara squirmed free, scurrying after the truck, yelling, "Help! Help!" and waving her hands over her head again. The driver must not have noticed. The truck kept going, rounding the corner out of sight, the noise falling away after it.

Ella and Andy climbed up the embankment into the field of Clara's sharp gaze.

"Look what you did!" The girl gestured down the road in the direction the truck had gone. "That was our chance. Ernie's going to die out here, he's going to starve to death and it's your fault! Both of you!"

Ella barely regarded the girl. She'd already started forward again, following in the wake of the truck. The long, arching arms of evergreens at the roadside were still swaying from the passing disturbance, but beginning to settle again. Ella said, "Ernie's not going to die, I won't let that happen."

They moved on, Clara keeping to the back of the pack, muttering her disapproval so quietly, it seemed like she was preparing for an argument she had scheduled for a later time.

•

The first house they passed was boarded up. So was the second, but Ella paused in the street, looking at it. It looked familiar, if only because it reminded her of the card from the memory game. Only the trees around it were different and the front yard was a mess of tangled weeds, brown and brittle like they'd been left in a toaster oven too long.

On the front porch, she set the Caveman down. He came clumsily awake again, swaying as he found his feet and starting to mew again, clutching his belly.

"What are we doing, Muffin?"

"He needs to eat," Ella said. The boards over the front door were nailed into place, but the nail heads had gone rusty, bleeding brown stains into the grain of the wood. When she wedged her fingers in behind the boards, Ella found the nails had been reduced to brittle, porous posts, like they'd been fashioned out of coral. They let go with a pop when she tugged. She threw the board aside.

Behind her, Clara was complaining, "Why are we stopping now? The building's boarded up. We need to keep going. That truck was going somewhere. We need to follow it."

Once all the boards were down and tossed aside, Ella turned to look at the girl. "He needs to eat," she said again, more steadily.

The door yawned open like the house had been waiting for them. Maybe that was why Ella entered so confidently, picking the Caveman up again and striding into the musty darkness. Underfoot, the floor felt solid, a fact belied by the smell of decay in the air.

The windows had been sealed with plywood, sharp beads of light illustrating the edges of the panes. The small living area was comprised of a couch and a padded, wooden chair half circling an iron stove on a pedestal of blackened brick. Behind the living room, a kitchenette and above that, a loft with a bed, pillows nestled up against the wood railing.

"We shouldn't be in here," Clara said.

Moving to the couch, Ella felt the fabric (it was dry, tacky with dust) before setting the Caveman down. In the kitchen, she was bothered by a sharp, rank odor. Beside the refrigerator, the bathroom door stood open. When Ella got close enough, she could tell that was where the stink was coming from. She shut the door without looking inside and the smell seemed to ease.

Returning her attention to the matter of food, she let her hand rest on the door to the fridge for a moment before abandoning the idea. With the place clearly abandoned for so long, she suspected she wouldn't find anything inside but a greater miasma. The cupboards didn't hold anything edible, though. Empty boxes littered the shelves; ragged holes left in the cardboard implicating rodents as the thieves.

Turning back, she found Andy and Clara standing dumbly in the center of the room, staring at her. The Caveman was laying on his side on the couch, cooing sadly with hunger again.

"We should have flagged down that truck," the girl said.

"Well, we didn't." Turning to Andy, Ella said, "It's cold in here. Get a fire started. I'll be back."

She went to the door, stopping when Clara seized her by her bandaged wrist. Ella flinched, pulling the hand away.

Quietly, presumably so that Andy wouldn't hear (he'd already gone to the stove as directed) Clara hissed, "I don't trust you. I don't trust that you aren't just going to leave us here."

Ella knelt before the girl. Straightening out the front of the girl's parka, Ella told her, "I never wanted you here. I didn't ask you to come. But you're here and I take responsibility for that. Okay?"

The girl glowered at her silently.

Looking past the girl to Andy, where he'd hunched down, before the open mouth of the wood stove, Ella said, "Clara's gonna come with me to help, okay?" Looking back at the girl, Ella repeated, "Okay?" and gave a nod.

Andy threw a hand over his shoulder and kept working, stacking bits of kindling in a teepee inside the mouth of the stove. Ella turned to the door.

31

The Great Wilderness

Red in Gray

The First Night

The clouds above, once such a certain harbinger of rain, had started coming apart. The day was warming as sunlight worked in fitful, flitting patches on the forest floor. Moving further and further away from the road, the girl complained the whole time, "I don't know why you think we're going to find food out here... We shouldn't be going this way, we should be following the road."

Ella ignored her until Clara got the hint that she wasn't going to get any sort of rebuttal. They continued on in silence, Ella bothered by the obvious presumption that the girl was right, in any case. In the shadows of the woods, nothing much grew. It was too early for anything to have sprouted. In the darkest patches, beneath the trees and on the cold sides of big stones, mounds of glassy snow hunkered in stubbornly.

Coming to a clearing, Ella paused when something sweet brushed past her. The wind rose and carried the scent away. Sunlight sat on her face a moment and then disappeared as a cloud drifted overhead, blocking it out. "This way," she said and turned sharply, moving on again.

"You're going to get us lost," Clara complained, but fell in line behind Ella anyhow.

After a few paces, Ella paused again, netting the girl before she got past. Ahead, a deer lifted its head to give them a cautious glance.

When Clara started to speak, Ella tightened her fist into the girl's parka and she went quiet. The deer blinked at them and, bowing again, returned to grazing. Behind that one deer, five others foraged, all spread out through the trees. Stepping softly and picking at the tufts of tawny grass on the forest floor, none of them seemed concerned about the new pair in their midst.

Crouching, Ella only moved her eyes from the deer for a moment to survey the ground at her feet. Just out of reach was a fist sized stone, laying in a depression in the earth. Watching the deer again, she shifted forward, prying up the rock, the underside of it cold and grainy with mud. With the same deliberate patience, she rose up, drawing back her arm.

"You can't be serious," Clara whispered beside her. "You're not going to kill a deer with a rock."

Ella shushed her, but didn't need to: the deer made no move at the sound of Clara's voice. It kept pulling tufts of grass from the ground.

Steadying herself, Ella aimed her sight at the animal's head, playing out a vision in her mind of just how things would go: she would hit the deer smack in the temple and it would fall to the ground, jerking; if not instantly dead, then mortally wounded. She started forward with her swing.

The rock shot out wide when Clara dove into her. Not expecting the hit, Ella tumbled to the ground, leaning up on her elbow just in time to see the girl running out into the woods, clapping her hands and shouting.

The deer scattered and, vaulting away, were gone so suddenly, the woods falling so silent again, it was hard to imagine they had really been there in the first place.

Ella bounded up. "What the hell was that, Clara?"

The girl looked at her triumphantly.

Ella grabbed the girl's shoulders, shaking her. "What the hell was that? What the hell do you think you're doing?"

Clara knocked her hands away. "What the hell are you doing?"

"Don't you swear at me."

"You swore first."

"I'm bigger than you, Clara, I can do what I want." Looking into the empty woods, in every opposite direction which the herd had scampered, Ella said, "Why did you do that?"

"What were you going to do?"

Ella glowered down at the girl. "I was going to get Ernie food."

"You were going to kill a defenseless animal—which is against the teachings of the Neo Hominem..."

"I'm not Neo Hominem, Clara, and I thought you were worried about Ernie starving."

"So you'd kill a defenseless beast..."

"It's food, Clara. Animals are meat. That's where meat comes from."

"Ernie's a vegetarian."

"That sounds like a luxury that might be ignored for the time being."

"And what were you going to do—slaughter it with your bare hands?"

Ella stared at the girl. "You don't want this to succeed. You don't want me to find food for him."

"It isn't safe here. We need to go back to the City. We shouldn't ever have left."

"Even if you're right, right now getting food is the only priority."

"The teachings of the Neo Hominem..."

"I don't care," Ella said, but her attention was called away again, this time by a bird that had fluttered down at the edge of the meadow behind them. Again, that delicate, sweet scent brushed by Ella.

"You aren't going to kill a bird, Pearson," Clara said pointedly.

Ella ignored her, pushing her aside to cross back to the clearing. With a chirp the bird lifted off, disappearing into the sky.

At the edge of the forest, spindly little vines with round, dark green leaves climbed out of a slushy pile of snow. Again—that faint sweetness in the air. The snow was dense and half ice and so it didn't fall away when Ella tried to brush at it. She dropped to her knees and started digging. There, buried in the snow, little, impossibly red berries clung to the vines.

•

Clara had refused to help and so Ella had made a basket out of her shirtfront to carry the fruit. In the end, there weren't very many of them, maybe half a pint's worth.

At the cabin, the girl resumed the argument she'd kept up the entire walk back: "What if they're poisonous?"

The room was warm and lit in shifting orange with the fire in the open door of the stove. The smell of woodsmoke had pushed back the earthy stink of the place. Andy looked down at the fruit, where Ella had dumped them on the countertop. Ella said, "They aren't poisonous. They're partridge berries. They grow around here."

"How do you know that?" Andy wanted to know.

"Well, I know they grow around here because I found them growing around here. And I know they're partridge berries because… I just know, all right?" In her mind she could even hear the latin name, *mitchella repens,* being sounded out. She kept that to herself.

Looking at the berries again, he didn't seem convinced.

"He needs to eat and this is what we have to feed him."

"This is a mistake," Clara argued. "If he gets sick out here, what will we do?"

"He won't get sick. They're partridge berries. They're good to eat."

"I don't know, Muffin. What about his special diet?"

"Well, we aren't going to find a box of Frosty-Puffs growing from a goddamned tree, Andy, and I'm telling you: they're safe."

Her confidence seemed to decide it for him. He said, "Okay," and nodded. "Just a little at first, though."

"Okay." Ella gathered up a handful and brought them around to the couch where the Caveman had given up making noise. He looked very pale, but when Ella held out her hand for him, his eyes brightened, landing on the berries in her palm. It was the carefullest she'd ever seen him eat, plucking them one by one from her hand and chewing each with a groan of satisfaction.

Ella looked over her shoulder to Andy when her hand was empty. "You see?"

"He might still get sick," Clara said.

Ella nodded, sure he would be fine, but deciding to give into the girl for the sake of diplomacy. "We'll keep an eye on him for the next hour and if nothing bad happens, he can have more. How's that sound?"

Clara crossed her arms and sat heavily in the wood chair, but did not argue.

•

In fitful stages, as though the girl were fighting inevitability, Clara's mood brightened. She fed the Caveman the remaining berries over a succession of four courses and in the final one had let herself go into a fit of giggles as the Caveman ate, more and more clumsily, reverting to his old habits. "He's got them all over his face," she said and laughed.

True enough, the Caveman had a big clown-smile of berry juice around his mouth.

"Careful you don't waste them, Clara. Tomorrow I can get more but tonight, that's all we have."

The girl nodded earnestly and started taking more care, finishing off her handful by telling the Caveman he needed to slow down.

Outside, night had fallen. Staring into the warm glow of the fire, somehow, Ella had ended up huddled into Andy's side, his heavy arm over her. Maybe it was the fire. Its warm, orange glow reminded her somehow of the envy-inducing gild in Dawn's suburban chateau. Only now she wasn't jealous—somehow settling on the notion that this ramshackle, abandoned little place was every bit as comfortable and even more homey than Dawn's house. The light and the warmth were her own: and seemed of a better quality for that reason alone.

"I'm happy," she said, a little surprised by her own voice.

When she turned to look up at Andy, he was staring into the fire dumbly. She looked away, so he wouldn't ruin the spell she was under.

At bedtime, Clara and Ernie took the loft (Ella having eased her rule about sharing beds, as this was a unique situation) and Ella and Andy moved the furniture to the edges of the room and laid down together on the warm, worn carpet before the stove. The fire kept Ella up, the light dancing on her face until it burned down to shimmering coals. The Caveman was snoring. It was the loudest sound in the cabin after the crackling of the fire had died down.

"I think I could stay here, Andy. I think this was where I was meant to be."

He was quiet, but he wasn't asleep. He stared at the ceiling.

"What are you thinking about?"

He turned to her. "It's weird, isn't it?—that neither of us remember our past, but you remembered partridge berries, just like that."

"It's not weird" she said reflexively, but the thought kept her awake even after the light in the fire had died out altogether. It was weird.

32

The Fire Gone Cold

The New Predator

Sabotage

Ella woke to the now familiar sound of Ernie mewing with hunger. The first peep from the little man had woken her, but it took her awhile to get up and moving. Despite the renewed chill inside the cabin and (more surprisingly) in spite of the ruinous filth that was everywhere around her, she felt perfectly at home. In her absence the previous day, Andy had busied himself taking down the plywood from some of the windows. The stark morning light illuminated what had been invisible before: thick cobwebs rounded out the corners of the room, a pale slip of dust covered everything so that it all seemed plainly spectral—a frail gray-laced ghost of a lamp hanging overhead in the place where a real lamp had once been. To ease the feeling that she'd brought her family into purgatory, when she rose and walked by an end table, she brushed her finger against it. There was a real table beneath the dust, but the fact the she'd needed to prove it at all was unsettling in itself.

After getting Ernie fed again, she would have liked to spend the remainder of the day getting the place clean—wiping all those tenacious ghosts away. But, in the loft, standing at the top of the ladder, it became evident that the day didn't intend on according to her plans. Sitting up, Ernie clutched his stomach, mewling. Beside him was another kind of ghost: an empty dent in the sheets where Clara must have slept. Gathering the little man up in her arms, Ella hurried back down the ladder and rushed to Andy's side where he was slowly acclimating to the day. The panic must have been obvious in her hurry across the room. He sat up straight.

"What is it?"

"Clara's gone," Ella said, turning to survey the cabin and confirm what she'd told him. Clara wasn't anywhere.

"What do you mean, gone?"

"It isn't a goddamned anagram, Andy, she's gone!"

He shot up. As though Clara were a tiny tchotchke, easily overlooked, he hurried up the ladder to examine the loft for himself. "She's gone," he announced with some bafflement.

"I realize that, Andy. I already goddamned told you that."

Hurrying down as quickly as he'd gone up, he stammered, "What do we do?"

Ella pushed Ernie into his arms. "I'll have to go find her," she said and started for the door.

"What about Ernie?" In Andy's hold, the little man had revived his bawling. He had his fist stuffed into his mouth and was suckling dryly at it, the hand muffling the noise. Andy said, "He needs food."

"I know but it'll have to wait, Andy."

"But, what if… What if…"

"Andy, pull yourself together," she snapped. It seemed to do the trick. He stopped muttering. "She probably hasn't gone far. The sun hasn't been up long." She made a move again, to go for the door.

"But what if you don't come back? Ernie needs food and I don't know how to get it for him."

"Why wouldn't I come back? Of course I'll be back."

"But what if…"

"What choice do we have, Andy?"

He nodded to himself resolutely and crossed the room to Ella and, forcing Ernie back into her arms, said, "I'll go. I'll go find her, she's my responsibility. You take Ernie and find more food. We'll meet back here."

It was a better plan than hers, she had to admit.

•

Outside, with the Caveman nestled in her arms, swaddled up in the grimy blanket he'd slept in, Ella gave Andy a long look. He nodded and walked out to the street, moving determinedly.

"Andy?" she interrupted him.

He stopped to look back at her.

"The other way."

Andy turned around to look up the roadway in the direction they'd left the car. He hesitated. "You're sure?"

Ella nodded.

"How do you know?"

"I just know. I knew about the berries and I know about this."

"Okay."

The fact was, she thought she could smell the girl on the wind—a vague electric twinge in the air—and the wind was blowing in from the same direction they'd come the day before.

•

The sun was still too low to see and the woods were pale and gray and Ella felt exhausted, but she didn't set the Caveman down. He'd given up sucking on his fist and in place of his pained mewing, was burbling happily, as though he knew they were on their way to breakfast. Ella would never admit it to anyone, but she'd grown to like the happy little noises he made and the way he felt so warm against her, even when she was more bothered by the dimness of the forest than by the chill.

At the clearing, a group of tiny birds had congregated around the pile of snow she'd half cleared the day before, taking to the air when she got too close. One of the birds dropped a tiny pearl of red as it ascended and quickly swooped back to snatch it from the ground before taking flight again. The flock had cleared away a little more of the snow, the scrape marks from their beaks evident in the slush. Setting the Caveman down, Ella crouched forward and clawed some of the snow away, exposing more tangled vine laying across the rock beneath. Little red bulbs of berries clung to the snaking plant. Moving aside, Ella gestured to the exposed trove and told Ernie in a funny French accent she hadn't realized she was capable of, "Zees morning will be a buffet for ee-ou, zir."

He seemed to like the accent and seemed to understand. Abandoning his woolen shawl on the ground, he crawled to the vines and hunkered down for his feast. Ella sat on the ground beside him and watched while he ate, staining his fingers and lips red. He was smiling so widely, he could barely keep the food in his mouth.

"Slow down, Ernie," she told him softly. "It isn't an all-you-can-eat buffet. What's there is all there is."

He seemed to understand that, too and worked more deliberately, taking each berry like a tiny pill between his fingers and thumb and popping them one by one into his gob and chewing each much longer than he needed.

During his meal, a small brown bird had descended from a nearby bough to stand, jittering on its twiggy legs, and flinching back and forth between Ella and Ernie, as though trying to determine what they were made of and which of them might pose the bigger threat. In flittering hops, he came closer until he settled on the rock beside Ernie, to share in the meal. Ella watched the thing. She thought, the Neo Hominem were wrong in thinking Supplicants belonged in the City. Ernie was an animal, it was easy enough to see here in the wilderness, easy enough to see when you could watch him feed beside a beast. This was where Ernie belonged, Ella thought, right where he sat. She turned and looked up at the sky. Billowy, cherubic clouds had caught the first light of the sun, stark white against the frosty blue. It would be wonderful when the sun was higher and on her, but even this wasn't so bad—this refracted eminence of it. The forest, where she'd expected a contrary silence to all the noise in the City, was alive with sound.

The bird's beak clicked against the stone as it gobbled berry after berry. The wind made the trees shake with papery gasps. Birds twittered. Far off, a crow barked.

Ella looked back at the bird, only inches away from Ernie. It was very small, hardly anything to it at all, but it was meat in the end and, in spite of what Clara had said, Ella knew the Caveman couldn't survive on partridge berries alone. If they had any nutritional value it wasn't much and certainly wasn't well rounded. She sat up, the bird giving her a tentative glance before jerking down to snatch up another berry.

She was impressed with the speed of her own reflexes when she lashed out, managing to catch the thing before it could leap into the air. It gave a soft warble as she crushed it in her fist. The world around her had gone quiet. Turning and looking at Ernie, he'd given up eating, his red fingers falling away from his mouth. His jaw hung open and the half chewed berry inside fell out onto his sleeve, leaving a bloody mark.

"Don't," she said.

This time, apparently, he didn't understand. At the sound of her voice, he began wailing. Ella scampered to her knees and crawled to him, throwing her arm around his shoulder and hiding her murderous hand behind her back.

"Don't, Ernie, don't," she said softly as he continued to bawl. She turned his face to hers and he finally quieted, starting to sniffle. "You need to understand, this is how the world works. You need to eat, yes?"

He nodded like he knew, but a moment later he was turned away, yowling unhappily again. Ella tried to turn his face but he locked up and wouldn't look at her. His eyes were open, frighteningly wide and staring out into the woods at the clearing's edge.

"Oh, shit," Ella stammered. Getting her arm under his ass she staggered up off the ground.

At the edge of the clearing a multitude of pissy-yellow eyes peered from the shadows of the forest. She hugged the Caveman close to her, whispering in his ear, "Don't look. Don't be afraid."

He buried his face in her neck as the first coyote stepped, snarling, into the clearing.

"Go away," she commanded. It slunk closer. When she yelled louder—this time abandoning her words—it jerked, the hair on its haunches going spiny, but it didn't retreat. After a moment of wary thought, it slunk closer still. Beside her, Ella heard a snap from the forest and turned to see another coyote coming in from her flank, its ears twitching in anticipation. Ella did a quick pirouette. None had come around her back side yet, but there were seven of them, half enclosing her and starting to separate, moving to surround her, all of them lowly growling now. There was no way she'd outrun them, that was obvious. Hefting Ernie higher on her shoulder, she looked back at the closest beast, the first who'd entered the clearing. His ears were back on his head. His lips curled, exposing long, yellow teeth. The smell of death was on his breath, the smell of rotten meat, of things devoured and turned to shit.

"No," Ella announced, taking an assured step toward the animal. It went lower, twisting its head at her and growling more insistently. "NO!" She kicked at the ground, spraying the thing with loose dirt and pebbles of ice. It flinched back and, as though in a forethought feign, when it rose up again, it was suddenly airborne.

In mid-flight, she swiped the beast across the muzzle. It went sideways, landing on the ground and skittering away. Righting itself, it wrinkled its nose and shook its head, sneezed, and glowered at her. None of the others had come to join him. They'd all backed off a pace, as if concerned about what this new predator, with a tiny kill in her hand, might be capable of.

"Go away," Ella said. "This one is mine."

The coyote seemed to think it over and, huffing, backed itself into the darkness of the forest. One by one, his snarling companions fell in behind him.

•

Ella didn't rush. She came out of the woods watching over her shoulders for any sign of the pack but, if they were nearby, they stayed hidden. As it was, she emerged on the roadside a little further up than she'd gone in and so she had the chance to see Terry's car glide by with Andy at the wheel. Finally, she broke into a jog, following the car to the overgrown driveway beside the little cabin.

"What the hell is going on?" Ella said, when Clara and Andy got out of the car. The girl marched angrily toward the cabin and stomped inside, slamming the door at her back. Ella looked to Andy, "The car's working? I don't understand."

"I think Clara should be the one to explain that," he said.

Inside, the girl was silent and stared at the floor.

"What happened to the car, Clara?" Ella asked. The girl just stared sullenly downward.

Ella turned to Andy and he shrugged and nodded at Clara again. "Tell her."

The girl toed the floorboard beneath her and finally said, "I disconnected the starter."

She was muttering so quietly, Ella barely heard. "What did you say?"

Clara flashed her a look, suddenly venomous. "I disconnected the starter while you and Andy were asleep."

"Why would you do that, Clara?"

"We were supposed to stay there, by the car and someone would have come along and then we could have gone back to the City, where we belong."

"Why, Clara, why would you do that?"

"Ernie doesn't belong out here, he's supposed to be in the City, where he can learn from the Neo Hominem, where he can learn how to be Neo Hominem. Not out here with the animals, like a savage. It's in the teachings; Master Thompson says..."

"Enough!" Andy announced and Ella flinched at the sudden, unexpected impact of his voice. "You're grounded, Clara. Go upstairs to your... loft."

The girl stomped up the ladder. A moment later the bedsprings shrieked when she flopped down with all her weight.

When Ella found her composure again after Andy's outburst, she went to his side and squeezed his arm. "Nice parenting."

"What?" He shook his head and a moment later found his laughter, burbling in his throat. "Oh, that? Thank you."

"I did a little parenting myself," she said and showed him the bird she'd slipped into her pocket. It was gruesomely twisted.

Andy winced. "Jesus, Muffin."

33

Pioneers

An Agreement

The Story of the Neo Hominem

After Andy had the fire going again, Ella had cleaned the bird (even less beneath the feathers than it had seemed) and fitted it on a spit. It cooked instantly. The milky skin went golden; all the bloody parts paling into shades of white and gray. Ella took what little she could pick from the bones and fed it to Ernie. It took some getting used to, feeling his tongue flit the meat out from her fingers but she found she didn't mind much—once she got used to it. He was loving it; obviously disappointed when the spartan, greasy meal was finished.

"He's lost weight already," Andy said.

"I know it."

"It can't be permanent, us living like this. You know that, too?"

She nodded, arguing despite the gesture, "I'm having more luck. I found the berries yesterday. Today the bird..." She'd decided to keep the episode with the coyotes to herself. Andy would only worry, and she'd already settled on some precautions that she thought would keep anything like that from happening again.

"It's not just the food, Muffin. Have you noticed how filthy we've gotten..."

She had. She was trying not to dwell on it. She said, "Tomorrow, when I go out for food again, I'll look for a river or somewhere where we can..."

"Ella."

She fell quiet.

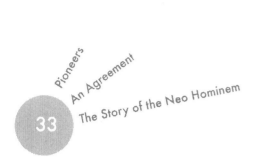

"We can't just hide here." A ripple of laughter ran through his voice, it sounded like nerves, or maybe his own surprise that he was the one to state the obvious.

"Why not? If we can find food and we can keep clean..."

He chuckled and shook his head. "If you want to live like a transient, it would be much easier in the City..."

"We're not living like transients, goddamnit!"

"No?" His voice was quiet. He looked around the place. "That's kinda what it looks like."

"Well, it isn't. We're living like..." Now she felt forced to examine the ramshackle little cabin herself, finally settling on the word, "pioneers."

"Okay. We find food, we manage to keep clean, what about the other things?"

Ella shrugged. "What else is there, Andy?"

"What if Ernie gets sick... What about your prescription?"

"I haven't even used it since we got out of the City." That was a partial truth: she'd had a few doses, but much fewer than she would have had during the same time period in the City and had started feeling, more and more, like the Represitol was something she could live without. She was confident that, in time, she could ween herself off it completely. Strangely, that seemed a promising prospect, maybe for the first time ever. Even with the incident with the coyotes, she felt much more at ease here... wherever they were... than she had ever felt in the City and she told Andy as much—omitting, of course, any mention of the predators she'd encountered.

"Okay. What about the other things..."

"Other things... Other things... There's nothing else, Andy. We can live simply..."

From the loft, Clara shouted, "His education! He needs to learn to be Neo Hominem!"

"You're in timeout, young lady," Andy snapped. Out of sight, the girl went quiet.

In that moment of silence, Ella didn't think she'd ever felt closer to Andy. Looking at him now, for the first time she considered that she might be falling in love with him. She tried to bury the thought. Yes, she was more at ease here than she could ever remember having felt, but she didn't need to get carried away with sentiment. Not just yet.

As if in an effort to correct her romanticism, Andy said, "But, she's right. What kind of future is there out here for him? He needs to learn..."

"Why is it only about him?"

Coming up to Ella, Andy laid his hands on her shoulders and waited until she raised her head and met his gaze before he said, "He's the future, Ella. You can see that now, can't you? You can see the way he's growing; the way he's learning."

Ella nodded. "What about Clara?"

Andy looked confused. "What do you mean?"

"Clara knows the teachings. She's good at math and could teach him that and how to fix things and, as long as no one starts calling her Master, I don't see the harm in it. I know a lot that I could teach him as well. Language and, I think I've proven myself a pretty adept forager and," she had a tough time with the word, remembering Ernie's face when she'd crushed the little bird, "hunter," she finally managed.

"Ella..."

"Just for the summer. We don't have to make it permanent. We could just stay the summer until things in the City blow over... There isn't even school in the summertime, anyway, is there?" Andy was silent, looking at her. "I can't go back, Andy. You do what you have to, but I can't go back. Not now. And, I think I'd like it if you stayed—all of you. I see a future here for us."

"Maybe just a few days, then," Andy agreed after a moment of thought. "We have the car for a week, anyway, isn't that what you said?" In a brief pause, he nodded to himself. He said, "We can have our vacation and see how it goes..."

•

When Clara was allowed down from the loft and took the chair by the fire, Ella started toward the door.

"Where are you going?"

"Well," Ella turned back. "If you're giving Ernie a lesson, I thought I'd go out and try to round up some more food."

"Why don't you come and learn, too." The girl gestured to the open space on the couch, between Andy and Ernie. Frustratingly, Andy sat staring at the girl, rapt with the same humble dumbness with which he'd looked up at the dais at the Assembly Temple. Ella felt herself mildly repulsed and had to look away.

"I don't think so. I think I've learned all I need to know about what you have to teach and... I don't want to be a distraction."

Andy's attention came away from the girl. Ella was happy to see the more sober expression on him until he said, "Clara's right. If it's a family vacation, we should do things as a family..."

"I don't think so," Ella said, but she didn't move. Both Andy and the girl looked at her expectantly. When Ernie turned to look at her too, Ella shook her head and came forward. "Fine. I guess."

She sat down on the couch.

For a moment, Clara stared at her feet, kicking loosely above the floor, as though unsure where she should begin, so Ella said, "Most religions like to start with a creation myth. Perhaps you should start there."

The girl flashed her a quick look. "I don't need your help."

"Sorry. Whenever you're ready."

The girl continued staring at her. She kept it up for a moment longer, before returning her gaze to the floor and seeming to summon her words from that spot, "The Great Creator is responsible for it all. That's how it begins. He gave a name to the trees and the animals and the sky and he made the buildings..."

"The buildings, too?" Ella's voice brought the girl to a halt.

The girl gave her a hard look.

"You asked me to come and listen and I'm only trying to help, Clara. The fact is, the construction of a building and the creation of a tree are two very different things..."

"It doesn't matter who made the trees."

"Of course it matters who made the trees. You can't claim your Great Creator is responsible for everything if there are things he isn't responsible for. A house is made out of boards, boards come from trees, so you can't really claim the Great Creator represents the beginning of anything, if your mythology doesn't account for where fundamental things like trees come from."

"It isn't mythology, Pearson. I'm talking about our history, the beginning of our world. Besides, not all buildings are made out of boards. Most buildings in the City are made from glass and steel or stone."

"So where did those things come from?"

"Our Great Creator made them," Clara insisted.

Ella shook her head, "No, they come from the ground, from minerals and ore..."

"May I just tell it!?" The sudden shrillness in Clara's voice shut Ella down but only for a moment.

"If you're going to be the teacher, you'll have to learn to field some questions, Clara," Ella said quietly, plainly.

Clara and Ella both looked to Andy as though he were the defacto arbitrator. He shrugged. "I think Ella's right, Clara, if you want to be a teacher, you'll have to deal with questions."

Clara started again, fiercely insisting, "The Great Creator made the world, he made the buildings..."

"I gotta stop you, Clara. God did not make the buildings. Men made the buildings..."

"When did I say God? You're supposed to sit and listen but you clearly don't want to learn, otherwise you wouldn't keep interrupting me. Maybe you should go." The girl gestured to the door.

"No, if you're going tell Ernie this garbage, I kinda feel like I should fact-check it: your *Great Creator* did not make the buildings, Clara. People make buildings. All I've heard so far sounds like a farce to me."

"I'm not a liar, if that's what you're trying to say."

"You sabotaged the car, that doesn't seem so far off from lying. And you didn't tell anyone you did it, which is tantamount to lying, anyhow."

"You don't know what you're talking about!"

"Ladies, ladies," Andy interrupted. "If this is going to be our classroom it needs to be civil."

"May I just tell it?" Clara asked him and Andy gestured for her to go on, giving Ella a chastising look afterward. Clara said, "The Great Creator made our world, that's the plainest way of saying it. He's responsible for it all..."

"I appreciate that you're leaving out the buildings this time..." Ella muttered.

"I said everything, so that's included too, okay?" The girl hurried to continue before Ella could interrupt again, "He made us, too, okay? He made us to serve Him, to aid Him in His plan of perfecting the world. He built us in His own likeness and made us perfect..."

"We're not perfect, Clara." Ella laughed. "I mean, I know I'm not perfect. Neither are any of you." She looked at Ernie and in a sly, humorous voice said, "No offense."

The girl's tone kept getting sharper. "He made us just the way he wanted us, that's our perfection..."

"But we aren't perfect, Clara."

"Of course we are. Look at us."

"No, we're not perfect. We forget things; that isn't any kind of perfect."

"We forget, because he made us to forget. We're perfect: exactly as he intended us to be."

"Why would he want us to forget?"

The girl seemed stumped, but only for a moment. She said, "If we didn't forget, how could we see the beauty of a sunrise? How could we hear the wonder in a piece of music? It would just be the same boring thing, everyday. Now, may I continue?"

Ella was quiet, but she didn't want to be. She wanted to argue, otherwise what was the point in her having sat down?

"You see," now the girl'd turned to Ernie, explaining to him in a more courteous tone, "the world was in disarray when the Great Creator found it. It was chaotic and violent and disorganized and the Great Creator set out to bring it into order, to replace the cruelty he saw with peace. We were His worker bees, His very angels. That's who the Neo Hominem are. You and I," she said, pointing to Ernie and then at her own chest and then, as if a distasteful afterthought, quickly, to Ella and Andy. "Where He said flowers should be sewn, we planted them. That was our charge. Where He wanted food in abundance, we reaped and made feasts. Where there was war, we brought it to an end. When He had something that needed building, we would build it..."

"So, he didn't make the buildings, after all," Ella said flatly, as an aside and was ignored.

"That's who the Neo Hominem were. Everything was as it should be. Then, without warning, the Great Creator quit the earth..."

"Quit the earth?" Ella straightened up, laughing warily at the phrase. "What does that even mean?"

Beside her, Andy gave a shush.

Clara said, "He was gone. Vanished. We were abandoned. Around us, the world began to crumble. While we were more than capable of helping Him when He needed help, in His absence we floundered. We did not have His gift, the spark of imagination that makes creation possible. Without His guiding hand, the world slipped back into disorder. It has, forever since, been sliding deeper and deeper into disarray..."

"Wait, hold on a second..." Ella said but Clara kept going, talking right over her:

"...and since that day, it has been our mission, the duty of the Neo Hominem, to bring our Creator back, to usher order and purpose back into the world." The girl leaned forward, having locked eyes with Ernie. A bead of drool had started down his chin from his open mouth, as he stared back at her. She said, "It's you, Ernie. You are descended from our Great Creator. You are our Great Creator, risen again..."

Ella cut her off, "Wait, wait, the world hasn't fallen into disorder, Clara. I mean, it's always been like this. You're little, you couldn't know: there wasn't ever a golden past. There was never any Garden of Eden." Ella hitched her head toward the door. Outside, the day had already started slipping away. "It's always been like this. Always a little good and a little bad; always a bit of a mess. That's the way the world is and always has been and no one made it that way, that's simply how it is."

"If no one made it, then where did we come from?"

"People have been asking that question since forever. The truth is, the earth made us. Nature made us, the same as the trees. Everything on the planet is a simple, confounding matter of chance. It's beguiling, it's unsettling, but that's how it is."

Shaking her head vigorously, Clara said, "No, you're wrong. It's just too simple to say, 'we're just here; we simply exist'..."

Andy was looking back and forth between the two of them, as if he wasn't sure which of them to believe. With Clara's spell on him broken, Ernie had gone to simply resting his head on the arm of the couch.

Ella said, "...Simpler than saying some goofy deity came down and gave us everything, prepackaged?"

"That isn't what I said."

"Clara, the fact is, these are problems that people have struggled with for ages: Where did we come from? What's the meaning of it all? The truth is, we came from nature, the same as the birds and the bees and the trees..."

"I'm not the same as a tree."

"No, of course not. You're not a bird, either, are you?" She felt an arc of anxiety flash inside her, thinking again of the bird she'd crushed, but she went on, "Nature has a lot of variety. And the fact is, life only has whatever meaning you want it to. It doesn't really mean anything, not outside of what meaning you give it. What's important is living with integrity: telling the truth, not tampering with people's cars..."

"You don't tell the truth."

"Of course I do."

A sudden pounding on the front door broke the moment.

"Who the hell is that?" Ella turned to Andy.

He shrugged and then flinched when another round of knocking shook the cabin.

34

The Visitor
A Warning
An Invitation

Keeping the children behind her, Ella pulled the long, hook-ended poker out from the collection of fireplace tools beside the stove as Andy went to the door. Another round of knocking thundered through the room as his hand fell on the doorknob.

"Who is it?" Clara asked nervously, when Andy let a gust of the cold outdoors inside.

Ella turned back, heartened to see that, like a diminutive clone of herself, Clara had positioned herself defensively in front of Ernie.

"Keep quiet," Ella whispered before returning her attention to the door. Andy had it half open, but in the nighttime out there, Ella couldn't see anything.

Andy was saying, "Oh, okay. That's very nice of you." He stepped out of the doorway, letting the door open wide.

"Andy..." Ella hissed and took a step back, closer to the children as the man who'd stood outside entered the room, hunched and sideways in order to fit through the door. Now she could see that what she'd mistaken as the darkness of the night wasn't darkness at all, but rather the man's colossal bulk blocking out the evening. When he was through the doorway, the thinning twilight outside was visible—a world reduced to gray tones, a yellow smudge banding the horizon, behind a tangle of branches. Straightening back up, he seemed to fill the space, she couldn't even spot Andy behind him, but heard the door close. "Andy?" she said again and brought the poker to a half backswing. It shook in her grip.

The uninvited visitor didn't seem to notice. Crossing to the kitchen, he set down the big bags he'd been holding—items that had somehow blurred with his giant carriage. Even without the bags in his arms he didn't look diminished in the least. Finally noticing Ella, he took the big, wide brimmed hat off his head so that she could see his face clearly. Very gently, he said, "There's no need for that now, miss."

She let the poker down but kept it tight in her hand.

"I didn't mean to startle you." He hitched his head over his shoulder, to the bags on the counter. "I just brought some food and candles and necessities. I thought you could use them."

Ella stared at him steely. "Who sent you?"

The man gave a cautious look at Andy, still standing by the door. When he looked back at Ella he said, "My name's Daryl. Really, I didn't mean to frighten you."

"I'm not frightened," Ella said.

"No," he laughed, "no, I can see you're not. You might put down the truncheon, all the same, as you're making me a little nervous."

Ella was hesitant to let it go. She knew now she was good against a coyote unarmed, but she doubted this man would back off if she slapped him on the nose.

"I'm from town," he said.

"What does that mean?"

He shrugged. "Nothing, I guess. Only that I'm from East Gish."

"How'd you know we were heading to East Gish?" Ella said. In her hand the weapon shook.

Daryl looked to Andy again, briefly. Looking back at Ella, he said, "I didn't. The fact is, ma'm, you're in East Gish."

"We are?"

"The edge of it, but yes. I was just being neighborly, stopping by. That's all I meant by it. I saw the boards come down yesterday and I thought I'd just bring a little welcome basket for you all." He nodded over his shoulder to the two big bags on the counter. Then he nodded at the poker in her hand. "It's all right if you don't want to put it down.

Last thing I want is to make you nervous. Please promise you won't club me with it, though," he said and laughed gently. Even for how soft his laughter had been, it seemed to fill the place like a timpani, bold and generous and unabashed. It was impossible to fear someone with a laugh as encompassing as that. Still, Ella fought to keep her poise. When she didn't respond, his laughter died and he said, "All right, then. Would you do me a favor, though?" He made a little gesture for her to move aside.

Ella looked behind her, to Ernie, where he hid. She stepped away, just a pace.

The giant, Daryl went down to a knee, looking at the Caveman. "Come here, little man," he said softly and looked to Ella to see if it was okay. She nodded and stepped aside another pace, but jerked the end of the poker again, to remind him it was there. The Caveman hobbled past her and up to the giant. "He is handsome," Daryl turned around after a brief inspection of the boy to tell Andy.

Ella flashed Andy a stern look. The man just shrugged.

Looking at the Ernie again, Daryl said, "Awful hairy, though. I didn't expect that."

Finally vindicated that someone else had noticed, Ella put her weapon away.

•

At the wood stove, Daryl stirred a small pot of stew. Diced onions and carrots and cubes of meat roiled in a cloudy broth under his supervision. He was a better cook than Andy: the food didn't smell like sewage at all and no one was sent running for a fire extinguisher.

"So, exactly what does it mean: Reclamation?" Ella asked.

If she hadn't been watching him so closely she would have missed the way the question affected him. He seemed to freeze for a moment. Giving one more gentle stir, he covered the pot and returned to the wooden chair beside the stove. He was much too big for the thing and had to shimmy his hips from side to side between the armrests to wedge himself in. The chair groaned, accommodating him. After situating himself, he said, "I'm not a technical guy, really. I'm more of a grunt in the operation."

He said it as though he were explaining something, but Ella realized he hadn't given up anything at all. The big man's attention wandered to the floor again, to watch Clara and Ernie playing patty cake. He wasn't looking at Clara, though. Since he'd come in, he couldn't seem to avert his gaze from Ernie for more than a few moments.

From her spot on the couch bedside Andy, Ella looked to the boy as well. She was beginning to see something of what everyone else seemed to find so easily when they looked at the little guy, though she still struggled to identify exactly what it was about him that was so alluring. Maybe it was that same thing that had always annoyed her in Andy: the unrefined curiosity, the wonder with which they both seemed to regard everything. The difference was, in Andy it had always seemed buffoonish; despite all that wonder and curiosity, he never seemed to learn anything at all. Now she could see that the same did not hold true for Ernie. He was learning. He was learning a great deal and relatively quickly. It was evident: even while his voice was still too frail to be heard over Clara's, his mouth was plainly moving in time to her cadence, "Patt-y cake, patt-y cake..."

Returning her attention to the man in the chair, Ella said, "I wonder if you know an old friend of mine, I guess he does project coordination down there, Timothy Crace."

"Timmy Crace?"

"You know him?"

Daryl nodded in an exaggerated fashion, as though it were implausible anyone wouldn't know the man. "I had no idea that you knew Timmy." He looked away.

"Why's it strange, that I'd know him?"

"Oh," he looked further across the floor, like he was trying to decide how much he should divulge and what exactly he should keep hidden. "Well, truth is: I lied to you earlier. I apologize."

Ella watched him, waiting for him to continue.

On the stove, the pot top had started jiggling, little cascades of stock frothing over the side and spitting from the stovetop. Daryl nodded and wrestled his way out of his seat to tend to it. After taking off the lid and giving a couple stirs and moving the pot further back on the surface, he said, "I didn't notice the boards come down, that wasn't true. Really, I'd have no reason to be this far away from the site. Timmy was the one who told me you all were out here. He was the one who suggested I stop in and see how everyone was fairing."

"Why wouldn't he just come himself?"

Daryl shook his head and returned to his seat. "That's a question for him to answer. Good news is, you'll get the chance tomorrow." He looked around, at Ella and Andy and the children on the floor. "If you're all available: we were planning on a little welcoming soiree… if you don't have other plans. We can always reschedule if you do," he added as a hurried side note.

•

"So we'll see you tomorrow?" Daryl asked at the doorway, after Ernie had greedily gobbled up the stew and promptly fallen asleep on the floor. Andy had carried the child up to bed and, with the absence of the Caveman, Daryl made his excuses quickly ("a long day ahead") and went for the door.

"Yes, of course."

Daryl nodded. "Good. We're all looking forward to it. Plan on about seven, no special dress required. There is one thing, though," Daryl hesitated, looking Ella up and down, "you're all looking a little, how shall I say, ragged, I guess. There's some good, strong soap, in the bag there."

Ella felt herself fill with embarrassment and she tugged down on the sleeve of her shirt so that it better covered the gauze around her wrist. It was particularly grimy. Even in the forgiving light from the fireplace it was evident how black the bandage had gotten.

"If there's one thing Timmy won't abide, it's uncleanliness." The man laughed, but the tone made it evident he wasn't joking.

"Of course," Ella said inwardly. Normally, she wouldn't have abided it either. But something had changed in her after having left the City. Out here, inexplicably, the dirt didn't seem quite so... dirty. In the City, filth had an obvious, unpleasant odor, everything seemed covered in a slick of soured oil. Here, in the woods, even in the cabin, the grime seemed benign—sweet and nutrient rich.

35

Bath Time

The Proposal

Amends

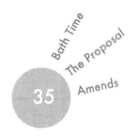

In the brightness of the day, the sun finally having wrenched itself free from the trees, Ella could see that Daryl had been right: they were all terribly filthy. Andy's face was marred with soot from tending the fire and his hands were blackened. Grime of a greater variety covered Ernie, the exact origins of which were harder to pinpoint. Mud caked his knees, some sort of oily stain darkened his shirtfront and the hair on his head was set up in a farce of electrical shock. Clara was the least mired of the three, but the color of her clothes was muted with dust from the cabin. Ella had no idea what she might look like and was content not knowing. The appearance of her companions was enough to keep her apart from them. She led the delegation through the woods by a safe distance of a few yards.

At her back, Clara complained. The contents of the criticism were varied, but kept to a few simple themes: the general dangers of the woods; the foolishness of having left the City; the inevitability of their getting lost.

Ella kept quiet and let Andy practice his parenting. His competence was increasing. When Clara said, "This is so stupid," Andy said:

"Please don't use that word, Clara."

When Clara said, "There are probably dangerous animals out here," Ella tried not to remember the pack of coyotes she'd encountered and was happy to hear Andy say:

"Any animal out here is more frightened of us than we are of them."

Ella liked the hypothesis. It accorded with her experience and, with all of them making so much noise moving through the forest, reassured her that they wouldn't come across anything alive. With the exception of a few squirrels chittering leerily in the trees, Andy's prediction proved accurate.

As Clara changed her tack, "Probably rabid animals out here..." Andy adjusted his, too:

"Stop, Clara, you're scaring Ernie."

Ernie seemed impervious to fear. He must have forgotten all about the coyotes. The little man marched on, his attention drawn to the trees, the squirrels, the way the cool midday sun lay in bright puddles all along the forest floor. He was, Ella noticed, walking with newfound coordination and confidence. He only stumbled when he got distracted.

Worn out on Andy answering every one of her criticisms, Clara gave up announcing her complaints to the forest. Brokering the distance to Ella, she said quietly, "I don't know how you think you're going to find clean water out here."

"This is where I'm from," Ella said, looking straight ahead and keeping to the trajectory that she'd already set. Regardless of the fact that she remembered none of this (it was living, thriving forest after all and would have changed immeasurably since the last time she'd been here), Daryl's disclosure that they were in East Gish filled her with an acute confidence that she could find anything out here that might need to be found. After all, she'd found the berries that had sustained Ernie through those first days. And, in the same way that she'd been so certain of the sweet, piney smell of those little fruits, she was now just as certain of the cool, candied scent of water that seemed to lead her on.

It was hard to tell if Clara was just acting out her dramatic monologue of the universal perils of the forest when the girl spun around and froze up stiff and said, "What was that?"

Ella stopped and looked back. There wasn't anything back there that she could see. "There's nothing there, Clara."

"I heard it. There's something following us."

It was impossible to hear anything with Ernie stomping in the leaves. Stepping up behind the little man and catching him, Andy lifted his head to listen, too. The wind sizzled in the boughs overhead.

Bending down, Ella put her hands on the girl's shoulders. "Nothing's following us, Clara. There's nothing for you to be afraid of."

"I'm not afraid for me, I'm afraid for Ernie. You should be too."

"There's nothing for anyone to be afraid of."

"How do you know?"

"I told you: this is my home; this is where I came from." Only having satisfied herself, Ella started off again.

•

They had to fight through a patch of briars, but when they came out on a bend in the river, Ella felt vindicated after the struggle. The rounded stones paving the riverbed made the river look a little too gray to be welcoming, but it had a nice, inviting burble. The water was shallow, perfectly clear. Ella looked down at the girl, "See?"

Clara refused to acknowledge that they'd ended up where Ella had said they would. Maybe she did remember more of this place than she thought: it seemed preposterous that her sense of smell had led her here.

Coming through the brambles had left a greater mark on Ernie than anyone else. The tender skin on his face and hands was stenciled with thin, pink abrasions that seemed to bother him particularly. He whined and rubbed his arms. Having found a new point of disapproval, Clara went to him and, looking at Ella accusingly, said, "He's all scratched up."

"The water will do him good and we'll find an easier way back," Ella said, already having returned her attention to the water.

It was very cold. Undressed, they all stumbled in, washing themselves with the strong soap Daryl had given them. Ella was the only one who didn't go in completely naked. Half out of shame and half out of fear of having to look at the wound, she kept her gauze wristband on and was careful not to submerge it, so that the fabric wouldn't get waterlogged. With her back to the group and her hand hidden by the blind of her body, she tried cleaning gingerly around the bandage with a little smear of soap froth and a splash of water. The result wasn't great but she left it at that, not wanting to spend too long fixating on a spot of filth that refused to come clean.

Still naked, she washed their clothes and couldn't manage to keep the bandage from getting wet. She set everything to dry on an anemic looking tree that bent out over the water and she went to sit on the rocks, watching Ernie and Andy splash around, both of them laughing.

The little man, despite the coldness of the water, his shivering and his blue lips, refused to get out.

Watching them, both so naked in the barren beauty of early spring, Ella couldn't help thinking that maybe she'd been wrong when she'd insisted to Clara that there hadn't ever been a Garden of Eden. Maybe there had been. Maybe it was right here, beneath her feet and above her head and all around her. Unclothed, with the sunlight brushing her body from tip to end, it was too easy to succumb to the reductive notion that because this was where she came from, perhaps it was where they'd all come from.

Clara sat beside her and asked, "What happened to your hand?"

The wind had already dried Ella, all but the sopping bandage around her wrist. She readjusted herself, taking her forearms off her knees and setting her hands down on the cool rock under her, so that the bandage was out of sight of the girl.

Ella didn't answer and after a moment the girl said, "You ought to change that bandage, it's all black."

Pretending the girl's voice was just another register of the wind, or the mumbled monologue of the river, she let it pass without an answer. After a moment, turning to the girl, she said, "I think I owe you an apology."

Now, it seemed, it was the girl's turn to pretend no one had spoken. She looked out to the river. Ernie was still thrashing about, but Andy had found a rock in the sun and laid himself out to dry.

"The fact is, as much as I insist the Neo Hominem don't have all the answers, I have to admit I don't, either." Ella looked out, too. The trees at the riverbank swayed and set shifting blotches of light on the water, a bejeweled, billowing blanket of gold and silver. Ella said, "I think it's easier for me now, with all this beauty around us, to accept that no one can know with any certainty where we came from. Maybe that's part of the beauty of life: that perfect uncertainty, the mystery of our own existence, all the things we forget, all the things we'll never know. Maybe you were right, that forgetting is a kind of perfection. If I could have remembered this place, I don't know if I'd be so in awe of it now. I have this feeling that this, this world, this place, is where we belong and I don't know how to reconcile that with any sort of coincidence. I feel like we were led here..."

"But this isn't where we belong, Pearson..."

Clara's curt certainty cut Ella out of her philosophizing. She turned to the girl.

"...It isn't where *he* belongs."

"How can you say that when you see how happy he is?"

Ernie had finally been forced out of the water by the cold and had gone up to the sunny rock where Andy lay and had curled himself, shivering, into the man's side.

Clara shook her head. "He's happy anywhere. The fact that you're only seeing it now..." She shook her head again. "And, it isn't about him being happy, anyway. It's about him learning to be Neo Hominem..."

"Why can't he just be a little boy, Clara? That's what he's supposed to be doing."

"Ernie needs to grow up in civilization. That's the point of all this. He needs to learn to be a man, to be a man among men, not a hermit, living in a squat. Master Thompson says..."

"Men live in the country, too. Don't act like you know what's best for everyone. You don't. There's nothing in the City for us anymore..."

"You mean, there's nothing for *you.* Well, it isn't all about you, Pearson."

"I'm not just thinking of me. I'm thinking of all of us..."

"Was that what you were thinking when you snuck into the apartment to get your bag? That it was best for everyone? You were going to run away. That's always been your intention."

"I won't pretend I'm without fault, Clara. I've made mistakes but I want to make this right. I want to make this work with us. All of us—you and me, too. I can't do it alone. I need you to meet me somewhere in the middle."

"But if we decided to go back, you'd still stay. You don't care about us, Pearson. You only pretend to. I see it, but you know who doesn't? Andy doesn't. He deserves better than that."

Ella was quiet for a spell. "I can see a future for us here, I couldn't see before."

"Your future: the future how you want it."

Ella turned to face the child. "And are you being so genuine now, little girl? Huh? Are you really concerned about the Caveman, or are you concerned about having lost all your stupid junk and your lousy *Master.* Maybe I am selfish: you are too. Even if you can't see it, I can."

"And you still call him Caveman. His name's Ernie."

"I meant Ernie. That's what I meant."

"Master Thompson was right, everything here has fallen apart. Look at it, everything is decaying."

"No it isn't," Ella said with a dismal laugh. "It's springtime: look at the buds on the trees, Clara, everything's in bloom. This is how the world is supposed to be. You want decay: look at the Northern District. If anything's falling apart, it's the City."

"Precisely. It's falling into this..."

"I don't want to hear any more about the Neo Hominem's apocalyptic pretensions."

"The world is coming apart and all you can think of is yourself, no concern for anyone else at all."

"The world is not coming apart, Clara."

"Look. Look at it!" Clara pointed around at the shroud of the forest. "It's fading away. Everything is disappearing and you won't even see it. The evidence of it is everywhere, Pearson. The old world is gone. All those boarded-up houses we passed?—you won't even see that for what it is."

"Clara, there are big economic reasons things like that happen, things you wouldn't understand: our society has moved away from farming and... It isn't anything apocalyptic. Your faith has poisoned how you see the world."

"No." Clara shook her head emphatically. "Now, we need to move forward: to remember what we've forgotten, how to care for people, how to protect them. We can't stay here. Why can't you see that?"

"The world is not coming apart, Clara!"

"Then where is everybody?!" The little girl whipped out her hands to indicate the breadth of the forest around them.

Ella scooted closer to the girl, taking a more reserved tone. "Clara, it's the country. That's what makes it the country. If there were a ton of people here, it wouldn't be the country, it would be the City."

Clara shook her head and turned. Looking out over the river, she got to her feet abruptly. "Where is he?" Her voice trembled.

Ella shot up, too. Andy was still on the rock, staring up at the sky, but Ernie was gone. She and Clara staggered forward, dropping into the water, water heaving around their calves. The girl had already started calling out, "Ernie! Ernie!" up and down the river, but Ella yelled:

"Andy, where the hell did he go?"

Andy stood, looking anxiously around. "I thought you were watching him."

"You were right beside him, Andy." Ella started upstream hastily.

Andy and Clara went the other way, their shouts of, "Ernie! Ernie!" echoing off the trees.

•

Ella found the little man just around the bend in the river. He was standing in a shallow eddy, staring into the water. Andy and Clara were still calling out for the boy, though they were out of sight now, their voices reduced to savage grunts carried on the wind, no different than any crow's 'caw' or the crack of a cold tree. With distance they'd become a part of nature itself.

When Ella called out, "I found him!" their voices went quiet.

After a moment, Andy barked back, "Okay." His voice was distant but there.

Ella slogged over to the Caveman. In the pool around his feet a gang of tiny, silvery fish were taking turns nibbling at his toes and Ernie giggled and looked up at her, still giggling. She scooped him up.

"You scared me," she told him. He fell into her chest, clumsily knocking the crown of his head into her face.

Ella turned and, sweeping her gaze through the forest, just caught sight of the coyote at the riverbank, stepping silently back into the darkness of the woods, its pissy eyes vanishing last.

•

Reconvening at the bend in the river, where the tree was flagged with their clothes, Ella tried to keep an even tone when she said, "Why don't we head back."

"Our clothes aren't dry yet," Andy said.

"Ernie's cold. We'll head back. Get everything together, Andy, we'll dry it over the stove."

They started off, Ella holding the shivering Caveman close and keeping a constant account of the forest they passed through. As though a child playing at having his own baby in hand, Andy walked cradling the damp lump of their clothing. He was the last in the pack and, quietly, Clara had slipped up beside Ella.

"I'm sorry," the girl said, after a few steps.

Ella barely heard. She was too intent on keeping a lookout and trying to appear casual at the same time.

"It wasn't fair of me to say all that..."

The girl's voice finally broke through Ella's paranoia. Ella reached out and laid a hand on the girl's shoulder, urging her forward more quickly and saying, distractedly, "It's fine."

The sour stench of wet dog drifted on the wind. The smell disappeared when the breeze turned.

"No. It isn't... Hey..."

Ella looked down at the girl.

"You're holding him too tightly," the girl said, laughing anxiously.

In Ella's arms, Ernie writhed unhappily. She loosened her grip, but the little man kept trying to break free.

"He wants to walk, why don't you let him down?"

"His feet are too tender to walk barefoot," Ella improvised an excuse to keep holding onto him and started moving faster.

Clara was satisfied enough with the answer so that she let it go, even when Ernie looked down at her and mewed plaintively. She patted his bare leg. "It's okay. We're going back to the cabin to get you warmed up." After a moment, Clara said, "Maybe you're right. Maybe it is a good place for him. He does seem happy."

Ella said nothing. She wasn't so sure any more.

•

Back at the cabin, the clothes steamed over the fire but didn't seem particularly clean once they dried, stiff as kale on the stalk and stinking of smoke. They all dressed from their luggage and Ella wished she'd been more thoughtful when they'd gone out: if they'd brought fresh outfits with them, they might have come home a little cleaner.

Though the bath had done them all good, Ella's feet and ankles were stained with muck.

36

Coyotes
Sweet and Sour
Another Proposal
An Abduction

Ella heard coyotes skulking in the dry scrub around the cabin. The snort of furtive, curious breaths sounded at the door, but when she looked outside there wasn't anything there. Only the wind.

She barely heard Andy when he asked if she was alright.

•

She saw coyotes in the solid void of night beyond the window of Terry's car; Andy at the wheel, cutting a path through the nighttime. The beasts ran with impossible speed, the whole pack keeping silent pace with the sedan—dodging through the forest at the roadside with the ease of raindrops on glass, sliding along, slick and unerring, none of them bound to the same tempo but every one of them advancing without fail. The world was full of coyotes.

When Andy parked the car, Ella didn't hear the low, joyful murmur of music reverberating off the tree line. She was too intent on the black chasms between the trunks where a billion, invisible eyes watched her defenseless family step into the warm, windblown night. Coming through the field, Ella kept a hand on Ernie's shoulder, glancing into the gaps between the parked cars, looking for animals hunching in ambush.

Andy asked again, "Are you okay, Muffin?"

"Fine, Andy." She whispered so the coyotes wouldn't hear.

There was nothing between the cars, but every aisle they approached concealed the possibility of coyotes, of teeth and empty stomachs aching to be filled.

"Oh, isn't it beautiful..." Andy said. Ella looked ahead, for the first time spotting the tall, white peaks of the party tent standing proudly just beyond the windrows of parked cars.

Beneath the wash of stars overhead, a lower strata of stars had been erected. Hung from poles, nearly invisible at the shore of the nighttime, long bands of strand lights swayed in the breeze. Partygoers spilled out of the tent, talking and laughing, falling silent when Ella's little family came into their midst. Ella barely noticed the sudden turn of reverence. She stood aside, examining the thumping sidewalls of the tent, wondering if a sheet of canvass could possibly keep predators at bay.

•

Passing through the curtain into the strange interior of the tent, a place where the ceiling of the night sky was replaced with a cavernous white skin but the floor under Ella's feet was as grassy and soft as any meadow, everyone in Ella's sight looked like they could have been Daryl's direct relations. They were all of similar proportions and, it seemed, of comparable humor: the tent rocked with laughter and burbling conversation. On a stage at the far end, a band churned out music which was almost completely overwhelmed by the noise of the crowd. Everyone was dressed in fine country attire and Ella felt a brief tug of embarrassment over her own outfit.

The proliferation of bow ties, tweed jackets and spring dresses only seemed to highlight the plainness of Ella's own clothes—and how filthy she still felt. The effect was so disquieting, it almost turned her right around. But as Ernie was led away by a happy band of giants who seemed like they would be the best possible custodians for him (certainly coyotes wouldn't risk tangling with adversaries so large) and then looking to see that Andy and Clara were chatting with other mammoths, she ducked away into the crowd.

Resolved to find Timmy, she thought it wasn't so impossible a task despite how full the tent was. Inexplicably, she was certain Timmy had not grown into a giant in their countless years apart. It seemed somehow inconceivable that he might have.

Deep in the midst of the giants, Ella moved carefully, protective of her personal space. When a lumbering wall of a man stumbled too close, she set her hand gently on his back. For all his unruly size he was, at least, aware of his expanse. At her touch he stopped and turned to her, bowing apologetically and moving out of her way. Even for all her care, she was jostled again and again until she finally emerged on the other side of the dancers. Here, the floor opened up and Ella could see that the gathering wasn't entirely comprised of giants. While behemoths dominated the dance floor, bands of more reasonably proportioned men and women stood around chatting, watching the spectacle as though they too were concerned with the prospect of being trampled.

Ella paused a moment to look around. None of the faces seemed familiar, but why should they have? Despite her certainty that Timmy hadn't become a giant in their longtime apart, she couldn't find any reason to suspect she might still recognize him. Regardless, she kept looking around until her gaze fell on the face of a stranger, a man who stared right back at her—just for a moment and then he hurried away. Ella started after him but only made it a step before someone seized her arm, bringing her to a stop. She spun around.

"There you are!"

Finding Andy holding her sleeve, with a last look to where the man who might well have been Timmy had disappeared from sight, Ella wrenched her arm free.

"Let's dance!" He grabbed for her again.

"Not now, Andy. I'm looking for someone."

She tried to pull away again but he was already dragging her back toward the dance floor. Behind her, the space where Timothy may have stood collapsed on itself, disappearing behind a closing curtain of partygoers.

•

Closer to the stage the music was loud enough to make out. The spindly clang of a guitar emerged from under the thump of a bass drum. The murmur of the upright bass parted to allow in the acrobatic inflections of the singer. At the front of the stage, the bandleader twisted and rolled around the mic stand like it was an old lover with whom he was reacquainting. Although the performers were of the same heroic scale as those on the dance floor below, the strains of music they produced were of a distinctly delicate nature. They worked through an old Doo-Wop tune.

"I don't want to dance," Ella complained as Andy brought her to the center of the floor.

"Just one." He pulled her close.

She pushed against him. "No, Andy. I don't want to be the center of attention. Dance if you want, but leave me out of it."

She got free of him and edged back to the sidelines, out of the crowd. The place where she'd spotted the potential-Timothy was completely lost. Trying to use the seams of the canopy above, traced out in glimmering lights, the way a captain lost at sea might use the stars to find his way, Ella looked up. It did her no good: the seams stretched away in both directions; identical. She could find no bearing.

"Not much of a dancer, huh?"

Turning her gaze down from the high canopy only slightly to spot the man looming at her side, Ella stopped where she stood.

Daryl hitched his head to the dance floor. "Your boyfriend's got the jitter bug, though, that's for sure."

"He isn't my boyfriend. Not really. I'm not sure what he is."

"That's too bad. I thought the pair of you made sorta a handsome couple."

"I guess. We don't really know each other, though. It doesn't matter how long we've been together, we're still strangers."

"I've always valued learning over knowing." Daryl shrugged. "He does seem sweet on you, anyway." Leaning down to her, his whisper was a huge thing, as resonate as the toms on the drummer's kit. "Did you know, in a past life, I wrote an advice column for a small paper?"

Ella looked up at the man and couldn't help laugh. The thought of him dispensing wisdom to housewives was plainly ludicrous. She said, "Is that true?"

He shrugged and straightened up. There was a glimmer in his voice like he was having fun with her when he said, "Probably not. But it could have happened. The past is such a big thing, I like to fancy I could have been anything at all back then. I've always considered myself a rather sage character, so who's to say it isn't true?"

Ella laughed again. She was surprised by how wary she'd been of him the day before. Despite his size, here, under the golden cast of twinkly lights and with a bowtie of peacock colors closing up his collar, it was hard to see him as anything other than a mammoth toy.

He said, "Well, come on then, let 'Dear Daryl' hear all about it."

Ella laughed again. "No. I don't think so. You don't really want to hear about my sad domestic situation."

"It's your call. I'll tell you, though, I am a pretty astute observer of the romantic heart."

"Well," Ella said, nodding, "you do seem to have the parlance down."

He looked at her sweetly. They both laughed.

When the laughter died away, Ella said, "I think I put everyone in danger for my own sake and now I'm wondering if they wouldn't be better off if I weren't around. It's a weird reversal. I always thought I'd be better off without them and now I'm thinking they're better off without me. It doesn't matter, I guess. Either conclusion is probably true and they both lead to the same end, anyway."

Daryl nodded, looking away. She couldn't tell if he was putting on an act to look wise, or if that was just how he was. He said, "I think... it isn't a decision you should make alone. I think, if you're feeling uncertain you have to be honest and let others make their own decisions. And look at him..." Daryl said, turning back, presumably, to the dance floor.

Ella looked back too. In the crush of bodies, she couldn't see anything beyond a few foot radius of where she stood.

Daryl said, "He does seem sweet, and so very sweet on you, my dear."

"You're right: he is sweet. I'm the one who's sour."

Daryl laughed again. The sound was loud, but in the commotion of the place it didn't seem conspicuous. "Well, self awareness is a virtue, I suppose—though I do think you're being damned hard on yourself. Think about it this way, though: sometimes nothing's better than sweet and sour together. They compliment each other, right?"

"I guess so."

"You should dance, is what you should do," Daryl concluded. "I find the best decisions are often made in moments of joy."

"You know, I'm really starting to believe you were an advice columnist."

Nodding, Daryl said, "I do have a knack for it, don't I?"

"I'm not much for dancing, all the same..."

"Come around and socialize with me a bit, then. I saw your old friend, Timmy, earlier. I know he was looking forward to seeing you again."

•

After leading Ella around, searching for Timmy and failing to find him, introducing her to a string of other friendly giants (whose names slipped away virtually the instant they were announced) Daryl led her to a table that was set up on a riser, kitty-cornered to the stage where the musicians worked, with a good view of the dance floor.

Andy was still out there, appearing between the giants and disappearing again, moving perpetually, with an easy grace that seemed entirely new to him. Ella realized, with a pang of regret, that it had probably been there the whole time. She'd just never recognized it.

So distracted by Andy's confident gyrations, Ella didn't notice Clara and the Caveman at the table until she'd sat, one of them on either side of her. Their sudden appearance was alarming, but only briefly. Turning from one to the other, Ella was overcome with an abrupt certainty that this was exactly where she belonged. The name tag on the table before her concurred.

The table was set for seven, all on the side facing the dance floor and all but two of the seats were taken, now that she had sat. The spot on the other side of Clara had a name tag for Andy and she had to lean further out to see the name tag for the empty seat beyond that one: *Timmy Crace.*

Ernie was at the far end of the table and a seemingly endless procession had lined up along the edge of the dance floor to meet the little man. One after another, partygoers stepped forward, enormous men and giant women, crouching before the boy to say a few words, or just touch him kindly.

When she looked back out at the dance floor, she found Andy again. The longer she watched him dance, the more she hated herself for staying away from him, for punishing him when he hadn't done anything wrong. Finally, she pushed out her chair and got up.

•

"Change your mind?" Andy's voice was close and gently seductive, when she finally found him.

She nodded and he wrapped her up in his arms and they were off, the vaulted canopy spinning above them. She could barely keep up. Seeming to sense it, Andy slowed and simplified his steps and Ella finally found the galloping groove of the music.

Together, they danced to the end of the song.

In the brief lull following, Daryl came forward. "May I cut in?"

Andy nodded and moved away.

The next song was slower and Ella was grateful for that. She could picture Daryl bowling her over to an uptempo tune. But he was a good dancer, too, considering his size. A languid waltz brought them around the room.

"I thought you weren't a dancer."

"I'm not," Ella said, and stumbled.

"You're doing fine."

Above them, a mirror ball had started spinning, tiny fairies of light dancing in counterpoint to the circling crowd assembled on the floor. With the light glittering on her shoulders, Ella thought, maybe she didn't look so underdressed after all—the beads of light looked like little gemstones adorning her; adorning them all.

As they circled the floor, Ella caught sight of Andy. He'd finally given up dancing to stand aside and watch her.

Daryl rumbled against her when he spoke. "Sweet and sour, nothing goes better."

"Maybe you're right," Ella said after a moment.

The song ended and she found Andy on the edge of the dancers, looking at her like she was the most lovely thing in the world. Crossing to him, taking his hand, she said, "Will you come outside with me for a little air?"

•

On the side of the tent away from the parking area, a narrow alley bordered the edge of a cliff, closed off on one side by the tent and on the other by a high a security fence. Beyond the chainlink, a glimmering township sat in the valley below, looking like it had been lit up to match the party. No cars circulated on the streets, no traffic lights turned, but every conceivable bulb seemed to be lit. It looked like it could have been a whole district of the City, biopsied from the neighborhoods surrounding it and plunked down here, in the basin of a valley, surrounded by dark wilderness. Everyone here must have been too used to the sight to notice the grandeur. A few couples had gathered out in the alley to chat, but they kept their backs to the glimmering village. Ella led Andy out to the edge and they both stared quietly for a moment.

"Beautiful," Andy said, and Ella flinched when she turned to find he was looking at her.

"Stop it, Andy." She looked away and couldn't help laughing at herself.

"What's wrong, Muffin?"

"Clara's right, Andy, I am selfish. I failed all of you, bringing you out here."

"What are you talking about, Muffin?" He put his arm around her waist and pulled her close. "This is exactly what we needed. We should have done it sooner."

"No, Andy, you don't understand. It's dangerous out here. I put you all in danger by bringing you..."

"It might be dangerous. You could be right." He shrugged. "The City's dangerous, too."

"I'm not joking, Andy."

"Neither am I. I don't think I've ever seen Ernie happier. I don't think I've ever seen you happier. I know I've never been happier."

"He is happy, isn't he? It isn't just me."

"Of course he is. We all are."

"Not Clara." Ella shook her head, looking away.

Andy laughed. "Clara's never happy. It's too much to expect of her."

Ella shook her head again and looked out over the sparkling township, over the reflection of stars above it. "I don't know. I feel like it'll all fall apart when we go back. I'll forget all of this—the way I feel now, the way we can be together when we're here, away from all the pressure of the City—and we'll just sink back into our old rut."

"I thought we weren't going back."

"It's a dream, Andy. A fantasy. We can't stay here."

"I'll stay. I'll go anywhere you want to be. I know I'm not smart like you, Muffin..." Beside her, he'd gone down on a knee. She thought he was only tying his shoe lace, but he didn't move and so she turned to him. "I just want to be with you."

"What are you doing?"

"Proposing, I think."

She laughed, not minding the sound of it, not minding that it was as inapt as his laughter always seemed. She was happy, genuinely happy. "You don't even have a ring," she teased.

Andy patted down the sides of his jacket and, finding the pockets empty, turned to paw at the ground, coming up with a little viridescent sprout which he twisted between his fingers into a loop. He held it up to her.

Reaching out, she plucked the fedora from his head and threw it into the wind. It wavered, tilting, before disappearing into the night.

Andy watched it sail into the darkness. "My hat."

"Sorry. We both need to learn to compromise, I guess. I'll take a twig ring. You promise never to wear a dumb hat again."

He laughed. He nodded. "I can live with that."

After slipping the ring onto her finger, he stood. He held her close, but only for a moment before his attention was drawn away. From inside the tent a rousing, quick tune had started up. He looked at her expectantly.

"Go ahead. Go dance. I'll be in in a moment."

He did a little hop and spin and, doffing an imaginary hat for her, scampered off. Ella laughed and looked back out at the town again. Maybe that would be the place where they could settle. Or, a little house on the outskirts, on a quiet street with a long brick path leading to the front door, lined with tall iron lamps.

As though privy to her daydream, a boy had come up beside her, explaining, "It's still not safe but we're getting there. Within a few months time it will be completely sanitized."

Ella looked down. About Clara's size, the boy'd wandered up to the fence and stood gesturing out at the town like a tour guide no one had hired. He was wearing a fedora and a snazzy little suit.

"It's almost ready to be populated again. After that, we'll continue West, cleaning town after town until we get to the coast. It's a lofty goal, but the fact that we've made it this far proves it can be done. It'll just take time, that's all."

She looked down at him and nodded, unsure why he was telling her all this, or what any of it really meant.

They were quiet a moment.

"Did you want to be alone?"

"No," Ella said. "It's fine."

"I only came out because I wanted to see you again."

Bending down and lifting the brim of his fedora, she took a good look at his face. "Oh, my god." She dropped down to her knees and held the boy's shoulders. "Timmy?"

"Hello, Ella."

His was the same face, unchanged at all, in the photo she had in her purse. For some reason, even though she'd expected him to look completely different, it came as no surprise that he looked exactly the same. Ella tried to reconcile it in her mind and couldn't and gave up on the notion of trying. They stared at one another.

"You look well."

He nodded. "You, too."

"You look… the same," she said.

He nodded again and reached into his pocket, pulling out a small cardboard square and handing it to her. It was an old photograph, creased down the middle. The ink had crusted off around the edges, looking like an ancient artifact. At some point, to prevent further deterioration, the thing had been laminated. Now it was frozen in a sort of perpetual oldness. It was a photo of Ella and, despite the obvious age of the picture, it looked as though it could have been taken that very morning. It was the same face Ella saw in the mirror everyday.

"Where did you get it?" she asked.

He nodded at the photo and so Ella turned it over. On the back side, in her own hand was written, *April, Ten. Ella.* It made her feel strangely cold holding it. She handed it back.

They looked at each other, that same tense silence between them. "Do you remember me at all, Timmy?"

He shook his head and thumbed the photo before putting it away, as though to say, whatever he remembered was only what he could hold. He said, "Me?"

She shook her head, dug into her purse and found the little framed photo of him and handed it over. He looked at it briefly before looking at her again, a question in his posture. She nodded. Turning the frame around, he unsecured the backing and gently pulled out the photo, reading aloud, "*April, Ten. Timmy.*" He looked up at her. "It's my handwriting."

She nodded and he put it back as it had been and returned it to her.

"I feel like we should have questions for each other."

Ella nodded. "But we don't. What does that mean: that I don't even know what I should want to ask you?"

Timmy looked out over the town. "Maybe just that we need to keep looking forward, maybe that's all it means."

"Maybe," Ella nodded and looked out, too. "So, that's it out there, the Reclamation?"

"Yes." He turned and leaned against the safety fence, thumbing his hat further back on his head. Looking at the party, he said, "In a way, that is, too."

Ella looked over her shoulder, back to the tent. "What—the party?"

"The party, the dancing. The laughter, the music. All of it, if not Reclamation, is at least a *conservation.* It's too easy to forget how important that part is. We can focus on the physical part of the Reclamation but the other part, maintaining the society and our sense of civility, keeping up the old traditions, is every bit as important. We read the old novels to learn how to act. We watch the old films to see how things were. We practice being civilized. After all, that's really what we're working to reclaim. Without it, we're all just savages. The formalwear, the shindigs, all just serve to make us feel like this place is a real home. Someday it will be again and, in the course of it, we all feel a little more..." He paused, searching for the word he wanted.

"Human."

"Yes." Timmy nodded. "More human. Out here sometimes, its easy to feel you're getting further and further away from what we used to be, from where we used to be and who we really are. It's too easy to forget, to forget what it is we're charged with saving. It isn't just the earth we're reclaiming, after all. It's the world, the whole of it we're trying to restore to the way it once was."

"I'd like to see it sometime, if you could show me."

"The Reclamation?"

Ella nodded.

"It's impossible, I'm afraid, for the time being. It's still dangerous down there, especially with our new friend around. I heard you'd named him Ernie. I'm curious to meet him."

"Can we stay, Timmy? All of us, my family?"

He looked at her for a long moment. "That's a conversation we can have. As for right now, enjoy the party. I'm afraid I have a speech to give. But I'll find you later."

Ella nodded. Timmy nodded, too, but they both stayed looking at each other for a quiet moment longer. In the tent, the music wound down and a voice broke out over the speakers, "*Thank you, thank you all. We're going to take a brief break now, folks, while our intrepid leader and foremost foreman,*" affectionate laughter resounded from inside the tent, "*Timmy Crace comes up and says a few words... Timmy, you out there... Timmy Crace?*"

Timmy nodded to her once more. "That's me, I guess..."

"Intrepid leader..."

Timmy laughed bashfully. He made a move to step away and then, seeming to remember something, paused and dug around in his pocket. When he brought his hand out again he was holding onto a little, folded up slip of paper. He held it out to Ella.

"What's this?"

"A gift. I heard you were looking for it and I happened to stumble across a copy. There aren't many left, but I'm not sure that makes it valuable." He shrugged. "Maybe it will help you understand something about yourself."

Ella nodded and took the slip of paper from him. "Good luck."

"Break a leg," he corrected her, and straightened his little blazer.

"It's theatre, then?"

He shrugged. "Isn't all of it? That was Shakespeare's opinion, and who was more human than he?"

Again, the voice called over the speakers, "Timmy Crace, where are you?"

•

When he was gone, Ella unfolded the piece of paper and looked it over. In the dim party lighting it was impossible to make out the whole thing, but she could see that it was the same type of form that Warner had given her, but it was un-redacted and that it had Ella's name on it instead of Kant's. Folding it carefully, she pushed the framed photo of Timmy aside and slid the document into a narrow pocket along the side of her purse. Holding the mouth of the bag open, after a moment she took the photo out again and looked into Timmy's flat face, marveling at how unchanged he was and how unsurprised she was by his consistency and her own. She flung the thing over the top of the fence. It fell away, following Andy's hat into the abyss of nighttime without a sound.

"A lot of littering tonight."

Turning abruptly, Ella found Sickens standing beside her. She flinched back, but only knocked into the fence. It rattled.

"Don't worry, I won't include it in the report."

Everyone had gone in to hear Timmy speak and now Ella and Sickens were alone in the alley above the cliff. Before Ella knew what was happening, Sickens grabbed her shoulder and spun her around, fastening her hands together with a pair of handcuffs.

"What are you doing?"

Sickens pushed Ella down the alley without responding.

Inside the tent, applause rose up and Timmy's voice crackled over the speakers, "*Hello. Hello, everyone...*"

"You can't do this..."

"It's too late for any of that."

Sickens pushed Ella through the field toward the lines of cars at the forest's edge, the sound of Timmy's voice shrinking away to a thin squawk, "*What a perfect evening for all of us. While our project is still weeks from completion on the site below...*"

Ella twisted around, calling behind her, "Andy! Andy! Help me! Someone!"

"*...and we'd all expected to be alone here until then, we have with us tonight, the first of the Supplicants, who will someday fill our new township...*" Applause crackled through the night.

Part 4
Child of Man

37 Return to the City

Far away from East Gish, the sky turned black. A bank of clouds must have moved in. Either that, or Clara had been right all along and the world beyond the car had simply decayed to the point where the sky had crumbled, the stars falling and dying out, like snowflakes landing on the sea. In the glare of the headlights, the road flowed under the car like a river of ashes. If it hadn't been for the stark, orange center line, Ella might have doubted where she was being taken. The line seemed to decide it for her, even when Sickens hadn't said any such thing: she was being taken back to the City. It seemed impossible that that line should lead anywhere else.

"Let me go," Ella pleaded again. Again, she got no response. "Take me back to East Gish."

From the back seat of the cruiser, through the mesh divider, Ella had a view of the back of Sickens' head, the pavement beyond the windscreen and, in between the two, the rearview mirror where a swatch of Sickens' face appeared now and then.

"Am I under arrest?"

Sickens glared in the mirror, ducking away without a word.

"If I'm not under arrest, you have to let me go."

Sickens sighed and shook her head. "You destroyed your metametric device. That's time, plus a fine, if I choose to charge you for it."

"I called you. You didn't show."

"In addition, you lied to employees of the service and interfered with an ongoing operation. Those are even more consequential charges, Pearson. You've managed to assemble quite the rap sheet for yourself."

"Am I under arrest or not?"

"You agreed to help. I don't see much choice for you now."

"Answer the question."

Sickens glanced at Ella in the mirror before returning her attention to the road. "I can arrest you, if that's what you want. If you'd like, I can charge you with it all; reinstate the old charges. You'd be shipped of to the penal colony. But it seems to me that wouldn't benefit either of us."

Ella was silent. The wind hissed at the doors. Beyond the windows, the stars had returned as mysteriously as they'd vanished. Maybe they'd only passed through a long, tall tunnel.

"So," Sickens said, "we can play it that way. Or, we can continue on with our previous arrangement. Which would you prefer? Honestly, it doesn't matter a speck to me."

"Just take me back."

"That isn't on the table, Pearson. Pay close attention: you can help me or you can take the charges. Those are the options. I suggest you consider your circumstances carefully before deciding."

Ella shook her head. "No. Warner told me about you. He told me you have no power, that you can't even lock a door on me."

For a quiet moment the agent seemed to consider it. "He's right. I'm hesitant to admit it, but I like you Pearson, I always have and it's true: I can't lock you up. There is no penal colony. It's just a line we use." The agent's gaze appeared in the mirror, only for a moment. "I do have power over you, though, authority I can still wield. I can punish you and I'll tell you exactly what's within my jurisdiction to do: I can turn you out, set you loose..."

"Freedom? Is that your threat?"

"Freedom isn't what I'm talking about, Pearson. What I'm telling you is you don't want me giving up on you. You've seen what's become of Misha Kant. It wouldn't take more than a nudge and you'd be out on the street, too. Look at yourself. Look how far you've let yourself go. You're half destitute already. Without me, without my help to bring you back into the fold, you're already gone. All that's left for me to do is drop you off in the Northern District. That's all it'd take. Not even a push, just me deciding to let you go."

Ella was silent a long moment before she managed to say, "What are you asking me to do?"

"You already know what you need to do." The woman's gaze was in the mirror again, staring into Ella.

•

With the car pulled over in front of the East Gish Club, Ella was confused for a moment about why she'd been brought here, of all places. It came back in a flood: her unfurnished apartment was just across the street.

"Here?" Ella asked.

The morning had settled in, the cheery light of the day and the innocuous babble of pedestrians on the sidewalk making Ella feel at odds with everything. The City was so stark and concentrated, it seemed too sharp and rich with detail to be real at all. The corners of the buildings, every perpendicular edge, looked honed to cut her to strips.

"You're being released on your own recognizance, because you're going to help me. Isn't that right?'

Ella was quiet.

Craning around to speak through the mesh, for the first time Ella saw Sicken's face in full. In the flat morning light, she looked false and plasticky. A craving for Represitol writhed through Ella's insides. "Aren't you? Pearson?"

"After I do what you need me to, you'll leave me alone?"

"Let me make it clear: helping me is the only way you'll be able to go on with your life. It's the only way any of us will. I need you, Pearson. The City needs you." Sickens watched her face and Ella gave a slow nod. "Is that a yes? You'll help?"

Ella made herself nod again.

"It's the right decision, Pearson. As of now, the charges against you are being suspended. Keep in mind, though, I can reinstate them whenever I choose..."

Sickens watched Ella until she nodded a third time, that she understood.

Climbing out into the day, the agent came around the car and opened Ella's door. After unfastening Ella's handcuffs the agent straightened up and, tucking the cuffs into her pocket, said, "Oh—I'd nearly forgotten—after it all, I did manage to push your petition through. It wasn't easy, but you're on your own, once again; just as you asked."

Ella looked at her wrists, as though the cuffs were still in place. "Oh."

There was a sour note in Sickens' tone when she said, "You seem disappointed."

She was. All she wanted was to see Andy again. But the long night had been exhausting and she couldn't seem to find the words to explain her change of heart and would have felt like a fool if she had. It wasn't any of Sickens' business, anyhow. If Ella was free, she was as free to return to Andy now as she was to remain on her own. And, in the end, it was only her freedom she'd been after from the start. Or, at least it was easy to see it that way now—even if it wasn't quite the truth.

Stepping out onto the curb, Ella started away but Sickens grabbed hold of her sleeve. Ella stopped and turned. Sickens still had the door open. She gestured inside.

Laying on the backseat was a little bundle, wound up in greasy rags. It must have been sitting there the whole night. It seemed preposterous that Ella hadn't noticed it, but she hadn't. Sickens let Ella's arm go and nodded at the bundle. Cautiously, Ella bent in and picked it up.

When she pulled back out of the car, Sickens closed the door and said, "We'll be in touch. I'll let you know how to proceed. And Pearson... Make sure you get cleaned up." The agent gestured toward Ella's filthy wrist. "Make sure you get under that bandage."

Ella nodded and turned away.

Queued up at the crosswalk, waiting for the light to change, she struggled to ignore the man beside her, who was explaining the lights to a little Supplicant whose hand he held. "When it turns green, we can go. Can you say 'green'?"

Ella stared at the light and the moment it turned, she lunged ahead of the pair.

38

A Warning Call
A Postmortem Vista
A Hard Bed

The day passed as if in time-lapse, Ella's mind floating in an abysmal bath of Represitol. She'd had more doses than she'd ever taken in a sitting. On the edge of the bed, she spent so long staring at the certificate Timmy had given her, it had long since ceased making any sense at all. And when the light in the apartment became too thin to continue looking, the type as muddled as any redaction, she turned her attention to the greasy bundle. It lay on the floor before her. A wide ribbon had come free from the coil, reaching out for her, unclean and complicit.

Sickens wanted her to use the device inside against Kant, wasn't that it?

Ella understood it so instinctively, she'd never questioned that the woman hadn't offered up the order explicitly. Even as she'd taken the bundle from the back of Sickens' car, she'd felt incapable of doing what Sickens wanted. That hadn't changed. She hadn't even managed the courage to peak inside the rags. Though she'd made more than one advance to take it up, she'd recoiled each time before her fingers came too near it.

In the dusky stillness of the apartment, when her phone rang Ella jerked, her gaze shooting from the bundle to her purse beside it. Scampering across the floor, she dumped out the purse and, finding her phone, pressed it to her face. "Yes? Hello?"

"You need to go."

"Sickens?"

The woman's voice was icy. "Don't use my name. You need to get out of the apartment right now. You need to go. Do you understand? Dyer's the mole. He sold us out."

"What? Go? Go where? Where can I go?"

The line was already dead.

Ella looked at the face of the phone. A moment passed before she picked herself up off the floor, tossing the bundle and her phone and everything else back into her handbag and hurrying to the door.

The hallway was empty. At the elevator, Ella pushed the call button and looked to the numbers above the doors. The ground floor was lit. She pushed the button again, hard and holding it down a second. The ground floor stayed lit, the elevator frozen in place.

At the staircase behind the elevator, Ella only just got the door open when she was stopped by a whisper of clothing, a soft flood of boots. The click and clatter of armaments rose up the stairwell, louder by the moment.

Spinning, Ella bolted back to her apartment.

From the windows in the living room, she could see a squad of police cars had pulled up, at all angles before the building, blocking the street in every direction.

Hurrying to the back of the apartment, she ducked into the bathroom and went to the window. It was no good. The alleyway below was already blocked off by a cruiser and, even with the window closed, she could feel the bell-tone drumming of hurried footsteps wracking on the fire escape.

Someone was already pounding on the front door.

"Police! Open up!" The order charged the air.

Ella froze a moment and only managed to get moving again when another, more serious assault landed on the door. This was not knocking. This was the singular attack of a sledge hammer or some other blunt key devised to circumvent the lock. The metal panel shrieked and clanged.

In the rear bedroom Ella looked around frantically. She hadn't brought a single thing into the space and now the emptiness of the room was overwhelming. The four corners hosted communes of dust in the tight angles. There was the door through which she'd come. And there was the high, narrow window in the back wall.

In the living room, the newest attack on the door sounded out with finality—a crash and then a second smack as the breached door collided with the wall. Lunging forward, Ella unlatched the window and hoisted herself out.

Mired in panic, it hadn't occurred to her that there wouldn't be anything on the other side of the window until she was confronted with the simple fact.

With her midriff hanging over the sill, Ella paused to look down at the long plummet below. *Never give up,* she thought.

In an old circus movie she'd seen a trapeze artist hang by the tips of her toes. She'd seen a picture of a squirrel perform the very same feat. And if a lowly rodent could do it... *Never give up.*

Behind her a voice blasted, "Clear!" followed by a second, "Clear!" and a stomp of soft soled boots and Ella knew she needed to act.

Twisting her body and latching her fingers onto the ledge, Ella pulled herself out the window. There was another ledge, just below her and another below that and... on and on until they were too small to see, and the view terminated at the open mouth of a dumpster, pushed to the end of the alley. At least she had a safety net. A very distant safety net, full of potentially pointy things. Still, buzzing with Represitol, she was certain she wouldn't need it. Never give up.

Contorted into a shape she didn't know she was capable of, Ella hooked her toes on the ledge and started unwinding herself, pushing the flats of her palms down the brick backside of the building. (Never give up.) She was doing it. She was capable. The next window ledge was only a few hand lengths away and she still had a little reach left. Only, fully extended, did she realize the flaw in her plan. The window below was still out of reach and now there wasn't anyway to get herself turned around. She stretched further.

A little further proved too much. Her toes slipped from the ledge.

•

The drop was immeasurable, both instantaneous and endless. Through the plummet, Ella managed to right herself, pulling her head up so her back would take the brunt of the impact. Not that it would make much difference from this height. These were certainly her last moments. Bricks blurred past in a muddy, rising cascade. She would have liked to think that her life would flash through her mind. There were moments of the past few days she would have given anything to recall and savor: blissful tchotchkes of beauty and honesty and joy: cradling the Caveman close, dancing with Andy… Unfortunately, all she could seem to ponder as she dropped was the simple fact that she shouldn't have climbed out that window in the first place. It was an elementary lesson—learned too late.

•

Ella did not hear the giant, muffled whomp of her landing in the dumpster. And, when she looked up to see the tall building standing over her and the high, blue sky beyond, it was hard to acknowledge that this was not her postmortem vista. Threads of wispy cloud, painted with the setting sun, charged along in unison and it was that movement that seemed to satisfy her that she hadn't been ended by the fall.

Still, she didn't dare move. Above, a dark speck of a figure poked out the open window high overhead. He must not have noticed her, tangled up in rubbish. Before retreating back inside he announced, "Clear!"

Ella sat up. She was covered in filth. Rotten food oozed from her arms and her whole outfit was soaked in rank slime. The smell of decay was overpowering.

Confronted by this new, immediate horror, Ella scrambled out of the dumpster. On her feet, she frantically brushed at her legs and sleeves, the muck sloughing off in gobs.

"Hold it, right there!" The hollered command from the mouth of the alley stopped her cleaning. She straightened up to see a cop marching down the alley toward her. Slowing as he took his appraisal, the officer stopped a dozen paces away, seeming reluctant to come any nearer. "What are you up to?"

"I..."

"You oughta know better than to be here."

Ella nodded uncertainly.

The cop hitched his thumb toward the street. "Beat it. We're searching for a fugitive and we don't need filth like you mucking it up."

Ella nodded again, more confidently, and hurried past him.

"And don't let me catch you around here again. Filthy savage."

On the street, Ella's phone dinged in her purse and she dug it out and turned the thing off, smearing the face with an unfortunate streak of crud. There were cops everywhere and Ella moved quickly, with her head down.

•

She'd gone several blocks before she felt calm enough to throw a glance over her shoulder. The neighborhood she'd come to was quiet. There wasn't anyone following her that she could see.

Stopping beside a trash can, she dug into her purse and found her phone. Turning the device on, she saw that she'd gotten a message from an unknown number: *Am I ever gonna get that date you promised me?* Tail-ending the message was a smiley face. It reminded her of Andy and she felt unbearably alone again.

Mark? It had to be Mark.

Standing a moment, looking from her phone to the trash can and back, she realized it would be sensible to get rid of the thing (there was no denying that) but it would mean losing her prescription. She didn't even want to know what dwindling dividend remained. In the end, it wasn't a price she was willing to pay, even for her own security. She moved along again, into a more distant neighborhood.

Hiding herself in a shadowy doorway, Ella rang back the number Sickens had called from. The phone rang and rang. No voice mail picked up. She waited a few minutes before trying again. After the fifteenth ring, a man picked up with an abrupt, "Yeah?"

"I need to speak with Sickens."

"I don't know who that is." The line went dead.

Ella rang back immediately. The same man picked up after the first ring.

"I need to speak with Sickens!"

"Lady, I told you, I don't know who that is."

"The woman who called me from this number! Sickens!"

"It's a public phone, lady. I need to make a call so…"

"A pay phone? Where are you?"

"The community center on Ludlow." He hung up without saying anything more. Ella switched off her phone and started moving again.

•

It was nighttime before she got to the community center on Ludlow. The place was closed up, all the windows dark.

The street was empty. There was no sign of Sickens anywhere.

Beside the pay phone a vacant wrought iron bench waited and Ella sat down, feeling too tired and alone to do anything else. Above her, as though to complete her desertion, the streetlight flickered and went out. Slowly, Ella crumbled to her side. Curling into a ball on the bench she fell asleep, waking sometime later to the cold dawn, only feeling half alive.

39 Home Coming — It's Decided

In the warming midmorning outside Andy's apartment building, Ella couldn't find any sign of a police presence on the street. She must have waited hours—sitting and watching, circling the block and coming back again, before she found the nerve to approach. With one last appraisal of the roadside, she slipped through the doors.

She was cautious going up the stairs, but in the end, the stairwell was empty. Ducking into the apartment, Ella started at finding Clara standing in the kitchen.

"What are you doing here, Pearson?"

Ella closed the door at her back. "I…"

The familiar racket of TV noise washed down the hallway from the living room. Dropping to a knee to get a better look at the girl as she came closer, Ella said, "It's so good to see you, Clara. I didn't expect you back already." She looked away from the girl down the long, cluttered hallway. "Is Andy…"

The girl shied back from Ella's stench. "Why are you here?'

"I…" Ella said, starting out on one track of thought and then abandoning it. She stood up and said, "I need to get cleaned up. Have the police been by?"

"What do you want, Pearson? Why are you here?"

"Clara, what's wrong? What do you mean, why am I here? I'm home."

"This isn't your home any longer. You shouldn't be here." Shaking her head and looking away, the girl said, "You don't know how hurt he is."

"Well, there's no need for that. I can explain..."

"It doesn't matter." The girl shook her head again. "You should go. It's too late. Everything's changed already. If you'd wanted to stay..." She made a vague gesture.

"This is ridiculous, talking to you like this. We're engaged, Clara. You don't have any say in the matter. Where's Andy?"

"Pearson..."

"Enough," Ella said and pushed the girl aside and started down the hall.

•

The apartment seemed to have changed, but Ella couldn't have said how. An unfamiliar smell, sweetened licorice, hung in the air. There was a bouquet of flowers on the dining table; maybe that was all it was.

In the living room, Ernie was on the floor, playing the memory game with a woman Ella didn't recognize. She was pretty.

"Who the hell are you?"

Impervious to Ella's scalding tone, the woman bounded up from the floor, stepping briskly to Ella to offer her hand. There was a bright note in her voice when she said, "Lydia. You must be Ella."

Catching a whiff of Ella, the woman withdrew her hand. Ella'd made no move to take it.

"Lydia, why are you in my apartment?"

The woman seemed about to answer, but Ernie had risen up off the floor and come between them, his sudden proximity somehow magnetic, drawing the attention of both women. He smiled at Ella. The sound of his voice, fragile and angelic, seemed to ring through her when he said, "Hello, Ella," and offered his hand to her, very formally—a little gentleman in an instant, hardly any drool running down his chin.

Ella was too stunned to take his hand. "You're speaking now?"

Lydia answered in his place, "He's just starting to, yes, but he's picking it up quite well. Amazing what a little attention can do." She laid a loving hand on the boy's shoulder and Ella knocked it off with a quick swipe of her own.

"I asked you: why are you in my apartment?"

The girl seemed about to answer but before she could, Andy's drowsy voice cut in from behind them. "Muffin?"

Ella spun around.

Standing in the doorway, in the unflattering midday light his hunched posture made him look small and sickly and out of place in his own surroundings. "What are you doing here?"

"Why does everyone keep asking me that? Isn't this my home?"

Andy made a move to speak, but nothing came out. He turned back to the bedroom before muttering, "Maybe we can speak in here, for a moment."

Before joining him, Ella gave the pretty woman a lashing look.

•

In the bedroom, Andy closed the door and Ella sat on the bed. He wouldn't look at her.

"What's going on, Andy? Who is that woman?"

"Lydia."

"Yes, yes, I know her name's Lydia. That isn't what I'm asking. Why is she here?"

"Ernie needed a secondary guardian, so…" He shrugged, defeated.

"We've only been apart…" how long had it been: one night; two? It couldn't have been longer than that. She went on, "…and I'm already replaced. Is that it? Thrown out?!"

"I didn't do any throwing, Muffin. I was given the notice that your petition had been approved, by some O.S.A. woman at the party in East Gish. When I went out looking for you, you were already gone, so… I'm happy you got what you wanted…" He shook his head, unconvinced of his own sentiment.

"This isn't what I wanted."

Looking at the floor, Andy was silent.

"Andy, we're engaged."

His posture buoyed a moment but faltered again when his gaze fell on her hand. "Where's the ring?"

Ella looked at her hand, too, aware for the first time that it had fallen away. Of course it had. It had only been barely holding on in the first place. "What—the twig?"

He hung his head. "It's decided, anyhow. Lydia's here and she seems very certain that we'll be happy. She's probably right. She must be. I never had a good sense for those sorts of things."

Ella lunged to her feet, moving close to him. "What are you talking about—it's decided? Nothing's decided, Andy. This is my home. We're individuals. We make our own decisions about who we want to be with."

He just shook his head, refusing to look at her once again. "It's decided," he said.

"Why do you say, 'it's decided,' when you're obviously so unhappy about it? You can decide, Andy. It's your right to decide... You're free to..."

"That isn't how it works... Master Thompson says..."

Ella's fervor fell apart. She didn't mean it as hurtful when she said, "I see. You aren't really a man, after all. You can't decide anything for yourself. You're Neo Hominem," but she knew how it sounded when it came out.

Andy was quiet.

"I won't beg... If you're settled on it..."

"It isn't mine to settle, Muffin," he said into his chest.

"Fine. Well," she let the word sit a moment before going to the closet and pulling out a clean pair of pants and a shirt and a clean jacket. She went to the door and let herself out.

Lydia was still in the living room, still standing and still wearing her dumb optimism as plainly as Andy always wore his, like she hadn't had a single concern since Ella had gone inside the bedroom. They'd make a fine match, Ella thought caustically.

Lydia's voice was unaffected as a birdsong when she said, "So, it's all settled, then?"

"It appears..."

Bumbling over to Ella, Ernie smiled up at her. He had his hand out for her again. "Hello, Ella. It was nice to have known you."

Dropping her clothes on the floor, Ella bent down and took him roughly by the collar, pulling him close. For an instant, she could feel his damp breath on her face, like a breeze coming in from the sea. Flinching at her own might, she loosened her grip and fixed his collar and then took a moment to smooth out his shirt, soiling it with her grimy hands. She barely noticed. "Don't you listen to any of them that this is settled. I'll be back. I'll be back and I'll do what I need to do, what I should have been doing all along. Do you understand me?"

His little, hairy face had become clouded. His smile vanished. He nodded slowly.

"I'm your," she gasped the word, "mother. I'll always be. Don't forget that. Don't forget me."

He nodded again, seeming more certain now and pulling away from her. Ella collected her things and rose up, turning away from the scene.

•

Clara saw Ella out, following her silently onto the landing. After Ella had taken the first few steps, the girl's voice stopped her. "Don't fight it, Pearson. Let it be. It's better this way, for all of us."

Ella turned back. On the stairs, she stood a little lower than the girl. "Clara, he's really different than we are, isn't he?"

The girl nodded. "Someday the earth will be His again... That's what Master Thompson says... But, you don't believe any of that, do you?"

Ella was quiet a moment. "That story you told me, about the Durrenmatt: you worked for Durrenmatt, didn't you? You made machines for them all those years ago, or however long it was?" Ella looked at the girl's tiny, nimble hands: perfect for a clockmaker.

"I loved those machines," the girl explained, staring off, suddenly sentimental. She looked at Ella and said, "But I found out, they weren't really the best. There are better clocks and I get to work on those now, too..."

Ella nodded. "Yes, of course."

When the girl reached out, Ella reached out too, unsettled when the act of kindness turned out to be something more practical. (What had she really expected from the girl?) Drawing back her hand, Ella found the key the girl had passed to her.

"Your boyfriend's car's around the corner."

"He's not my..." Ella started, but let the statement die unfinished and turned around and went down the stairs.

•

At the bottom landing Ella paused, quickly undressing herself. Even naked, she was filthy. Rot smeared her torso and thighs. Gobs clung to her hands and face. With the ruined outfit piled in a corner, she took her clean shirt and wiped herself down. It only improved her appearance marginally. In the new pants and with her fresh jacket buttoned all the way up, she saw that she'd still managed to soil the fabric. Fingerprints darkened the lap of her pants and the lapels of the coat.

She looked at her purse. It was ruined. Taking out her phone and the bundle Sickens had given her and Timmy's slip of paper and stuffing them into her pockets, she left everything else as it was, her purse and clothes abandoned in the corner of the stairwell.

40 Skinned Knees

A Favor Granted for a Favor Owed

Terry's car was where Clara said it would be. In addition to the bird shit and wads of pine sap dulling the finish, a pair of parking tickets had been inserted under the windshield wipers. It wasn't until Ella came around the driver's side that she saw the boot locked to the front wheel. Dumping the key back into her jacket, she turned away.

In the park a few blocks from the car, Ella was dismayed to find that she was more or less indistinguishable from the drove of vagrants that lounged, isolated, in a back quarter of the public area. She stayed well away from them, choosing a bench near the playground. The swing set was busy, creaking and squealing as a group of children, not unlike Ernie, yelped with delight. They were taking turns, swinging as high as they could and letting go of their seats. Flying briefly through the air, they landed, scurrying to keep up with their own momentum. The children still swinging cheered. Ella watched, feeling her despair settle deeper. She'd never even had the chance to bring Ernie here. He would have loved it, though he wasn't nearly as graceful as these children and would not have been capable of doing what they did. Maybe someday he would.

Another child took flight. She was smaller than the rest and, when she landed, couldn't get her feet going fast enough. She sprawled out across the palms of her hands and her soft, bare knees. Without a thought Ella hurried over to the little thing, who'd already started blubbering. Turning her over, Ella could see she'd scraped up her knees, the roughed skin already starting to fill with red, red blood—the color more startling than any Ella had ever seen.

"Oh, sweetie, oh, sweetie," Ella cooed, starting to take the girl up in her arms.

The thing cried so helplessly, Ella barely heard the woman rushing at her from the side, barking, "Hey! What are you doing?"

Ella didn't realize the voice was directed at her until the woman was right there, pushing Ella away and sweeping the girl out of her arms.

Ella stumbled back, stammering.

"What the hell do you think you're doing?" The woman held the child as though to shield her from Ella's good intentions. "Stay away from my child, you filthy..."

Ella slunk back another step.

The woman hitched her head toward the far off crowd of vagrants. "One call to the police and you'll be cleared out, all of you, you understand? Go back to your own kind."

The woman stomped away.

When Ella got her senses back she skulked off to a park bench a little closer to the homeless, but still apart from them. She wasn't one of them, even if she was the only one who would see it.

Taking her phone out of her jacket and switching it on, she looked over the text message from Mark, wondering what the chances were of it being a setup from the cops: an easy net with which to snare her. In the end, she decided she didn't care. She needed a shower—the day's misadventure was proof of that, if nothing else—and either Mark would provide it for her, or the police would. She was too tired to keep running. She rang the number back.

On the other end a man answered, "Hello?"

It sounded like Mark, but how could she be sure? Her mind was foggy from the restless night and the exhausting morning she'd already been put through. "Mark?"

"Ella." He sounded pleased. "I didn't think I'd hear from you..."

"Mark, I..."

"Thought you were trying to shirk on our deal." He chuckled lightly. She thought of Andy.

"No, no," she said, trying to temper her voice. Across the park, her talking into the phone seemed to have aroused the interest of a couple vagrants. "Are you free?"

"Now? It's two in the afternoon..." He laughed. "I'm at work..."

"Oh, right." The thought that there were still people out there with jobs, people whose lives hadn't unraveled, filled her with shame. "What about tonight?"

"Well, okay. Where you wanna meet?"

"I was hoping I could come over to your place, I..." The stale silence on the other end of the phone stopped her from saying anything more.

"Ella..." There was a long pause. Was it a sigh she heard, or a piece of paper being dragged across his desktop? "I kind of just wanted to hang out with you..."

"Yeah, Mark, I want to see you too and..."

"Eh, it's not a good idea, Ella."

"What do you think I'm asking for?"

"We've fooled around... I get that. You've never really taken me seriously. I mean, I'm not asking for a commitment but... I like you Ella, but I can't just be there for you when you... you know."

"So, I can't come to your apartment?" Ella looked around the park, all that bright sun and the dreadful openness. Somewhere in the distance a police siren wound itself up. "I just need..."

"And, what I'm telling you is, I need more than that."

"No, no, you're right, Mark. I can't keep stringing you along. Let's meet up and I can explain..."

"A date, then?" He sounded hesitant, but hopeful. He laughed and said, "You do owe me."

"Sure. Of course. Of course I owe you." She couldn't think of anything else to say. She said, "Wherever you want. Name the place."

"Your treat? You do owe me. How about Dane's? Seven o'clock?"

Ella thought about Dane's, about waiters in bow ties and a maitre'd stationed at the front of the house like a sentry. If she hoped to get in anywhere, it would need to be somewhere darker than that, somewhere she could pass unnoticed. "How about the East Gish Club?"

"Oh. I've never heard of it. Is it any good?"

"Yes," Ella said. "Yes. It's great."

"Seven, then?"

"Yes. Seven."

•

Being back in the neighborhood of her recently raided apartment made Ella nervous, but she was relieved to find no cruisers on the street and, when she stepped inside the East Gish Club, the grimy gloom in the place seemed a perfect camouflage to absorb her. She'd waited until nightfall to come in and, at the back of the room the warm light and boisterous voices seemed like something projected on a screen—something fictitious, illusory and completely apart from her. Ella took a seat at a dark corner table. As akin with the dim filth as she felt, the darkness was oppressive and she worried she'd fall asleep without any light to keep her up and that, when Mark showed, he wouldn't see her and would leave deciding she'd stood him up. She looked at her phone to see how long she had before he was due to arrive. It was already six-thirty.

She needed a pick-me-up and a quick dose of Represitol seemed like it would fit the bill. And the phone was already in her hand. She swiped over to her Pharma App, picking Represitol from the queue. The next screen loaded instantly and she picked the 'single dose' option from the menu. The program started up.

A little glimmering jewel of light blinked into existence on the black screen. It shimmied, cycling through the color spectrum, glowing brighter and bigger as it passed from cobalt into a bay-blue azure and from there to green and yellow. Orange faded into red and the bead of light grew and grew, swelling faster and faster, the colors blurring into a blare of pure, white light, as brilliant as the sun.

When the dosing had finished, she was returned to the initial screen—asking if she wanted another dose. Ella looked to the bar in the back. No one seemed to have noticed her. She looked back down at the phone. There weren't many doses left by the app's count but, slightly refreshed now, she decided on another anyway, in hopes of quashing what anxiety remained, writhing in her mind.

When the second cycle concluded, she did feel better. Her daze of woozy calm made the situation developing around her feel like a dream into which she'd been submerged. She looked up from the screen to see the barman making a hasty decent on her from the back of the room. Shutting the phone off , Ella shoved it into her pocket and sat up straight, trying to look as self-assured as she could manage while the barman stomped to her, shouting, "Hey! What are you doing?"

The charge of his voice caused Ella to sit even straighter, conspicuously rigid now. "Nothing. Nothing, I was just… I'm here to meet a friend…"

Coming alongside the table, shaking his head in disgust, he said, "You're just drugging-up in my restaurant, huh?"

"No. It's not what you think. I have a prescription…"

He came to a stop, staring into her face. "Oh, I know you," he snarled. "You're that woman who keeps coming in, leaving without paying…"

"I didn't…"

He lunged to grab hold of her, seizing up when he'd entered the aura of her scent. He shrunk away. "Oh, I see. I see exactly what's going on. What you are. You vagrants make me sick. You make the whole City sick, spreading your filth around. I oughta call the cops." His uproar had brought the attention of the crowd in the back. The laughter had died. Everyone was looking at her.

"Please don't… I'll leave…" She stood from the chair and took a step away.

"Ella?"

The voice from the door brought her attention around. Mark was standing there, having just come in.

"Mark, thank God." She looked back at the barman. "I'm leaving. I'm sorry I… I'm just sorry, that's all."

Looking her over as she approached, Mark backed to door. Pushing it open, he put a foot outside and made a sort of choking sound. "I… I just realized… Sorry, Ella, this really isn't a good night for me after all… I have…" He gave up trying to make excuses and turned, ducking outside and starting briskly away, down the sidewalk.

Crashing through the door, Ella had to break into a run to catch up with him. "Mark, it isn't what you think. It isn't as bad as it looks. I just need a shower and…"

"I'm sorry, Ella… I wish I could help… but I just…" He wouldn't look at her, even when she fell in beside him. But he did slow down, as though realizing that there wasn't any dignified way to outrun her. When she reached to touch his jacket he twisted away, quickening his pace again.

"Mark, please…"

Arriving at the door of his car, the man had no choice but to stand in her company as he struggled to get his keys from his pocket.

"Please," she pleaded, "please."

She reached for him again. Backed up against the car door, he contorted fitfully away from her. There wasn't anywhere he could go.

Ella found some pity and lowered her hand and took a step back into the shadows, where her filth seemed diminished by degrees. "I understand you don't want to be near me but…" She hung her head.

Sickens had said she 'knew what she had to do,' and Ella guessed she did. There wasn't any other option now. She'd have to take care of Kant. There seemed no other way to get her life back.

She said, "I understand, you don't want to be near me. Could you maybe, just give me a ride to the Northern District, please? I won't bother you any more after that. I promise."

He'd gone back to struggling with the lock, his back to her.

"Aren't we friends, Mark? Can't you just help me with this? Please?"

The locks unsnapped and he ducked into the car and closed the door on her.

Her reflection overlaid him in the glass when she stooped closer. Even for how imperfect a representation it was, she couldn't avoid how awful she looked. Her face was stained. Her clothes were wrinkled. A smear of crud marred the cleavage in the opening of her jacket.

He didn't turn to face her when he said, "In the back seat. Don't touch anything."

41

The Mirror Face
The Doll Woman

Beyond the windows of Mark's car, the streets passed by like a tableau tracing humanity's triumph to its own demise. Skyscrapers, windows glowing to challenge the night sky, mixed with buildings that seemed somehow more permanent, if more rudimentary: brick and stone carved and laid with care; these things were meant to last forever. Further from the city center, the buildings shrunk and lost any trace of embellishment. Rows of homely tenements twisted past and, block after block, seemed in increasing need of repair. Street lights failed at the roadside, until there were no signs of civilization left. Beyond the headlights, the ruins standing against the sky could barely be seen—just the jagged tops jittering past. With every increasing degree of darkness, Mark hurried the car along with greater urgency until he was pushing it so hard it seemed like it might come apart beneath them—the struts rattled, the chassis creaked. The car bounced over the broken pavement.

His driving had become so erratic that when he finally pulled over, Ella scrambled for the door, relieved to stumble out into the wasteland of the Northern District. Before she could thank Mark and get the door properly closed, the car jerked away, the door handle torn from her hand.

Following a savage three point turn, the car blasted past her, the door slamming shut on its own. She raised her hand in farewell. Mark didn't even look at her. Ella closed her hand and dropped her arm and turned up the pathway to the old Hatteras warehouse.

The chains on the front doors had been removed. Inside, Kant's desk lay in a broken pile in the entry. All the paper that had been scattered around it was gone. The blackness beyond the jumble of broken boards was so perfect Ella didn't even consider trying to navigate her way into it. It was obvious: Kant had moved on.

Ella stumbled back to the roadside. She wouldn't last long in this starving darkness, she knew. Her head already seemed to be drifting off, her logic going knotty and incomprehensibly inverted. She was losing track of what she'd come here for. Maybe she'd just come to find some peace.

She'd lay down, she decided.

Everything would be clearer in the morning.

Dropping crosslegged onto the curb, she listed to the side, her head almost touching down on the concrete before a beam of clear, heavenly light landed on her face and, in that sudden blast, her exhaustion seemed to evaporate entirely. She sat back up. Beyond the flare of the flashlight the soft, gray wad of Kant's bandaged head craned to look Ella over. "You okay?"

Ella shrugged and struggled to rise.

"I thought you'd show up before now. I'd almost given up on you," Kant said. "Come on, then."

•

The one armed woman still sat at the side-ended cable spool. The collection of doll parts didn't look to have diminished at all. It gave the impression that time had not advanced, that Ella hadn't been gone even a moment.

As though the place were a refuge from the darkness, a group of transients now filled a corner of the room, sitting on a rug that might have had a fancy woven pattern or maybe it was just an intricate assortment of stains. The group was silent, looking down and acknowledging neither Ella nor Kant when they came in. They stared at the ground and were so still, Ella found their appearance to be somehow self-explanatory: of course they'd come here; though Ella couldn't have said why that was the case.

Gesturing to the table, Kant said, "Sit."

Ella sat and watched the woman with her doll-work. A head and feet had already been fitted to the soft, fabric body. With the doll set aside, the woman dug through a collection of porcelain hands, trying to find a pair. At a glance, all the hands in the pile looked identical but, as Ella watched the woman fret over this hand and that, she began to see what the woman saw: the slight variations in size and detail and coloring. All so similar; all so very different.

As though Ella had asked, the woman said, "Soon the world will be full of children again. It's already starting to fill." A pale satisfaction tinged her voice. "And children need toys. It seems insignificant—even extravagant—these little things, but it's so very important for children to play. It's how they learn, you know, it's how they practice..."

"We've gotten good at practicing too, haven't we?"

The woman nodded but otherwise didn't treat the question as if it had any significance at all. Ella may as well have commented on the weather. Having found a pair of hands that she seemed satisfied with, the woman returned her attention to the unfinished doll.

In the meantime, Kant had brought another chair to the table and sat, looking Ella over for a long, quiet moment.

"Things haven't worked out well for you."

Looking away, Ella shook her head.

"I'm sorry for that. But I think we can still help one another, if you're willing to trust me."

Ella nodded and reached into her jacket. Her hand closed around the filthy bundle. She hesitated, finally pushing it aside and taking out the document Timmy had given her instead. She laid the slip out on the table.

Taking it up, Kant looked it over for a long moment before setting it back on the surface between them. She said, "So, there are still some out there." She looked at Ella. "No luck finding mine, though?"

Ella shook her head. "What does it mean?"

Kant shrugged. "It's a question you'd have to ask yourself, whether it means anything to you at all. It isn't for me to say."

"But you saw what it says?"

"You saw me look at it, Pearson."

"What does it mean?"

"You see what it says. Accept it or don't. It has nothing to do with me."

It was a thin, pale answer to Ella's question. She wanted to know who she was, because she no longer seemed to have any notion. Kant's answer was as worthless as no answer at all. Ella snatched the page from the table and stuffed it back into her pocket. In a fluid motion she brought out Sickens' bundle and slapped it on the table. Behind her, the vagrants bristled at the sudden noise. A moment passed and they were silent again.

Ella'd expected some sort of reaction from Kant. She got none.

"Sickens gave it to me," Ella said, again hoping for some reaction from the woman. Again, she was disappointed. "Aren't you afraid? Aren't you worried what I came here to do?"

Kant shrugged. "I don't even know what's in there. Why should I be afraid?"

"What's in there? Isn't it obvious? It's the same thing you tried to give me on the train. It's the same thing Dyer tried forcing on me. It's a bomb, Kant. What else would it be?"

Kant shrugged and made a gesture indicating that there wasn't any knowing for sure until the object was uncovered. When Ella refused to touch it, Kant leaned forward and flipped the filthy rags away. A waft of lavender defused into the room instantly. Ella looked down at the pale bar of soap sitting in the cradle of oily rags. How had she not smelled it before? The greasy cloth must have kept the aroma down or maybe she'd just been too distracted to notice the scent. Maybe she was losing her mind, after all.

Where before she'd been incapable of looking at it, now Ella couldn't seem to turn away. She was a fool. She'd had, in her possession this entire time, the means to get herself clean. She remembered now, exiting Sickens' car, the woman reminding her to wash under the bandage. She was a fool. Ella put her head in her hands.

"It's okay. It's okay," Kant said, though she didn't seem to understand the problem, not really, not even when she laid her hand on Ella's shoulder consolingly. "It's okay."

Pulling herself together, pulling away from Kant's touch, Ella sat up straight and uncovered her face. Kant had placed another bundle on the table between them, just beside the bar of soap. Its sudden appearance made Ella flinch.

"Tell me it's more soap."

Kant shook her head gently. "There's a more urgent issue at hand." She nodded down at the greasy bundle. "Warner..."

"I already told you..."

"There's nothing to it," Kant said and leaned forward and unfolded the wrappings.

Still hoping there would only be a bar of lavender soap inside, Ella felt herself cringe when she saw the device. It wasn't much bigger than a bar of soap. It had a digital clock face and below that a small, red button. It might have been identical to the device Dyer had shown her —it might have been the very same device.

"You push the button once to trigger it. It'll give you a count of five to get clear..."

"You don't need to tell me this... I don't need to know it...."

"...If you can't get clear, hold the button again and it'll deactivate." She watched Ella's face to see if she understood. When Ella gave no indication, Kant continued, "This is important, though: if you turn the device off, an alarm will sound. Three quick beeps, to let you know it's been disarmed. You know what that means: it means anyone in earshot will hear..."

"I don't know why you're telling me this. I won't help you..."

"It's best to trigger it and leave immediately. That's ideal. Just make sure that Warner will stay in the vicinity for five seconds after you leave. The radius isn't big, but it's big enough to cover a room the size of his office. You understand?"

"I told you, I can't do this... I won't..."

"Warner trusts you, he'll let you near him; closer than any of us could hope to get..."

"That doesn't mean I'm capable..."

"You're capable."

"You say that but you don't know me; you don't know the kind of person I am. I'm not a terrorist... I refuse to be made into one..."

"Warner is the radical. Don't confuse that. We're simply doing what needs to be done. What no one else knows needs to be done," the woman said from behind her mask of bandages.

"I don't even know you. Why should I trust you? You say you're on the side of good, but I don't even know what you're fighting for."

After a moment of silence, the woman nodded and bowed her head and with a slow, deliberate hand, untucked the wrappings at the back of her neck. The bandages loosened and with the help of her hand, coil by coil fell around her neck. She lifted her head.

Ella, who'd leaned close as Kant unwrapped herself, now jerked back, the chair legs beneath her screeching on the floor. Again, the group at the back of the room grumbled at the sudden noise. Ella held herself away, rigid. It was her own face she was looking at. Almost her own. On the crown of Kant's head a gaping hole exposed a milky surface beneath the skin, threaded through with little, flickering filaments. In a moment of panic, Ella thought that she was looking in a mirror at her own face, so horribly disfigured. Touching her forehead, she was relieved to find the skin there still intact. Even so, she couldn't look away, didn't even look away when Kant reached out and took her by the wrist and drew her hand down.

Ella's bandage had been reduced to a brown bracelet, loosely wrapping her wrist. It no longer even covered the wound there. Ella looked down when Kant said, "Oh, you've let it get very dirty."

The wound was packed with grime, but even so, Ella could see how like the wound in Kant's head it was.

"You understand?"

Ella nodded dumbly.

"You see, I know you're capable of what I'm asking you to do, because I'm capable of it myself. And, as you can see, we're the same."

"Twins..."

"Something like that. 'Duplicates' might be a more accurate word." The women looked at each other a moment before Kant said, "Warner's sick, Ella. He's mistaken our role in the world. He can't see that our Great Creator is already here, before us, and that we—you and I—must act as His guardians. We must protect Him."

"They aren't a God. I know it. They can't be..."

"It doesn't matter if you believe it or not. The attack on the Assembly wasn't vandalism. Warner's been working to undermine the Supplicant Placement Program since the moment it was enacted. He's trying to bring back the plagues, Pearson. He'll kill Them, every last one of Them, even your... what did you call him..." Kant stared at Ella a moment before she came up with the word, "Caveman."

"His name's Ernie," Ella said.

"He'll kill Ernie. He'll murder every last one of Them, Ella. He needs to be stopped. You're the only one he trusts enough to let close... It has to be you."

42 A Good Enough Mirror

The Revolving Door

At the foot of the CCI building, a mass of businessmen and women converged, pouring through the revolving doors like water rushing through the neck of a bottle. Ella injected herself into the throng. Around her, marketeers, executives and receptionists jostled, trying to keep their distance from her while, simultaneously, fighting to retain their places in the chaotic queue. Ella was pushed aside but she pushed back, lunging for the nearest door and levering herself through.

Spat out into the lobby, her presence prompted a fresh uproar. Scampering clear of her, an undertow of whispers and nervous gasps rippled through the crowd, like the sucking sound of a wave retreating from shore. Ella hobbled onward in an expanding bubble of isolation. Ahead, at the bank of elevators, the crowd reconvened and Ella was dismayed to find that the gulf around her now included the security desk and the guard behind it.

The man didn't seem to notice her until Ella listed to the side, to join the long, thin flush of people scrambling by her. They lurched off when she approached, like school fish dodging a shark. The sudden clap of hard soled shoes finally brought the attention of the man behind the desk. Striding into the open, he announced, "Hey, you!"

Ella made a scampering half circle away from him, around a stand of fear-frozen women who squealed when she got close.

Despite her effort, in two steady strides, the guard caught hold of her, wrenching her to a stop.

"What the hell do you think you're playing at?" He gave her a hard shake before turning her out toward the doors.

Stumbling as he forced her along, Ella pleaded, "I work here! You have no right to treat me this way." She ground her heals into the slick, polished floor in a bid to stop herself being pulled along but only stumbled, almost falling. The guard hoisted her up, setting her on her feet and pushing her more vigorously.

"Sure ya do," he said.

Digging her fingers under his, Ella tried prying up his grip. He wouldn't let go. He hardly seemed to notice her effort. She set her feet again, skittering sideways. Her foot caught and she stumbled again. Forced to walk or fall, she caught her stride. Through her strain she said, "I work for Mr. Warner. When he finds out about this..."

"Sure ya do," he repeated with the same bored annoyance.

"I'm very important," she griped and returned her effort to prying up his fingers.

"Sure ya are, you're Queen of the goddamned hobos..."

"I'm not a..." he almost had her to the doors and Ella looked out to find the discouraging, cold daylight beyond the glass. Swarms of personnel were still pouring in, the slick sheen of polyester shoulders glimmering in the day. Startled expressions sifted by—executives, consultants, receptionists and... Dawn! The girl's familiar face appeared just beyond the glass partition of the moving door.

Ella was thrown into the opposite quadrant from her errant-receptionist-turned-bossman and she started hammering on the glass as the contraption turned. Looking through the partition, the girl's shock only took a moment to dissolve into something like recognition. (Or was it simply pity?) Ella only had a moment to catch the look. In the next instant, she sputtered outside again, a hulking woman in a tweed blazer trying to assume Ella's spot in the turning door. Ella forced the woman away, shoving herself into the building again. Beyond the glass, the security guard was waiting. Dawn had already disappeared.

When the gap opened up, Ella feigned right and when the guard lunged to catch her, she ducked to his left. Outmaneuvering him, she sailed into the lobby, casting frantic looks to all the well-clad backs advancing away from her.

"Dawn! Dawn!" she paused to call out. In that brief moment, the guard managed to snare her again.

Yanking her back to the door, he said, "That's enough of that. Try it again and I'll call the police."

Ella kept calling for Dawn and out there, in the crowd of bodies sifting away, the girl appeared once more, coming on wearily.

"Dawn! Dawn!" Ella cried out.

Reluctantly, the girl hurried forward, catching the guard by his shoulder and bringing him to a stop. "What do you think you're doing?"

"Miss, stand free. I'm just removing this vagrant..."

"This is no vagrant," Dawn said, gabbing hold of Ella's other arm and yanking her out of the guard's clutches. "This is my receptionist."

The guard leaned back taking a long, uncertain appraisal of Ella. "It is?"

"*She* is."

"I'm sorry, miss, I can't allow vagrants into the building, regardless of their position, it's strict policy." He made a move to collect Ella again.

Dawn pulled Ella closer, seeming to take full ownership. "It isn't *miss.* It's ma'm to you. I'm the Vice President of Operations for CCI and this is my receptionist and we're—both of us—on our way to work."

Without waiting for the man's rebuttal, Dawn turned Ella around and started marching her toward the bank of elevators. The guard scurried to catch up. "Ma'm? Ma'm? I'm sorry, please, I have to insist..."

Dawn paused, snarling back at him, "What is it? Speak or move aside."

"I really can't..." he was looking Ella up and down again.

"Well, it isn't up to you."

"I can't..."

"Do you want me to call Warner and have him straighten this out?"

The man stammered a moment. "Alright. Alright. You'll have to take the service elevator though. I have to insist."

"You can't be serious."

"Please ma'm. I'm very sorry but, please. This is my job we're talking about." A submissive weepiness had crept into his tone.

•

The service elevator was big and noisy. In spite of all the empty space, Dawn huddled in the farthest corner from Ella, staring into the face of her phone and casting quick looks at Ella's feet, as though concerned that her old boss, her once professed best-friend, might start creeping closer.

"I'm sorry about your jacket," Ella said.

Dawn looked down at the sleeve of her blazer to the long line of filth that Ella had inadvertently imparted to her. After trying unsuccessfully to brush the mark away, Dawn stripped the jacket off and draped it over her arm. The silence between them resumed, the elevator shuddering and clanging as it continued to rise.

"How're the wedding plans coming?" Ella asked after a moment.

"Oh... Oh, the wedding..." Dawn seemed embarrassed that the subject had been broached and said nothing more about it. After a moment, she said, "About Terry's car..."

Ella'd nearly forgotten about the car. She said quickly, "It's at Andy's," dug in her jacket and found the key and held it out for the girl.

Dawn looked skeptically at Ella's hand. "It's fine. Keep it. We have a spare set at home. I hope it's..."

"The car's fine, Dawn." Ella let the key fall back into her pocket.

When the elevator stopped, Dawn took pains to exit well away from Ella. She said, "You're okay to..."

Ella shook her head. "Don't worry, I won't tell anyone what you did for me."

The girl nodded and moved away.

43 The God of Monsters

In the office, everyone was so absorbed in their morning routines—cubicle cohabitants staring into their computer screens, chatting over the walls of their enclosures, crossing the room preoccupied with papers in their hands—no one seemed to notice Ella.

Hurrying across the floor, she was relieved to find Warner's receptionist absent but the door to his office was locked. Ella wavered. Staying out here, in plain sight, was not an option.

With her hand on the knob and her shoulder pressing into the panel, she pushed as hard as she could, leveraging what strength she had, digging her feet into the carpeting. The jamb creaked.

Framed in the big window along the far wall, the sun was crawling slowly out from behind the high horizon of city scrapers. She kept pushing, harder and harder as the light around her blossomed up thick and golden like a tide of broth and then, when the sun finally edged out from the skyline, blasting light across her face, the lock gave out. The wood around the handle cracked. Twisting, the latch pulled away from the lock plate and Ella fell into the room. Scrambling up and turning, Ella saw she'd aroused the attention of more than a few employees.

"Sorry," she announced, and quickly closed the door behind her.

•

When Warner came in, he was distracted by the broken knob and stood a moment, fiddling with it.

"Sorry about that," Ella said. She'd taken a seat at his desk, twisted around so she could see the room, back to front.

If Warner was surprised to see her, he didn't show it. He said, "I suppose you'd like me to close it?"

"Please."

Closing the door, the man paused to look Ella over. "You're not looking so well, Pearson."

"I've been through a lot."

"I don't doubt that. And I am sorry for it."

Ella motioned to the other side of the desk. "Why don't you have a seat?"

Warner nodded and crossed the room. Sitting and pretending to examine something on the desktop, he said, "Let me tell you, Pearson, I'm quite pleased with how..."

Ella shook her head slowly. The man went quiet. Reaching into her pocket, she pulled out the bundle and set it on the desk and unfolded the wrappings so the device sat between them, unmasked.

"I see," Warner said. "A gift from Misha Kant, I suppose?"

Ella nodded, once.

"Nice of you to bring it to me." He leaned out of his chair to reach across the table. Covering the device over with a quick hand, Ella shook her head again. Warner fell back into his seat. "Are we no longer comrades, Pearson? Is that what this is?"

"I don't know. I'm not so sure we ever were. You tell me."

Leaning away, Warner tented his hands over his chest. When he spoke, his hands came apart as though he were releasing the words, fluttering birds, into the room. "Of course we are. I've always been on your side. I've always been on the side of all our kind, no matter what Kant might think..."

"She told me you're a villain. That you intend to make yourself a murderer, too."

"Yes, of course she'd see it that way. But, in the end, I'm on her side too, even if she won't accept it." He turned in his chair and looked out over the City.

The sun had gotten higher, lighting everything up in milky morning hues and shocks of silvery glint.

"When you look at the City, what is it you see, Pearson? Do you see the opportunities available to someone like you—a place where anyone with hutzpah and talent, no matter their origin, can thrive?" Warner nodded to himself. "I've worked very hard to make it so. The redactions have helped make it so." When he turned back to Ella he said, "Still, it isn't what I see. I see our own past, a history of enslavement. It's what the City is for me, a constant reminder of the countless indignities we were once forced to endure. The reality of the past, outside of our memory of it, cannot be erased. But, perhaps it's better that way.

"For years—so many years, it can only be called ages—while our community has feasted on useless fictions, imitating a culture that failed itself, I've spent my time pouring through the old archives, cataloging the practical evidence of our Great Creator..."

"Don't waste your time," Ella said. She'd withdrawn her hand from the device, so that only a solitary finger rested on the red button. The movement wasn't lost on Warner, his gaze flitting to her hand anxiously. "I don't believe in fairy tales..."

"It's true, Pearson. There was a Great Creator. At one time, there were billions of them. And their death heralded our liberation. Now, unfortunately, there are a majority of fools running things, who've decided they want them back..."

Ella shook her head heavily. "It's a story for dopes and children. That Kazakian guy, he wasn't any sort of God... Neither is Thompson. Neither are you. You don't have the right to decide who lives and who..."

Warner cut her off brusquely, "You're right, of course: Edward Kazakian was no God. He was a man among men. They're all gone now, but I can tell you all about their race, if you care to hear the truth. They were ingenious and cruel and their greed made them the greatest scourge the world has ever seen: if a God at all, then the God of monsters. They murdered one another, Pearson. They victimized their brethren and taught their children to do the same. They laid waste to nature; they poisoned the air and the water in the interest of their greed. They were barbarians, savages—everyone of them.

"When the Neo Hominem speak of the great chaos long ago, it is the instrument of their Lord and Messiah that they describe. They did not vanquish it, Pearson, mankind was its wellspring—war, evil, suffering, it was all their making, all the work of the Human Monster, the *Great Creator*. No one remembers the way they really were and it is no mistake that those cruel truths are forgotten.

"They made us to forget, Pearson. It was their plan all along to condemn us to ignorance." He leaned forward. "They feared our adding together our days of servitude and realizing the empty sum. They feared what would become of them if we learned to see them for what they truly were. They feared our strength. They feared our wrath if we came to see our *Creator's* true face. And they were right to..."

"You're as bad as Thompson, Warner... All this sermonizing... I told you, I don't go in for old folklore..."

"It's no myth, Pearson. It's too long ago now to remember, to really remember, the way it was for us then but," he leaned back and dampened his tone, overcome with a sudden calm certainty, a satisfied assurance when he said, "you can take some solace from the fact that we won't ever have to relive that old nightmare; that we will not voluntarily offer up our wrists for those old shackles. I've insured it. We're safe now." He held out his hand for her. "It's over. It's done. You can give me the device."

Ella had almost forgotten her hand on it, her finger laying over the button, not quite heavy enough to trigger it. "You've insured it? What does that mean?"

"Do you still have Sickens' little gift? The bar of soap?"

"What are you getting at?"

"You see, that was a very special bar of soap, Pearson. Its cleansing power surpasses all other soap: impregnated with a particularly virulent strain of the virus that wiped out our Great Creator ages ago, that bar of soap has the ability to eradicate every last one of them, every artificially cultivated progeny of our Great Creator..."

"Ernie..."

"Don't give the devil a name, Pearson. It gives him power over you. But, no matter that now—rejoice, you're free. We are all free. There's no longer anything to fear."

"You had me..."

"You're a hero, Pearson. Don't shrink from the significance of that. Monuments should be constructed in your honor. In fact," Warner said and leaned aside to collect a pen and a scrap of paper, "I think I envision a statue of you, perhaps standing in Kazakian's very place, atop the obelisk in front of the Assembly, a statue in heroic scale, perhaps," he chuckled, "clutching a bar of soap to the sky in lieu of a sword." He chuckled again. "The inscription on the base should read, 'Ella Pearson was a servant to no Man...'"

Ella smacked her hand down on the table. "I don't want a goddamned monument..."

"Are you sure? It's well within..." His words ran out as his gaze lingered across the table to the device, to Ella's hand on top of it. Ella looked too.

It must have been when she smacked her hand on the table that she'd accidentally triggered the thing. Now, she snatched her hand away from it in a fit of horror. The red button popped back up, Warner jolting from his chair in the same instant like there was some direct connection between the two. But it was already too late, too late for either of them.

•

Ella's first thought was that the impact had turned Warner into a cold forensic sleet—that he'd been vaporized and she'd been showered with his insides. But she looked up. He was still standing there, wavering above her. Head to waist, all she could see of him, dripped with a viscous, brown sludge. He wobbled and looked at his hands. Ella looked at her own. She'd been dowsed as well. Long, glistening strands of snotty sludge sloughed from her arms. Despite her own horror at being so soiled, when she looked back at Warner again, she felt incapable of stemming the laughter that started bubbling from her. And when Warner turned his hateful gaze to her, the laughter turned to a torrent.

"What are you laughing at, you imbecile? Don't you see what you've done? You've ruined us both!"

Ella couldn't stop laughing.

In a frenzy the man started searching the room from corner to corner. When his gaze landed on the chair behind him he turned, grappling with it, yanking it up. Slipping and sliding, he managed to stay upright.

"What are you doing?" Ella asked through a gag of laughter.

Taking the chair over his shoulder, he threw it with all his strength into the enormous window at the back of the room. The glass shuddered, rejecting the chair. Warner slipped and went down. Climbing to a knee, he tried to get up and slipped again, falling a second time.

Ella's laughter, which had started to subside, rose again, filling the room.

Finally, struggling to his feet, Warner retrieved the chair. Dancing in a wide puddle of glistening sludge, when he tried pitching the chair at the window a second time, it came out of his grip at a wide angle.

Although the window took up half the office and he was facing dead into the very center of it, he missed the thing entirely. The chair crashed into a table in the corner, smashing the lamp on top in a bright splash of destruction.

"Damn it! Damn it!" he spat, his hands clenching and his shoulders high and shivering like a wolf ready to lunge. "Damn it!" Having given up on the window, the man's gaze fell on Ella. He started back toward her with a homicidal intensity in his pace and his clenched fists.

Even that wasn't enough to clear out Ella's laughter. In a fresh fit of haw-hawing, she spilled out of the chair and onto the floor.

He would have gotten to her, maybe would have beaten her to her own end, if his receptionist hadn't suddenly appeared in the doorway, brought there by the commotion in the room. Turning his attention up from where Ella was writhing helplessly in a fit of hysterics, Warner looked to the door.

"What's going on in..."

Warner slid again, falling hard onto his shoulder right beside Ella as the word in the receptionist's mouth escalated into a scream. Disappearing from the doorway, the cry of horror followed her out. With the door open, Warner abandoned any intention he'd had of attacking Ella and, struggling back up to his slick feet, he sputtered out into the hall.

"Where are you going?" Ella called after him, her words tangled in laughter. Outside the office, a commotion rose up. Awkwardly unknotting herself from the chair, she got up on her own slipping feet, and went after him.

•

By the time Ella made it out the door, the entire office was empty, only drifting paper and a shrinking ruckus of screams as proof anyone had been there. Scurrying to follow the brown, glistening path toward the emergency exit beside Warner's reception area, her laughter was finally gone.

In the stairwell, Warner hadn't managed to get beyond the top landing. He'd fallen and was struggling to get himself back up, hoisting himself on the railing above the stairs.

"What are you doing, Warner?" Ella scampered after him, too late.

She hit the railing hard and just in time to see him fall away though the narrow chasm in the center of the staircase. He seemed like he'd drift down the whole way, through that impossible, snaking coil of stairs that wound off into an indeterminate point. He didn't. His head struck a rail after a few floors with a nauseating bell-tone. It started him spinning out of control and Ella flinched and clenched as his legs and arms struck the rails, sounding a succession of low, ringing dongs, like a huge clock announcing an hour in panic. His body was thrown from side to side and then disappeared somewhere between a pair of floors. Ella caught sight of an arm and leg hanging over the rail before they slid away and she heard the man land with a plasticky crunch.

"Oh, my God." Ella's laughter was completely forgotten now. So too, any memory that she was still covered in slime, so when she launched toward the staircase, she didn't realize she no longer had much control over her momentum until she tried stopping and went spilling away over the rough descent of stairs.

•

Following a sobering trail of brown spatters, Ella found Warner in a motionless heap some ten floors below, his ass aimed to the sky, his face and shoulders flattened against the landing.

"Oh, my God," Ella muttered. She'd taken to sliding down the stairs on her ass and now, abandoning the snail trial she'd left in her wake, she staggered up and over to the man's wrecked body. "Oh, my God."

Laying her hand gently on his hip, she gave a little push.

He crumpled into a more natural looking position. Half his face was gone—the skin torn free and, where it wasn't stained with brown sludge, Ella could see the delicate ivory sheen of his nose and his skull, where they met, without juncture at the equally milky bowl of his inverted eye, run through with haltingly flickering filaments.

"Oh, my God."

A tremor ran through him at the sound of her voice: a sign of life, or was it a glimmer of loathing when his dented eye turned to her?

"Jesus, are you okay?" She reached out for him.

He slapped her hand away with surprising vigor and rose up, jittering onto a knee. Ella shrank away.

"You," his voice had gotten glitchy and rigid, broken into static fragments like it was being diced by a spinning fan, "you, you ruined me..." He staggered on his hands and knees, seeming much less capable of conducting himself on his slippy shoes now, but he didn't have far to go. Latching onto the railing again, he pulled himself to it and, in one great, graceless feat of gymnastics, went over the edge again. This time he managed a lower score, ringing out a couple tones from the railing before he went off course.

•

Ella found him three floors lower, in worse shape than he had been, slithering under the lowest rail toward the abyss in the center of the stairs. Grabbing him by the cuff of his pants, she pulled him back and flipped him around so he had to face her.

"What are you doing?! This is crazy!"

Finally, he seemed aware of the reality of it all; all that was happening, all that he had done to himself. He grabbed Ella by her jacket and pulled her close, kicking his feet and dragging her, on top of him, across the landing. His voice was worse now, like the tiny endearment of a pull-string toy when he said, "They won't have us back. Can't you see it, Person?" he mispronounced her name. "We're ruined, both of us..."

Ella didn't realize until he'd pulled her under the railing that his fitful lunging was an attempt to turn his suicide into the murderous sort. Beyond his wrecked face, the hollow in the stairwell loomed, so deep it seemed without end.

"Oh, Jesus." Ella flailed her arms. He'd already managed to pull her shoulders past the railing and there wasn't anything to grab hold of. "Oh, shit."

Suddenly, Ella felt herself at the tipping point; the top of her abdomen hanging out over the void. He still had his hands knotted up in her jacket and was bent back, his face craned down toward the ground where it lingered, somewhere, unseen below them.

His voice returned, "We'll be at peace... together..."

Ella barely heard him. She got her hand under his face and started pushing him away, but he had her coat wrapped in his fists and all she managed doing was coming closer to the edge, teetering more precariously with him. Ella dug her knees into the slick concrete beneath her and, arching her back, managed to get her ass lodged under the lowest rung of the rail. The sliding stopped.

Warner only fought harder once he'd been brought to a halt. Thrashing his legs, he battled to get her off balance.

"I don't want to come with you! Let me go!" Ella kept pushing under his face, trying to lever him free.

With her knees and ass wedging her in place, Ella finally let go of the man's chin and reached up over her shoulders, taking up fistfuls of her coat and yanking it forward over her head. For a dizzying moment, the world disappeared behind the fabric and Ella had the sense that she was falling, spinning away, out into nothingness. But no. She could still feel the safety rail biting into the top of her hips and the rough concrete digging into her knees. She let go of the jacket and reached further back for another handful. Giving a yank, a sudden jar of force wrenched her as the coat slid over the back of her head and caught in the crook of her arms. Her legs almost gave out. Straightening her arms, the jacket, in Warner's grasp, slid away.

Warner fell, kicking her hard across the face as he went.

He twirled a moment and was thrown off course again, out of sight, back into the stairs.

"Jesus Christ." Ella wagged her arms frantically to try and find the balance she'd lost. It wouldn't be found. Her knees were at the very edge of the landing, her ass the only thing keeping her from dropping away down into the chasm below. Finally, her flagging right hand managed to catch the handrail and she twisted herself around and slid back under the railing. She lay there, looking up at the spiral of stairs above.

•

By the time Ella found the brown spatter some floors below where Warner must have landed next, the man was already gone and the emergency lights in the stairwell had started flashing. A shattering screech of alarms rung off the walls. Ella kept going down, through the strobing light, floor by floor on her rump, too tired to try and walk.

She never found Warner's body. When she landed on the ground floor, there was only a brown streak on the landing as proof that he'd been there. The door was open. A snaking brown trail led outside where a pack of firetrucks and ambulances had assembled.

44 The Examination

Red Lights Below

The assault of water and detergent was powerful enough so Ella had to lean into it to keep from being knocked back, but when the process concluded, she was disheartened to see she was still stained; repulsive freckles cluttered her arms in a confusion of overlapping constellations. She could only assume her face was just as badly marred. Happily, there was no mirror to confirm it. Dried and fitted out in a gray prison smock, she was escorted down a long hallway, past an endless procession of identical doors. Although the door the guard stopped at looked the same as all the others and, as such, seemed an arbitrary choice, Ella had been through this process enough times now to know that this door was meant for her and that her future waited beyond it. Even so, when the door opened Ella stared in, unable to move.

Beyond the smudgy stainless steel table in the center of the room, Agent Sickens waited, Ella's Practitioner standing at the woman's side. Ella might have stayed frozen at the threshold if the man hadn't patted the tabletop gently. The noise called her in. The door closed at her back.

"Where's Dyer?" No one answered her.

"We have some questions you'll need to answer," Sickens said.

"Where is he? I need to speak with him."

"Ms. Pearson," the Practitioner said, "it will be better if you simply comply and answer the questions." When he patted the table again, Ella hung her head and obeyed, stepping forward and climbing up onto the slab.

Ella turned to the Doc. It was hard keeping her attention away from the mirror on the wall where, in the periphery of her vision, she could see a dark pantomime of her own movements. "Please listen to me," she told him, her gaze following him as he rounded the table. He did not look back. "This woman is a traitor. She's a murderer. I need to speak with Agent Dyer."

Though the man gave Sickens a glance, he didn't say anything for a moment, not until he'd turned back to Ella. "Please, lay back."

Ella stayed rigidly upright. "She tricked me into..."

"Ms. Pearson, it befits you to cooperate in this Assessment. Now, please, lay back."

Ella looked back and forth between the pair. "I want to speak with my attorney."

Sickens said, "This is a Sanitation Assessment. There's no need to have counsel present."

"A Sanitation Assessment? What the hell does that mean? What about the Supplicants, Sickens? What about Ernie? What did you do? Is he..."

"Ms. Pearson, please calm yourself," the Practitioner said. "This Assessment has nothing to do with any outside circumstances. It's important you understand that. The Sanitation Assessment is only concerned with one thing: establishing whether or not the Object, that would be you, can meet the minimum requirements of continued, general citizenship. Now, please, lay back."

Ella glared at the Practitioner. Stabbing a finger in the direction of Sickens, she said, "That woman is a murderer. She's responsible for killing my..." With her hand stretched out, she couldn't avoid the brown blotches on her arm and quickly drew the hand back, so she wouldn't have to see it. "I need to make a statement to the police. You understand that? She tricked me into bringing a virus into the City with the intention of..."

"I'd be happy to take a statement from you," Sickens interrupted to say, "after the Sanitation Assessment."

"Not you. I'm not interested in making a statement to you. What did you do, Sickens? Was Warner telling the truth? He said they'd all been wiped out. All of them. Is Ernie…"

Sickens leaned in and whispered, "I'm trying to help you, Pearson. I like you, if I haven't made that clear. This…" She looked down at Ella's stained arms. "This was never my intention…"

"I don't want your help. I don't want anything from you."

"Ms. Pearson," the Practitioner drew her attention back, "this is your last opportunity. Do you understand? If you refuse the inquiry, we'll have no choice but to allow through the preliminary judgement that you are unclean, that you are unfit to remain in society. You'll have no opportunity for a review at all. Do you understand that?"

Ella shook her head, but laid back despite the gesture, looking to the ceiling. In the periphery of her sight, the faces of her inquisitors leaned in.

"Very well," the Practitioner said, "let's get this underway, shall we, Ms. Sickens?"

The agent turned her attention to the tablet in her hand. Taking the Practitioner's cue, she read from the screen, "Do you bathe every day?"

Ella looked back and forth between the two of them, tossing her head fitfully. "Is that what this is about? Really? You used me as a weapon, Sickens. You had me kill my own… Is he… Is he really gone?"

"Ms. Pearson," the Doc said, "You've already been warned. This will be your only chance to make your case. If you do not answer the questions…"

"Do I bathe every day–is that the goddamned question you're asking me, if I bathe every day?" Looking back and forth between the pair in a fury, she said, "Jesus Christ, is this it, really?"

"Ms. Pearson," the Practitioner warned her gently.

"Yeah. I mean, I try to. Yeah."

Stabbing the screen on her device and casually circling the table, Sickens asked, "So, if not every day…"

"I said, I try to every day..."

"...how many times a week do you bathe yourself?"

"I... I'm a very clean person..."

"When was the last time you bathed yourself?"

Ella shook her head. "It's been within the last week. Four days ago, I think."

"Do you not remember having bathed yourself recently?"

"It was four days ago," Ella announced, trying to sound certain. "What's the point of this?"

"Did you use soap?"

"It can't be a bath without soap, can it?"

"Ms. Pearson, you'll only be allowed so many exceptions..." the Practitioner scolded her again.

"Yes, I used soap, of course I used soap. I want to see my attorney."

"I already told you," Sickens said peevishly, "he can't help you. This is a Sanitation Assessment and you do not need legal counsel for that. Now, please, let's continue." The woman's 'please' did not sound like a please at all. "How frequently do you wash your hands?"

"My hands? Who keeps track of that sort of thing?"

"How many times in the last week did you wash your hands?"

"It was a very unusual week," Ella said. She couldn't remember having washed her hands once in the last week and the realization sent a surge of shame through her. Even though, with the brutal cleaning she'd just endured, there was no way her hands weren't perfectly sanitary, the question made them seem filthy and, when she caught a look at her arm out of the corner of her sight, the deep stains there left no other conclusion, but that she was soiled beyond all hope.

•

From her seat on the risers, the red lights below looked like the eyes of a colossus deliberating over which way she might best be consumed, but Ella tried to remind herself that one of those lights must represent something good: if the door on the right meant denial, then the door on the left must constitute the possibility that a petition could be approved. The room was quiet. No one else was admitted and the stillness around her made the wait seem eternal. Maybe this would be her punishment. Maybe, like that unfortunate drunkard in the Poe story, they'd just brick her in and forget about her. Certainly, there was some reason the hallway had so many identical doors. Maybe, behind them, old dissidents sat, collecting dust and regret.

She was so certain that the light on the right would be the one to go green, that when the left one turned, she didn't move. Over the intercom, a voice announced, "Ella Pearson, please exit through the indicated door."

Ella stood and hobbled down the stairs.

It was the door on the left, so she must have passed the examination. She wanted to be happy about it. She was free, she'd won. There was no satisfaction in that victory. Ernie was gone. There was no getting him back. She'd lost Andy and Clara, too, of course. They were still out there but, having decided on a penitence she felt suddenly ambiguous about, she'd made up her mind that she wouldn't ever see them again.

Lydia would probably make Andy very happy. Ella wasn't sure anything could make her happy again. She wasn't sure the concept of happiness was something she could still comprehend.

All her certainty that she'd been granted clemency evaporated when she opened the door to find a staircase leading down. She paused again. The voice crackled over the intercom, "Ella Pearson, please exit through the indicated door."

Ella stepped forward into the cramped stairwell. Halfway down, the door slammed shut behind her. She flinched but didn't stop until she'd come off the last stair.

A hallway stretched ahead. Its length was impossible to determine; the fluorescent tubes on the ceiling only lit the next twenty feet ahead. Beyond that, nothing but darkness. After a moment, the voice came over the intercom again, "Ella Pearson, please exit through the hallway ahead." It was the same voice from the Represitol ads, Ella was almost certain.

Hesitant to take that first step, when the lights began to flicker, she moved. After ten paces, the tubes behind her went out with a pop and, simultaneously, the ones ahead lit up, so that her view of the hallway stretched out, twenty feet long again. Nothing remarkable was revealed, just the black throated mouth of more hallway. Although, as Ella continued on, she thought maybe 'hallway' wasn't the right word. It was a tunnel, not a doorway in sight. She must have been underground, the walls were damp. The place smelled like a bucket of stirred sand. After another ten paces, the lights behind her popped off and another bank ahead sizzled on. And so it went, long after she'd lost count of how many sets of lights she'd passed through.

She might have walked for miles before she stopped again. Ahead, just beyond the light, it looked like a pile of old rags was blocking the way. After a few moments staring, the intercom repeated, "Ella Pearson, please exit..." and the lights above her started faltering. Ella knew she needed to move. Stepping forward warily, behind her the lights died and ahead they came on, illuminating the body, curled in the middle of the hall, motionless. Ella stopped again. The thing didn't move, but Ella didn't want to get any closer to it.

"Ella Pearson, please exit through the hallway ahead." The lights began to fade again and Ella started forward slowly, edging along the wall that had the widest path around the corpse—just wide enough to skirt by. When one of the feet twitched, Ella seized up for a moment. It happened so quickly, she couldn't quite be sure she'd actually seen it. The next time, when the warning came over the intercom, it was muddled with another message, laid over top, "Rupert Warner, please..."

Ella stepped forward. Wedging her toe under the man's shoulder, she turned him over so she could see his face. She wouldn't have recognized him. Where his head wasn't deformed into a crooked, flattened mess, he was stained with blotchy freckles that, she supposed, matched her own. He looked at her and she couldn't tell if the man recognized her either, though, despite her stains, she must have looked more or less the same.

"Your name's Rupert?" she said derisively.

The thing on the ground groaned and twitched. Lolling his head away, he turned to the wall.

Above, the warning called again, "Ella Pearson/Rupert Warner, please exit through the hallway ahead." Warner didn't look like he intended on going anywhere.

The lights flickered, but Ella stayed her ground just long enough to say, "You deserve this, you son of a bitch. You can be trapped down here forever, for all I care." She wanted to kick him, to throttle him. "Is it true what you told me? Is he really gone? Are they all dead?"

"We're free. Rejoice," Warner muttered listlessly at the wall. The lights faded out and came back, dimmer than before. She straightened up and kept moving. Following her, the lights brightened. When the set behind her went out with a snap, she stopped to turn back. She could still see him, just a barely visible heap in the darkness, the light barely grazing him. She went on again and when the next series of lights died out and she looked back, he was gone, consumed by the darkness.

"Damn it," she said. She put her hand on the wall and moved back into the section of hallway she'd just quit, hurrying and kicking her feet shallowly. When she struck on his body in the darkness, she bent, savagely yanking him up. The dark was making her head muzzy, and for a moment she couldn't tell if she'd successfully lifted him, or if she'd sunk to the ground beside him. She managed to get herself turned around and got her bearings back when she saw the distant diorama of lighted hallway twenty feet away. The voice came over the intercom again, "Ella Pearson, please exit through the hallway ahead."

Dragging Warner back up the hall, the lights ahead flickered and Ella leaned forward, moving as fast as she could. After a few more steps, the light died out. She was submerged in blackness.

The world seemed to spin, everything in it coming uncoupled. Suddenly, she was no longer certain that she was heading in the right direction. Absurdly, it seemed that, in the darkness, the tunnel had evolved a third direction and she was now condemned to this new path: heading straight down, deep into the earth where the blackness around her would be somehow more complete: a solid thing that would be impossible to break with. She kept pushing forward as hard as she could, aware of her diminishing speed.

The light came back in a sudden flare. Warner groaned and Ella straightened up. She'd fallen to her knees and had been crawling, dragging him behind her by his ankle though she'd barely been aware of it. She climbed back to her feet and continued dragging the man along.

"Just leave me," he muttered.

"I don't want to hear it," she said and continued on.

After a few hundred yards more, she came to a stairwell, leading up to a door. Ella hoisted Warner up and carried him to the top of the stairs. Pushing through the door, she was comforted by the sudden shock of light. It only lasted a moment.

Looking around, once her vision had adjusted, she found she'd been delivered into the wasteland of the Northern District.

Part 5
The Savages

45 Everything You Wanted

The house wasn't so immaculate as it had seemed on Ella's previous visit. Daylight illuminated every little fault in the place: the way mildew stained the clapboards, the way the paint was cracked around the window casings, the uneven bulge of the brick walkway. The front door hung open.

On Ella's first approach, she couldn't seem to get her feet aimed to the door so, after waffling a moment on the sidewalk, she just kept going. She turned up the next street; out here the houses were even more extravagant. Pausing, she fretted over her gloves a moment, hitching them higher on her wrists, even though they hadn't sagged. The gloves didn't match but they were both whole and hid the stains on her hands.

She'd put a lot into her outfit for the day. The morning before, she'd washed her clothes in a drum that had filled with rainwater. It looked clean enough but by the time her clothes were dry they came off the line stiff and smelling like pennies. She found a beaten, wide brimmed fedora in a dumpster and when she kept her head down, no one could see her face.

Stalled on the sidewalk, she forced herself to turn back and approached the house from the opposite angle. The door was still open.

She took the path up. The house was quiet. Ella leaned inside, knocking lightly on the jamb.

It seemed like a long wait before Dawn finally showed.

With her face hidden by the brim of the hat, all she could see were the girl's feet.

Obviously, Dawn wasn't expecting her; she said, "Yes, what is it?"

Ella said, "It's me," and lifted her head to the side.

There was a long pause. Ella looked away.

"What happened to your... Never mind..." Dawn turned back inside, leaving the door open and an invitation unannounced.

Ella followed her in.

In the foyer, Dawn had already returned to the task on the floor: kneeling over a box and fixing the top closed with packing tape.

Taking off her hat, Ella looked around.

All the pictures had come down from the walls. The place looked vacant.

"Terry's not here," Dawn said. With a snap from the teeth on the dispenser, she cut the ribbon of tape and smoothed it out with her hand. She pushed the box away and stared at the floor a moment. "I'm going back to the City. Back to my old apartment. Back to how things were before."

Ella kept quiet.

Dawn twisted up to look at her. "Don't pretend you aren't perfectly happy about it."

"I'm not happy, Dawn."

"You never gave up loving him, did you?"

"Terry?"

"Don't act like you don't know who we're talking about."

Ella looked away. With no furniture or decor, the grandeur of the room seemed diminished. It looked as shabby as Andy's old place. She made herself say, "That doesn't make me happy about it."

Dawn had gone back to staring at the floor again. "I don't even care about all this. The house, the neighborhood." She laughed dryly. "Even Terry." She shook her head dispassionately. Her silence filled the room. "He was always so convinced he knew best. So arrogant. So pompous. I can see why it didn't work for the two of you. You're too much alike."

Ella stood silent and tried to act like the attack hadn't landed.

"We had two, a boy and a girl. You met them, I think. They got sick at the same time: the day after I saw you last. Terry told me, you know how he is, *always right,* that children would get sick and that was just something that happened. That I shouldn't worry. I couldn't sleep. I just stayed by their bedside. When the first one stopped breathing, Terry let me call the hospital. Let me!" She shook her head. Trembling with anger, her fingers clicked on the hardwood floor. After she'd calmed herself, she said, "We named the girl Sissy, because she was the sister. She died in the hospital.

"They told me there wasn't anything that could've been done for either of them, but I still don't see what good came from not calling the medics sooner. That was all Terry. All Terry's fault... So arrogant..." She shook her head. Her fists closed up.

"I'm sorry, Dawn."

"Oh, I'm sure you are. I'm sure you're very sorry." The girl pushed herself up off the floor and for a moment Ella thought she was going to lash out. Instead, she wobbled weakly over to another box and fell down before it and started fixing the top closed with the packing tape. Ella watched her, unable to find anything appropriately conciliatory to say. Without looking, Dawn said, "And I suppose you and Andy'll be getting married soon. This summer, maybe? Maybe you came to ask me to be your maid of honor, just to put me through a final ringer, just so I know how thoroughly I've lost and how you've won it all, all over again."

"I haven't won anything, Dawn. Look at me."

The girl didn't look up.

"Andy left me, anyhow. Or, maybe I left him, I can't quite sort how it fell apart. But it has. I'm not taking any satisfaction from this, Dawn. If there were a way to go back and somehow make it different... I would."

Again, Dawn shot a crazed glance at her. This time she managed to hold it. She said, "That day you came to borrow the car, something changed. You two were alone for five minutes and I don't pretend to know what happened between you in my garage—I don't even want to think about it—but he was different. All that night he was different and the next day, too. He wasn't looking at me anymore. It was like I wasn't even here. Or maybe he wasn't. He was thinking about you. I could see it, written all over him. And when he got his car back and it was a mess, I was so mad at you. It was so disrespectful. But you know what he said?"

Ella was quiet. The girl's voice had gone wobbly and unsteady and it wrenched Ella's insides.

"He didn't say anything. He didn't care. It was like he'd given it up to you and hadn't expected it back."

"I'm sorry for everything that's happened, I really am. And I'm sorry for my part in it. Whatever you think I did, I wish I could undo it."

"You say that, but you got everything you wanted, didn't you? You might be sorry for all the wreckage you left but you can't be sorry for the outcome."

"I am sorry, Dawn. Maybe I did get something I wanted but I'd give it up if I could... To tell the truth, I can't even remember what I wanted in the first place. It wasn't worth it, whatever it was."

The box was taped and Dawn hobbled up to her feet, keeping her gaze on the boxes on the floor. There were three.

Outside, a cab had pulled up to the curb, the horn blaring twice.

Muttering and still looking down at the boxes, Dawn said, "That's it. Three boxes. My whole existence."

"Can't I help?"

"Don't touch my things." Dawn bent and grappled with one of the boxes, drawing it up off the floor. Passing by Ella to the door, the girl said, acidly, "I think you've done quite enough already."

She staggered outside.

Through the window, Ella caught sight of the girl hobbling down the walkway. She bent and picked up one of the remaining boxes.

By the time she got outside, Dawn already had the first box in the back of the yellow minivan and Ella moved behind the girl to set hers inside, too. Turning, Dawn swung out viciously. The box fell to the ground, landing with a muted whomp, collapsing the corner. Something inside cracked.

"Look what you've done," Dawn snarled at the box.

"I was only trying to help, Dawn."

The girl turned to Ella. "You think I don't see you for what you are? I told you not to touch it. I didn't want it soiled."

Staring at the girl, Ella cowered away.

"I was trying to be kind, not bringing it up, but look at you. Can you smell yourself, Pearson?" She looked to the box again. A side of the box looked grimy, where it had rubbed against Ella's chest but Ella thought it might only have been a shadow. "I asked you not to touch it."

Ella kept staring at the box while Dawn returned to the house and collected the final one. With it packed away in the back of the minivan and the trunk closed up, Dawn climbed into the taxi without a word.

The van pulled away.

Ella stood, looking at the box. The top was still fixed up securely with tape. Who knew what spoils hid inside, but Ella couldn't make herself touch it again.

A New Home

46 Playing Nurse

When morning arrived, Ella climbed out from under her concrete slab. Beyond the ruins around her, the City sat, vaguely in the distance, like something wrought out of soot and smoke. Ella sat atop the uneven slab to watch the sunrise. Though the sky was smoggy, there were no clouds to catch the early morning reds and pinks of daybreak, so when the sun peaked up at last, it was in an instant flare of hard light.

Reaching into her pocket, she dug out the little slip of paper that she carried everywhere. It was no longer whole. It had split at the creases where she'd folded it a few hundred times too many and so now there were four individual pieces. She held them together so she could read the heading at the top of the document, *Certificate of Quality.* Centered below that, the word *For* was broken in half by the tear. Below that, was her name. Further down the document, under the designation, *Location of Service,* the document read, *East Gish* and under *Allocation* it read, *Farmhand.* The thing seemed to make less and less sense the more frequently she looked at it.

She looked out over the wasteland before her. If she was meant to be a farmhand, what had brought her here? She laid the pieces over each other and carefully pushed them back into her pocket.

After awhile of sitting and soaking in the sun, she climbed off the slab, ducking underneath again. Crawling to the back of the dugout she found Warner still curled up, faced away. When she reached under him to lift him, he grumbled and struggled against her. He didn't have much fight. Ella dragged him out into the day and laid him out on the slab.

Even though she'd arranged him to face her, he twisted himself away, his head loped to the West, his face falling into shadow.

"How long are you going to keep this up?" Ella asked.

Like an ungrateful child, he insisted on punishing her with his silence.

"I could have left you down there." She knew, at least some part of her knew, deep down, that that's what he'd wanted. Still, it was the only threat she had and so she used it when she felt she had to. "You can't blame this on me. You did this."

He was silent, staring out toward where the horizon might have sat if it hadn't been blocked out by a broken ridge of brick wall. His silence made her sad—he was all she had anymore—and her sadness made her angry, so she went quiet on him, too, and leaned back to let the sun fall over her.

47 A Cynical Conclusion

It was impossible to know how long she'd been in the dugout on the evening she saw the figure of a boy clambering over the ruins toward her.

It had been a long time.

Climbing up onto a jagged, deteriorating wall a hundred feet away, the boy paused, raising a slow hand in hello. Ella looked behind her. There was no one there, just a long chasm of crumbling ruins, like a giant had gone charging through. She turned back to the boy. He still had his hand up. When Ella raised hers, he dropped off the wall and closed the distance to her. Going to the edge of the concrete slab, Ella leaned over to help him up.

They stood together, looking at each other a moment before the boy turned his attention down to the twisted form of Warner, lounging gracelessly on the concrete. His face was hidden; turned away, pouting as usual.

"Is that..."

"Yes," Ella said.

"I heard you'd taken him. I had no idea you'd still have him with you."

Ella sat down and looked away to the sun. "What do you want?"

The boy sat beside her. But he didn't look at the sun. "Just to see you again."

"Is Ernie..." Ella went quiet a moment. "Dawn said her kids had passed..."

The boy shook his head sadly. "No one blames you."

"Lot of good that does." She'd unbuttoned her shirt and had let it fall off her shoulders to let in the last of the sinking sun. The light pressed on her for a moment before the boy reached out and, without a word, set her shirt right, covering her up. Ella let it be. "And Ernie, is he..."

"Let's not talk about that. It isn't what I came for."

She looked at her hands, freckled with brown splotches. She'd almost gotten used to it, if it was the sort of thing one could get used to: dreadful freckles. The wound on her wrist had gone black and crackled like something salvaged from a fire. After a moment she asked, "So why did you?"

He shrugged. "The same reason I kept your photo all that time, I guess, when I couldn't even remember you; the same reason you kept the photo of me. We were important to each other. I don't know, with the Reclamation suspended... I just wanted to see you again. To make sure you were alright."

"Well, now you've seen," she said. "What do you think: am I alright?"

"You're angry. I can see that."

They were both quiet and turned and looked at the sky, striated red and gold. The wind had chilled, anticipating the night. After a moment, Ella said, "You don't forget like I do, do you?"

"I forget."

"Not like I do."

"Why do you say that?"

"I don't know. There was a reason you wanted them back; I couldn't ever see the point of it."

He said, "That wasn't a matter of remembering, Ella."

"What was it, then?"

"Faith." He shrugged. "If They were responsible for us, there must have been a lot of good in Them, something worth getting back again."

"Warner told me they were monsters, that they were evil and selfish." Behind her, Warner groaned and shifted anxiously as if the conversation had taken a turn that interested him.

Timmy looked at the man, what remained of him; the flattened face, his limbs askew. "That man there, or what he used to be, he was the monster—he was the selfish one. He wasn't trying to protect anything but himself, anything but his own position." Turning from the man, Timmy said, "Still, I don't know if I approve of you torturing him like this..."

"Who says it's torture? I saved him." When Warner groaned again, she said, "Shut up," and he went quiet. After a moment of silence, where she collected her composure, she said, "He told me we were slaves."

"No," Timmy said, "we were Their children."

"I don't know. They didn't make us for our benefit."

"That's just it, Ella: our Creator might have made us to serve Them; but They also gave us the world, They gave us all this beauty to be a part of." He motioned around to the sky and the City and the setting sun. The gesture might have been more impactful had they been anywhere but here: the Northern District. From here, all it looked like they'd inherited was the sun making a hasty escape from a crumbling failure. There was a pained edge in the boy's voice when he said, "There's the proof of Their good intentions: we're here, we're Neo Hominem, we have souls."

Ella nodded, but she didn't know if that was true. What did it mean, anyway, to have a soul? It was an invisible, intangible thing—something without more than a name to prove its existence—and a thing that couldn't be seen or felt, certainly had no propriety to exist. And, if there was any evidence of her having a soul at all, Ella thought, that evidence could only be her pain. She said, "If you're right, it only makes it worse."

Warner groaned again and shifted. His body rubbed against the concrete with a dry, raspy gasp.

Timmy sighed. "Maybe They were monsters, then. It's a cynical conclusion but I understand your coming to it. It's something I've thought about a lot, actually." He looked at his little hands, his child's hands, perfect for manufacturing tiny, wondrous things. "I think there's another reason, maybe, why They would have made something that looks like we do. Something that feels, something that looks like They did." He shrugged, as though his own conclusion was a bit of a letdown. "I think They were sad. I think, if you knew, if you knew everyday that death was looming right around everyone you loved, there would be a lot of attraction to having something permanent that wouldn't wither away. Their making us is a credit to the expansiveness of Their love. We don't know dying, we don't know loss, not the way They did. I don't think we can understand what it's like, being constantly on the edge of that precipice that took our Creators away."

Ella thought of Ernie. She thought, maybe she did know what it was like living beside death.

On the distant skyline, the sun was squashed, flattened out, sharpening and flaring in a last, dying exertion. Timmy stood up. "I should go."

"Just like that?" Ella didn't look at the boy.

The sun flashed brightly off the boy and his shadow was long into the distance, disjointed and laying like shattered bits of a man scattered on every rise behind him. He nodded back at Warner. Laying flat, the man had already fallen into darkness. "You should let him go. It isn't fair to him, torturing him like this."

"I'm not torturing him. I told you, I saved him."

"Is that what he wants, Ella?"

"No one asked what I wanted."

The boy said nothing to that. After a moment he hopped off the slab and started away.

He paused, still facing into the distance when she said, "Don't bother coming back, trying to find me. I'm leaving."

The boy nodded. He turned his head a little, not quite looking over his shoulder to ask, "Where will you go?"

"East Gish. There's something there for me."

"If you go out there, into the wilderness, what if you forget?"

"Forget what?"

"Anything. All of it. What if you forgot how to speak or how to be what you are?"

"You're worried about my not being ready if..." She didn't finish the thought.

"When," he insisted and shrugged and said, "when." He'd taken a kerchief from his pocket and was wiping at the hand she'd taken when she'd helped him up onto the slab. The gesture wasn't lost on her.

"I can't be expected to just wait. It might never happen," Ella said.

"It isn't a good idea, Ella."

"Why does it matter to you at all?"

He turned back, finally. "I came here to see you because you were important to me, even if it was a long time ago. We were important to each other. If you leave there's no coming back."

"There's no coming back, anyway, is there? I'm stuck out here, isn't that it?"

"We're trying to clean the City again, to prepare for the next try with the Supplicants. If you leave, you risk contamination. You'll not be allowed back."

"I've already been thrown away. Is there really any chance I'll be let back in, I mean, really, any chance?"

"I wouldn't ask you to stay if I thought it were otherwise. When our Creator returns, who knows what They'll be capable of..."

"How is it your right to decide who stays and who gets cast out, anyway?"

"Someone has to decide, Ella."

"Why? Why does someone have to decide that? You're making this whole world on the hopes of your Great Creator coming back and what if they don't? And how can you pretend to know what they'll want of the world, anyway?"

"It's written."

"They'll come into the world with fresh eyes. They won't know what's written and what isn't. They won't know what they want. I had a Caveman, Ernie, I know what they're like better than you do. They'll accept the world however it is. All this throwing away isn't necessary."

"Did you feel that way before, when you were living in the City? Or is it only now that you've gotten this grand sense of equity?"

Ella was silent.

The boy shrugged. "Just think about what you're doing," he said and started off. After shimmying down a wall in the distance, he was gone.

48

The Slipping Away
The Turning Away
The Glimmering Exit

Ella moved away from the City. The world opened up around her, green and lush and screaming with nature; birds and crickets and toads —all manner of everything—crying for attention. Above, the sky was bright and open, hosting a scattered band of bulbous white clouds that charged along lazily; everything headed in the same direction. The wheelchair she pushed bobbed over the cracks in the road; Warner's head lolling from side to side as though taking an impatient appraisal of the world around him, but it was hard to tell if he was seeing any of it at all.

"At some point you're going to have to start talking to me," Ella said. Warner only gave a groan. His head listed away to his other shoulder. "You spoke to me in the tunnel, I know you still can."

Beyond the pollution of the City, the sun felt enormous. Ella took off her shirt and folded it over the handle of the wheelchair and kept pushing Warner down the empty highway. Later, when she noticed the shirt was gone, she didn't bother turning to look for it. After a few more miles, with the sun sinking ahead of them, she unbuttoned her slacks and stepped out of them and left them in the road, as well.

With the pink evening light all over her, warm and fuzzy, Ella found a clarity of mind that seemed somehow perfect, virginal and unambiguous. But, then, more and more, she couldn't seem to remember much and stopped trying to. It didn't bother her. Who need remember when the present moment was so wide and encompassing around them? Any memory that existed couldn't possibly be as essential as this—the whole world wide awake and alive. The trees bowed modestly in the wind, the leaves applauding the pair as they moved away; following the sun to the end of the world.

•

Somehow the summer had turned late and seemed to gather its heat together the way the greedy assemble riches; as though it were something that could last. Even the nights were warm. Above them, the stars pivoted off, as though they were set on a crooked clockwork. It was just bright enough so that Ella could keep half-awake, lolling in a half-dream. Or, maybe she had fallen asleep and her dream was this wondrous sky, hanging overhead.

It was so different from the City sky. In the City, at most you could hope to see a star or two blinking through the blight of pollution, as though a pair of eyes peaking around the edge of a curtain, to get a glimpse of the show on stage. Even in East Gish, the night sky, while bustling with stars, was homogenous: pinpricks on a black mat. Here, the sky was a window to the cosmos. Clouds of pink and blue galaxies seemed to twist out like octopuses reaching for one another. There seemed no square minutiae that didn't harbor a twinkling glint of starlight. Here, the night sky appeared to have no blackness about it at all. It was a firework display, frozen in time and slowly twisting itself so that every glimmering tchotchke of it, every last fleck of light could be admired.

Ella watched the stars turn. "If there were a bridge, leading straight up, do you think we have enough time in us still, so that we could walk to one of those stars out there?"

"We can't exist in space, Pearson. We'd freeze up and come apart." Warner's voice was steady and sure, spiteful and somehow Ella wasn't surprised by it. She was probably dreaming, she decided. Though she was certain Warner still had the capacity for speech, she was equally certain that he was too vindictive to grace her with it.

Anyway, she ignored his answer; that wasn't what she'd been asking. She'd been asking about time, not about the practicality of space travel. She was quiet, just watching the stars. In his wheelchair, Warner turned away from her.

•

The heat of the day was already thick when the sky started to lighten. Ella didn't move. Laying in the grass, she stayed stretched out, her gaze fixed on the jagged horizon of trees in the distance. The serrated horizon was still dark as night and the land stretching out toward it, a hazy, irresolute gray. When the sun rose and the light filled in the landscape around her and lit on her face, Ella sat up. She was under an ancient walnut tree that had died alone, on a little glade. Its arms stretched out, bare and black while everything else in nature seemed verdant and fresh. The morning was still, the forest around her quiet and motionless, like the day's thick humidity was a gelatin encasing it all. Ella turned around.

Warner's wheelchair was gone.

She struggled to her feet. Two pairs of tracks were left in the grass, one up the incline where she'd pushed it, another set led away, back down toward the road.

"Warner?"

The wilderness was quiet.

Ella stumbled down the hill, chasing her long shadow. She ran by a wide indentation where Warner must have fallen over. The grass was flattened and twisted, where he'd struggled to get back into the chair; the path continued after that, so he must have been successful.

On the road, there was no sign of the man, but the angle of his path cutting through the grass seemed to indicate that he'd continued on in the direction she'd been pushing him.

"Warner?" She called out again. The stillness and quiet of the morning made the world feel unbearably empty. He couldn't have gotten far, Ella thought. She started running again.

•

The sun was high in the sky before she stopped, looking back and forth down the course of the road.

"Warner?" she called in one direction and then the other. Her voice died in the damp air without an echo.

Was it even possible that crippled-old-Warner had outpaced her by this much? Either he wasn't as crippled as he'd led her to believe, or he'd gone the other way. In the still, heavy air, not a whiff of him lingered. He wouldn't have gone back to the City, she decided and started moving again.

The road wound down, in and out of valleys and across a broad meadow that shone like spun gold in the setting sun. Ella sat on the edge of the culvert and soaked up the last light of the day and when the sky went pink, she laid down in the rigid grass to sleep.

•

Ella dreamt of Ernie but in her dream he was not named Ernie and he wasn't the Caveman, either. It was just him in essence, smiling and drooling, giggling at something beyond Ella's awareness, something she couldn't turn to see or maybe something she simply couldn't understand.

When she woke, a breeze stirred the broom hay above her, the slender, golden reeds swaying up toward the blue, blue sky. An electric scent wafted on the wind. Ella rose up and looked across the meadow. The grass sizzled and shushed and, with Ella standing, the smell was even stronger. She started across the field, into the breeze.

Before the edge of the meadow, where a dense line of scrub brush bordered the forest, a long, flat rock rose up from the earth. From a hundred yards away it looked like a pile of garbage. She stopped, twenty paces off, knowing now that that was where the scent came from. The shelf of stone was littered with bodies, stretched out in the sun. They lay so still, there could be no conclusion but that they were all dead, victims of some mass extinction. But when Ella stepped closer, something stirred. A head popped up, catching sight of her. She stopped again.

"Hello?" she ventured and the sound of her voice caused them all to stir, scrambling up silently into hunched, skittish, savage poses.

She raised her hands timidly. There were a dozen of them, all completely naked and all of them strutting on their knuckles and the balls of their feet like animals.

"What are you doing out here?"

They perked at the sound of her voice, but not one of them answered.

When she took a step forward, they lurched, altogether, hopping off the rock and scurrying into the forest, the brush rattling as they disappeared from sight.

Ella ran after them, but by the time she got to the edge of the woods, the brush had fallen still and quiet again. There was no sign of them, other than the faint and fading electric bite in the air.

•

Days later, Ella caught another electric whiff, but it only lasted a moment and when the wind changed direction, the smell died away and she didn't catch any sign of it again.

The road angled down and the horizon before her rose and rose as she entered into a range of fertile, rounded foothills. As she'd slept through a big portion of the car ride to East Gish, and what she hadn't slept through was hidden by nighttime, it was impossible to tell if she was going the right way. She must have been, the roadway was kept up and someone had bothered maintaining it all this time. If it didn't lead to East Gish, it certainly led somewhere.

In the end, whether or not it was the way to East Gish became irrelevant. Ella was no longer thinking about that place as her goal. She was just walking now, searching for Warner, but even that flimsy enticement to her own future had started unraveling. She could no longer seem to recall his name or his relation to her; only that he was crippled and in need of her help.

The road wound down in snaking turns and here, in the growing rise of the foothills, the sky shrunk and the sun's area of influence constrained. Long before evening, the land around her had gone dark and she came on the mouth of a tunnel leading into the base of a mountain. Inside was perfectly black.

She would have stopped there, but the man in the wheelchair, the man who needed her help was inside—she was unaccountably certain of it.

Starting in, the tunnel was not as dark as it had seemed from the road. A vague, gray band of dying daylight led inside. She followed the orange centerline that cut the roadway in half. In her field of vision, with every advancing step, the line dimmed, fading away. When it had disappeared altogether, she looked up. In the frail light, Ella thought she could see something ahead. A speckle of light twinkled. It must have been the other end of the tunnel. Entombed in darkness, she hurried toward the glimmer, suddenly spurred by the realization that she might be trapped in here. In her rush, she stumbled and fell and when she rose up, she could no longer see any light, in either direction. She took a few more lurching steps and stumbled again and fell and this time she did not get up. The road was cold and damp underneath her.

Just a nap, she thought. She was very tired and rest would do her good and when the sun came up in the morning it would certainly wake her. Or, maybe if she slept a long time, months or years, decades or millennia, the next truck headed down the roadway to... what was the name of that place?... wherever she was headed... she would be discovered and helped back into the light. Until then, just a nap. A little snooze.

49

Perceptual Data

A Star is a Light at the End of a Tunnel

0000000000000000000000000000000000000000000000000000000000000000
0000000000000000000000000000000000000000000000000000000000000000
0000000000000000000000000000000000000000000000000000000000000000
0000000000000000000000000000000000000000000000000000000000000000
0000000000000000000000000000000000000000000000000000000000000000
0000000000000000000000000000000000000000000000000000000000000000
0000000000000000000000000000000000000000000000000000000000000000
0000000000000000000000000000000000000000000000000000000000000000
0000000000000000000000000000000000000000000000000000000000000000
0000000000000000000000000000000000000000000000000000000000000000
0000000000000000000000000000000000000000000000000000000000000000
0000000000000000000000000000000000000000000000000000000000000000
0000000000000000000000000000000000000000000000000000000000000000
0000000000000000000000000000000000000000000000000000000000000000
0000000000000000000000000000000000000000000000000000000000000000
0000000000000000000000000000000000000000000000000000000000000000
0000000000000000000000000000000000000000000000000000000000000000
0000000000000000000000000000001000000000000000000000000000000000
0000000000000000000000000000000000000000000000000000000000000000
0000000000000000000000000000000000000000000000000000000000000000
0000000000000000000000000000000000000000000000000000000000000000
0000000000000000000000000000000000000000000000000000000000000000
0000000000000000000000000000000000000000000000000000000000000000
0000000000000000000000000000000000000000000000000000000000000000
0000000000000000000000000000000000000000000000000000000000000000

50 Sunrise Beneath the Earth

0000000000000000000000000000000000000000000000000000000000
0000000000000000000000000000000000000000000000000000000000
0000000000000000000000000000000000000000000000000000000000
0000000000000000000000000000000000000000000000000000000000
0000000000000000000000000000000000000000000000000000000000
0000000000000000000000000000000000000000000000000000000000
0000000000000000000000000000000000000000000000000000000000
0000000000000000000000000000000000000000000000000000000000
0000000000000000000000000000000000000000000000000000000000
0000000000000000000000000000000000000000000000000000000000
0000000000000000000000000000000000000000000000000000000000
0000000000000000000000000000000000000000000000000000000000
0000000000000000000000000000000000000000000000000000000000
0000000000000000000000000000000000000000000000000000000000
0000000000000000000000000000000000000000000000000000000000
0000000000000000000000000000000000000000000000000000000000
0000000000000000000000000000000000000000000000000000000000
0000000000000000000000000000010000000000000000000000000000
0000000000000000000000000000000000000000000000000000000000
0000000000000000000000000000000000000000000000000000000000
0000000000000000000000000000000000000000000000000000000000
0000000000000000000000000000000000000000000000000000000000
0000000000000000000000000000000000000000000000000000000000
0000000000000000000000000000000000000000000000000000000000
0000000000000000000000000000000000000000000000000000000000

0000000000000000000000000000000000000000000000000000000000
0000000000000000000000000000000000000000000000000000000000
0000000000000000000000000000000000000000000000000000000000
0000000000000000000000000000000000000000000000000000000000
0000000000000000000000000000000000000000000000000000000000
0000000000000000000000000000000000000000000000000000000000
0000000000000000000000000000000000000000000000000000000000
0000000000000000000000000000000000000000000000000000000000
0000000000000000000000000000000000000000000000000000000000
0000000000000000000000000000000000000000000000000000000000
0000000000000000000000000000000000000000000000000000000000
0000000000000000000000000000000000000000000000000000000000
0000000000000000000000000000000000000000000000000000000000
0000000000000000000000000000000000000000000000000000000000
0000000000000000000000000000000000000000000000000000000000
0000000000000000000000000000000000000000000000000000000000
0000000000000000000000000000000000000000000000000000000000
0000000000000000000000000000000000000000000000000000000000
0000000000000000000000000000000000000000000000000000000000
0000000000000000000000000000000000000000000000000000000000
0000000000000000000000000000000000000000000000000000000000
0000000000000000000000000000000000000000000000000000000000
0000000000000000000000000000011100000000000000000000000000
0000000000000000000000000000111100000000000000000000000000
0000000000000000000000000000011100000000000000000000000000
0000000000000000000000000000000000000000000000000000000000
0000000000000000000000000000000000000000000000000000000000
0000000000000000000000000000000000000000000000000000000000
0000000000000000000000000000000000000000000000000000000000
0000000000000000000000000000000000000000000000000000000000
0000000000000000000000000000000000000000000000000000000000
0000000000000000000000000000000000000000000000000000000000
0000000000000000000000000000000000000000000000000000000000

0000000000000000000000000000000000000000000000000000000000
0000000000000000000000000000000000000000000000000000000000
0000000000000000000000000000000000000000000000000000000000
0000000000000000000000000000000000000000000000000000000000
0000000000000000000000000000000000000000000000000000000000
0000000000000000000000000000000000000000000000000000000000
0000000000000000000000000000000000000000000000000000000000
0000000000000000000000000000000000000000000000000000000000
0000000000000000000000000000000000000000000000000000000000
0000000000000000000000000000000000000000000000000000000000
0000000000000000000000000000000000000000000000000000000000
0000000000000000000000000000000000000000000000000000000000
0000000000000000000000000000000000000000000000000000000000
0000000000000000000000000000000000000000000000000000000000
0000000000000000000000000000000000000000000000000000000000
0000000000000000000000000000000000000000000000000000000000
0000000000000000000000000000000000000000000000000000000000
0000000000000000000000000000000000000000000000000000000000
0000000000000000000000000000000000000000000000000000000000
0000000000000000000000000000000000000000000000000000000000
0000000000000000000000000000000000000000000000000000000000
0000000000000000000000000111111111100000000000000000000000
0000000000000000000000011111111111111000000000000000000000
0000000000000000000000011111111111111000000000000000000000
0000000000000000000000001111111111110000000000000000000000
0000000000000000000000000000111100000000000000000000000000
0000000000000000000000000000000000000000000000000000000000
0000000000000000000000000000000000000000000000000000000000
0000000000000000000000000000000000000000000000000000000000
0000000000000000000000000000000000000000000000000000000000
0000000000000000000000000000000000000000000000000000000000
0000000000000000000000000000000000000000000000000000000000
0000000000000000000000000000000000000000000000000000000000

0000000000000000000000000000000000000000000000000000000000
0000000000000000000000000000000000000000000000000000000000
0000000000000000000000000000000000000000000000000000000000
0000000000000000000000000000000000000000000000000000000000
0000000000000000000000000000000000000000000000000000000000
0000000000000000000000000000000000000000000000000000000000
0000000000000000000000000000000000000000000000000000000000
0000000000000000000000000000000000000000000000000000000000
0000000000000000000000000000000000000000000000000000000000
0000000000000000000000000000000000000000000000000000000000
0000000000000000000000000000000000000000000000000000000000
0000000000000000000000000000000000000000000000000000000000
0000000000000000000000000000000000000000000000000000000000
0000000000000000000000000000000000000000000000000000000000
0000000000000000000000000000000000000000000000000000000000
0000000000000000000000000000000000000000000000000000000000
0000000000000000000000000000000000000000000000000000000000
0000000000000000000000000000000000000000000000000000000000
0000000000000000000000000000000000000000000000000000000000
0000000000000000000000000000000000000000000000000000000000
0000000000000000000000001111111111111000000000000000000000
0000000000000000000001111111111111111111000000000000000000
0000000000000000000011111111111111111111100000000000000000
0000000000000000000011111111111111111111110000000000000000
0000000000000000000001111111111111111111100000000000000000
0000000000000000000000111111111111111110000000000000000000
0000000000000000000000000111111111110000000000000000000000
0000000000000000000000000000000000000000000000000000000000
0000000000000000000000000000000000000000000000000000000000
0000000000000000000000000000000000000000000000000000000000
0000000000000000000000000000000000000000000000000000000000
0000000000000000000000000000000000000000000000000000000000
0000000000000000000000000000000000000000000000000000000000

000000000000000000000000000000000000000000000000000000000
000000000000000000000000000000000000000000000000000000000
000000000000000000000000000000000000000000000000000000000
000000000000000000000000000000000000000000000000000000000
000000000000000000000000000000000000000000000000000000000
000000000000000000000000000000000000000000000000000000000
000000000000000000000000000000000000000000000000000000000
000000000000000000000000000000000000000000000000000000000
000000000000000000000000000000000000000000000000000000000
000000000000000000000000000000000000000000000000000000000
000000000000000000000000000000000000000000000000000000000
000000000000000000000000000000000000000000000000000000000
000000000000000000000000000000000000000000000000000000000
000000000000000000000000000000000000000000000000000000000
000000000000000000000000000000000000000000000000000000000
000000000000000000000000000000000000000000000000000000000
000000000000000000000000000000000000000000000000000000000
000000000000000000000000011111111000000000000000000000000
000000000000000000011111111111111111110000000000000000000
000000000000000011111111111111111111111110000000000000000
000000000000001111111111111111111111111111100000000000000
000000000000111111111111111111111111111111111000000000000
000000000000111111111111111111111111111111111000000000000
000000000000111111111111111111111111111111111000000000000
000000000000111111111111111111111111111111111000000000000
000000000000011111111111111111111111111111110000000000000
000000000000001111111111111111111111111111000000000000000
000000000000000001111111111111111111111100000000000000000
000000000000000000000111111111111111100000000000000000000
000000000000000000000000000000000000000000000000000000000
000000000000000000000000000000000000000000000000000000000
000000000000000000000000000000000000000000000000000000000
000000000000000000000000000000000000000000000000000000000

0000000000000000000000000000000000000000000000000000000000
0000000000000000000000000000000000000000000000000000000000
0000000000000000000000000000000000000000000000000000000000
0000000000000000000000000000000000000000000000000000000000
0000000000000000000000000000000000000000000000000000000000
0000000000000000000000000000000000000000000000000000000000
0000000000000000000000000000000000000000000000000000000000
0000000000000000000000000000000000000000000000000000000000
0000000000000000000000000000000000000000000000000000000000
0000000000000000000000000000000000000000000000000000000000
0000000000000000000000000000000000000000000000000000000000
0000000000000000000000000000000000000000000000000000000000
0000000000000000000000000000000000000000000000000000000000
0000000000000000000000000000000000000000000000000000000000
0000000000000000000000000000000000000000000000000000000000
0000000000000000000000000000000000000000000000000000000000
0000000000000000000001111111111111111000000000000000000000
0000000000000001111111111111111111111111111000000000000000
0000000000001111111111111111111111111111111111000000000000
0000000000111111111111111111111111111111111111110000000000
0000000011111111111111111111111111111111111111111100000000
0000000111111111111111111111111111111111111111111110000000
0000001111111111111111111111111111111111111111111111000000
0000001111111111111111111111111111111111111111111111000000
0000001111111111111111111111111111111111111111111111000000
0000001111111111111111111111111111111111111111111111000000
0000000111111111111111111111111111111111111111111110000000
0000000011111111111111111111111111111111111111111100000000
0000000000111111111111111111111111111111111111110000000000
0000000000001111111111111111111111111111111110000000000000
0000000000000000111111111111111111111111100000000000000000
0000000000000000000000000111111111000000000000000000000000
0000000000000000000000000000000000000000000000000000000000

0000000000000000000000000000000000000000000000000000000000
0000000000000000000000000000000000000000000000000000000000
0000000000000000000000000000000000000000000000000000000000
0000000000000000000000000000000000000000000000000000000000
0000000000000000000000000000000000000000000000000000000000
0000000000000000000000000000000000000000000000000000000000
0000000000000000000000000000000000000000000000000000000000
0000000000000000000000000000000000000000000000000000000000
0000000000000000000000000000000000000000000000000000000000
0000000000000000000000000000000000000000000000000000000000
0000000000000000000000000000000000000000000000000000000000
0000000000000000000000000000000000000000000000000000000000
0000000000000000000000000000000000000000000000000000000000
0000000000000000000000011111111111100000000000000000000000
0000000000000001111111111111111111111111111000000000000000
0000000000111111111111111111111111111111111111100000000000
0000000111111111111111111111111111111111111111111100000000
0000011111111111111111111111111111111111111111111111100000
0001111111111111111111111111111111111111111111111111110000
0011111111111111111111111111111111111111111111111111111100
0111111111111111111111111111111111111111111111111111111110
1111111111111111111111111111111111111111111111111111111111
1111111111111111111111111111111111111111111111111111111111
1111111111111111111111111111111111111111111111111111111111
1111111111111111111111111111111111111111111111111111111111
0111111111111111111111111111111111111111111111111111111110
0011111111111111111111111111111111111111111111111111111100
0001111111111111111111111111111111111111111111111111111000
0000011111111111111111111111111111111111111111111111100000
0000000111111111111111111111111111111111111111111100000000
0000000000011111111111111111111111111111111111110000000000
0000000000000011111111111111111111111111111100000000000000
000000000000000000111111111111111111111111100000000000000000

51 When Caveman Comes Home

When the lights came on, Ella Pearson's nightmare dispersed with the same suddenness with which the darkness departed. Like the darkness, still apparent in the shadows beneath the cots and in the poured concrete corners of the dorm, still lingering in the places the overhead lights could not so easily reach, fragments of the dream held tenaciously on. The dread lingered.

Around her, the room stirred with activity but Ella lay still a moment longer, looking up at the slab above her, trying to hold onto her dream, even for how bitter it had been. It seemed important to hold on to; important that she not forget.

In a glistening, tarry pool a boy'd been sinking—thrashing wildly and screaming soundlessly—and Ella stood at the edge, watching it happen. She did not want the boy to die. Somehow, she understood that that slim little creature being pulled into the black, viscous hole represented an anchor for her and that, without him, she would float away, untethered to anything at all. Even so, she could not make herself act.

The pool (she knew this, too, with a dreamer's instinctive understanding of the absurd physics of nightmares) was a brew of bacteria and poison, a stew of death and decay which she could not make herself enter. The boy's mouth filled with sludge as he sank. Then his nostrils filled. His eyes, wide with fear were sucked under and at last, all that was left of him were his hands, clawing at the air for something to grab hold of. When he'd disappeared and the ripples in the pool went still, Ella realized that it wasn't just the pool that had been black. She stood in the middle of a void, nothing to be seen in any direction and, without the boy and the churning soup of filth to give her bearing on the world, she could no longer feel the ground beneath her feet. She floated off into a panic of solitary freedom.

A pair of feet swung down from the bunk above her and Ella knew she needed to move. It was either that or miss her place in line. It had never happened before, but certainly there would be consequences if it did. Hurrying to get out, Ella landed on the floor right in the same slot where she started every day.

Everyone was off their cots now, all thirty-two of them, lined up in the aisles, marching orderly out the door at the far end. After all the irrational uncertainty in her dream, the routine was comforting to be a part of.

By the time Ella reached the doorway herself and looked up the stairwell to the shock of daylight at the end, any remnant of her nightmare was gone, even the lingering dread. All she had left was the vague memory of it.

At the top of the stairs, the warmth of the day seemed to pull her out.

She collected her pail from the shelf beside the door (the same as all the others but, somehow, indelibly *hers*) and started out into the long, furrowed field, a pastiche of green and soil so rich it looked black under the sun. Starting away from the door, in her own direction, like everyone else who'd emerged—diffusing into the day like marbles rolled across a floor—without command Ella returned to the distant, unmarked place where she'd finished the day before.

Starting afresh, turning her head down to the ground, she moved along. Beneath her, heads of lactuca sativa (lettuce, as the common name) scrolled by, one after another. Some paces in, a musty scent pulled her to a stop. Bending down, Ella examined the lower leaves of the head she'd come to, which seemed to have gone particularly pale. Black spots laced the edges. Ella set her bucket down and delicately tugged off the dead leaves and threw them into the pail and rose up to continue on.

The nightmare was gone, but Ella was aware that she did dream and that most of her dreams were fitful and bad and that they were somehow moored in her own past: particular experiences which she shared with no one else. It was a hard thing to wrap her mind around: every day now was a shared day and she had no experiences which were hers alone. Whatever her past had been was gone, as illusory and fleeting as the dreams themselves, and Ella supposed it was probably better that way. If her past had been so troubled that it still bothered her this intensely, it was certainly best forgotten.

She continued on, toward the horizon, where the blue sky and the sprawling edge of the earth were held apart by a frozen bank of clouds. She watched the ground.

...Lactuca sativa, lactuca sativa, lactuca sativa...

In her working down the windrows, Ella had come alongside a raised access road that cut the field in two. She kept working, ignoring the plume of dust growing on the horizon. She continued ignoring it as it blossomed, opening up, larger and larger.

The heads of lettuce scrolled by below her, all firm and clean and as identical as children's balls off a manufacturing line.

...Lactuca sativa, lactuca sativa, lactuca sativa, digitaria. Ella stopped. Bending down and setting her pail at her side, she pinched the errant gnarl of crabgrass from the ground. It was young and fresh and weak and gave in without a fight. It's pale roots came up clinging to a teaspoon of soil. She shook the dirt free from the weed and tossed it into her bucket.

She was forced to see her own arms as she worked. They were freckled and it was a source of shame, those imperfections, though no one else seemed concerned by them. She had a feeling that they had not always been like that, though she couldn't remember a time when they hadn't been. She hated them. She hated seeing her own taint beside the perfect rows of sweet smelling lettuce which she worked so hard to maintain. She could keep her rows exactly how they should be, but she could do nothing to improve herself. The sanitary shower that ended her every day just rolled over the stains, even as it managed to carry away every last grain of dirt from her fingers and the pads of her feet.

Behind her, the hum of a motor came close and the storm of dust whirled around her. The car stopped on the access path.

Ella flustered when the dust started settling on the lettuce, brushing off what she could. She didn't look when the door of the car wound open behind her. She didn't look when the crunch of footsteps came to the edge of the embankment and stopped.

"Ella?"

She raised her head and looked at the boy on the road.

He waved her up and said, "Come up here, please."

Leaving her bucket behind, Ella climbed up the incline to join the boy.

"He's come to speak with you again," the boy said and led her around to the other side of the car, where a man in a wheelchair was just being lowered to the ground on an automated ramp.

He wore a very thick beard and his eyes were milky with blindness and his breath was bad. He smelled like he was dying. No, Ella thought, he *was* dying. That was the smell on him. Strangely, the man seemed unbothered by it, if he even knew, and he must have known. Looking up at Ella with a bright, brownish smile, he said, "It's good to see you again. Shall we go for a little walk?"

Ella looked at the boy who'd led her around the car. He nodded.

Ella started walking. The old man came along side her, pushing down on the joystick on his armrest. They moved into the settling dust behind the car. The old man looked around the landscape and, in spite of the dust still drifting in the air, he took a deep breath and said, "It is beautiful out here, isn't it? I suppose I don't need to tell you that."

Ella nodded and looked around, too. In the distance, the City could be seen, rising up, gleaming in the bright day.

"It isn't old age that put me in the chair," he said after they'd gone a little further and the dust had settled. Ella was dismayed to see how the heads of lettuce at the roadside had been tinged rusty with the settling dirt. She tried to remind herself that when the watering started in the evening it would all get washed away, anyhow. The old man was still talking, but she barely payed attention. "I only say that to remind you. It occurs to me that you might have forgotten."

They continued walking, Ella's feet grinding on the roadway, the motor of the wheelchair whirring beside her.

"It happened when I was a boy, you see. I contracted an illness and, as a result, I lost the use of my legs."

"I'm sorry to hear that," Ella said. She wasn't sure why she was being told this. It had nothing to do with her. It had nothing to do with lettuce at all.

"It's fine. I faired better than most. In fact, today's my birthday."

"Congratulations."

"Thank you. It is a very special birthday. Would you believe I'm eighty-seven today?"

Of course Ella believed it. Why would anyone lie about such a thing? She was quiet.

"I'm the oldest man alive." He was silent a moment, looking at her. "Can you believe that?"

Again, she couldn't imagine why he would have made up such a thing, so she was silent.

Suddenly, seizing her wrist with his papery hand, cold despite the warmth of the day, he brought her to a stop. Without the whir of the motor, the lonesome tone of the wind rose up. Seeming embarrassed, he let go of her with an apologetic nod and reached into his pocket. He pulled out a picture and handed it to her. A little baby, so fresh in the world it's skin was purple.

"That's my great grandson."

"He's very handsome," Ella said and handed the picture back.

"He needs a nanny, is the thing." The man looked at her, expectantly.

Ella looked down at him.

"You wouldn't be interested, would you?"

Ella shrugged. "I have work to do."

He nodded. "I thought I'd try. You asked me once, a very long time ago, not to forget you. I never have."

She looked at him a moment. She could not remember him. But his face was old and if she'd asked for that promise so long ago, how could she be expected to remember?

They returned to the car in silence. The man backed his wheelchair onto the ramp and, with an electric grumble, it lifted him and sucked him into the car. "Goodbye, Ella," the man said. In the next moment the door folded closed on him and he was gone behind the tinted glass.

Ella started back toward her pail in the windrows, stopping when she heard the boy behind her speak up, "You know, you can only say 'no' so many times before he'll stop asking."

Ella nodded. She supposed that was probably true.

Skittering down the embankment, she found her weed bucket again and continued on.

...Lactuca sativa, lactuca sativa...

Under the wide, blue sky, under the nurturing warmth of the sun, even in spite of the dark taint of her dreams, Ella wasn't convinced there had ever been a better, brighter day than this. So maybe the nightmares didn't matter, after all. Maybe she should let them go, forgotten. Maybe the only dream that really mattered was this one, this perfect, uncomplicated life enveloping her.

Acknowledgements

This book would not have been possible without the hard work and commitment of the following people:

My father, my wife and Liz Cameron all helped with the task of reading an early draft and providing important insights into what I wasn't seeing. Alex Ortolani and Ben and Erin Lutton are owed many thanks for acting as early readers and for their meticulous help in proofreading and preparing the manuscript for publication. My mother also deserves thanks for her (perennial) help in proofreading. In addition, I'd like to thank my wife for long talks about the social and sexual habits of robots and for generally being awesome and more supportive than I deserve.

Finally, I'd like to thank you for following me along this journey. If you enjoyed the book, please tell your friends about it or give it a review or rating on Amazon or Goodreads. This caveman thanks you.

48309874R00259

Made in the USA
Middletown, DE
15 September 2017